Dedication

To my mum Jean,
whose wisdom inspired me to write,
I dedicate this book to thee.

My love of writing stemmed from when I was a child, it was a time of innocence in which I would become lost in a world of fantasy. However, for seven years I lost my way, feeling that taking a different path would ultimately be best for me. That all changed one day in January 2006 when I was inspired to rekindle my love for writing by my mother.

The Genesis Project: The Children of CS-13

R.S. Johnson

THE GENESIS PROJECT: THE CHILDREN OF CS-13

AUSTIN MACAULEY

Copyright © R.S. Johnson

The right of R.S. Johnson to be identified as author of this work has been asserted by him in accordance with section 77 and 78 of the Copyright, Designs and Patents Act 1988.

All rights reserved. No part of this publication may be reproduced, stored in a retrieval system, or transmitted in any form or by any means, electronic, mechanical, photocopying, recording, or otherwise, without the prior permission of the publishers.

Any person who commits any unauthorized act in relation to this publication may be liable to criminal prosecution and civil claims for damages.

This book is a work of fiction. Names, characters, places and incidents are either the product of the author's imagination or they are used fictitiously. Any resemblance to actual events or persons, living or dead, is entirely coincidental.

A CIP catalogue record for this title is
available from the British Library.

ISBN 978 1 84963 054 2

www.austinmacauley.com

First Published (2011)
Austin & Macauley Publishers Ltd.
25 Canada Square
Canary Wharf
London
E14 5LB

Printed & Bound in Great Britain

Acknowledgements

This is my moment to acknowledge the many wonderful people in my life who have been with me on this often testing journey.

To my mum, Jean, and stepdad, Stephen. I thank you both for all the love, support, encouragement and guidance you have shown me throughout my life. Special recognition must go to my mum who was the first to read this book, and who offered me so much for which I am grateful.

To Elaine and Richard. I thank you both for the help you provided me when no other option seemed available.

To my fiancée Rachel, the most wonderful woman in my life. I thank you from the bottom of my heart for putting up with so much over the past four and a half years, and thank you for pushing me when I needed it the most.

And to the rest of my family and friends. I thank you all for the support and encouragement you have given me throughout.

To Austin & Macauley who saw potential in me and my book. I thank you for giving me that much needed break. A special mention must go to Annette Longman who answered every question I put to her without any hesitation.

A special mention to the following for their help: Darlington Borough Council Library, H & M Revenue and Customs, drakensburg.kzn.org.za, the Squares Management team at the Greater London Authority and the American Library United States Embassy in Pretoria, South Africa.

And last, but by no means least, to you, the reader. I thank you the most for taking the time to read what I have written.

Prologue

The Descent into Darkness

April 18th

The bombing was sudden and unexpected.

And in that fragment of a second, when the day seemed like any other in the capital, everything around Joseph Harris – a Marine Security Guard stationed at the American embassy in South Africa – was ripped apart, consumed by flames and debris.

His world became a sudden blur. He felt himself hurtling through the air, and in that instant he could do nothing but shield his head and face with his arms. And as the shouts and screams from those that had survived the blast echoed throughout his mind, his own thoughts were a swirling torrent of fear and regret, for he feared death and he regretted not telling his wife how much he loved her.

Then everything presented itself in front of his swollen, bloodshot eyes. He was lying on his front, half-buried under the wreckage from the explosion, with one side of his face covered in dust, the other in blood, and with fire and thick black smoke engulfing everything in sight.

And it was then, through the pain and suffering all around him, that Joseph Harris felt his own body admitting defeat, wavering on the fine line between existence and the abyss of death.

With his battered and bruised body shaking and jerking violently, and his lungs burning from the smoke inhalation, Joseph Harris closed his eyes and pictured his wife as he whispered his last words to God. He asked for forgiveness. He asked for the Lord to protect his wife and family. But most importantly he asked for his death to be quick and painless. As the flames devoured the embassy, as the walls began to crumble, his final prayer was answered.

Chapter One

The Welcome Home Celebration

Seated inside a grand, white marquee enclosed in one of his many great gardens, Franklin Julian Lane tapped his champagne glass with a dessert spoon and slowly stood. Once gaining everyone's attention, he cleared his throat and began to talk into the microphone he held in his hand.

'Ladies and gentlemen ... Friends and family ... Welcome home Robert.'

At the sound of these words, the entire marquee erupted in an applause of cheers and claps. Feeling flushed, Robert Lane buried his face in his hands while his older brother, a tall, well toned figure of a man with hazel eyes and very short dark hair, seated directly to his right, wrapped an arm around him and whispered something into his ear. The applause began to fade after a few seconds had passed, and Frank, who was now smiling broadly and looking directly at his youngest son, continued.

'It's good to have you back.'

And as he picked up his champagne glass and stared deeply into his son's eyes, the next words he spoke were said in a way that Robert had never heard before. For never once had his father spoke with so much affection, especially to him.

'I just want to say that I love you Robert, and I'm extremely proud of what you have achieved.'

The words seemed unreal to him and yet they had completely numbed his body. For years he had longed for them to be spoken, and now, at the age of twenty-six, he had finally experienced what every man – whether he admitted it or not – craved for, recognition from his father.

Frank raised his glass, staring out into the crowd as he said proudly, 'Ladies and gentlemen, to my son ... Robert.'

In unison all the guests raised their glasses and shouted, 'To Robert.'

And as the last of the guests uttered his name, there was a brief silence before someone shouted from the back, 'SPEECH ... SPEECH.'

Frank could not hide his amusement as he held out the microphone for his son to take hold of. Robert was suddenly brought back to his surroundings and he looked taken aback. Leaning back in his chair and crossing his arms in defiance, he repeatedly mouthed the word, 'No,' as he shook his head.

But it seemed to do little, as more and more began to join in, clapping their hands in an rhythmic fashion as they all shouted, 'SPEECH ... SPEECH ... SPEECH ... SPEECH.'

Finally, with dread etched upon his now deeply reddened face, Robert grasped the microphone, took a deep breath and stood to mass applause.

'I'm not really one for unprepared speeches,' he admitted, 'so you'll have to bear with me on this one.'

He looked around the table he was seated at, feeling a pang of sadness as his eyes came across the empty space his late mother would have occupied.

'Ladies and gentlemen I am truly honoured to see you all here today,' he began. 'I know many of you have travelled a long way, so I would like to welcome you and thank you all for being here, to share with me this amazing day. I truly appreciate your company.'

He began to walk around the large circular table, laying a gentle hand on Frank's shoulder as he passed.

'I can't stand here without giving acknowledgement to my father, who has always been there for me with support and guidance in every big decision I have ever made in my life. So I must take this opportunity to thank you, Dad, not only for your wisdom but also for planning and executing such a wonderful day as today.'

Still he walked around the table.

'As I look around this marquee I realise what dear friends and family I have. And although this welcome home party has brought us all together today, I am reminded of the fact that my mother is not here celebrating with us...'

His voice suddenly grew soft and sombre.

'...I just hope I made her proud.'

He picked up his glass and held it aloft; staring upwards as he said the words, 'To my mother Margaret, perhaps the greatest woman I had ever known.'

All of the guests, some of whom were now dabbing the tears from their eyes, picked up their glasses and toasted once again.

'To Margaret,' they said in unison.

Handing the microphone back to his father, Robert breathed a sigh of relief and sat down to a standing ovation.

'I just want to add one final thing,' Frank said after the clapping and whistling had settled down, 'this is a celebration, so I want to see everyone having a good time. And I must insist that each and every one of you are on *that* dance floor by the end of the night.'

As soon as he sat, the band positioned in the far corner began to play while the tuxedo dressed waiters began to walk among the tables, bearing silver trays with glasses of champagne and sandwiches. The buffet tables were laden with all manner of exotic foods, whilst the bar stocked every drink imaginable.

'An impressive speech son,' Frank said to Robert from across the table, 'you certainly don't get your natural ability for public speeches from me. What you have my son is a gift, you'll make an inspiring president one day.'

Robert, who had turned round to grab some food off the waiter bearing one of the trays with row upon row of sandwiches placed upon it, quickly faced his father. He no longer desired nor was interested in food; his attention now was solely on Frank. How long he was waiting for him to continue he did not know, but each passing second was as agonising as the last.

'I've spent thirty-five years developing and expanding CyberTech Defence Systems,' Frank finally said. 'But as well as being a businessman I'm a realist, the popularity of CyberTech had been dwindling before the new commercial was aired.'

Frank could see Robert was about to object, but he shook his head.

'No, no,' he said quickly, 'you have no reason to be modest; there is no shame in basking in your glory.'

He paused briefly to take a sip of his champagne.

'What you achieved in Italy surpassed everything the board and I had predicted. We had been discussing for some time that the company needed to head in a new direction, and, well we've all agreed that you are the man that could take CyberTech Defence Systems to new heights.'

Frank took another sip of his champagne and looked at Robert, who was completely dumbfounded.

'So what do you think son?' he asked, raising his eyebrows a fraction. 'Ready to become president of one of the most powerful defence companies in the world?'

From Frank's tone and expression it appeared that he wanted it answered quickly, but there was a lot to consider. CyberTech Defence Systems had companies established throughout America, France, Germany, Italy, Australia and the United Kingdom, it employed over five hundred and fifty-six thousand people, how could he accept that sort of responsibility with only a few seconds to think about it?

But then something deep within him, whether it was the champagne flowing through his body, the opportunity of a new challenge, or something else he didn't know, seemed to burn away his unwillingness. He heard his voice suddenly accepting the offer his father had made him.

Frank held up his glass, and in turn Robert held up his, and together they clinked them. Congratulations were offered from around the table at that point.

'My brother, president,' said Mark Richard Lane admiringly. 'I'm proud of you kid.'

'Your mother would be so proud of you,' said Sylvia Lane, his grandmother who was sitting across from him.

'Congratulations Robert.'

The softly spoken words from Lisa Anderson made Robert look at the woman seated directly next to his brother. She was beautiful, with long soft curling brunette hair, which fell in ringlets, soft brown eyes and pale skin which had a radiance about it. For a moment he just stared at her, his heart pounding relentlessly against his chest, while his stomach tingled, as though a hoard of butterflies were fluttering inside of it.

But then reality came crushing over him, his eyes were drawn to the diamond ring sparkling on the third finger of her left hand. And in that instant he knew that he and Lisa Anderson could never be; her heart belonged to another.

Robert smiled, but did not reply, his mouth had gone completely dry.

'So what was Italy like?' Mark asked, as he took a couple of beef sandwiches from a passing waiter.

'Even if I described it as beautiful, it still wouldn't do it justice,' Robert said truthfully.

'So you would recommend it for me and Lisa to go on our honeymoon there then?'

The words felt like a knife piercing through his heart. Robert took a sip of champagne and, although this was the last thing he wanted to say, he said it through a forced smile, 'Yes I would, and to prove it I'm going to send you both there as my wedding present to you both.'

Mark put an arm around his brother and patted him. 'First class and a five star hotel?' he said with a cheeky grin.

'Pay no attention to him Robert,' said Lisa, and she gave Mark a look that suggested that she wasn't amused by what he had just said, 'that's really nice of you to offer.'

As the afternoon merged into evening, the celebrations grew more and more lively. Mark and Lisa were now on the dance floor, holding each other very closely as they swayed to the rhythm of the music, while Frank and a few of his business associates were laughing and joking in a corner. Making his way through the crowd, he tried to escape the continuous attention of tipsy women who wanted to dance with him, Robert was contented enough to just sit alone at one of the tables and watch the beautiful woman with the softly curling brunette hair who was dancing with his brother. He tried to subdue the indescribable feelings he held for her, but it seemed only to deepen his love.

'Is this seat taken?'

The woman's soft voice pulled him out of his pining state.

'No,' Robert said, pulling out the chair next to him and offering her the seat, 'please.'

He grabbed a champagne glass off a passing waiter and placed it in front of the woman who had straight golden hair, which came down to her shoulders and soft ocean blue eyes, her tanned skin had a glow about it. The sparkling black dress she wore was low cut and her matching shoes were peep toe with a very high heel.

'Thank you,' she said, holding out her hand. 'I'm Katherine Adams.'

'It's a pleasure to meet you Katherine,' said Robert pleasantly as he shook her hand. 'I would introduce myself but seeing as this is my party you'll know who I am.'

Katherine took a sip of her champagne and leaned inwards.

'Oh I know who you are,' she whispered, smiling, 'you probably hear this all the time but I'm such a great fan of yours.'

'I do,' Robert said smugly, 'but I never tire of hearing it.'

Katherine playfully tapped him on the arm, and as she did a voice reached them through all the talking and music.

'Finally,' the voice said softly and sincerely, 'a chance to talk to my grandson.'

Sylvia Lane suddenly appeared, dressed in what only could be described as a unique style. His grandmother had turned seventy several months ago, and to mark this birthday milestone Robert had bought her a cottage in France, a country she had loved and always wanted to retire to. Sylvia was short and slim and gave the impression that she was frail looking, although she was anything but. Her light grey hair had been curled especially for this party and her hazel eyes were bright, soft and behind slim, oval shaped glasses.

'Grandma,' said Robert quickly, 'may I introduce Katherine Adams.' He looked at Katherine. 'Katherine this is my grandmother, Sylvia Lane.'

'Please to meet you,' Katherine said politely, extending her hand.

But as Sylvia looked up and down at the woman sitting next to her grandson she took an instant disliking to her and as Sylvia was the type of woman who would tell it how it was, she would not mince words in the process.

'Let me give you some free advice,' she said frankly, looking at Robert now, 'never trust a woman who dresses that provocatively.'

Katherine was taken aback by the remark, but then she looked at Sylvia, her expression suggesting, *well you're one to talk*. And her biggest mistake was letting Sylvia catch hold of this look.

'There's a fine line between being classy and being common,' said Sylvia, staring deep into Katherine's ocean blue eyes, 'you my dear are the latter.'

And having the last word, Sylvia grabbed hold of her grandson's hand and pulled him effortlessly to his feet, leaving Katherine reeling in shock. Robert turned and mouthed the word, 'I'm so sorry,' before disappearing into the crowd.

'You didn't have to be that rude to her Grandma,' he said as they walked through the marquee.

'Girls like her are after one thing and one thing only,' Sylvia said in disgust, 'trust me I've saved you from a lot of aggravation.'

'We were just talking,' Robert said, feeling it was important to explain that what he and Katherine were doing was totally innocent, 'surely there's no harm in doing that.'

'Of course not, but it's what you do after the talking that matters.'

Robert knew better than to argue with his grandmother. He linked his arm through hers as they walked outside. The cool early evening air felt nice and refreshing against their faces as they walked across the finely cut grass towards the bench under the small oak tree, which had been planted as a memorial to his mother.

As the pair sat on the bench they talked about the glorious weather that they had been experiencing then the conversation turned to the French cottage, which his grandmother was happy to take part in, but then she got onto the subject of Lisa Anderson, a territory which Robert felt was unnecessary and his cheeks began to flush slightly with the embarrassment of his grandmother knowing of the love he felt.

'I'll never forget what you said to me when you first saw Lisa,' she said cheerily, looking up at him, 'you told me that she must be an angel because she was the most beautiful girl you had ever seen.'

'What did I know,' Robert said, avoiding his grandmother's gaze, 'I was six at the time.'

'You must have known something,' said Sylvia, 'it's lasted twenty years.'

Robert looked into his grandmother's soft, wrinkled face, and felt uncomfortable and frustrated. Did she really think it would be easy for him to talk freely about Lisa, that he could simply switch off the love he felt for her? Didn't his grandmother understand that this was the last thing he wanted to talk about?

'But believe it or not I know how you feel,' she said, and Robert looked at her now as she continued. 'I was sixteen and fell madly in love with my best friend's boyfriend. His name was George Williams, he was tall and handsome and the first man I fell madly in love with.'

She went quiet and her eyes seemed to moisten that much more, as though this particular recollection was quite painful for her.

Robert looked at her for a long time before saying softly, 'What happened?'

'I met your grandad,' she said comically, 'and we all know how that ended up.'

'Do you ever regret meeting grandad?'

Sylvia smiled brightly and stood. 'That's something we can talk about some other time,' she said, 'now if you will excuse me I must continue my mingling with these lovely people.'

She walked off, leaving Robert to sit alone. He looked down at the letters engraved on the bench back and ran his fingers over them.

Margaret Lane
Wife, Mother & Friend
Sadly missed but always in our thoughts

'Well here we are again, Mom,' he said, unsure if he believed the idea that his mother could actually hear him, wherever she was, 'sorry that it's been a while since I last was here. I don't know if dad had told you but I was in Italy...'

He grew quiet, it was difficult for him talking like this and his eyes began to sting as the tears tried to come.

'I miss you so much,' he said, fighting hard to stop them from forming. 'I really hope I've done you proud.'

He blew a kiss to the sky, sat a moment longer and then wandered back inside the marquee. He stood by the entrance, watching Lisa who still danced with his brother, unaware of the five year old girl who came running over to him, her arms spread out in joy.

'Uncle Wobert,' she said cutely, hugging his leg, 'will you dance with me pease.' And she smiled brightly, showing her small white teeth.

Robert looked down at his niece and smiled. She was wearing a white dress with pink frills and her brown hair was braided in two bunches. He knelt down so that her soft, innocent-looking brown eyes were level with his, she had the look of her mother about her, there could be no mistaking that.

'Melissa,' he said, his voice was no higher than a whisper, 'I would love to.'

Her giggles turned to shrieks of laughter as he whisked her off her feet. The band began a new song as he made his way to the gleaming dance floor. He ignored all of the disbelieving stares from the single women he had tried to escape, he just held onto Melissa as he twirled her round the floor.

'Are you enjoying the party?' he asked, manoeuvring her around the dance floor.

'Yeah, it's weally, weally good,' smiled Melissa brightly.

And as Robert looked over at where Lisa and his brother were standing, he watched as Mark broke apart from her. He fished inside his trouser pocket, pulled out his phone and put it to his ear. Whoever was ringing him hadn't had much to say, because he was putting his phone back inside his trouser pocket within seconds. Then whispering something to Lisa he hurried past everyone and made his way out of the marquee.

Lisa looked a little lost, and as the song came to an end Robert put Melissa down.

'Will you save me a dance later?' he asked.

Melissa held the bottom of her dress and swayed where she stood.

'Hmm,' she said, 'okay.' And she giggled as she ran off into the crowd.

Lisa was still on the dance floor, her left arm was held across her stomach while she bit the thumb nail of her right hand. Rubbing the sweat that had gathered on the palms of his hands, Robert took a deep breath and slowly approached her. There was nothing wrong with what he was about to do, he was just going to ask for a dance, it was totally innocent.

But with each step he took he became more and more conscious of the way he was walking, it was sort of half casual, half rigid. But this was the least of his worries, what would he say to her?

Hi Lisa, he began to rehearse in his head, *I was just wondering if you wanted to dance.*

Absolutely pathetic, he fumed.

He started again.

Lisa, how about this dance?

Would you like to dance with me?–

'Ah Robert,' a woman said, 'I'm glad I found you, I've been wanting to offer my congratulations to you all day, you've been a difficult man to find.'

'Oh sorry Aunt Muriel,' said Robert, who felt himself cringe. He recognised the voice immediately and turned round to see a short plump woman with auburn hair, dressed in an olive green trouser suit hurrying over to him. 'I've been meeting and greeting, you know how it is. I was just coming over to find you.'

It was totally fabricated but his auntie was unaware of it, she smiled, leaned inwards and kissed Robert on his cheek, leaving a smudged red lipstick imprint on his skin. It was clear that she had been enjoying the celebrations; he could smell the alcohol on her breath when she stepped back.

'So are you enjoying yourself?' he asked, wanting nothing more than to turn around to see if Lisa was still standing there.

'I'm merry,' she admitted, 'but I'm not drunk, I haven't slurred my words yet so that's a good sign.'

She began to laugh and Robert rolled his eyes discreetly, he was going to be stuck with his aunt whether he liked it or not. But then a voice reached them through the music, it was a voice that carried hope.

'Muriel,' Sylvia called out, 'have another drink of champagne.'

She made her way effortlessly through the mass of people with two glasses held in her hands.

'I've already had too much my dear,' Muriel said at once, 'one more and I shall be on my back.'

'Nonsense,' said Sylvia, handing over the champagne, 'you can never have too much champagne.' She put an arm across Muriel's shoulder and slowly led her away from Robert. 'Why don't you tell me about the time you met Sir Nicholas Ross.' And very discreetly she switched off her hearing aid.

'Ah well,' Muriel began ecstatically, 'he wasn't a Sir back then…'

Robert didn't watch the pair walk off, he turned quickly and was delighted to see that Lisa was still standing on the dance floor. He walked over to her but before he could say a word, Lisa hurried past him saying, 'Excuse me,' before leaving the marquee.

Chapter Two

New Chapters

The high definition television in Frank Lane's living room was a colossal flat-screen, the best that money could buy, it was mounted against the far wall opposite the large chestnut leather suite. Mark's caller, a fellow compatriot of the United States military, had told him to simply check the news. He wasn't quite sure what to expect but none of that mattered now; because even if he was told what he was about to witness, he still wouldn't have believed it.

The image being played before him was broadcasted live from a news helicopter. It slowly circled, showing the United States Embassy in its awful reality. Its walls were caving inwards and crumbling and flames devoured everything that stood in their way, leaving behind faint wisps of smoke and ash.

'If you are just joining us,' a female voice said, *'then you are looking at a very disturbing live scene here ... That is the United States Embassy in Pretoria, South Africa and we have reports coming through, confirming that a large explosion has occurred at the Embassy.'*

There was a momentary pause as the helicopter circled again and continued to feed the live images. The newsreader started talking once again, trying her utmost to remain professional.

'Here at the American News Network Centre we have been working on the story since the news first reached us, calling all of our sources in the attempt to get a clear understanding of what might have happened at the Embassy, but clearly something devastating has occurred in the capital –'

Mark changed channels in the hope of finding out more details on what exactly was going on.

'–we must make clear that we are not implying that this is a terrorist attack,' a man's voice said, as video segments from the remnants of the Embassy played above the statement:

BREAKING NEWS: EXPLOSION AT UNITED STATES EMBASSY IN SOUTH AFRICA

'No,' a woman replied, it sounded like she was holding the discussion via the telephone, *'but we can't rule out the possibility of this being a deliberate attack upon the United States.'*

Words suddenly appeared on the top left hand corner of the screen, saying:

VOICE OF JAQUELINE SIMPSON
AUTHOR OF INTERNATIONAL BESTSELLER
TERRORIST IDEOLOGIES

'There has been growing unrest in the country since the acquittal of three United States Marines,' the male news presenter said, *'would I be wrong in saying that this could be the root cause of the attack?'*

'It's too early to speculate, no group has claimed responsibility–'

Mark began flipping through the news channels once again, annoyed that they were even discussing the idea of this being an intentional strike against America. The whole thing was just ridiculous, an attack of this magnitude, delivered on US. soil would be impossible to achieve.

But it seemed the news channels didn't share his view, as each one was running the same story but with different theories and ideas attached to it.

'–the feeling here is that this could be the work of–'

'–however this turns out, this is going to be a day that is going to live in the history of the United States and South Africa –'

'–we have James Hoffman on the line for us; he's a frequent guest of ours and a terror expert. James is it too early to speculate –'

'–this could be one of the most horrifically planned attacks against the United States –'

'–I believe that we are going live to our African correspondent Jeff Simmons who is at the scene in Pretoria, Jeff what can you tell us? You would presume that the staff at the

Embassy prepares for this type of thing day in day out, but this must have come as a complete shock to them?'

The screen switched suddenly to a young male reporter standing on a quiet street somewhere in Pretoria.

'Well Kate,' he said. The street seemed to emanate an eerie way about it, *'no amount of training or preparation could have helped the staff at the Embassy for what happened to them.*

'South Africa has never experienced an attack on this scale before. I can confirm that South African security forces are now on full alert; they are extremely concerned that there might be additional attacks across the country. Normally when you have a situation like this occur they would immediately get in touch with the various intelligence agencies around the world, trying to get an idea of who might have been planning such an attack. But right now, the first order of business has to be to protect the South African people against a second or third attack, the likelihood is that more attacks are going to follow.'

'Has there been any word from the South African President?' the newsreader asked.

'President Zandberg delivered a statement forty-five minutes ago. In it he said that he had been in constant contact with the American President Jack Carter since the Embassy explosion, he was deeply saddened by the loss of so much human life and he made it clear that if this was a terrorist attack he would assist with the tracking down and capturing of any suspects.'

'Okay thank you, our African correspondent Jeff Simmons there...'

Lisa Anderson, who a few minutes ago had been enjoying dancing and socialising in the blissful ignorance of the events unfolding in South Africa, was now standing in the doorway, watching in numbed horror at what was being broadcasted.

She did not know how much time had passed before she summoned up enough strength to move inward, nor did she care, but as she knelt with Mark, gripped his hand with hers and stared at him with moist eyes, the words she wanted to say, needed to say, were now lodged firmly in her throat.

So she said nothing and simply stared at what was being shown, squeezing his hand every so often, hoping that he would return the pressure, reassuring her that everything was going to be okay, but the reassurance never came. And it was then that she knew that this was no longer an accident, that this was an attack delivered on United States soil and that the repercussions of this were going to ripple out across the entire globe.

'What's going to happen?' she asked breathlessly, not being able to look at him. 'Are they going to send you over there?'

'Of course not,' his tone was soft and compassionate, 'this was just an accident, nothing more.'

Despite everything she had heard and watched, her naivety wanted to believe him. But in that instant it was ripped away from her, for she caught hold of a yellow bar materialising at the bottom of the screen. And she stared at it for a long time, her body now physically shaking as the bar continued in an endless loop; replaying the same black bolded text.

BREAKING NEWS: EXPLOSIONS HAVE BEEN REPORTED AT THE UNITED STATES CONSULATES IN CAPE TOWN, DURBAN AND JOHANNESBURG, SOUTH AFRICA

'We are receiving some breaking news,' the female newsreader said, sounding suddenly unsettled, *'there are reports coming in that explosions have occurred at the United States Consulates in Cape Town, Durban and Johannesburg, South Africa.'*

Chapter Three

The Address

Seated at the HMS Resolute in the Oval Office, the President of the United States felt an unusual sense of isolation despite the fact that he was surrounded by his most senior of advisors. All were reassuring him that it wasn't his fault, that he couldn't have predicted this, but he was letting the words wash over him, for they were meaningless. His job as President was to protect the American people, he had failed in his duty.

It seemed now that an invisible barrier separated him from his aids and advisors, the offers of reassurance could not suppress the two minute and thirty-seven second video that was now overwhelming and tormenting his brain.

It was made clear from the beginning that this was no accident, the President knew this: Four explosions, all on United States soil, happening on the same day. *Accident? Impossible!* It had been organised and executed by a well-known terrorist network. But as the hours passed none claimed responsibility, until something quite unexpected happened.

Exactly one hour after the Consulate bombings, a video was placed upon the internet. The statement was addressed by a small, thin man with a bald head and thick dark moustache named Zuberi Jacobs, admitter of all the American bombings and leader of a group calling themselves the Liberators of South Africa.

This man Zuberi wore no mask, no military uniform nor was he holding a weapon. The video was not filmed underground or in a cave but rather in a simple looking room. And from the moment President Jack Carter had finished watching it, it seemed to nestle into his mind, infecting it with every passing second.

And in that moment of total solitude, the haunting words Zuberi Jacobs had told the whole world with, began to echo inside his head once again.

'My name is Zuberi Jacobs,' he had begun in flawless English, his voice was deep and powerful, *'and I am a terrorist.*

No doubt that is what the President of the United States will condemn me as.'

He slowly stood from behind the desk he sat at and lifted up his dark green T-shirt to present his toned physic to the camera.

'No explosions strapped to my body, no weapons concealed, or in this room. I am just an ordinary man.'

He sat, his cold dark eyes staring deep into the camera lens.

'However, today has become a dark chapter, there is no escaping that fact, but I address these words regarding the bombing of the American Embassy and Consulates. The bombings can never be justified, so I will neither bore nor waste your time in trying to, but I will tell you this: I desire to live in a peaceful South Africa, but in order for this to happen, I must lead the brothers and sisters of the Liberators of South Africa into battle. A terrible injustice has occurred and those responsible must be held accountable.

'The road to victory will be long and many will die on the way, but their deaths will not be in vain. Once we become free men and women, we will turn South Africa into a country worthy of those who bravely gave their lives.

'If history has taught us anything it is the fine line between freedom fighting and terrorism, those who condemn me will portray me as a terrorist, but in time I will be hailed as a freedom fighter and a patriot.'

The address had put President Carter at a crossroads: apprehend those who were responsible, then many could, and most probably would, die, ignore the Americans who died, then justice would never be. Whatever decision he chose, it would be wrong in the eyes of some.

How does one way up human life? he thought deeply, *does punishing the wicked to avenge the virtuous accomplish anything? How can one justify going to war? An eye for an eye?*

He sighed and stared out at the mass of people.

Without war there can be no peace.

One by one, the senior advisors offered their support before they walked off into the mass of people, leaving the President to think about the many great American leaders before him, and how they coped in the face of their adversaries.

We are at war with terrorists ... this is the hardest decision I have ever had to make.

'Mr President,' the man by the camera said, bringing him back to his surroundings, 'you're live in five ... four...'

His voice grew to a whisper.

'...three ... two ... one...'

Taking a moment to compose himself, President Jack Carter drew a deep breath, stared directly into the camera in front of him and began to deliver *the* most important speech of his life.

'Good evening...'

*

The sheer fascination of human tragedy mixed with terrorist involvement had drawn millions of people across the globe toward their television sets. Fear and dread had settled over the whole of America and the atmosphere inside Frank Lane's stunning mansion was no exception.

Those that were staying for the night had gathered in the magnificent living room, each man and woman watching with increasing anxiety as the President began his much awaited address.

'Today,' his gloomy tone echoed out, *'our fellow Americans stationed at the United States Embassy and Consulates in South Africa came under attack in a series of well organised and deadly terrorist attacks...'*

Sitting next to Mark, with Melissa fast asleep in her arms, Lisa found it very hard to listen to the words, when she already knew what was going to happen. She had been a part of Mark's military career long enough to know what action would be taken when a situation like this occurred. But there was a small fragment of her that hoped the President would make the right decision, that he would look past the people who had died and see that going to war would not bring them back, nor would it help the United States of America. But she was naive to even think that, and she could not sit here and listen as her worst fears were confirmed. She leaned inwards towards Mark and whispered, 'I'm taking Melissa to bed.'

But Mark did not answer; he was enthralled with what the President had to say.

Lisa positioned Melissa so that her head was resting on her shoulder, then she held her close, stood and walked out of the room. The President's voice could no longer be heard when Lisa walked into the bedroom where Melissa would be sleeping. She gently laid her daughter onto the bed and pulled the covers over her.

'Is daddy going to go away again?' Melissa asked, her eyes now open.

'No, of course not sweetie, daddy isn't going anywhere,' Lisa said, not at all convincingly.

'Then why are you crying?' asked Melissa, half concerned, half curious.

'I've just got something in my eye, that's all.'

Melissa tilted her head to one side, her expression leaving little doubt that she knew her mother was lying.

'Nothing gets past you, does it,' Lisa said quietly.

'Nope,' Melissa said with a confident smile.

Lisa tucked in the duvet and kissed Melissa on the forehead.

'I don't want daddy to go away.'

The confident smile Melissa had shown only moments earlier was now gone, and Lisa knew that it was only now, before she was to close her eyes and drift off to sleep, that could have forced Melissa to reveal how great and sincere the fear of losing her father was.

'Nobody does sweetie,' Lisa said softly, 'try not to think about it.'

She stood a moment, staring and smiling down at her daughter before she turned and headed for the door.

'Sleep well,' she said not looking back, and she turned off the light and left a sliver of a gap in the door.

When Lisa arrived in the kitchen, there stood Mark, rummaging through the large silver refrigerator, clinking glasses as he pulled out three bottles of beer.

'Are you going to be sent?' she asked.

Mark did not turn.

'Most probably,' he said quietly.

Lisa made no attempt to hide her anger and frustration, cursing, and sighing deeply, she scraped the legs of the kitchen table chair against the stone flooring and dropped down into the seat.

'I love my country very much,' Mark said.

Lisa turned, but Mark did not look at her, still standing in front of the open refrigerator, he welcomed the cool air brushing against his flushing face.

'And what about your daughter and fiancée?' she asked, her tone one of outrage. 'Are we given a second thought?'

Mark closed the refrigerator door, walked over to Lisa and crouched down so that her face was a fraction above his.

'Everything will be fine,' he said quietly.

'No it won't be,' Lisa said, unable to look at him now, 'I've been watching the news...'

Mark tried to hold her hand to give reassurance, but she pulled away.

'...Your words mean nothing, you think they reassure me, but they don't.'

But before Mark could reply, there was an awkward clearing of a throat. And there was Robert, standing by the kitchen doorway.

'Sorry to disturb you both,' he said with an uncomfortable look, 'I just wanted to get the drinks.'

'I've got them here,' Mark said.

He looked at Lisa for a fleeting moment, before he stood and walked out of the kitchen, handing Robert his beer as he passed.

Alone now, Robert wasn't quite sure what to do, he wanted to comfort Lisa, offer her some sort of reassurance, but what would he say?

'He probably won't even get sent,' he said, 'the last thing America and the President need is to get involved in another war.'

'I'm not a little girl, Robert,' Lisa said indigently, 'you don't have to tell me fairytales.'

'Yeah,' said Robert – why were his cheeks burning? Why did they have to go red now? – 'I'm sorry.'

As soon as he said it, he knew that his apology was feeble. *I'm sorry,* he cringed at the very words, surely he could have thought of something better to say.

He was about to leave when Lisa threw back her hair and turned around. Despite her puffy red eyes and cheeks streaked with mascara, she looked even more beautiful and captivating. And in that moment, where his eyes met hers, Robert fell in love with Lisa Anderson all over again.

'It's been a long night,' she said, smiling. 'I'm sorry.'

Robert accepted the apology and he walked over to the large freezer, pulled open the door and reached for the tub of strawberry ice cream.

Then, without saying a word, he picked up two dessert spoons resting on the draining board and sat down opposite Lisa at the table. Taking off the lid, he slid the tub to the middle and held out one of the dessert spoons for Lisa, who took it with a smile.

They both were happy enough to just sit in silence while eating spoonfuls of ice cream.

Chapter Four

South Africa's Saviour

May 24th

'Right Melissa,' Mark said quickly, as he stood in front of the resplendent pine bookcase with letters from the alphabet carved intricately all around it, 'which bedtime story would you like read to you? Now remember, you can only have one tonight, it's already an hour past your bedtime.'

'Okay Daddy,' she muttered as she climbed into her bed with her favourite doll and pulled her pink flowered duvet cover up to her shoulders.

Mark ran his finger across the books that lined the bookcase, reading out the titles as he went.

'*Angel's Incredible Journey* ... *Rupert Rabbit and Friends* ... *The Great Encyclopaedia of Mammals* ... *The Land of the Fairy Princess* ... *The Castle on Princess Hill* ... oh look...'

He pulled out a large, thick shiny book; a picture of a white horse with a horn protruding from its forehead was beautifully illustrated on the front of it.

'...*The Legend of the Unicorn*, you haven't had that read to you in a while.'

He looked over at Melissa, who was merely straightening the hair of her doll, but she said nothing.

'*The Legend of the Unicorn*,' Mark repeated, showing the front of the book to Melissa, 'would you like me to read it to you?'

'No,' Melissa mumbled, speaking to the doll as she continued to straighten its long black hair.

Mark slid the book back in its place and continued to read out the titles, albeit in a more whispery tone.

'Daddy,' Melissa said, tilting her head to one side, looking rather puzzled, 'why do you have to go away?'

Mark stopped suddenly. Drawing a heavy breath, he looked at his daughter sympathetically. Ever since South Africa had fallen in disarray and America was preparing to send its finest to put an end to the violence, he'd been expecting this question, even preparing himself for it. However, this was the last thing on earth he wanted to talk about, especially with his five year old daughter.

'Well Melissa,' he said softly.

He walked over to the bed, sat next to her, and looked directly in her small, innocent eyes. He wasn't quite sure how to tell her, or if in fact he should, it seemed such a complex issue to explain to such a young girl. Just as he decided to say nothing, and to simply change the subject, Melissa put her doll on the single drawer chest and pressed the matter further.

'I saw mommy watching the television,' she said, rubbing her tired eyes with the back of her hands, 'the people were talking about a war somewhere in the South – South—'

'South Africa?' Mark prompted.

'Yeah,' said Melissa brightly, 'they said that soldiers were going over there to fight and that's when mommy started to get upset.'

Mark considered for a moment what he should tell her.

'Well Melissa,' he began softly, 'the reason why mommy got upset is because the American President has ordered lots of soldiers to go over to South Africa in the hope of stopping the war there.'

'Soldiers like you, Daddy?' Melissa said, looking up at Mark.

'Yes that's right,' Mark said, 'soldiers like me.'

The room suddenly fell silent. Melissa's eyes moved from her father's back towards the doll resting on the bedside chest, a moment later she picked it up and began straightening its hair once more. Mark put his arm around her, and as he pulled her closer, he kissed the top of her head.

'Is war a bad thing, Daddy?' Melissa asked finally, speaking to the doll.

'Yes,' Mark said, understanding his daughter's desire to know why he was going away. 'It's a very very bad thing. It's something that should never, ever happen, but well sometimes it does.' He paused for a moment. 'It's difficult Melissa,' he continued, 'to try and simplify it all so that you will be able to understand.' Again he paused for a moment. 'War happens when people in a country try and hurt other people in that same country or in a different one.'

'Is that why you have to go away?' Melissa asked, she had stopped straightening the doll's hair and was now looking up at him. 'Do you have to stop the bad people from hurting the good people?'

'That's right, it's my job to go to South Africa and help the good people.'

Melissa nodded slowly. Seemingly satisfied she smiled up at her father and cuddled into him.

'Okay,' Mark said, getting to his feet and walking back towards the book shelf, 'so what story would you like me to read to you?'

'Hmm, I would like … *Rupert Rabbit and Friends* pease, Daddy.'

Pulling out the small brightly coloured book, Mark lay next to Melissa and cuddled into her. He turned over to the first page, and cleared his throat.

'This story begins with –'

'Daddy?' Melissa said quietly.

Mark closed the book, but did not answer.

'Daddy,' she continued, her voice now growing with worry as her hand gripped her father's, 'are the bad people going to try and hurt you?'

What should he tell her? The truth? Melissa would certainly have nightmares. Then what? He was going to war, there was always a possibility of him being injured, or even killed. But was it right to hide this fact from her? Would she think any less of him if he told her a fairytale? What if he told her a tale and something did happen to him? It seemed that there was no easy option for him to take.

'Well,' he said, sighing, 'yes, Melissa, they're going to try, but daddy is going with some of his friends, and we won't let that happen, I promise.'

For a moment they just sat in the silence, simply staring at one another, before Melissa smiled up at him.

Mark reopened the book and started to read.

'This story begins with –'

'I don't want a story now, Daddy,' Melissa said suddenly, shaking her head. 'I want to go to sleep.'

'Oh,' Mark said, unable to hide his disappointment, 'never mind. Are you too tired to give me a kiss goodnight?'

Melissa giggled, then she knelt up, threw her arms around Mark's neck and gently kissed him on the cheek.

'Don't forget to give Lucy a kiss, Daddy,' she said, holding out the doll.

Mark took hold of it and stared at its small black beady eyes, a moment later he was planting kisses over its face, much to Melissa's giggling delight.

*

Wandering into his bedroom, his thoughts now a swirling creation of worry, regret and empathy, Mark sat on the edge of *his* side of the bed, took off his watch, put it on the bedside table and ran a hand across his shaved head. The television, although muted was playing in the background, and in the adjacent room he could hear the faint, steady stream of a shower.

In his preoccupied state of mind, he hadn't noticed the white candles dotted around the room, flickering elegantly, the rose petals scattered evenly in the centre of the bed, the champagne bottle nestling in the ice bucket, or the two crystal glasses and strawberries resting by the television.

Lisa had gone to great lengths to make this evening one to remember. Smiling broadly, he jumped to his feet and hurried over to the television. With his finger poised over the power button, he glanced quickly at what was being shown.

The room was monumental. Brightly lit from above, the entire screen was filled with row upon row of rising blue fabric chairs, all of which were occupied by both men and women, young and old. They were all staring down at something and a moment later the majority showed stern expressions and were shaking their heads.

The camera suddenly switched focus to a young African-American gentleman dressed in a smart burgundy suit with his hand raised.

Despite being fully aware, Mark didn't know why he was doing it, why he was pressing the volume button, why he kept pressing it until the man's voice was no higher than a whisper and why he leaned in closer to hear the conversation.

'I would like to ask the panel their views on the decision the United States Government has taken to send military personnel to South Africa?' the man said, lowering his hand.

'This is of course,' said a professional female voice out of nowhere, *'the news in which President Carter has ordered American personnel to South Africa in an attempt to end the violence there.'*

The screen switched focus again to seven people – three men and four women – seated in leather chairs at a large, rectangular glass table. Mark recognised one of the faces instantly.

In the very middle of the group sat Kelly Prescott, the beautiful doe-eyed brunette who hosted the highly popular, yet often controversial, debate show, *Questions & Answers Time*.

'Okay,' Kelly continued, *'Erm ... Professor Koller? Your answer please.'*

The camera zoomed in towards the short gentleman positioned at the very end of the table. He was portly and clean shaven, with long silvery hair that flowed over his shoulders and oval-shaped glasses that perched on the edge of his nose. White bold lettering suddenly appeared under him.

PROFESSOR HANS KOLLER
TERROR EXPERT

'Well,' Koller said in impeccable English, despite him having a thick German accent, *'the South African war is such a controversial subject, people are divided on the matter, and I feel – no, no, I know that America was condemned from the very beginning over which action to take.'*

He paused for a moment, pushing his glasses further up his nose as he leaned forward.

'But let us not forget that before the assassination of the South African President, he had asked America for their help in fighting against the Liberators of South Africa. So that it itself had put Jack Carter at a crossroads.

'So was America right to send four thousand troops?' Kelly asked, although the camera did not move away from Koller.

'Difficult to answer,' Koller said, and he took several sips of his chilled sparkling water. *'America sent troops to South Africa to put an end to the war and hold those accountable for the Embassy and Consulates bombings, so was it right? Yes I believe it was.'*

'Okay, thank you Professor Koller,' Kelly said, the camera now returning to her, *'Jessica Mayer, your answer please.'*

The camera switched to the woman who sat next to Hans Koller. She was beautifully dressed in a dark green suit, her hair was tied in a ponytail and her manicured fingernails were painted black which perfectly suited her slightly tanned complexion. As with Professor Koller, white bold lettering appeared under her.

JESSICA MAYOR
WRITER AND BROADCASTER

'There has been a lot of emphasis on Zuberi Jacobs and the reasons why he targeted the American Embassy and Consulates and descended South Africa into a state of war,' Jessica said softly in her British accent. *'But the bottom line is the Liberators of South Africa are terrorists and no amount of vindication could ever defend the massacre of over fifty-six hundred innocent men, women and children—'*

'THAT IS ABSOLUTELY RIDICULOUS...' a strong, powerful male voice boomed nearby.

Gasps and murmurs began to run through the audience, they all knew that this discussion was going to get quite heated. The camera suddenly zoomed towards the thin gangly man sitting to the left of Kelly Prescott, a moment later white bold lettering appeared under him.

JAMES ALBA
CREATOR OF INTERNET WEBSITE: LIBERATORS OF SOUTH AFRICA: TERRORISTS OR FREEDOM FIGHTERS?

'...the Liberators of South Africa have never killed civilians; America used that propaganda to justify this war –'

'And you say I am ridiculous,' Jessica Mayer said, laughing heartily now as the camera turned focus back to her, *'America have never once used propaganda to justify this war, and you say the Liberators have never killed civilians?'*

She paused a moment to allow her adversary to respond, but James Alba remained silent, so Mayer continued, *'Well what about the massacre of Cape Town?'* she asked in a pugnacious tone.

Again she paused, but there was still no response.

'One hundred and thirty-three men, women and children were lined up, and over a four hour period, they were shot one by one.'

The camera quickly focused on James Alba, who was smirking as he stared out at the crowd, before returning to Mayor.

'But they were not content with this mindless killing. After shooting the last of the civilians the Liberators of South Africa then stripped-naked the bodies and then hung them from the homes they had once occupied –'

Mark switched off the television, threw himself backwards onto the bed and closed his eyes in an attempt to savour and appreciate the soft glowing ambience and silence. Once again the South African war presented itself, tormenting his mind and thoughts. And in the next few weeks he would be there, fighting against the Liberators of South Africa, doing his utmost to restore peace and hope to the country. He, along with thousands of other servicemen and women were, as the former South African President had so passionately put it, South Africa's Saviours.

However, the American people were divided on the prospect of their military getting involved in South Africa's conflict, and Mark was no exception. The problem was that he had always been encouraged by his mother to fight for what he believed in, but what if he didn't believe in the cause? Should he still fight? Would it make him less of a man if he didn't?

His past tours had been so clear-cut: *We are freeing these people from tyranny … Fighting in this country will help towards winning the war on terrorism … This is so our loved ones can live in a world of peace.*

The faint streaming coming from the bathroom suddenly stopped and Mark opened his eyes and rolled his head towards the adjacent room. It was at times like these – when he felt alone or worried or scared – that Mark needed to hold his soul mate, to inhale the fragrance of her hair, to feel the warmth of her skin, to see the hope in her smile.

And as he got to his feet and pulled off his white T-shirt, he felt a slight draft pressing against his bare chest. Across the room he could see the curtains swaying ever so slightly. Dropping his shirt onto the bed, he crossed over to the window – which had been left open a shade – and closed it shut. And as he stared at his disorientated reflection in the thick gleaming glass, a pair of soft hands suddenly, but gently, covered his eyes.

'Surprise,' Lisa whispered into his ear.

Mark gripped her wrists, slowly pulled her hands away and turned and stared into a pair of soft brown eyes, which were gazing back at him. Lisa looked captivating in her peach satin dressing gown, while her shiny, slightly damp, brunette hair flowed elegantly over her right shoulder.

For a moment they just looked at one another, before Lisa walked over to the champagne bottle and lifted it out of the ice bucket. Water droplets dripped onto the chest of drawers as she filled the two crystal glasses, and as she held out one for Mark, a mischievous glint seemed to twinkle in her eye.

'Champagne?' she asked, smiling seductively.

Mark stepped forward; his fingers brushed against Lisa's as he took the glass and offered his thanks.

'I hope you believe in God, Mark Lane,' Lisa said, as she stood before him with her hands on her hips, 'because I'm going to take you to heaven.'

But before Mark could even comment on the alluring use of words, Lisa pulled at the tie of the dressing gown and allowed it to fall to the floor.

And as Mark stared in wonder at the nakedness of Lisa, the fear he had towards the South African war – which had infested his thoughts and weighed heavily on his heart – seemed to lessen.

'I love you,' he said finally. 'I always have you know.'

And with one swift motion she was upon him, arms wrapped around his waist, kissing him deeply. And in that moment, Mark closed his eyes and became lost in the embrace.

In spite of everything; the long and unknowing path set before him, the possibility of him dying in South Africa, he felt himself fortunate to be spending his last night with the woman he loved.

Chapter Five

The Liberators of South Africa

August 18th

Washington, in part the whole world, had all predicted, expected even, for the war in South Africa to last no more than six months. But as the fifteenth month approached, the war that had so far claimed the lives of three hundred and seven Americans, two thousand and seventeen Liberators of South Africa and over fifteen thousand civilians, still raged, and showed no sign of ending.

The simple truth was that the Liberators of South Africa had been severely underestimated. Zuberi Jacobs and his high ranking associates were calculating, swift, but above all methodical. They had ingeniously developed and constructed an underground network of tunnels and rooms throughout South Africa, they had perfected hit and run attacks and ambushes – which had the desired effect on the morale of the American soldiers – and perhaps most importantly, every man and woman was ready to give their lives for the cause.

However, as darkness began to fall over the Drakensburg Mountains, a lone marksman ran hard across the grassy plains, ignoring the escalating gunfire echoing in the distance and the eight black-backed jackals feeding hungrily on an oribi (slender legged, long necked small antelope) carcass. Gasping and panting, the marksman slowed, staring through the semi-darkness at the large stones partially hidden by thick clumps of dead grass. He was a bearer of grave news, news which would undoubtedly be the turning point in the South African war. He was returning from Pretoria after he had been sent on a perilous journey to the capital fourteen days ago.

For one teetering moment, while the gunfire from the far off battle and the sound of the jackals ravaging the carcass broke the silence and stillness, the marksman dropped to his knees, and looked around. Satisfied that he had not been followed, he crawled towards the grassy clumps and slowly and very carefully he began to remove the stones one by one.

Soon his fingers brushed against rough, splintery wood, and there, resting upon the earth sat a square door with a piece of looped rope attached to it. It was secured to planks of wood which ran all the way round, framing the square hole. But weather and age had rusted its hinges, and as the marksman gripped the piece of rope and pulled it towards him, it seemed to resist. Harder he pulled, and eventually it succumbed to the force, squeaking in protest.

A blast of cool, earthy air rose from the entrance. The marksman sat at the edge and dropped down onto an earthy ledge. Staring up at the last remnants of light in the sky, he fumbled for the rope and pulled the door shut, with much less resistance.

Now in the darkness, the marksman crouched. Rummaging through his pockets, he pulled out a satin chrome lighter so to illuminate his way.

A sheer drop faced him, he leaned forward, lighter in front of him and saw a wooden ladder, which disappeared into the darkness further down. He tried to remember how many rungs there were, but with his brain bearing this gravest of news and him wondering whether this ladder would still hold his weight, it was impossible to remember.

There was nothing for it. He lowered himself onto the ladder, clicked shut the lighter and slowly descended the rungs one by one. At last his feet touched firm ground and the marksman used the lighter once again to illuminate his way. It was cool, narrow, claustrophobic and damp underground. The marksman moved down the long tunnel, his back bent due to the low ceiling. But as he moved deeper, a realisation came to him. Would the high-ranking members of the Liberators of South Africa still be here after all this time? Two weeks had passed since he was last here and the South African war had changed so much in that time. The Americans and British were advancing everyday, had they uncovered this underground network of rooms and tunnels? He stopped and listened attentively in the darkness, to the silence all around him, half-expecting to hear foreign whispers or the cocking of a gun. He slowly moved down the tunnel once again, slipping his weapon off his shoulder as he went, holding it firmly in his hand.

Up ahead, two tunnels branched off to the left and right of the main one. And as the marksman approached this junction, he stopped and once again listened to the silence. The two tunnels that branched off led to the sleeping quarters, and as he chose to take the right, he held his rifle at the ready and slowly and very quietly inched down.

The tunnel sloped and as the marksman followed it down he came to the entrance. There was no door, it just went straight through into the room. Holding the lighter out in front of him, he crawled through into the sleeping area. Every one of the makeshift beds was occupied with members of the Liberators of South Africa, each one plainly asleep, their dreams unaffected by the death and destruction occurring not far from here.

Satisfied that this underground network had not been infiltrated, the marksman turned swiftly and silently, slid his weapon across his shoulder and crawled back up the cool, damp earth. And as he crawled back onto the main tunnel, he turned right and continued to follow it down, after ten or so metres a light breeze flickered the lighter's flame and with it came faint words.

'…with all due respect sir, we have no idea if Gazini ever made it to Pretoria; we have had no word from him since he began his journey to the capital –'

'Gazini is a great man,' a deep voice said. 'I sent him to Pretoria safe in the knowledge that he would not fail me.'

'But sir, South Africa is falling all around us, we must act now if we are to win this war…'

And there, up ahead, the marksman could see patches of dull light streaming through the gaps in a wooden door. He clicked shut the lighter and put it in his trouser pocket. Then he crawled a little further, knocked several times on the door in a sort of rhythmic fashion, pushed it open and crawled through.

The sparsely furnished room was filled with high-ranking associates of the Liberators of South Africa, all of which were seated at a long, simple looking table. Illumination, though scarce, came from oil lamps, which were scattered evenly throughout the vast room. And as the marksman's eyes adapted to this inadequate lighting, a cold, deep voice issued from the head of the table.

'Gazini,' it said through the eerie silence, 'our brother returns, welcome back.'

The marksman could barely make out the faint outline of the speaker, but he recognised the voice instantly. Drawing nearer, the dark, cold eyes of Zuberi Jacobs could be seen through the dimness.

'Sit here,' Zuberi said, motioning to the empty seat on his right.

The eyes around the table continued to follow the marksman as he removed his weapon, made sure that it could not fire off a round and rested it against his chair, then he took up his allocated place. Once he was seated, they all looked back at Zuberi.

'So what news do you bring from Pretoria?' Zuberi asked.

Gazini hesitated only for a brief moment, 'It is under the control of the Americans and British sir,' he said dryly, 'there is nothing left, none survived the onslaught.'

The men and women around the table watched Zuberi apprehensively; many of them pulled their stares away from him and simply stared down at their laps, fearing that any sort of eye contact would single them out.

Zuberi's persona had gradually altered over the last fourteen months. At the dawn of the South African conflict he took a philosophical approach to everything, his strategies and tactics were long and thought out and all were met with success. However, thirteen months on, the effects of the war had affected him deeply, so desperate he was to end it, he made critical mistakes, which he did not accept responsibility for. His tolerance towards failure dwindled and soon his wrath became infamous across South Africa, and no man or woman sitting here tonight wanted to experience it due to the loss of over a thousand Liberator lives.

But Zuberi, for whatever reason, said nothing. Instead, he leaned back in his chair, which creaked loudly and drummed his long fingers on the table.

'No doubt our brothers and sisters would have fought valiantly,' he said finally in a sort of philosophical tone, 'but the British and the Americans will hail this as a great victory, however, their over confidence and ignorance will be their ultimate downfall.'

He leaned forward, his dark eyes glistening in the oil lamps illumination as he rested his elbows on the table.

'This is the turning point in the war,' he said, staring at each of the faces, 'and so we must choose our next step wisely ... Momentum favours the Americans and British due to their successful capture of Pretoria, the next step for them will be to try and retake Johannesburg.'

All of his followers were nodding their heads in agreement.

'The last thing they will expect is for us to bide our time and retake Pretoria.'

The men and women around him became suddenly unsettled, and murmurs quickly circled the table. The announcement was most unexpected. Halfway down the table, Tau Myers, a tall, thickly set man, with a dark leather patch covering his left eye, leaned forward.

'With such a force there sir,' he said, his voice was as deep and cold as the earth that surrounded him, 'maybe it's time for us to discuss other alternatives.'

'We have no other alternatives,' said Zuberi softly, 'I am not blind to see that South Africa is falling all around us. Pretoria is where it all began; we must retake it that is the last thing they will expect.'

'Sir, with all due respect,' Tau said, bravely squaring his shoulders, 'we cannot defeat them in the capital.'

Zuberi curled his hands into fists and slammed them on the table, 'DO NOT TELL ME WE CANNOT DEFEAT THEM!' he roared.

Most of the Liberators were neither looking at Zuberi nor Tau now, they just sat in silence, staring down at their own laps.

'We bombed the United States Embassy and Consulates,' continued Zuberi, his rage now subsiding, 'we have killed many of our enemies ... many claimed that the war would last no more than six months, the fifteenth month is approaching and we are still fighting...'

He stared at Tau, who was bravely staring back into the dark, detached eyes.

'...so never tell me that our enemies cannot be defeated.'

Tau did nothing more than nod his head curtly.

'As I was saying,' Zuberi said, looking again at the faces of the men and women who sat around him, 'we will bide our time and retake Pretoria.'

He paused for a fraction of a moment. This time no one cast doubt on his strategy, his followers sat in their chairs, silent.

'Once we have successfully retaken the capital the end will soon be in sight.'

The faces around him showed that they did not share his optimism.

'The South African Saviours continue to fight because they have little choice, if they withdraw now then those who have given their lives, have done so for nothing. But how many lives will it take for the politicians to realise that they cannot win this war?'

It was a rhetorical question, he was continuing before any of the men and women could answer.

'The road will be long and many more will die along the way but we will never withdraw. We will fight and we will not stop until we win this war.'

The silence that followed the words was only momentarily.

'Sir,' the timid voiced speaker said, looking down the long table.

He paused a moment to allow Zuberi to answer, but Zuberi did not, he looked to be lost in thought, so he continued, 'Sir, the Brotherhood of –'

The words brought Zuberi out of his trance-like state immediately and he stared at the man with such intensity that he subsided at once. Of all the things Zuberi had been told this evening, nothing had seemed to unnerve him like these words had.

'Arapmoi Sebothoma,' he said, his lips quivering slightly from saying the name aloud, 'the renowned philosopher who is to bring about my downfall. What of him and his so-called Brotherhood of Sakarabru?'

'They grow influential everyday,' the man said truthfully, 'Lenka Shone has on many occasions spoken of the growing relationship he and the rest of the Council have with the Brotherhood.'

'Yes, yes,' said Zuberi softly, 'but that will all change soon. The brother who I sent to infiltrate the Council has succeeded. Soon he will plant the seed of mistrust in Lenka Shone's mind, convincing him that the Brotherhood is going to bring about the collapse of the Council.'

He stood, placed his hands behind his back and began to walk around the room.

'And yet, having been told about the Brotherhood of Sakarabru steadily gaining power and support troubles me deeply. There can be no denying the fact that Arapmoi Sebothoma is a great man, but he is no greater than me.'

Still he walked, looking at the faces of the men and women as he passed them.

'We both love our country, we are both methodical in our approach and we both are gifted in inspiring the people to fight for our causes.' He stopped behind the bald-headed man who sat at the opposite end of the table to him. 'So what does Arapmoi offer that I do not, Moswen?' he asked, laying a hand on the man's shoulder.

'He offers nothing sir,' Moswen Karpel said at once, glancing briefly over his shoulder, 'you are far greater than he.'

A faint smile curled upon Zuberi's lips. He patted Moswen on his back and began to walk once again.

'If what you say is true Moswen,' he said softly, 'and I believe it is, then our problem must lie with you.'

'Sir?' Moswen said blankly.

Every man and woman was looking at Moswen now, he was in charge of recruiting and each of them wondered whether this failure was going to result in his death.

'You were one of the many politicians, who publicly condemned me over the Embassy and Consulate bombings,' Zuberi said, his tone was serene, musing.

'I was wrong,' said Moswen calmly, 'I did not know all the facts.'

'No you didn't,' said Zuberi silkily, 'but that did not stop you or indeed anyone else from speaking out.'

'I can only offer my apologies,' Moswen said, as tiny beads of sweat began to gather on his forehead.

'Oh how you fell from grace,' Zuberi said, narrowing his eyes a fraction. 'The outspoken politician who fell to his knees, begging me to spare his life. And I was kind to you, placing you in charge of recruitment because of your relationship with the people. But would you presume me to be that ignorant that I would not have you watched closely.'

Moswen's lips parted but no words came from his mouth.

'You should know that every wall has got ears. I know all about the deal you have with Lenka Shone.'

Moswen's eyes widened when told this. And in that moment, the cleverly thought out plan to assist in the capture of Zuberi, in effect ending the war, came crashing down all around him.

'Sir – I-I –'

'Assist in the capture of me and you would have been offered a place in the new restructured Government,' said Zuberi. 'Deputy President of South Africa I believe it was.'

'No sir.' Moswen wiped away the gathering sweat from his forehead. 'That is not true, whoever told you that is wrong.'

'Such lies, Moswen,' Zuberi said softly, 'the Americans know all about this underground facility.' He looked at his small watch with fading leather straps. 'And they intend to strike in little over three hours.'

The faces around him displayed nothing but shock, every man and woman looked down the bottom of the table, in deep disgust at the man sitting there.

'Sir, I beg of you.'

Zuberi's laugh was so deep and thunderous that it made him sound a little mad. Moswen looked at the man and woman sitting either side of him, hoping that they would come to his defence; they both were involved in this intricate plan, surely they wouldn't just sit there and say nothing. But that is exactly what they did. They both looked at him, their eyes beginning to soften, both regretting what they were about to do. The pair turned away, unable to watch what was about to happen to him.

'The final words from a desperate man,' said Zuberi coldly.

And with one swift motion he pulled the pistol from out of its holster and aimed it directly at the man sitting opposite him.

'Please sir,' Moswen said.

He stood, raising his hands in defence, but it accomplished nothing. The deafening gunshot echoed throughout the room, some of the Liberators jumped out of their chairs, and time seemed to slow from that point. The bullet hit Moswen squarely on the left side of his chest, the fear had not faded from his rugged face, but his eyes widened in shock. He fell backwards into his chair, his arms splaying, his breathing coming in short, wheezy gasps, then both he and the chair hit the floor with a resounding thud.

The Liberators that had jumped to their feet quickly sat as Zuberi slowly walked around the table and stared down at the man whose bloody body was jerking violently on the floor.

'You gave me no choice,' Zuberi said, his voice no higher than a whisper.

A gurgling sound issued from Moswen's throat, and Zuberi raised his pistol and kept firing until Moswen Karpel moved no more.

The execution had drawn a shocked silence to the room. The man and woman who had sat either side of Moswen did not speak, they lowered their heads and closed their eyes, hoping, praying that they would not experience the same fate their co-conspirer had.

But Zuberi did not see this, nor did anyone else, and as he slid his pistol back into its holster, the main door to the room flew open and about a dozen men and women, who had been sleeping only moments earlier, poured in, their weapons held and ready to fight if need be, a few more arrived soon after. They all looked at Zuberi.

'Pack your things,' he told them all, 'and tell the others to do the same, we leave in one hour.'

They all said, 'Yes sir,' at different times, before hurrying off.

'Tau,' Zuberi said, looking over at the man with the leather patch covering his left eye, 'how many are there to fight?'

'Six, possibly seven thousand,' Tau said, 'I cannot give an exact number.'

He was not looking at Zuberi when he said the words. His dark eye was still fixed upon the body of Moswen, watching the blood as it pooled out from under it.

'That is not nearly enough to retake Pretoria,' said Zuberi truthfully. 'There have been too many mistakes; some I admit are from my own doing.'

He looked down at Moswen; he felt no sadness, no remorse. Everyone around the table watched him do so, unsure what to make of this sudden admittance of failure.

'The first move has been made,' he said, not tearing his eyes from the body, 'but the next step must be chosen wisely.'

He turned and walked away, without given so much of a backward glance.

'Tau, Gazini,' he said before leaving the room, 'you know what must be done with the body.'

Chapter Six

A New Plan

August 19th

What was left of Moswen after the animals and birds had had their fill was found by the Americans early next morning. The underground network was deserted and Moswen's body had been stripped naked and hung from a tree about three hundred metres or so from the main entrance.

Many miles away, residing in a grand memorial building that now housed the remaining politicians of South Africa, Lenka Shone's aide was hurrying down the carpeted corridor floor, sweat had gathered on his dark skin and had soaked his shirt underneath his armpits.

Luthuli Dros was twenty-five, but the South African war had aged him dramatically. He had not yet perfected the ability to survive on only a few hours sleep, like so many of the politicians in this building did, and it showed. There was nothing striking about Luthuli, he was of average height and his appearance and looks were plain. And it was because of this that many believed prompted Lenka to hire him as his aide. Standing side by side, Lenka Shone – a man with designer facial hair, expensive taste in clothing and handsome looks – stood out that much more. Although Lenka quashed this at once and said it was down to Luthuli's hard work, dedication and intellect.

Luthuli had almost reached the lone door at the end of the long corridor and as soon as he reached it he opened it and walked straight through without knocking. Lenka was sat behind his desk, smartly dressed, reading through a stack of official looking documents. He looked up and smiled as soon as he heard Luthuli enter.

'You're up early,' he said amused, glancing at his designer watch. 'Would you like a cup of tea?'

'Moswen Karpel is dead,' Luthuli said suddenly, 'the Americans found his naked body early this morning.'

'I see,' said Lenka, his smile now fading. But his pause was only momentarily. 'How about that cup of tea?'

'Sir,' Luthuli said, who was sure that Lenka had not heard him properly, 'Moswen Karpel is dead.'

Lenka placed a finger on his lips to silence Luthuli who did so at once, and then he stood and hurried quietly over to the door. He opened it a fraction and stared through the sliver of a gap, and once he was satisfied that no one was listening he closed the door shut and turned quickly.

'It is sad news about Moswen,' he said quietly, walking back towards his desk, 'but now it has become clear that someone within this building is working for the Liberators of South Africa.'

He sat behind his desk while Luthuli sat opposite.

'Sir, you cannot be sure of that,' he said, his voice no higher than a whisper.

'Yes I can be,' said Lenka confidently, 'we took every precaution to keep Moswen's actions anonymous to the Liberators, only the people here knew that he was working for us.'

Luthuli slumped back in his chair and looked down at his lap. 'What do we do now sir,' he said despairingly, 'Moswen was close to Zuberi, he was one of the select few of his high-ranking officers.'

'Moswen was not the only one who wanted Zuberi dead,' said Lenka quietly, 'we have many more that can replace him.'

Luthuli could feel his back straighten; he looked up and stared directly into Lenka's eyes.

'But I think it is best if their identities remain secret,' Lenka said, smiling, 'someone is working for the Liberators, it is safer for you not to know who is working for us.'

Luthuli understood completely; knowing any of their identities could put him in grave danger and he acknowledged Lenka's best interests by nodding.

'Now,' Lenka said, smiling brightly, 'how about that cup of tea.'

He stood and walked over to the kettle in the corner and clicked it on to boil.

Chapter Seven

A Shadow of his Former Self

August 20th

Robert Lane was fast asleep with the left side of his face resting upon his exquisite, handcrafted desk in his study. His right hand still clutched the glass tumbler he had been drinking from, and the newspaper he had been reading before he fell asleep in the early hours lay quite flat to the left of him, its headline announcing:

GLIMMER OF HOPE FOR AMERICA'S GOLDEN BOY?

Directly underneath, a colour picture of Robert, tired looking and unshaved, sitting at a table with six others took up most of the front page.

After his disastrous appearance on the controversial debate show, Questions & Answers Time, *last week, Robert Lane is rumoured to be retreating to a cottage somewhere in France.*
It has been an emotional fifteen months for the twenty-eight year old English born American, who is still trying to rebuild his life following the untimely deaths of his brother and father.
The retreat is said to be 'a last ditch effort' for America's golden boy who has already had several stints in rehab following his dependency on alcohol and sleeping tablets and who is currently seeing renowned psychiatrist Robin Haynes over his much published nervous breakdown and his on-going battle against depression.

Full Story: Pages 4-5
Robert Lane's Rise and Fall: Pages 6-7

Robert grunted in his sleep and he rolled his head, the right side of his face now resting upon his desk. The room he was in was perhaps the most unique out of the twenty-seven rooms which made up his American home. It was a carefully blended mixture of handcrafted walnut furniture with accessories from around the world, but it was the fine collection of framed photographs secured firmly to the walls that many thought demonstrated his true wealth and power. Shaking hands with the President of the United States and the Prime Minister of Great Britain, posing on the red carpet with glamorous British Actress Kate Morris, at a charity event with Sir Nicholas Ross, the list was endless and quite spectacular.

Robert suddenly shifted in his sleep, and his arm knocked the glass tumbler to the floor. He awoke; the glass smashing was like an explosion going off in his head. He sat upright, dazed, and looked around the room with his sore, tired eyes. It took a while for him to remember what he had been doing before he fell asleep, but as his eyes glanced upon the newspaper on the desk the night's events came rushing back to him.

The golden dials on his Jean-Paul Henry watch pointed towards five o'clock and Robert sat only for a brief moment before he threw the newspaper in the bin, stood, switched off the desk lamp and wandered out of his study.

Now in the hallway, Robert walked quietly along the carpeted floor, but instead of going directly to his room, he stopped outside the second bedroom he came to. Standing only inches away from the door; he ran his fingers over the polished grain of wood and closed his eyes.

Lisa would no doubt be asleep at his hour. He stepped closer to the door, his body now millimetres away. What he would give to sleep next to her, to feel the warmth of her skin, to hear the beating of her heart, to watch her as she slept, and at that precise moment, the hallway was suddenly illuminated by the outside security light underneath the window. The light pulled Robert out of his wondering state; he walked over to the window and peered through, trying to see what had triggered the light.

The figure that slowly walked across the dewy grass was about average height but the black suit with matching tie and white shirt he wore showed that he was muscular. Robert had hired four bodyguards in all – three were to protect him and one was to protect Lisa and Melissa – all former United States soldiers, all survivors of the South African war. But it was this blond haired, blue eyed man he was looking at now, called Michael Parker that Robert had an unlikely connection with. His brother had died while saving Michael when they came under attack whilst out on patrol, and although Robert didn't hold Michael responsible for Mark's death it was clear that Michael had an unimaginable amount of guilt pressing down on him, and felt protecting Robert was the best thing for him to do.

The other two bodyguards Robert had not the same rapport with, Marcus Smith was a tall, muscular African-American, who had a square jaw, extremely short hair and hardened brown eyes. Derek Matheson was, in some respects quite average compared to both Michael and Marcus, he had plain features and spoke very little. The only thing striking about him was his left earlobe had been severed by flying debris from an explosion in South Africa.

Robert had also spent an unimaginable amount of money on custom made armoured vehicles and this very mansion. There could be no denying the fact that CyberTech Defence Systems was, in some respects, prospering from the South Africa war. America had ordered twenty-five of the revolutionary Black Raven helicopters. France, Germany and Italy had all placed orders for the mighty Juggernaut tank and Britain had ordered a dozen of the Armoured Personnel Transport Vehicles.

And as a result of these record contracts many had questioned Robert's true motives: did he really believe in the South African war or was he just a greedy businessman who was only interested in making profits? Antiwar campaigners believed it was the latter, and from the moment Robert became president of CyberTech Defence Systems they began their protests and soon threats against his life had become a real concern.

The bodyguard disappeared back into the shadows of the garden and the security light extinguished soon after, plunging the hallway back into its original dimness. Robert glanced over at Lisa's door only for a brief moment before he went straight to his bedroom.

Switching on the bedroom light, he walked directly over to the cream wardrobe doors and slid them apart. It stretched out about six metres or so, countless designer suits, shirts, trousers, jeans, coats, T-shirts, jumpers, shoes and trainers were either side as Robert walked down, heading towards the ceramic sink with chrome taps at the far end.

He ran the cold water and splashed it over his face several times, rinsing his mouth out each time as he did it. He turned off the tap and stared into the oval mirror, watching the water droplets drip from his face. Then grabbing the white towel hanging on the rail, he patted his face dry. The cotton towel felt soft against his unshaved face, it seemed to reinvigorate his skin, giving life back to it. He re-hung the towel on the rail and then reached for his black suitcase which was stored on one of the overhead shelves.

But as he pulled it down, a thick magazine layered with dust fell to the floor with a thud. Its brightly coloured front cover bore the name:

HER MAGAZINE
PROUDLY PRESENTS
THE ONE HUNDRED SEXIEST MALES IN THE WORLD

His attention caught, Robert put down his suitcase and scooped up the magazine. He began flicking through the pages, scanning the array of faces as he leaned against the wall, some were familiar, some not so. He continued flicking through just as his own name jumped out at him. But it still took him a moment or two for him to realise that he was looking at a photograph of himself. Dominating the top of the page were the bold lettered words:

Number One – Robert Lane: America's New Phenomenon

Directly underneath the headline was one of the answers he had given when asked a series of questions about filming the new CyberTech Defence Systems recruitment advertisement.

"The camera never made me nervous. I felt naturally comfortable in front of it."

Studying the picture closer, Robert suddenly remembered posing for the photographs in Italy; he was standing barefoot on a golden beach wearing dark blue jeans and a crisp unbuttoned white shirt which revealed his toned, tanned body. The scene was elegantly created with the calming blue ocean and the sun turning a dull orange just before it set, adding to the beauty.

There was an article printed on the right hand of the page which accompanied the photograph.

In the four years that we have conducted this poll, no man has ever achieved number one status in their first attempt ... until now.

In the last 12 months, thanks to the new CyberTech Defence Systems *advertisement taking the nation (and the world) by storm, the handsome English born American has become America's most sought-after national treasure. And it's not hard to see why. With his flawless good looks, great fashion sense and perfect body, it's like God himself decided to make one perfect man to walk upon the world he created. Add a pair of soft brown eyes and a smile that could melt the coldest of personalities and it's no wonder that the twenty-five year old has even surpassed thirty-one year old Italian ladies' man Cristiano De Luca as the world's sexiest man.*

And now, he accepts perhaps the greatest accolade a man could achieve: the reverential acclaim of Her Magazine's *readership. Such was the enormous surge in votes during the first two weeks that, within eight days of the polls opening, he had an overwhelming lead. In fact, when the voting closed he had achieved a landslide victory, taking forty-seven percent of the votes.*

Perhaps there is only one more question left to ask: Is he perfect? Well, he's tall, handsome, charismatic and single, the girl's here at Her Magazine *think he is.*

Words by Sue Jackson
Photographs by Rebecca Adams

And as Robert finished reading the words, an overwhelming feeling came crashing over him. He closed the magazine and as he looked up he caught hold of his reflection in the mirror.

'What's happened to you?' he whispered, walking towards the mirror.

The last fifteen months had taken its toll on him. Not only was he relying on tablets to help him sleep and alcohol to get him through most days, but his eyes were drawn and hazy and a dark shroud covered his cheeks, chin and upper lip. His hair was long and untidy and his body had lost all of its former glory.

But above all else, he was now alone. His brother had been killed while out on patrol in South Africa and his father had committed suicide six months later, most people had said that Mark's death had been the deciding factor. Robert, however, could never and would never forgive him. Such was the burning hatred he felt that he now refused to admit his father's entire existence.

He stood only for a few more seconds before he walked out of his dressing room, dropped the magazine in the small metal bin as he passed it and headed straight for his en suite bathroom.

Sliding open the glass doors of the exquisite marble shower, Robert turned it on and allowed it to warm up before he undressed and stepped inside. Sliding the doors shut he allowed the powerful jets of water to massage his body and mind. And as he reached for his shampoo he switched on his shower radio.

'Breaking news this morning,' a female news reporter said, her voice was strong and professional, *'four US soldiers have been killed in an explosion in South Af–'*

Robert switched off the radio. The South African war had claimed another four lives, but he could not bear to hear it, it was all too familiar for him. He turned around and bowed his head, allowing the water to run down his thick mane of hair.

Chapter Eight

The French Cottage Retreat

August 25th

Robert had bought the French cottage as a present for his grandmother on her seventieth birthday. Two years on, this was the first time he had returned to the country to see the place.

His last memory of the cottage was of a derelict building overrun with weeds. So he was somewhat surprised when driving up the gravel path of the transformation that had occurred in such a short amount of time. The one and a half acres of land was entirely weed free, now it was picturesque: lusciously finely cut lawns, a gleaming pond teaming with fish and brightly coloured flowers dotted throughout the numerous boarders.

The cottage had also been extended and completely renovated, a guest bedroom had been built on just for Robert.

Robert had fully expected his grandmother, who had a no-nonsense approach to just about everything, to begin to sort through his life as soon as he arrived in France, but to his great surprise she did not push the matter.

And over the past four days they spoke very little to one another. Robert had already thought up his excuse for his lack of conversation on tiredness from the jetlag, but it was not needed.

And so it was now on the last day of his visit that Robert, his grandmother and Michael were sat at the table in the kitchen bowing their heads in prayer.

'Dear Lord,' Sylvia began, 'thank you for this wonderful food, thank you for watching over us on this day and please look after our loved ones that are no longer with us. Amen.'

Robert and Michael said, 'Amen,' in unison.

Laid out before them was a large red casserole dish and on the large oval plate next to it were thick slices of homemade buttered bread.

Sylvia opened her eyes, unclasped her hands and lifted the lid off the casserole dish. The smell of Rabbit, and home-grown potatoes, carrots, peas and leeks filled the room, it was mouth-watering.

'The food looks delicious Sylvia,' said Michael hungrily.

As soon as all the bodyguards had met Sylvia Lane she made it clear to them that they were to call her Sylvia and not Mrs Lane or ma'am. She also understood that they had a very important job to do, but that did not excuse them from having three hot meals a day. They would have to devise some sort of system but they would all at some time sit down at the table and have a meal.

'Well help yourself my dear,' said Sylvia with a smile, 'there's plenty to go around.'

Michael filled his bowl with the casserole and grabbed three slices of bread. And within a few minutes he had finished. He poured himself a glass of water, drank it in one and wiped his mouth with a napkin.

'That was the best rabbit casserole I've ever had,' he said, meaning every single word of it.

'You are more than welcome to help yourself to some seconds,' Sylvia said, smiling once again.

'I appreciate the offer,' said Michael, 'but there are two more mouths in need of feeding.'

And as he stood, nodded and smiled in appreciation to both Sylvia and Robert and left, Sylvia looked over at Robert. 'Have you been to Church lately?' she asked him. She grabbed another slice of bread, folded it in half and dipped it in her casserole.

'God and I stopped talking a long time ago,' said Robert quietly, staring down at his bowl, 'you of all people should know that, Grandma.'

'I just thought that it would do you no harm if you had a quiet word with Father Patrick.' She took another bite out of her bread and looked at Robert as she ate.

'And I suppose if I talk to him he will offer me some words of comfort and then everything will be alright, will it?'

There was a mocking in his voice that his grandmother didn't like.

'Don't be sarcastic,' she said sharply, 'it doesn't suit you.'

The silence they sat in was only brief before Marcus arrived in the kitchen.

'Help yourself, Marcus,' Sylvia said, 'there's plenty of food to go around.'

He pulled out a chair, said, 'Thanks Sylvia,' grabbed a bowl and filled it.

Marcus finished within a few minutes and Derek arrived not long after. And once everyone had had enough to eat, Sylvia cleared the table and walked out of the kitchen. She came back a moment or two later carrying a large grey lidded box. She set it down on the table and looked over at Robert who was holding a glass of water in his hand, taking tiny sips from it.

'Your father left this to you in his will,' she said, slightly out of breath, 'you can take it back with you when you travel home tomorrow.'

And as far as she was concerned it was end of discussion, Robert knew better than to argue with her, or so she assumed as she walked towards the kitchen sink.

'I love you very much, Grandma,' he said a moment later and Sylvia turned to face him, 'but I'm not taking that home with me, regardless of what you say.'

Sylvia arched her eyebrows. 'And you're going to stand firm on that are you?' she asked, somewhat surprised with Robert's confidence, his voice was clear and unwavering.

'Yes I am,' he said, there could be no mistaking the defiance in his voice.

'Well I'll have to respect your decision then, won't I?' She didn't wait for her grandson's response; she walked over to the sink, filled it with hot water and squirted some washing up liquid, which immediately began to foam. 'Here,' she said to Robert, throwing him a small checked towel, 'you can make yourself some use to me, seeing as your not going to accept what's rightfully yours.'

She put on her bright yellow rubber gloves and began to clean the plates just as Robert stood.

'That was quite a performance you put on last week,' she said, rinsing the bubbles off the now gleaming plate.

'You know about that then,' said Robert casually, already knowing where this would be heading.

'You more than anyone should know that bad news always travels faster than good.'

And there could be no denying the fact that Sylvia was right. She rinsed the soap bubbles off another plate and handed it to Robert, who said, 'No doubt you will be disappointed in me,' as he dried the plate and put it away.

'You've achieved a lot more than most men your age,' his grandma said truthfully, 'and I'm extremely proud of you.'

But, Robert thought, there was always a 'but', when something was said in that particular way.

'I have no right to judge,' she said, 'all of us at one time or another run away from our problems, it's all part of God's wonderful plan.'

'God's plan,' Robert scoffed, 'and for your information, Grandma, I'm not running away from anything.'

'That's the biggest pile of bull I've heard since leaving America,' Sylvia said plainly, looking at her grandson now as she passed him another plate.

Robert was taken aback by the words; he avoided his grandmother's eyes as he took hold of the plate and began to dry it.

'I know I'm being selfish when I say this to you,' said Sylvia as she continued to wash the remaining pots. 'I've already lost my son and grandson,' she said. She gave a tiny sigh and pulled the plug from the sink, watching the water swirling down the hole. 'I can't stand to lose you too.'

It was an odd moment as the silence suddenly crept over the kitchen. Robert looked over at his grandmother, who was still watching the water drain away. Throughout her life Sylvia Lane had always been strong and independent, a woman who showed little emotion; not a single tear was shed at any of the funerals she had attended. But this was the very first time Robert had seen this venerable side of her, the fear of losing her now only grandson had melted away the tough barrier she had encased herself in, exposing this scared, elderly lady.

'Everything will be alright,' said Robert softly, realising that he had spoken harshly to her and that she only had his best interests at heart.

But the reassurance he hoped would comfort her offered very little. Sylvia gave a sarcastic laugh.

'No it won't be Robert,' she said. The vulnerability she spoke in her words only moments earlier had now vanished, replaced by the sharpness she almost always spoke with. 'I know what the alcohol does to people; I've seen them throw their life away because of it.'

'I know what I'm doing,' said Robert, drying the rest of the plates and cutlery.

Sylvia pulled off her rubber gloves and hung them over the tap.

'And is that what they say to Lisa when she's told you're dead?' she said. 'That you knew what you were doing.'

The words were unexpected and the invisible wall Robert had constructed around himself began to slowly crumble. But he fought hard against this state of vulnerability; the ancient philosophy passed down through the generations of men in his family was that a breakdown of tears was a sign of weakness. Bearing the surname of Lane brought responsibilities, you were to be a protector, strong and dependable, you didn't show any sort of emotion. That's why Robert felt an odd sensation when his father said he loved him the day of his welcome home party. That was the first and only time he had said it, Frank wasn't a sentimental man, but none of that mattered now, he was nothing more than a coward and Robert used this hatred and resentment he felt to fight back his tears.

But his grandmother's words had unlocked something deep within him and he became overwhelmed with so many things. The harder he fought the quicker it spread through his body, and for the first time in years he began to sob, tears streaming down his cheeks. As soon as he wiped them from his face more tears came and he could do nothing to stop it from happening.

He just stood there, avoiding his grandmother's gaze, ashamed of the pitiful state he was in. Sylvia walked forward and parted her arms, but Robert instinctively took a stop backward. The last thing he wanted to do was hug her, to be that vulnerable in her arms, he could not bear to have this hug just out of pity.

'None of this is your fault,' she said softly, still walking towards him.

And as Sylvia put her arms around Robert, he pulled her close to him and everything that had happened to him: the death of Frank, the death of Mark, his alcoholism, everything was wept into her shoulder.

Sylvia smiled; her grandson was finally grieving.

Chapter Nine

The Last Declaration of Franklin Julian Lane

August 26th

Robert slowly opened his eyes, he was wrapped in a navy blue quilt on the pulled out sofa bed. The dark, cloud filled sky was visible through the thickly glassed window of the Titan. His specially built plane was quiet, except for the humming noise coming from the four powerful engines.

He rolled over onto his back and stared up at the darkened ceiling. Less than twelve hours ago he was in the company of his grandmother, oddly though, it felt like a lifetime away. He just lay there, thinking about his life; how he got to this specific point, and where he thought he would be heading.

The grief that had consumed him since his father's death had changed, it felt different now. The talk with his grandmother had partly numbed the hatred and loathing he held towards Frank, she gave him a different perspective on things.

He thought about his father now, his last moments in his plane, waiting for it to crash, he thought about the box left in his will, without explanation, and as he did, resentment started to develop in the stillness and darkness. Why didn't his father talk to him? Why couldn't he have confided in him? Wouldn't Robert have understood? Or was Robert nothing more than a pawn, someone to be manipulated and used to thrust CyberTech Defence Systems into the public eye, but never trusted with his father's darkest secrets? Robert thought back to the note left next to the telephone at his father's home, two pathetic words scrawled on a scrap of paper which read, *I'm sorry'*, and the anger he felt towards his father developed in the darkness.

The more he thought about it, the bitterer he became, until he could no longer just lie there with these thoughts as his only company. Desperate to numb every screaming part of his body, he threw off the covers, swung out his legs and walked out of the room. Out on the landing, Robert waited for the automatic lights. They flickered on and he slowly walked down the stairs. Now on the second floor, Robert entered the first room he came to on the left. The highly polished walnut door bore a brass name plate, which read: *Bar*.

Upon entering, Robert – to his surprise – found Michael and an auburn haired woman dressed smartly in a navy blue knee length skirt and blouse sitting on the cream leather couches, deep in conversation. But as the pair saw him, they both jumped to their feet.

'I should go and check on the pilots,' Carmen Williams said awkwardly, her pale cheeks now beginning to blush, 'see if they need anything.' She smiled at Michael, then hurried off, politely saying, 'Good morning, Mr Lane,' to Robert but avoiding his eye.

'I hope I didn't interrupt anything,' Robert said, walking over to the bar, 'I never knew you two were so close.'

'There's nothing between us,' said Michael quickly, feeling that he should explain himself, 'we just enjoy each other's company on these long haul flights.'

Robert was behind the gleaming bar now, clinking bottles and glasses as he walked back over to where Michael was. He set the bottle of whiskey and two crystal glasses down on the large round table and sat opposite.

'I should really get some sleep,' Michael said, 'we'll be landing in a couple of hours.'

'One won't hurt,' Robert said, picking up the bottle and filling the two glasses to about a quarter. 'Call it a nightcap.'

He set the bottle down, picked up his glass and clinked it with Michael's.

'To brighter futures,' he said.

Michael acknowledged the toast with a smile and reached for his glass.

'To brighter futures,' he said, downing the drink with one quick motion.

The silence was only brief.

'Have you ever been in love?' Robert asked, staring down at his whiskey but losing the desire to drink it.

'Yes sir,' said Michael, setting his empty glass down on the table, 'only the once though.'

'How was it for you?'

'She broke my heart,' said Michael truthfully. 'When I began my army training she wrote me a letter effectively ending the relationship, she told me she couldn't be with someone who if sent away might not come home.' He forced himself to smile, as though this particular recollection meant nothing to him, but it was clear from his softening expression that it was still painful for him to talk about it. 'I can understand why she did it,' he said, his voice breaking slightly, 'she wanted stability, to settle down and have lots of kids, I couldn't give her that.'

Robert set down his glass of whiskey next to Michael's empty one. He was about to offer his sympathies but reconsidered, saying it after all these years would sound so condescending.

'I never thanked you,' he said, breaking the awkward silence. Michael looked at him, his eyebrows arched in surprised. 'I know you risked your life to try and save my brother.'

'Yeah,' Michael said, nodding, and it was clear from his expression that the events of that day still hurt him deeply, 'but I didn't save him.'

Again they sat in the awkward silence which followed the words only for a couple of seconds before Michael stood, said, 'Thanks for the drink,' and headed for the door. Before he left, he glanced over his shoulder and wished Robert a good night.

Once again, he was alone. The large grey box that was left to him in his father's will was in the corner of the room. He just looked at it, a part of him wondering what it might contain. He glanced down at his glass and for a moment he thought about drinking it in one, knowing that the alcohol would give him the strength to search through the box. He stared down at the amber liquid, fighting hard against the desire to numb his body with it.

And without realising he was doing so, he was digging his finger nails deep into the skin and muscle of his left arm, overwhelming his longing with pain, with the drawing of tiny speckles of blood. In this silence, with nothing but his long, deep breathing and the humming noise coming from the engines as his only company, the days he spent at his grandmother's came back to him, the conversation he had with her on his final day returned to him, and in the silence, understanding of his father's actions slowly and very purposefully began to unfold.

And with this unfolding came a sense of disgust when he looked at the whiskey, he no longer burned with that obsessive desire to drink it, to feel the effects it gave him. He felt an indescribable amount of freedom, of liberation, as though the invincible force – originating from the alcohol – that had gripped and slowly diseased the inside of him had been smothered by the understanding.

Robert had no idea how much time had passed before he stood and walked over to the grey box. He stared down at it for a fraction of a moment before he picked it up and sat back down on the chair, and with it resting on his lap he took off the lid and looked inside.

A black vinyl briefcase sat at the bottom, it was the only thing the box contained. Reaching for it, he laid it on the table and dialled in the combination which he knew was the year his father was born. Then pressing the two buttons either side of the latches, the briefcase unlocked with a click.

Everything was neatly arranged inside and Robert began to slowly sort through it all. Four leather-bound, what looked to be like books, sat at the bottom of the case. Robert reached for the top one and quickly glanced through it. It was a journal, and from the dates it was written – unmistakably in his father's handwriting – a long time ago. It felt odd and at the same time eerie reading the words, Frank would have been a young man at the time of writing, twenty-seven, twenty-eight perhaps. Robert wouldn't have even been born.

He wrote mostly private things, how he felt on the eve of his wedding night, how he felt becoming a father for the first time, but as continued to glance through there was a particular section that caught his eye. It wasn't very long, barely making two lines but it was written in a way that Robert had never seen from his father before.

The time has come for my dream to become a reality (it began), *the road ahead will be long and at times difficult but this is my destiny*.

Robert read the words several times, hoping that it would make sense to him, but it didn't. He put all four journals next to the briefcase and began to sort through once again. Next he pulled out a stack of letters; there were about a dozen in total, all different sizes and colours.

The top one was a plain white unopened envelope which bore no name. Turning it over in his hands, Robert ripped open the top edge. He reached inside and pulled out a folded piece of paper, which he opened out on his knees. It was a letter that looked to have been typed by an old-fashioned typewriter, there was no date, no suggestion of when it had been typed.

Frank,

This is perhaps the most difficult letter I have ever had to write. I have thought long and hard over how I should tell you this and what I am about to say was a hard decision to make. A storm is beginning to gather. Once again the South African campaign is under the spotlight following recent disastrous events. As a result of this I have no other choice but to discontinue funding for your project.

There can be no denying that I saw great potential in your idea but I am also a realist. Although your idea in theory could save the lives of countless American soldiers the reality of it all is many won't see it that way.

We have been friends a long time and I will never forget the kindness and generosity you showed me during my many hours of need, but if anyone should uncover the project then I will publicly condemn you. I hope you understand why I must take this action, I have too much to lose.

Robert stared at the words a long time after reading them, whoever had typed this was not as good a friend as the letter suggested, there was no signature, no name, no way of knowing who had written it. He read it again, more slowly this time, more carefully, hoping that it might become clearer doing so. He said aloud the words, *I have no other choice but to discontinue funding for your project.* What did that mean? What sort of project? Frank had worked on so many over the years, it could have been anything. He refolded the letter and slid it back inside the envelope.

The half dozen envelopes he sorted through next were love letters written by his mother to his father. Robert only glanced through them, feeling that they were for his father's eyes only. Next was a large brown envelope, and as he picked it up he could feel it contained something quite bulky. He tore it open and dropped its contents on the table.

There were four stacks of photographs, each one held together by an elastic band. He picked one up, removed the band and began to look through, one photograph at a time. They were in no particular order, some were of him and Mark when they were younger and older. He stopped when he came across one that had caught his attention. It was of him, Mark and Lisa and they were stood, posing in that order.

Robert couldn't remember when it had been taken and it was only when he turned it over in his hands and looked at the date scribbled in the top left hand corner that he realised it had been taken just before he travelled to Italy.

Mark had his arm around both Lisa and Robert and all three were smiling. Lisa looked beautiful as ever and Robert sat there, looking deep into her soft brown eyes, wondering what she was thinking at that moment in time. And then, without realising he was doing so, he put his thumb over his brother's face. It was just him and Lisa now, if Mark wasn't in the middle then they would be next to one another, their cheeks touching. What Robert would give to share such a moment with her, to feel her soft skin against his, to have that closeness.

But then the guilt gripped hold of his body. Mark had fought and died for his country, and how did Robert repay him for that ultimate sacrifice? By trying to erase him from the photograph. The very thought sickened him but no matter how hard he tried he could not suppress the love he had for Lisa. He had spent two years in Italy and met the beautiful and wonderful Adriana Penna, but she was not Lisa Anderson, and if Robert couldn't have her, he would want no other.

He placed the picture on top of the others, secured the rubber band around it and put all of the photographs back inside the envelope. He began sorting once again and the very last one he came to was a letter oddly addressed to him. He ripped it open at once and unfolded it on his lap.

Dear Robert, (it read in his father's unmistakable handwriting)

I feel great regret when I imagine you reading my final words. The regret is partly for myself (I would not be so conceited to think entirely of myself at this time of writing) because I know if you have this in your keeping I am no longer here. My regret is also for you my son, for there is no doubt in my mind that the feelings you will now hold towards me are of hatred and betrayal. It is only natural, you have lost your mother, brother and now your father. But your hatred is not as powerful as it ought to be, and if you are willing I would like to take you on a journey of truth starting with the words:

The Genesis Project

In closing all I can say is this: be patient Robert and find it in your heart to forgive me.

Your loving father,
Frank.

The silence and stillness from that moment seemed to deepen that much more. Slowly and very carefully Robert read and reread the words several times, whispering a certain three each time.

'The Genesis Project.'

He had no idea what to make of the words. He stood, and with the letter still in his hand, he hurried out of the bar and headed straight to his room. Turning on the lights, he walked over to the small, recessed bookshelf and pulled out a large, grey dictionary. Standing underneath one of the circular wall lights, he began turning the pages until he came across the section of GE, then he ran his finger down the vast array of words.

And then he felt himself slowly walking backwards towards his bed, enthralled, as he stared at the two descriptions:

genesis *(jen-iss-iss)* n, pl *-ses (-seez) the beginning or origin of anything. [Latin, from Greek, generation, birth, origin.]*

Genesis *(jen-iss-iss)* n bible *the first book of the Old Testament, recounting the creation of the world and the establishment and the early history of Israel.*

Chapter Ten

The Inspirer of Men

September 3rd

The tale of why Arapmoi Sebothoma had returned to South Africa after twenty-five years of absence still remained a mystery to all those who fought with him, even after twelve months. It was common knowledge that he was a respected writer and a teacher of philosophy in England, in fact some of his books had become worldwide bestsellers, but whatever his reason for doing so, he had turned his back on all of his fame and glory to return to his homeland.

As soon as he arrived in South Africa and made his intentions clear that he was going to stop the Liberators of South Africa and put an end to the war, word quickly spread, and over time he was depicted as the man who towered over his enemies, and whose gaze scorched the very ground he looked upon. In truth, Arapmoi Sebothoma was short, with a gangly physique, small brown eyes and black afro hair. His legend had been exaggerated to such an extent that all new recruits for the newly formed Brotherhood of Sakarabru felt disheartened.

This man surely cannot be Arapmoi, they all thought upon meeting him, *he looks weak, how can he lead us into battle?*

But it was the passion delivered in his influential speeches and the heroism he showed in battle that made each and every one of them realise that they were witnessing someone very special.

And this was both demonstrated and made clear, for at that moment, deep under the derelict buildings of Johannesburg, Arapmoi Sebothoma, the man now dubbed the *real* South African Saviour turned the brass handle of a dark wooden door and entered into a room illuminated by nothing more than candles and oil lamps.

The story of how they captured this underground network of rooms had been told and retold so many times over the few days that they had spent here, that Arapmoi knew it would soon become part of South Africa's history. Naturally, it had been altered by everybody who had spoken of it, Arapmoi frequently heard people telling their own unique account of what happened. His favourite, he admitted, was of how he, along with a band of twelve brothers, who were outmanned five to one, stormed the fort and came out victorious but not before Arapmoi was shot six times. An exaggeration of course, but when first told of this, Arapmoi erupted in roars of laughter.

And with good reason, he admitted.

He adjusted the flame on each of the oil lamps and walked over to the quarter filled bookshelf which dominated the left wall. He stood before it and began to look at the various books on display, they were arranged in no particular order.

Africa's Terrorists: The Story of the Liberators of South Africa
John Lessing

Ancient Philosophies
Arapmoi Sebothoma

The History of Philosophy
Arapmoi Sebothoma

The Liberators Success: Terror Strategies used against the South African Saviours
Ted Rees

Origins of the Liberators of South Africa
Ruben Spears

Terrorist Ideologies
Jacqueline Jenkings

The Liberators of South Africa: Freedom Fighters or Terrorists?
James Alba

Zuberi: The Making of a Terrorist
John Quinn

Zuberi Jacobs: Behind the Mask of a Terrorist
Adam Hamilton

To defeat your enemy, Arapmoi had once told the young woman who had asked him about his selection of books, *you must first understand how they think and how they fight.*

Moving away from the bookcase, Arapmoi placed his hands behind his back and began to slowly walk around the room, wondering who might have once occupied this lavish place. From the desk and chair, soft rug, bookcase and camp bed set up in the corner, there was no doubt in his mind that it would have been someone of great importance. Perhaps Zuberi himself lived here once, but then again it could have been anyone.

Since his arrival in South Africa Arapmoi kept a war journal, it was a way for him to try and make sense of the horrific things that affected him and the country he loved. And so every evening without fail he would write about the day's occurrences. And as he sat behind the desk, he withdrew his pencil and notepad from the bottom drawer and opened it to a fresh page, then he wrote the date in the top right hand corner. Tapping the pencil against his lips, he wondered what he could write, considering that this had been a quiet day, but it did not matter.

At that moment, someone came bursting through the door. Tall and burly, the young man suddenly stumbled and fell in front of the desk of the astonished Arapmoi who had jumped to his feet.

'Tebogo, what is it?' he said, removing his pistol from the top drawer, fearing the worst.

'Sir, have you heard the news?' Tebogo Jeppe panted as he got to his feet and placed the palms of his hands flat on the desk.

'And what news would that be?' Arapmoi said, there was relief in his voice.

'Zuberi – he's – he's dead.'

The words had brought complete silence to the room. Arapmoi slowly sat; overwhelmed by emotions he longed for but never thought he would have the chance to experience in South Africa.

Zuberi Jacobs dead!

'By whom?' he asked, still reeling.

'The Americans are claiming responsibility sir,' Tebogo said, still breathing heavily but managing to raise a triumphant smile. 'The exact details of how it happened are still sketchy, but it looks almost certain sir.' His pause was only momentarily. 'I cannot believe Zuberi Jacobs is dead.'

There was a brief silence. Arapmoi sat motionless, a look of disbelief sprawled across his face as Tebogo wiped away the beads of sweat that had gathered on his forehead with the back of his hand.

'Is it over sir?' he asked, perplexed by Arapmoi's nonexistent celebratory mood. 'With Zuberi dead, there will be no one to lead the Liberators of South Africa; surely it will begin to collapse in on itself. The war has been won.'

Arapmoi stood slowly and began to walk around the room.

'Let us not get ahead of ourselves Tebogo,' he said quietly, looking directly in front of him as he walked, 'we must first wait for confirmation from the Americans; this could after all be some sort of plot to deceive us.'

'But what if it isn't sir?' Tebogo said, finding it almost impossible to contain his excitement. 'What if Zuberi *is* dead?'

Arapmoi walked over to Tebogo and laid a gentle hand on his shoulder. And as he stared into the young man's brown eyes he raised a smiled as he said softly, 'You must be patient Tebogo, first we must wait for confirmation from the Americans, then we will take it from there.'

Tebogo nodded, the excitement he felt only moments ago had now vanished, replaced by emptiness. Unable to look into the eyes of the man who he regarded as a father, Tebogo nonetheless was still disciplined enough to still show him respect. He stared straight ahead, saluted, and said glumly, 'Very well sir,' before spinning quickly on his heel and leaving the room.

Arapmoi sat back down behind his desk, and looked down at the journal still spread out before him. Sighing deeply he picked up the pencil and wrote in block capitals:

IS THIS THE DAY THE WAR ENDED?

He laid the pencil in the crease of the notepad and closed it. He sat in silence, a mixture of contrasting emotions was now running through him. Why he felt like this only he knew, but this was neither the time nor the place to start exploring his inner self. He put the notepad back inside the bottom drawer and stood, walking aimlessly around the room.

He always carried a golden locket discreetly on himself, and as he removed it from around his neck, he opened it and stared at what it contained. There were two photographs inside the oval shaped locket, the one on the left was a picture of a young man. He was eighteen, Arapmoi knew this because it was a picture of himself. It had been taken in a day of celebration. The young Arapmoi had large afro hair, he was smiling, an excited smile, because this was the day in which he would be embarking on a new chapter in his life. In a few weeks he would be studying philosophy at an English University, the man who was born into poverty had now become an undergraduate.

The photograph on the right was of a teenage girl who looked a lot older than her years, she was posing with a baby in her arms. The girl's name was Siphiwe. Arapmoi knew her well, they were once lovers. And as he stared at the woman and her baby tears began to develop in his eyes and started to run down his cheeks.

He closed the locket and wiped away the tears. Then he clasped his hands together – with the locket in the middle – closed his eyes and bowed his head, pressing his forehead hard against his thumbs.

'Forgive me,' he whispered. 'I have failed you both.'

Chapter Eleven

The Victory Celebrations

South Africa was a nation divided on the subject of the Council, some believed that they would play a crucial role in the rebuilding of the country, others believed that they would become corrupt and would satisfy their greed with the power they would soon hold. And there was a select few, like Arapmoi, that believed it was both.

Once Zuberi Jacobs had plunged South Africa into the darkness of war he soon began to concentrate on ridding the country of its politicians, in what he referred to as, 'political cleansing'. He felt betrayed after every single one of them publicly condemned his attack on the United States.

Those who managed to survive this deadly onslaught found themselves hiding in abandoned homes, starving and terrified. But there was one man, a man who came close to death, a man who united the remaining politicians, a man who created the Council, and his name was Lenka Shone.

And using the cover of darkness Arapmoi and Tebogo left the underground network and made their way towards the white Toyota Avensis that had been hidden away in an abandoned garage. With a torch in his hand Arapmoi carried out the routine search for explosives on the dirty vehicle while Tebogo, holding a R5 assault rifle stood closely by, watching intently for those still fighting for the Liberators of South Africa. Once Arapmoi was happy that the car had not been tampered with, he unlocked it and climbed into the back while Tebogo sat in the driver's seat, positioning the rifle within an arm's reach on the passenger's seat.

They would be the only ones travelling tonight, Arapmoi preferred it this way. A single vehicle brought less attention than a convoy of them, which was usually the procedure when transporting someone of high importance.

Tebogo began adjusting his seat, then altered the side and rear view mirrors. This was the first time he had travelled to see the

Council, he had studied the route carefully and yet he could not disguise or hide his nervous tension.

'Whenever you are ready to go Tebogo,' said Arapmoi pleasantly, his voice projecting from the hood of his long robe.

Tebogo took a deep breath to keep himself calm, then he slid the key in the ignition, turned it and brought the car to life. He drove out of the garage, they were quickly on their way along the quiet road, but after five or so metres Arapmoi leaned forward.

'Perhaps it would be beneficial to you if you switched on your headlights,' he said softly.

It was a stupid mistake and Tebogo could not hide the fact that he knew it. Cursing under his breath he switched on the lights and the road ahead became illuminated.

'I'm sorry sir,' he said, disappointed with himself. 'I'm just nervous about seeing the Council tonight.'

'You have nothing to be nervous about,' said Arapmoi still softly, 'the Council members are no different from you or I.'

Tebogo found that hard to believe, the Council members all came from privileged backgrounds, before the war they lived in luxurious homes, drove expensive cars and had important jobs within the government. It was an altogether different life to the one Tebogo had lived in. He grew up in poverty, starving, living without hope. He became separated from his parents when the disease of war ravaged South Africa. They talked about fleeing to the neighbouring country of Namibia but then, without warning the Liberators of South Africa arrived, killing those who opposed them. Tebogo's father had told him to run and not look back, Tebogo kissed his mother goodbye and that was the last time he had seen them both alive. He was sixteen at the time, alone, scared, hiding from the Liberators of South Africa when they began to forcibly recruit people of his age to their cause.

Arapmoi had found him shortly after his seventeenth birthday rummaging through rubbish, in the vain hope of finding food. Arapmoi had soft brown eyes and had a warmth about him, he became that much needed father figure to Tebogo, protecting him from the outside world, teaching and offering him guidance. Although over a year had passed since he last saw his parents, Tebogo still believed that they had safely made it to Namibia and would one day be reunited with them.

He took a left at the junction and after twenty or so metres had little other choice but to slow. Thousands had gathered to celebrate the news of Zuberi Jacobs's death; a mixture of emotion tumbled into the street, fireworks and gunfire illuminated the night sky and large flaming metal barrels roared on the ground.

'The people are rejoicing,' said Arapmoi quietly, his smile could not been seen from behind his hood, 'they are rejoicing the end of this terrible war and of the man who started it all.'

Beeping the car horn so that a safe passage could be made through seemed only to excite the gathering crowds even more, for men and women alike were now clapping their hands as they chanted the words: *'Praise the death of Zuberi, Arapmoi is our saviour.'*

'This is the first time I have heard the people say Zuberi's name aloud,' Arapmoi said in disbelief, now looking through the clean patches in the dirt streaked window, 'it had always puzzled me as to why they could never speak his name.'

'Praise the death of Zuberi, Arapmoi is our saviour ... Praise the death of Zuberi, Arapmoi is our saviour.'

'Never be intimidated by a name Tebogo,' he said in a pensive manner, 'most of Zuberi Jacobs's power came from the people's inability to say his name. How can you expect to defeat your enemy if you cannot even say his name aloud?'

It was a question Tebogo didn't have to think long about, and yet Arapmoi had expanded his mind further.

'I suppose you are right sir,' Tebogo said, 'but you are forgetting one thing.'

Arapmoi looked into the rear view mirror when the words were said, 'And what would that be?' he asked softly, and Tebogo could see him raising his eyebrows a fraction from behind his hood.

'Well,' Tebogo began with great admiration, 'perhaps you found it easy to say his name because, well, it was common knowledge that you were the only one Zuberi feared, and it was you that put an end to him. I would be amazed if this day wasn't going to be celebrated as your day, as Arapmoi Sebothoma day.'

'Praise the death of Zuberi, Arapmoi is our saviour ... Praise the death of Zuberi, Arapmoi is our saviour.'

'You flatter me Tebogo,' Arapmoi chuckled, 'but I know Zuberi feared no man, woman or child and as for me putting an end to him as you say, it was the Americans who accomplished that with their planes, not I.'

Tebogo glanced into the rear view mirror and his eyes met with Arapmoi's. 'You are modest sir,' he beamed, 'but you should take credit when it is due.' He cleared his throat and began his explanation. 'When the Americans arrived they brought with them their fancy weaponry and expensive planes and tanks but despite their superiority they never once managed to outwit Zuberi Jacobs or any of the Liberators of South Africa. They relied on luck to kill him in the end; it was nothing more than that sir.'

'Praise the death of Zuberi, Arapmoi is our saviour ... Praise the death of Zuberi, Arapmoi is our saviour.'

'It was you and you alone that brought us back from the brink of death,' Tebogo continued. 'You turned it around for every man and woman who had lost hope, you taught us all how to fight, how to survive. Your way of thinking helped save the lives of millions, you are a great man sir, and a great leader.'

Arapmoi had resumed staring out of the window whilst Tebogo had been talking, as he heard the kind words being spoken he moved his hand slowly towards his chest and pressed his palm against the golden locket hidden discreetly under his clothes.

'You are most kind Tebogo,' he said quietly, 'but a man of my 'apparent' greatness would have saved every man, woman and child. Many thousands still lost their lives.'

There was an incredibly long silence inside the car. Tebogo tried to end it, to think of a response that would ease Arapmoi's anguish, but nothing sprang to his mind. He could only listen to the crowd still chanting from outside.

'Praise the death of Zuberi, Arapmoi is our saviour ... Praise the death of Zuberi, Arapmoi is our saviour.'

'Sir is it true what *they* are all saying?' Tebogo asked, deciding that focusing the attention away from Arapmoi was the best option he should take. 'About how Zuberi was killed?'

It was obvious from his expression that whatever 'they' were saying, he wasn't going to believe a word of it until Arapmoi confirmed it was true. But as he looked into the rear view mirror waiting for an answer, it was apparent it wasn't going to come, for Arapmoi was still staring out of the dirt streaked window, seemingly lost in thought.

'What *they* are all saying,' he pressed on, 'is that Zuberi was holding a meeting in a building when an American plane flew over and dropped a bomb on it, destroying it completely.'

'Zuberi's death is still shrouded in mystery,' Arapmoi said quietly, not tearing his eyes away from the window, 'so naturally rumours are already starting to circulate on the streets.' He paused briefly. 'But yes, I too have heard that particular story.'

Tebogo thumped the steering wheel with his fist and made a triumphant laugh. 'I heard that Zuberi always insisted that his meetings were to be held underground, safe from bombs and explosions. How ironic that the first time he decided to hold a meeting above ground it resulted in his death.'

Again he sounded the car horn to clear the road and once again it only seemed to excite the gathering crowds. *'Praise the death of Zuberi, Arapmoi is our saviour,... Praise the death of Zuberi, Arapmoi is our saviour.'*

'Let us hope that he suffered a great deal before he finally died,' he said without hesitation or remorse.

The harshly spoken words had pulled Arapmoi out of his gaze from the window and into the rear view mirror once again.

'No one,' he said, his tone hardening slightly, 'no matter how evil they are, deserves to suffer before their death Tebogo, when he comes before our Lord then and only then will Zuberi be held accountable for all that he has done.'

And again the pair sat in the silence, although this time it was a far more comfortable one. And as the car began to pass the majority of the celebratory crowds, the men and women changed their chants, to a more fitting one, Arapmoi thought.

'Hail the Brotherhood and those who have died, God protect their souls,' could be heard, although growing fainter by the second.

'So why do you think Zuberi held his meeting in that building?' Tebogo asked as they finally passed the majority of the chanting crowds.

'I'm afraid we shall never know why Zuberi decided to change his mind,' Arapmoi said truthfully, 'perhaps one of his most trusted advised him to hold the meeting in that specific building. It is not unusual for followers to turn on their leader in times of despair. Zuberi commanded his men and women through fear, they fought *his* war knowing that if they didn't they too would be executed.

'To inspire men to fight Tebogo, you yourself must fight along with them. They will respect you for that, respect is a very important and powerful tool to have, because once you have gained their respect, they will in turn be ready and willing to lay down their lives for you.'

Once again Arapmoi had spoken with such wisdom that Tebogo couldn't help but admire the man. They had passed the crowds now but the chanting could still be heard, growing fainter.

'Sir, tell me about England?' Tebogo said intrigued. 'Is it true that they are a nation of tea drinkers?'

'There is more to the British than their love of tea,' Arapmoi said after he had finished chuckling, and Tebogo arched his eyebrows in surprise, as though he wasn't expecting this response. 'The people are passionate, especially about their football and the country has a rich and wonderful history and heritage and has some of the most beautiful countrysides I have ever seen.'

Tebogo looked impressed. 'Do you miss living there sir?' he asked.

'Yes of course,' Arapmoi said, 'I met some wonderful and very dear people, some of whom I thought I would never be able to see again, but in the light of Zuberi's death it appears that I can return home sooner rather than later.'

The silence which followed after the words was odd and for a long time Tebogo didn't know what to say.

'Sir?' he finally said with great uncertainty, he looked into the rear view at Arapmoi who was looking back at him now. 'What do you mean? – What are you saying?'

It appeared that Tebogo had finally asked the question Arapmoi was most anxious to talk about, the reason why he asked him – for the first time – to accompany him on this visit to the Council, because never once had he fixed Tebogo with such a determined stare as he did now. Throwing back his hood, he leaned forward and rested his forearms on the front seats. But despite rehearsing what he was about to say many times over in his head, he still found it especially difficult to say the words.

'My stay in South Africa was always going to be temporary,' he said regretfully, 'I came here to stop Zuberi, and although I didn't personally achieve it I still feel it is time for me to rest my weary bones and return back to England, this war has taken so much out of me.' He began to smile. 'Believe it or not Tebogo I am only forty-six.'

But Tebogo didn't find it humorous and at this point he could no longer drive, he brought the car to a halt and with the engine still running he turned in his seat to face Arapmoi.

'Sir, I don't know what to say.'

He paused a moment while a deluge of questions that he needed to be answered flooded his head.

'Who is going to replace you?' he said, thinking this was the most important question to ask first.

'You,' Arapmoi said. As soon as he said the word, Tebogo's mouth seemed to fall open dramatically. 'I will not lie to you Tebogo, you have much to learn, and the road ahead will be at times difficult, but you can take great comfort in the fact that I see great potential in you.'

'Hail the Brotherhood and those who have died, God protect their souls,' the faint words could barely be heard over the sound of the idling engine.

'I am most honoured sir,' Tebogo said, he faced forward and began to drive the car just as Arapmoi leaned back, 'but are you sure it is a good idea for me to replace you, I'm sure there will be many who will disagree with that decision.'

'If they are as loyal to me as they claim themselves to be, then they will all respect my choice.'

'I'm going to be sad to see you go sir,' said Tebogo glumly, 'you've been like a father to me.'

'I have merely kept that position warm for your father, you will be reunited with him and your mother soon, I am certain of that.'

Tebogo smiled and in no time at all they were driving out of the city, making their way towards the Clarence Sauer monument and museum which was set beautifully in the peace and tranquillity.

'Sir,' said Tebogo smiling, 'can I ask you something?'

'There is no harm in asking,' Arapmoi said pleasantly, 'but I cannot guarantee an answer to your question.'

Tebogo paused for a moment, thinking how it was best to ask this question. Many within the Brotherhood of Sakarabru had placed bets on the reason why Arapmoi had returned to South Africa. The pool now stood at five hundred and twenty-six rand, a nice amount if Tebogo could casually ask the reason why.

'Well sir,' he began, 'why did you come back to South Africa?'

Their eyes met in the rear view mirror only for a fleeting moment.

'What is the pool worth now?' Arapmoi asked.

Tebogo couldn't help but smile. 'Five hundred and twenty-six,' he said.

'An impressive sum,' Arapmoi said admiringly, 'but I was hoping that it would be at least a thousand by now.'

'So what was your reason for returning?' pressed Tebogo eagerly.

Arapmoi stared out of the window, watching the distant fireworks exploding into the night sky with a brilliant glow of red and orange.

'This beautiful firework display is the perfect way to celebrate this momentous occasion,' he said smiling.

Tebogo knew not to press the matter further. And as the sound from the celebrating crowds could no longer be heard, he realised that this was the first question Arapmoi had never answered.

*

The Clarence Sauer monument and museum had been completed eighteen months prior to the bombings of the United States Embassy and Consulates. Since then, the seventy-nine roomed building had incredibly held the test of time, it had never even suffered a scratch even during the war.

The monument and museum had been designed and built as a lasting memorial and named after the great man Clarence Sauer, who, despite the racial segregation embraced by the government at the time, dedicated over forty-three years of his life establishing and maintaining his orphanage, which accepted any child no matter where they came from. But now it acted as a sanctuary for all surviving South African politicians. The twenty-five men and seven women had been united and under the direction of the appointed leader Lenka Shone had called themselves the Council.

Tebogo rolled the car to a stop in front of a large metal gate, and as soon as the two security guards peered through the glass and recognised Arapmoi they opened it and waved the car through. The entire floor within the enclosed wall was paved with stone slabs and black granite benches created for contemplation, a large, grand plaque with each orphan's name inscribed on it stood in a quiet garden with a beautiful water feature.

Stepping from the car, Arapmoi breathed in the cold night air and stared up at the vast building, the windows gleamed in the moonlight while the grey stone columns which enclosed the entire flat roofed edifice gave the building a surreal look. Somewhere in the far off distance, fireworks and gunfire were still lighting the night sky.

This was not the first time he had been to the monument but it would be his last. The museum was excellently displayed, Arapmoi always felt it a sobering yet absorbing experience every time he set foot upon here, even though he had visited countless times. Inside, it explained the reasoning behind the orphanage by presenting the apartheid system imposed at the time. And despite it being named after Clarence Sauer the structure did not seek to glorify him or turn him into a heroic figure, on the contrary, it emphasised what an ordinary man he was, which in effect turned him into a legend.

For a moment Arapmoi stood before the grand, stone steps, admiring and savouring the beautiful craftsmanship and tranquillity of all that surrounded him. He found it hard to try and understand what Clarence Sauer had had to endure, that he had been judged by the colour of his skin. And yet he had stood up against this, he made his voice heard, never faltering in the darkness of segregation.

A minute or two passed before he started to walk up the stone steps. There were fifteen and as Arapmoi reached the final one and stood before the heavy set of double doors, he raised his fist and began to hit the right door in a series of knocks. *Thud, thud, thud ... thud, thud ... thud, thud, thud, thud.*

Chapter Twelve

A Meeting of Different Minds

The door swung open from within after ten or so seconds had passed. A giant, clean shaven South African man with black dreadlocked hair, dressed smartly in a dark green suit stood before them both, gripping the doorframe to steady his swaying body.

'Arapmoi – er, sir,' Mosegi Joubert said, utter surprise played across his face, 'what – what are you doing here?'

'Good evening Mosegi,' Arapmoi said softly, 'Mr Shone knows about my arrival, it seems very odd that he never told you, don't you think?'

And then as he paused for a brief moment, he caught hold of a faint whiff of alcohol from the guard's breath.

'Ah yes,' Mosegi said faintly, 'I remember now sir, Lenka – I mean Mr Shone did mention something about you coming to see him. Please, please come in, get out of the cold.'

He stepped aside at once.

'Well thank you Mosegi,' Arapmoi said pleasantly, 'you are most kind.'

The hallway was sumptuously decorated; deep-piled carpeted floors, large framed photographs mounted against the hand painted walls, and an impressive bronze statue of Clarence Sauer, which faced them.

And as Arapmoi entered and threw back his hood, he knelt down by this statue and stared up at it. The bronzed man stood over two metres tall. With short afro hair and large circular spectacles, he was proudly dressed in a smart three piece suit as he spread out his arms in joy. Knelt by his feet were children from all ethnic backgrounds, all of which were gazing up at him in wonder. Inscribed on the base were the words:

Life is never easy, and all of us in one way or another will have to withstand judgement and prejudice before we can be rewarded with our hopes and dreams.

Clarence Sauer

And as Arapmoi kissed the statue and stood, he noticed something was amiss, for brightly coloured ribbons were wrapped tightly around the neck and arms of the great man.

'This monument offered them sanctuary,' he seethed, 'and this is how they pay their respects, by defacing his memory.'

He tore the coloured ribbons violently from the statue, crumpled them all into one and threw them all to the floor.

'With the death of Zuberi Jacobs I assume that there have been a lot of festivities,' Arapmoi asked the guard, as he continued to stare up at the statue.

'Yes sir,' Mosegi said, unable to hide his excitement, 'the feast laid out in the main hall is fit for a king.' The words made him chuckle, Arapmoi and Tebogo, however, did not find it humorous.

'I would expect nothing less from the Council,' Arapmoi said, still staring up at the statue, 'they are known for their extravagance, and for their taste of alcohol. Which brings me to my next question, Mosegi.'

His eyes averted from the statue to the guard's heavy, dull ones.

'Has the finest of wines and spirits been flowing freely since the news of Zuberi's death reached here?'

'You should have seen it sir,' Mosegi said eagerly, 'they had arranged all the champagne glasses in the shape of a pyramid, and Lenka – er I mean Mr Shone popped open a champagne bottle and began to pour it into the top glass, it was like a champagne fountain.'

'I have seen it done once before Mosegi,' Arapmoi said softly, smiling a fraction, 'it was impressive to say the least. But no alcohol has passed your lips, you have of course remained professional all evening.'

'Yes of course sir,' Mosegi said with an awkward smile curving upon his lips.

Arapmoi nodded and narrowed his eyes a fraction, watching as beads of sweat began to gather on Mosegi's forehead.

'If you try and fool others Mosegi,' he said quietly, 'you are nothing but a fool yourself.'

The guard could no longer look at Arapmoi, he was staring down at the floor, the beads of sweat were rolling off his face and onto the carpet, leaving little watery marks.

'Well sir,' Mosegi said, looking up now, 'I may have had one ... or two ... or perhaps three glasses of champagne.' And then he quickly said, 'Mr Shone said it was okay to do so.'

Arapmoi stepped closer to the guard, his voice now growing to a whisper.

'These are still dangerous times Mosegi, even though Zuberi is no longer with us. You see what you have to understand is this, *he* never targeted this building, but his most loyal of followers may not share his sentimentality. Those left will be angry and will be seeking revenge, and they will not think twice in descending upon this grandest of monuments, killing everyone who have sought sanctuary here, and presenting their stripped-naked bodies for the whole world to see.'

The words seemed to have sobered the guard instantly. Clearing his dry throat, he closed the seemingly impenetrable door and slid across the thick metal bolt.

'I'm sorry sir,' Mosegi said regretfully, he knew that he had disappointed the man who had shown faith in him. 'I shall never fail you again.'

Arapmoi reached out and laid a gentle hand on his shoulder. And as he turned away and began to walk across the soft, deep red carpet with Tebogo behind him, he looked over his shoulder, and said, 'Nice suit Mosegi,' before winking.

'What you said to Mosegi,' Tebogo said after a few seconds had passed, 'about Zuberi never targeting this place, was that true?'

Arapmoi suddenly slowed and then stopped. He looked at Tebogo, who surprised by this, felt compelled to explain himself.

'I just find it hard to believe that Zuberi had that much sentimentality,' he said truthfully.

Arapmoi seemed to be thinking, long and hard he thought, before he nodded and said, 'Follow me, I think you'll find this interesting.'

And with that, he led him into one of the small rooms off the great hallway. The pair crowded in around a giant leather-bound book resting open inside a dust streaked display case. Arapmoi peered down at what it contained, glancing at the various words which had been written.

'On the left hand page,' he said quietly, running his hand across the thick dust that had gathered.

For a moment Tebogo stood before the case, wondering why this book was so important that it had to be encased by glass and wood. He shot a sideways glance at Arapmoi, who just simply stared back at him, before he moved closer and looked down at the page.

No words I feel I can write can really express my deep sadness for the loss of my good friend Clarence Sauer. South Africa is without question a lesser place without him. He was the truest man I ever had the privilege to meet. He took me in, saw real potential in me, inspired me to believe that no ambition of mine was ever impossible to fulfil. It saddens me to admit this, but I know in my heart of hearts that he is in a far more fitting place than the one he graced for sixty-seven years, and Heaven I know has already improved by his illuminating presence there. May you rest an eternity in the peace and happiness you truly deserve.

Your friend,
Zuberi Jacobs.

Tebogo read the beautifully handwritten words slowly and carefully, as though this was going to be the first and only time he would be able to, the final two words he spoke aloud.

'Zuberi Jacobs,' he said in utter disbelief.

He looked at Arapmoi who, to Tebogo's amazement, was smiling faintly. This was the very last thing he felt like doing, this revelation was immense. *Zuberi was an orphan?* he kept thinking, the whole idea was impossible to believe.

Never once had he pictured Zuberi as a child, innocent and alone. He had always imagined him to be just there, the man who killed innocent men, women and children, the man who brought the whole of South Africa to its knees and came close to destroying it completely. Then again, as he looked at Arapmoi, he realised that he had always imagined *him* to be just there, old and wise and the inspirer of men and women.

'That's why he never came here isn't it?' he whispered.

It wasn't a question merely a statement.

'He had too much respect for Clarence Sauer,' he continued quickly, 'how could he destroy the monument of the man who raised him?'

'Are you beginning to understand?' Arapmoi asked, still in his soft tone.

Tebogo read and reread Zuberi's words, holding onto the display case as he did each time, as Arapmoi continued, 'You see, like me, Zuberi's legend was exaggerated, and because people were even afraid to speak his name aloud, his power grew and he became more influential.' They walked out of the room and headed down the corridor. 'But despite all of this,' Arapmoi continued, 'despite all of the fear he had over so many people, despite him being depicted as a God, a part of him was still human enough to remember and respect the man who played the most important part in his life.'

They halted in front of a heavy wooden door which led into the showing room. But the usual sign which hung on the door announcing the time for the next airing of the life and times of Clarence Sauer had now been replaced by a handwritten note which read:

Enter those who seek to celebrate the death of Zuberi Jacobs.

Arapmoi tore it from the door, crumpled it and let it fall to the floor. They quickly walked through the dimly lit room, Tebogo's eyes wandered upon the large screen and fold down chairs as Arapmoi turned the handle of the next door and stepped through.

Never in his wildest of dreams could Tebogo have imagined such a spectacular place. The great circular hall, was without doubt, one of the most impressive rooms he had ever seen, the polished looking marble floor and the hand painted walls were both pure white, while a large, gleaming staircase – which was across the way – led up to the second and third floors. The whole room was lit by eight candle chandeliers which were suspended above six lengthy tables. Laid upon these were a green bean salad, corn on the cob, komkomer sambal (cucumber relish), hoender pastei (boer chicken pie), tomato salad, yellow rice, rock lobster tail salad, bobotie (beef pie), cape kidgree (fish and rice), green bean bredie (lamb and green bean stew), klappertert (coconut pie), green mealie bread (corn bread), sosaties (grilled marinated meat with apricots), yellow melon muscade (melon salad), raisin tart with sour cream sauce, soetkoekies (spice and wine cookies), green mango atjar (green mangoes preserved in spiced oil) and the champagne pyramid Mosegi spoke earlier of, although with fewer crystal glasses.

As they moved further into the grand room, laughter and clapping could be heard coming from one of the adjacent rooms, it seemed that the Council members were now in there, continuing on with their celebrations, leaving empty bottles of champagne and half-eaten food in their wake. Tebogo admired the framed colourful paintings Clarence Sauer had created throughout his life – all were secured to the circular wall – before his eyes fell upon the six tables.

'The food looks fantastic,' he said hungrily, feeling his stomach beginning to rumble uncontrollably.

Again the laughter and clapping could be heard from the other room.

'Well,' Arapmoi said softly, looking around the room, 'it seems they have retreated to another room to carry on with their celebrations. I'm sure they wouldn't mind if you helped yourself.'

'I'm not so sure sir,' Tebogo said, sounding a little unnerved, 'this food has been laid for the Council members, I wouldn't feel comfortable, I mean what if somebody said something?'

'We are all equals in this building Tebogo,' Arapmoi said, putting an arm around him, 'there is no social hierarchy, and if anyone makes you believe otherwise, you point them in my direction.'

He patted his back and headed for the staircase.

'Now feast,' he called proudly over his shoulder, 'I shall not be too long.'

He began to walk up the staircase, while Tebogo stood and stared at all the delicious food displayed in front of him.

Seventy-nine unique rooms made up the monument: some were large and grand, like the room filled with glass cabinets, displaying all of the trophies and framed certificates Clarence Sauer had been awarded over the years. While others were long and wide, like the one that contained the numerous suits worn by him during the many ceremonies and charity events he had attended to.

The first time Arapmoi had visited the Council, Lenka Shone's accommodation had been on the third floor, in the large library. So it was understandable, his embarrassment, when he knocked and walked in one day to find one of the female politicians changing her clothing. Trying his best to explain that he was looking for Lenka, the woman was hysterical, screaming that Lenka had moved to another part of the building. After that, it was difficult to keep track of Lenka's whereabouts; he always avowed that it was for security reasons, but Arapmoi knew of his 'unique' sense of humour.

Arapmoi stepped onto the second floor and made his way down the long corridor directly ahead of him. He passed countless framed photographs of Clarence Sauer, as he posed with many greats, past and present: Presidents and Prime Ministers, celebrities from all walks of life.

Having little time to stop and look at each individual photograph, Arapmoi stared straight ahead as he neared the end room. But as he stood in front of the dark door, gave it three hard knocks and waited, his eyes were drawn to the last framed photograph. Five people were grouped together, Clarence Sauer was in the middle, with a man, woman and two teenagers either side of him. They were standing on a red carpet and all were dressed smartly in black evening wear. The black italic writing underneath it read:

Pictured with Franklin Julian Lane, his wife Margaret and two sons Robert and Mark Richard at a charity event held in London.

The door opened a moment or two later, and Lenka's aide, Luthuli Dros, stepped out, holding a crimson coloured leather folder close to his chest.

'Mr Shone is ready to see you now,' he said as he walked past, he had an ill-mannered and ignorant way about him.

'Thank you Luthuli,' Arapmoi said, remaining polite.

Every moment he spent in the presence of Luthuli Dros, the more and more he disliked the young man. Taking another look at the photograph, Arapmoi turned the handle and stepped through.

When Lenka Shone had first appeared in front of television cameras, he was charming, inspiring and passionate; he was one of the people. Arapmoi had watched him closely during his rise to Council leader, and listened in admiration as he delivered a vigorous speech the day he was elected.

'The Liberators of South Africa will win if we as individuals stand by and do nothing,' he had said. *'I am ready and willing to lay down my life if necessary so that South Africa can be a free and just country...'*

And Arapmoi wanted to believe him. But as he stopped and stared down at the bald headed, expensively dressed man with designer moustache and beard, surrounded by cigar smoke, he was beginning to wonder whether he had meant anything he had said on that day. Had it been just an elaborate lie? Had he simply told everyone what they wanted to hear? Or was the power he received that day like a drug, consuming him, corrupting him? Outside of this building the South African people he had promised to protect were starving and dying and were beginning to lose trust and hope. Many had opted to join the Liberators of South Africa believing that this was the only way for them to survive.

I don't blame them, Arapmoi thought, *this man had promised them everything, and gave them nothing.*

'Arapmoi,' Lenka said brightly. He rested his cigar in the groove of the ashtray, then he stood, walked around his desk and embraced the man he believed to be a good friend, Arapmoi, however, didn't share the same view. 'Please, please, have a seat.'

Arapmoi took the seat facing Lenka's desk, while Lenka walked over to the array of fine spirits displayed in the corner.

'I know you're not much of a drinker Arapmoi,' he said, grabbing two crystal glasses and filling them each with brandy, 'but one won't hurt, will it?'

'I suppose not,' said Arapmoi.

He glanced around the room, and as he did, a fury began to develop deep within him. Everything in this room displayed luxury, in here you could become oblivious to the war raging outside of these walls. Lenka walked back towards the desk, sat in his chair and passed one of the glasses to Arapmoi who said a word of thanks.

'To the death of Zuberi,' Lenka said proudly. He clinked his glass with Arapmoi's and drank his brandy in one.

'To the death of Zuberi,' repeated Arapmoi quietly, draining about half of his.

The brandy warmed his throat and stomach, and with it came the realisation that he couldn't return to England, he had to stay here, he had to keep a watchful eye on Lenka.

'You know,' Lenka said, picking up the cigar from the ashtray, 'the Americans are confident that elections could be held as early as June.' He nestled the cigar in the side of his mouth and leaned back in his chair. 'Will I be able to count on your support,' he asked, hopeful Arapmoi would.

'I trust that if you are chosen to be President you will never allow the fallen to be forgotten.'

Lenka removed the cigar from his mouth and leaned forward, resting his elbows on the table. 'If I am elected Arapmoi,' he said clearly, 'you have my word that I will celebrate September the 3rd as Liberation Day. All of South Africa will unite as one and pay their respects to all those who fought against and died because of the tyranny of Zuberi Jacobs.'

'That's very poetic of you,' Arapmoi said, already convinced that he wouldn't. 'If you are true to your word then you have my support.'

Lenka smiled and put the cigar back in his mouth, it seemed to taste that much sweeter as he took a long draw from it. This was a major victory for Lenka, Arapmoi was loved by the South African people and a vote of confidence made publicly by him would almost guarantee the Presidency.

'Why don't you stay for the night Arapmoi,' he said, tapping off the ash into the tray, 'enjoy the celebrations, there are plenty of rooms that I could have a bed set up in.'

'I'm afraid I must decline that most generous offer,' Arapmoi said quickly, 'Tebogo is with me on this visit.'

'Ah yes, the young Tebogo Jeppe,' said Lenka brightly, 'I have been hearing great things about him. Well we have more than enough room here; I do not see a problem in finding somewhere for him to sleep.'

Arapmoi shook his head, 'Once again, thank you for the generous offer,' he said gratefully, 'but I must decline; there is still a lot of work that needs to be done.'

Lenka took a final draw on his cigar and then stubbed it out in the ashtray. 'So what will you do next Arapmoi?' he asked. He stared down at the crushed cigar for a brief moment before he looked up and leaned back in his chair. 'Will you be returning to England?'

Arapmoi thought long and hard, before this exact moment he would have said yes, but as he stared at the man sitting opposite him, the man who he knew was gradually becoming corrupt with the power he held, he knew that he could not return to England. He was needed here to watch Lenka closely and make sure that he didn't go down the same path Zuberi had.

'No,' he said directly, 'there is still a lot of work here to be done.' He paused for a brief moment. 'And that is why I have decided to step down as Brotherhood leader, I feel the time is right for me to do so.'

The silence which followed the words seemed long and awkward but it lasted only a few seconds.

'I see,' said Lenka slowly, 'well if that is how you feel then I must respect your decision.' He grabbed Arapmoi's glass and his own, and then he stood and refilled them with brandy. 'You are more than welcome to join the Council,' he said, passing Arapmoi his glass, 'I'm sure you would make a great addition, as long as you didn't run against me for the Presidency.'

He chuckled and Arapmoi forced himself to smile.

'In my heart I am a philosopher,' said Arapmoi, 'not a politician.' And he had to drain his brandy in order for him to say the next words. 'I shall leave that in your capable hands.'

'I would be lying if I said that I wouldn't be sorry to see you go,' Lenka said. 'If there is anything I can do for you, please do not hesitate to ask me.'

'That is very generous of you,' said Arapmoi pleasantly, 'but you have nothing to worry about, I will always be around, watching you carefully.'

He smiled and Lenka began to chuckle; he just allowed the words to wash over him. He stood and extended his hand, and Arapmoi knew that he had outstayed his welcome. And as the pair shook hands neither one said a word of goodbye.

Arapmoi turned and as he headed for the door he caught sight of a cardboard box, he hadn't noticed it when he had entered. It was filled with bits and pieces but at the very top sat a framed photograph of Clarence Sauer busy digging in his garden, but the glass used to protect the picture had been shattered, leaving tiny cuts on the photograph.

'I'm sorry about that,' said Lenka casually, 'one of the Council members had not perfected his aim when removing the cork from the champagne bottle.'

Arapmoi said nothing. He knelt and carefully and very purposefully removed the photograph from its frame.

'This monument shielded you from Zuberi Jacobs,' he seethed, 'and this is how you show your gratitude.' He folded the photograph perfectly and slid it inside his trouser pocket, then he stood and stared directly and determinately into Lenka's brown eyes. 'Never again disrespect this monument.'

The severity in Arapmoi's eyes made Lenka feel a little uneasy although he would not let it be known. But as he tried to offer his apologies, to say: 'sorry', or 'it will never happen again', or anything, the words seemed to become lodged in his throat.

Arapmoi turned swiftly and left the room. As Lenka poured himself another brandy and slowly appreciated its taste, a faint smile drew upon his lips; he had just witnessed, for the first time, a chillingly different side to Arapmoi Sebothoma's character, this could work in his favour.

Chapter Thirteen

CyberTech Defence Systems Research and Development Centre

June 17th

Robert sat alone at his desk in his study, out of all the rooms that made up his mansion he loved this one the most. He thought of it as his sanctuary, a place where he could come to forget about the outside world. Opened before him was the penultimate volume of his father's journals, he had been reading for about twenty minutes, stopping every so often to take a bite out of his beef, lettuce and cucumber sandwich and to drink some of his bottled water.

The weeks had turned to months and nearly ten had passed since Robert had read the letter written by his father. Learning the meaning of Genesis had only deepened his intrigue, and it was only going to be a matter of time before he began reading through his father's journals, searching for more on the project.

He lasted more than most would have in the same situation, but half an hour after looking up the definition of the word Genesis in the dictionary he returned to the bar, sunk into the leather couch and picked up the first of the leather-bound journals.

Robert thought he knew his father quite well, but after reading through the first two journals he was forced to consider the fact that he knew very little about him. It was as though Frank had lived an entirely different life to the one Robert had remembered when he was growing up, his father had been a married man when he had met Robert's mother, and they embarked on an affair that happened over three years before Margaret fell pregnant with Mark. Once told he was about to become a father, Frank did the only noble thing he could and divorced his first wife and married Margaret once he was legally able to do so.

Robert also had an uncle that he never knew existed. His father never spoke of him; Robert couldn't remember if his grandmother had ever mentioned anything about Fredrick, which was his uncle's name. Frank wrote very little about him, as a result Robert knew nothing about the man; his age, what he looked like, where he lived. But despite these revelations, the Genesis Project still eluded.

He took another bite out of his sandwich and he began to think about his father. The memories he had of him had been tarnished by his suicide and what had been written in the newspapers after his death. And although Robert at the time had been experiencing the same sort of personal attack he nonetheless believed what the papers had to say about Frank, so angry he was that he didn't even question if it was a complete fabrication, like most articles were. But his feelings had changed since he began reading the journals, the words had expelled the hatred, loathing and resentment from his mind, at last he was giving his late father the chance to explain.

Robert drank some of his bottled water and turned the page. He had started reading the third journal about a month ago, this one was different compared to the other two, while they were mainly about his personal life this one was about CyberTech Defence Systems, perhaps this was the journal that would reveal something about the Genesis Project.

I met the new director of the research and development centre today (he read). *I'm looking forward to working with Ruben Cross, our meeting was interesting and he brought some good ideas to the table.*

Research and Development Centre, Robert wrote in his notepad. This process of systematically tracing his father's footsteps was long and time consuming, but if at the end the Genesis Project still remained a mystery, then at least Robert had done all he could.

*

'Welcome to the Research and Development Centre, Mr Lane,' Ruben Cross said, as Robert stepped through the automatic doors with both Michael and Derek directly behind him. 'It's an honour to finally be meeting with you.' There could be no mistaking the 'Englishness' in the tone of his voice.

Robert extended his hand and Ruben shook it eagerly. The lobby the greetings took place in was small yet impressive, highly polished marble flooring, one way surrounding glass and a set of black glassed doors which were firmly closed.

'Your arrival has been kept secret,' said Ruben heartily, 'so naturally everyone knows.'

He ran his identification card through the security device on the black glassed doors and it flashed green.

'My office is just down here,' he said just as the automatic doors began to slide open.

This was some welcome, the entire evening staff had gathered and lined up either side of the corridor, as soon as they saw Robert walk through they erupted in claps. Taken aback by this warm reception Robert shook each of their hands and offered words of thanks.

'Okay ladies and gentleman,' Ruben said to the designers and engineers, 'the show is most definitely over. Now back to work everyone, "the defence of your country needs you."'

Laughter quickly circled among the group. Ruben leaned inwards and offered his apologies to Robert at once, 'I'm sorry Mr Lane,' he said, smiling, 'I couldn't resist.'

Despite being the centre of this ridicule Robert nonetheless found it amusing. 'The defence of your country needs you,' was the last words he had spoken in the new CyberTech Defence Systems recruitment advertisement as he pointed towards the camera. He accepted Ruben's apology gracefully and the staff quickly disappeared into their rooms soon after.

Robert and Ruben talked mainly about the miserable weather they had of late as they made their way down the long corridor. The blue carpet underfoot was embroiled with the CyberTech Defence Systems insignia every five metres of so, framed photographs of everything they had created were secured to the cream walls and large circular lights illuminated their way from above.

They came to a white door on the left, the silver nameplate read:

Ruben Cross
Director of Research and Development

Ruben slid his identification card through the security device and as it blinked green he turned the chrome handle and stepped through while Michael and Derek waited in the corridor. His office was like no office Robert had ever seen. At least three times larger than the most largest of office spaces, Ruben's looked to be part futuristic, part gothic. Lit by surrounding wall lights, the deep piled brown carpet was dotted with various pieces of furniture, three computers with flat screen monitors grouped together on a large corner workstation, a desk strewn with books, drawings, sheets of paper and boiled sweets, two black couches either side of a black glassed coffee table, a large bookcase filled with books on engineering, mathematics, physics and design and a black gleaming refrigerator with a kettle, cups, tea, coffee, sugar, a large bottled water unit, a biscuit tin with a plastic tray resting on top of it.

As Ruben closed the door behind them it was the fridge that he walked straight over to.

'Tea? Coffee?' he asked.

'Coffee,' said Robert, needing a boost of caffeine, 'no milk, one sugar.'

Ruben filled the kettle with the water and clicked it on to boil.

'I thought of writing to you on several occasions after your father had died,' he admitted, putting coffee, sugar and for himself a tea bag and milk in the cups, 'but I didn't know what to write. I mean how do you offer your condolences to someone you've never met?'

The kettle clicked off a moment later and Ruben filled the two cups with the boiling water.

'I believe my father liked to come here quite a lot,' said Robert, walking towards the leather couches.

Ruben put the two cups of tea and coffee with the biscuit tin on the plastic tray and walked over to the table and set it down.

'Yes, your father was once a regular visitor at one time,' he said, 'but after your brother's death, I saw very little of him.' He passed Robert his coffee and then took the lid off the biscuit tin. 'Chocolate biscuit?'

Robert grabbed two and dunked one in his cup.

'So what did you talk about,' he asked, taking a bite out of the soggy biscuit.

'An array of things,' said Ruben truthfully, 'he always spoke fondly of you.'

The last words spoken had unsettled Robert, he finished off the rest of his biscuit and took a sip of his coffee to try and hide the fact. 'Did he ever talk about the projects he was working on?' he asked, welcoming the coffee warming his throat.

'Only future ones,' said Ruben, leaning back in the couch, 'there could be no mistaking that Frank was a genius, some of our greatest creations had been thought up by him, but more often than not some of his ideas were just not practical.'

'Did he ever talk about the Genesis Project,' said Robert hopefully.

Ruben gave Robert a quizzical look.

'The Genesis Project,' he repeated quietly. He looked to be thinking, racking this brain for that particular project Frank might have once spoke of. 'That's a new one to me.'

Robert felt his heart sink; although he knew the chances of Ruben saying yes were minimal the disappointment still came crashing over him.

'But I wonder,' whispered Ruben. He stood and walked over to the computers with his tea in hand. He powered them up and sat in the black leather swivel chair, turning to Robert he said, 'We could search for the Genesis Project see what it brings up, you never know.'

Ruben took a sip of his tea then began tapping away at the keyboard just as Robert stood and walked over.

'Well I'll be,' said Ruben, taking another sip of his tea, 'it looks like you're in luck Mr Lane.'

There was no mistaking the utter surprise in his voice, Robert peered closer to the central monitor.

Name	Creator	Size	Type	Date Modified
The Genesis Pro...	Franklin Juli	857,358KB	File Folder	20:47 19/...

Your search has found 1 result.

Ruben double clicked on the folder but as soon as he did a message bar suddenly appeared.

Restricted access (it read).
This file is password protected please enter the password below.

'It appears that we have a problem, Mr Lane,' said Ruben, taking another sip of his tea.

'All I can think of,' said Robert, not averting his eyes from the screen, 'is my dad's date of birth.'

He told it to Ruben who in turn typed it in. He pressed the return key and as soon as he did, another message box appeared on the screen.

Password incorrect.
Warning!
For security reasons this file will permanently lock if one more incorrect password is given.
Please contact your administrator for assistance.
Please enter the password below.

'Obviously Frank didn't want just anyone looking through this folder.' Ruben sighed deeply and narrowed his eyes slightly. 'I've never seen anything like this before,' he said honestly, 'I mean we don't have anything like this secured on our files, they are password protected, but not to this extent.' He began to drum his fingers on the table. 'Your father really knew what he was doing here.'

The pair continued to stare at the blinking cursor.

'It's your call Mr Lane,' said Ruben, looking up at him now.

Robert read the warning message again.

'Who's the administrator?' he asked, pointing to the screen.

Ruben thought for a moment, looking back at the screen. 'At that time it would have been Larry Wilson,' he said.

'And there's no way of contacting him?'

'No,' Ruben said quickly, 'well not unless you can contact the dead ... Larry passed away six months ago.'

Robert drained the remnants of his coffee, hoping that the caffeine would clear his mind. He stared at the screen for a long time but then something suddenly seemed to occur to him, almost as if it were a revelation.

'Try my date of birth,' he said eagerly.

Ruben looked up at Robert once again, he looked as though he was about to say something, but then seemed to reconsider. He typed it in as Robert told him and was about to press the enter button when he stopped him.

'I think it's best if I do it,' Robert said, 'then if anything goes wrong it's my fault.'

Ruben understood and acknowledged it by nodding. He stood from the chair and Robert knelt in front of the monitor. With his finger hovering millimetres above the enter button, he began to question whether what he suspected to be the password was right. And like in many situations before, doubt began to erode his confidence, if it was wrong then the file would be locked, but before he would allow himself to go down the road of self-doubt, he hit the enter button and stood, waiting.

The screen looked as though it had frozen; for a long time nothing happened. And then, quite suddenly, the folder opened, revealing five other subfolders.

*Name	Size	Type	Date Modified
Catherine Sutton	1,021 KB	Word Document	20:27 19/...
Christina McNeil	998 KB	Word Document	20:28 19/...
Christopher Hayes	1,031 KB	Word Document	20:28 19/...
David Pierce	1,015 KB	Word Document	20:29 19/...
Diana Maria Houghton	1,019 KB	Word Document	20:30 19/...
Doug McAllister	999 KB	Word Document	20:31 19/...
Dylan Shaw	1,001 KB	Word Document	20:32 19/...
Eliza Louise Smith	1,016 KB	Word Document	20:33 19/...
Ella Greenwood	1,029 KB	Word Document	20:33 19/...
Evan James Whitehead	1,012 KB	Word Document	20:34 19/...
Eve Ellis	1,007 KB	Word Document	20:35 19/...
Fiona Cose	1,004 KB	Word Document	20:36 19/...
Franklin Julian Lane	1,025 KB	Word Document	20:38 19/...

Name	Creator	Size	Type	Date Modified
Equipment Desi	Franklin Julie...	470,693 KB	File Folder	20:40 19/...
Island Schemati	Franklin Juli...	101.964 KB	File Folder	20:41 19/...
Personnel Info	Franklin Juli...	107,927 KB	File Folder	20:42 19/...
Research and Spectre	Franklin Juli...	239,962 KB	File Folder	20:43 19/...
Inform...	Franklin Juli...	23,547 KB	File Folder	20:44 19/...

Robert clicked on the personnel file and it opened immediately.

Finally, the Genesis Project* like a ball of string was beginning to unravel itself.

'I'll need to print these,' said Robert.

But as he scrolled down the list of names, Robert came across one that made him furious with himself.

'William Davies,' he said, his voice no higher than a whisper, surely it could not be him.

He clicked on the document, but as it presented itself on the screen Robert slumped in the chair. He stared at the photograph which accompanied the personal information, staring into the blue eyes of the middle-aged handsome man, the man who had been Frank's best friend, the man who was Robert's godfather, the man who could have told him everything but who Robert had never even considered.

Chapter Fourteen

Meetings and Plans

June 20th

Grasping the brass door knocker of the single glass paned oak door, Elliott Ethan Grant tapped three times and stood, waiting patiently. He took in the moist night air in deep breaths while admiring the beautifully crafted fountain which stood in the middle of the circular gravel driveway.

A moment or two later the outside security light above the door came to life, and as Elliott snapped his head back round, the head of an African man, bald headed with designer facial hair could be seen looking at him through the glass pane.

The young man with long blond hair and soft, almost innocent looking, blue eyes watched as the door opened from within. The man standing before him was tall and dapper and looked to be in his forties, his expression left no doubt that he was expecting this visitor.

'Elliott,' he said with a smile, his voice was deep yet welcoming, 'the directions I gave you were okay I see, please, please come in.'

'Thank you Charles,' Elliott said politely as he walked into the lavishly decorated reception area, 'this is a really nice place you've got here.'

'It's a roof over my head,' Charles Piennar said modestly.

He requested Elliott's coat, hung it on the long wooden stand and then led him down the short hallway on the left.

'The others are already here,' he said before entering through the end door.

Elliott followed closely behind, his heart beating ever so slightly faster from entering the unknown. The dining room was a phenomenal size, two mahogany cabinets displaying Charles's finest china were against the far wall and a gleaming mini bar was in the far corner. But none of these compared to the fifteen foot mahogany table centred directly in the middle. All but three of the twelve chairs were unoccupied.

'May I introduce Elliott Grant to you all,' Charles said in an oration manner. 'Elliott, this is everyone, there will be plenty of time for you to get acquainted with them all later.' He pointed over at one of the empty seats and said, 'If you could sit next to Rupa and Limpho,' and then patted him on the back.

Charles took up his seat at the head of the table while Elliott, smiling politely at those he passed, took his place between a young Indian girl and a burly, middle-aged African man.

'Now that we're all here,' Charles said, straightening the stack of white papers directly in front of him, 'let us begin.'

The small, thin African woman with long black hair tied in a ponytail sitting three chairs down to the left of Charles suddenly sat upright, frowning, as her brown eyes darted from face to face.

'Shouldn't we wait for Uuka,' she said quickly, checking her watch, 'he should be here at any moment, it's not like him to be late.'

Everyone around the table looked at her now but the woman did not know why. Unsettled by the sudden attention, she slumped back down in her chair and avoided all of the intense gazes by staring down at her own lap.

'All of us are under immense pressure at the moment,' Charles said directly to the woman, who did not look up when he spoke to her, 'so I will forgive your lapse in concentration Mpho.' He paused for a fraction of a moment to look at the others seated at the table. 'For those of you, who might have forgotten,' he said indignantly, 'Uuka Fourie has returned to South Africa to attend the funerals of his mother, father, two brothers and three sisters.'

The room suddenly fell silent. Every man and woman – including the one that had raised concerns over Uuka's absence – now understood and knew what had happened, and each bowed their heads to acknowledge the fact. And as Elliott bowed his and closed his eyes, extracts from the newspaper he read the day after the atrocity had occurred in South Africa, suddenly appeared in front of his eyes.

It's already being hailed as the most atrocious act ever to come out of the South African war ... the massacre occurred after the British soldiers claimed that they came under attack during a patrol ... according to eye witnesses, the eleven men, seven women and nine children were then made to stand in a line and one by one the British soldiers killed all twenty-seven ... despite the British soldiers claiming that they were attacked first, local South Africans say no weapons were found on the dead and no bullets were fired other than by the soldiers...

'And it is because of this that I have asked you all here this evening,' Charles said, bringing Elliott back to the dining room. 'We have got a new leader and soon we will be heading in a new direction.'

Everyone around the table suddenly had their interests sharpened.

'Nine months have passed since the death of Zuberi Jacobs, and we have waited patiently for the South African Saviours to withdraw from our country. But still they are there, occupying the land that we all hold dear. And we have had no choice but to stand by and watch, as our loved ones and friends have been massacred by the very men and women who had been sent to protect them. We have bided our time, we have waited patiently, but now it is time for us to strike fear into the hearts of our enemies.'

Charles handed the stack of white papers to the tall, thin Afrikaner man with prominent cheekbones sitting directly on his right.

'Take one and pass them on,' he said. 'This article was taken from today's newspaper.'

And as the Indian girl handed the ever decreasing stack to Elliott, her soft fingers gently brushed against his. Elliott looked up; she was smiling at him and in that moment he took an instant liking to her, so he smiled back. She looked to be the same age as him, but that's where the similarities ended. Her long shiny black hair came down passed her shoulders and her eyes were soft and brown and sparkling, she wore no make-up and yet her complexion still radiated beauty.

'Thanks,' he said, as he took a sheet of paper and passed it on to the man sitting to his left.

The girl leaned inward, 'Hi Elliott,' she whispered, her voice was soft and heavenly.

'Hi,' he whispered back. And in that moment he couldn't think of anything else to say. He looked at Rupa, wanting to say more but couldn't find the words.

Just as she was about to look down at her sheet of paper he said quickly and quietly and without thinking, 'It's Rupa isn't it?'

'Yes,' she whispered, smiling brightly.

'I'm Elliott,' he replied quietly, and as soon as he said the words he immediately thought himself as stupid and started to blush red from the embarrassment.

'I know,' whispered Rupa, who had every right to laugh at him but didn't.

But before she could say another word, there was a clearing of a throat somewhere down the table. They stared at one another for a moment longer before Rupa looked down at her paper and started to read. Elliott still looked at her though, admiring her beauty, but he soon realised that everyone was reading and so tearing his eyes away from the most beautiful woman in the room, he did the same.

Protestors still set for Trafalgar Square demonstration
Simon Ashford

Despite serious health concerns, Samuel Potter is still going ahead and organising a mass protest in the heart of Trafalgar Square in August. An exact date has yet to be set, but sources close to Mr Potter say that the demonstration could be held on the fifteenth.

Outraged by the lack of equipment being supplied to the British soldiers fighting in South Africa, over 750 people have already signed up to become apart of perhaps the biggest pro-South African war demonstration ever to be held at Trafalgar Square –

'Surely you can't be serious?' Mamello Galpin said, who had finished reading the article first. 'Please tell me you're not considering this? Please tell me you're not considering killing seven hundred and fifty people?'

Elliott had only read two thirds of the article but he couldn't help but look up at the African man sitting opposite him. He was slender built with a gaunt looking face, and it was clear that the immensity of this war weighed heavily on his mind. His black eyes looked drawn and heavy tonight, dark stubble shrouded his cheeks, chin and neck and wisps of grey were beginning to advance in his short black hair. The woman sitting to his left had held his hand since Elliott had arrived, both Mamello and her wore matching gold wedding rings. There was nothing striking about her, her skin was slightly lighter then her husband's and her rather cold looking eyes were a hazel colour. Elliott, however, did admire the small shells hanging from her dreadlocked hair.

'It is not being considered,' Charles said coldly, 'is it being planned as we speak.'

'This is madness,' Mamello said aghast, 'these people are not our enemies, they have nothing to do with the war in South Africa.'

'Are you that conceited to think that these people, who want better equipment to be supplied to the soldiers fighting in our country are all innocent in this?' Charles asked.

'This is not what we stand for,' Mamello said bravely, knowing it was true.

'Do not tell me what we stand for,' said Charles, his voice now raised. 'I was there when war was declared; I have witnessed first hand what the South African Saviours have done to the country and its people.' He narrowed his eyes a fraction. 'And so have you Mamello.'

The words were like a knife piecing through Mandisa Galpin's heart. She tore her hand from her husband's and looked away, trying to hide the tears now forming in her eyes and running down her cheeks.

'I say to you Mamello and to everyone else in this room, how many more of our people will be slain before the South African Saviours leave our country? How many more buildings will be destroyed by their bombs? How many more schools will fall? How many more Uuka Fourie's will there be, without any family left?'

Nobody had the courage to answer the question; there was no mistaking the pure anger and contempt in Charles's voice now.

'They claim that they have provided us with hope,' Charles said, his voice now softening. 'The fact is that they have taken what little we had.'

Mamello slumped back in his chair and remained silent.

'Do not be fooled into believing that these people are innocent,' Charles said, picking up his sheet of paper. 'They support the war, they support the destruction of our country, of our people, so how can they be innocent?'

Once again no one answered.

'The answer is simple.' His pause was long and dramatic. 'They can't.'

He placed the sheet back on the table, rested his elbows on the table and interlocked his fingers.

'We have a lot to organise,' he said, 'I will contact you all shortly.'

The meeting was now over, and Mamello, through gritted teeth, had to accept the fact that this was the end of the discussion. He was the first to leave, offering Charles a half-hearted goodnight as he passed him. Mandisa quickly followed him out, wiping the tears from her cheeks and smiling a watery smile politely to everyone as she left.

The man sitting to Charles's right was next to stand, but before he could leave his arm was grabbed and Charles pulled him closer.

'Keep an eye on Mamello will you,' he whispered in his ear, 'I don't want him doing anything unnecessary.'

The man nodded and left immediately after. Charles offered his 'Goodnight', and 'drive safely', to the rest of his guests as they passed him. He stood and followed Elliott and Rupa – who were the last ones – to the front door.

'I have great things planned for the both of you,' he said, just as they grabbed their coats and stepped outside. They turned and Charles smiled at them. 'Goodnight,' he said pleasantly, 'have a safe journey home.'

'Goodnight Charles,' Elliott and Rupa said at different times before he closed the door.

Walking towards his black, sleek Audi TT, which had been an eighteenth birthday present from his mother and father, Elliott felt heavy drops of rain on his face. He glanced over at Rupa, who was putting the hood of her waist length coat over her head. He waited a moment, wondering if she was going to climb into one of the other cars, but as each one passed her, it appeared that she was going to walk home.

'Can I offer you a lift?' he called out, knowing there was nothing worse than walking home in the rain.

'No, thank you anyway,' she said, looking over at him now, 'I don't live far from here. Besides I like to walk.'

'You like walking in the rain?' he asked, there was a hint of sarcasm in his voice. 'I don't find that odd at all.'

The rain started to get heavier, the droplets now pounding off the gravel driveway.

'You can't walk home in this,' he shouted over the downpour. 'Stop being so proud and get in.'

Elliott unlocked his car, climbed into the driver's side and brought the Audi to life. A moment later Rupa opened the passenger's door and dropped into the leather seat.

'Thanks,' she said, throwing back her hood and wiping the raindrops from her face.

Elliott switched on the car's lights, set the windscreen wipers to the fastest setting and drove out of the cast-iron gates and onto the privately owned road, which was boarded on both sides by high manicured hedges. They sat in the silence until they had turned onto the main road.

'I'm sorry about your dad,' Rupa said quietly and sympathetically.

Elliott quickly averted his eyes from the road to Rupa, who was looking out of the front window.

'How do you know about that?' he asked surprised, looking at the road again.

'Everyone knows your story,' said Rupa, who still stared directly in front of her, 'it's not everyday you get someone from your background joining up to fight against the injustice in South Africa, you caused quite a stir when Charles first talked about you. You need to take a left at the roundabout.'

Elliott indicated, glanced over to the right to make sure the way was clear and turned. He wanted to press the matter further on why he caused quite a stir but as he thought about it, it became clear as to why.

'So what's your story then?' he asked, keeping his eyes firmly on the soaked road.

'My dad was a cameraman,' she said quietly, 'he was filming the intense fighting between British soldiers and the Liberators of South Africa with reporter Dennis Clark. The Land Rover they were in was hit by a grenade; Dennis Clark died instantly, my dad died three days later from the burns he received. The investigation is still ongoing, but neither the British nor the Liberators have admitted the attack, both have continually blamed one another.'

'And I suppose with you joining up to fight, you think it's the British.'

'I do not think it was the British soldiers,' she seethed, 'I *know* it was them, they have done nothing but hinder the investigation. What could they be possibly hiding if they are innocent?'

It was a self asked question Elliott was all too familiar with; he had asked himself a similar one about the Americans when his father had died. It was still as painful to him now as it was back then, because it was a question that could never be understood or answered and could drive you insane if thought over long enough.

'I'm sorry to hear about your dad,' he said, knowing it was perhaps too late to offer his condolences but knowing he felt better by doing so.

'Thank you,' Rupa said, smiling emotionally. 'You need to take this left.'

Elliott indicated and turned into a quiet road with large, impressive semi-detached houses on either side.

'That's where I live, there,' Rupa said, pointing toward the house with the silver Mercedes parked in driveway.

The rain had eased when Elliott rolled to a stop in front of Rupa's home. He stared up at the building, no lights were on, everyone would probably be asleep at this late hour. Elliott's home was at least two, perhaps three times as big as this one, and yet this one he looked at now felt more homely.

'That's a nice house you've got,' he said admiringly.

'It's my aunt's,' said Rupa quickly, 'I'm living with her at the moment, my mother has been finding it difficult lately. You probably understand with your mum being in the same situation.'

For a fraction of a moment that seemed to contain an eternity, Elliott thought about his mother. He thought about how the death of her husband, Elliott's father had unfazed her, how she seemed to be carrying on with her life without even a care for the man she promised to love forever, how she was becoming increasingly close to business tycoon Edward Harrison.

'Yeah,' Elliott lied, trying to flush the images of his mother from his mind, 'I understand.'

Rupa opened the door but before she stepped out, she leaned over and kissed him gently on the cheek. 'Thank you for the lift home,' she said, smiling.

'You're welcome,' he said, becoming momentarily numbed by the kiss, 'anytime.'

And as she stepped out of the car and closed the door, the rain began to fall heavy again. She buttoned up her coat and shielded her face against the downpour as she ran to the front of the house, putting her key in the door and opening it. Before she stepped inside, she turned back and waved.

As Elliott waved back he waited until she had closed the door before driving off. He suddenly began to smile. This was the happiest he had felt in a long time.

Chapter Fifteen

William Davies

June 22nd

The twenty-second of June was always a difficult day for William Davies, today was his son's birthday. But what made it particularly difficult this year was the fact that his son would have been twenty-one, a celebratory milestone in any young person's life.

When Jack Davies had heard that America was going to war in South Africa, he followed the tide of patriotism that swept across the country and enlisted, much to his mother's disapproval. She knew the realities of war, American soldiers were laying down, giving their lives in South Africa everyday, their deaths seemed so meaningless, so pointless, and yet William was delighted with his son's news.

He himself had served his country in the army and always boasted to his son that it made him the man he was today. *'The United States army will teach you things no other job will,'* he continually said to him, *'you will see the world and it will make you into a man, son. I never regretted a single day that I served.'*

After completing his intense training he was sent to South Africa to fight against the Liberators of South Africa and rebuild the country. Before he departed, his father shook his hand and his mother threw her arms around his neck and hugged him tight, as though this would be the last ever hug she would ever be able to give him, Jack did his best to ease her worries.

'Don't worry, Mom,' he said, with a grin, 'everything will be okay, I'll be back in no time.' These were the last words spoken to his parents, nine weeks later Jack Davies was dead.

'Your son was out on a routine patrol,' William and Kaitlynn were told on a dark, cloud filled day, *'when they were ambushed by the Liberators of South Africa. I'm sorry to say that despite Jack's bravery he was killed.'*

And as soon as Jack's body had been flown home and laid to rest, Kaitlynn demanded a divorce; she could never nor would ever forgive the man who she held responsible for her son's death.

'JACK JOINED UP BECAUSE OF YOU,' she would rage, *'YOU SAID IT WOULD MAKE HIM BECOME A MAN, OUR SON IS DEAD BECAUSE OF YOU.'*

And that was the haunting reality. The dynamics of war had changed since William had left the military; it seemed so cleancut when he had joined up, he had served his country and was well respected because of it. But now, any war America participated in, whether it be justified or not was always controversial. People protested, voicing their opinions, defacing the memories of the brave men and women who had given their lives for their country, so that those protesting could live in a world free from terrorism.

Before Jack died, William believed it was honourable to give your life for your country, it was the greatest sacrifice you could give, but it was clear now that Jack Davies was just a statistic among many others. He had filled his son's head with fairytales, promising him a wealth of knowledge and experience, he had convinced him that joining the army would be the best option for him to take. It took away his life and William knew his that wife was right, he granted Kaitlynn her divorce and took early retirement.

Now, on a wet and blustery day, William stood in front of his son's grave, simply staring down at the white headstone which read:

Jack Davies
19 Years Old
Beloved Son and Patriot

A cold wind blew through the graveyard, rustling the dead leaves, but William ignored the numbness in his hands which clutched a beautiful bouquet of brightly coloured flowers. Kaitlynn had visited sometime today, the single red rose she always brought lay flat against the ledge which was the base of the headstone.

'Happy twenty-first son,' he said quietly.

He laid the flowers on top of the earth that covered his son's coffin and slowly knelt. He reached for the inside pocket of his coat and withdrew a small bottle of brandy and two small glasses.

'Don't tell your mother you've been drinking,' he said with half a smile, 'you know what she's like.'

He put one of the glasses on the ledge next to the rose, twisted off the cap of the bottle and filled it to the top. Then, once he had filled his own, he clinked them together and said proudly, 'Happy birthday, Jack,' before drinking his brandy in one.

The alcohol warmed his throat and belly and a moment later it seemed to warm the rest of his body, sending with it the realisation that his son was no longer here. Tears welled in his eyes but his anger stopped them from rolling down his cheeks. He stood and ran his hand over the top of the gravestone.

'I miss you so much,' he said.

He took a step back, saluted, turned on his heel and walked away.

*

William sat in silence all the way through the long drive home. As part of the divorce settlement, he was allowed to keep the country retreat: a large three storey house in the middle of nowhere. He enjoyed the tranquillity from the surrounding woodland, and he spent most days just walking through the woods.

As he turned off onto the private road, entered the four digit number to the gate which barred his way and drove toward the house, thunder could be heard overhead. He rolled the car to a stop and managed to get inside just before the downpour of rain started.

*

By the time Robert arrived later that evening the rain had stopped. When William opened the door to greet his visitor, Robert was unable to hide his shock. The last time he saw William he had thick, dark silvery hair and blue eyes that oozed with exuberance. He was suave; a man who took great pride in his appearance, he was always clean shaven, was always stylishly dressed, and always wore expensive cologne. He was a man who had charm and good looks and was like a father figure to Robert when Frank was away.

But everything that had made him a cut above the rest was now gone, he had dramatically fallen from grace and he looked terrible because of it. He was gaunt and pale, his hair had begun to thin and turn white and his eyes had almost become grey looking.

After their pleasantries William hung up Robert's coat and then led him into the smaller out of the three living rooms, which was in complete disarray. Empty bottles and dirt ridden plates and teacups were littered over the hardwood floor, newspapers, weeks even months old covered the couch and armchair and left over takeaway food still in their containers were scattered on the table in front of the couch. The room had a dark and depressing feel about it, Kaitlynn's influential style was sadly missing now, the bright flowers she proudly displayed in vases around the home that brought warmth and colour were now just a distant memory.

'Jack would have been twenty-one today,' William said, walking aimlessly around the room, 'I would ask you to join me for this celebration, but I know all about your journey in becoming teetotal.' He walked over to the quarter filled bottle of brandy and poured some in a dirty glass. 'But will you begrudge me in having one?'

'No, go ahead,' said Robert.

William held his glass aloft, 'To Jack, a patriot who I'm proud to call my son.' He drained his brandy in one and set his glass on the small table next to the armchair. 'Now how about a drink for yourself, what can I get you, how about a cup of coffee?'

'Coffee would be ni –'

'I know how you take it,' interjected William.

He disappeared out of the room and Robert heard him in the kitchen, clinging cups and filling the kettle with water from the tap. He began to walk around the room, looking at each of the framed photographs proudly displayed on the mantelpiece as he passed them. He crossed over to the window at the far side and peered through the drawn curtains. He could only see trees and bushes, the moon was high in the sky, illuminating the forest. William lived in the middle of nowhere, he had hidden himself away from the outside world, Robert didn't blame him, he had taken the death of his son hard. He turned away from the window just as William came back into the room, holding two teacups by their handles.

He passed the green-coloured one to Robert and sat down in the armchair, cupping his own coffee with both hands.

'So what do I owe the pleasure,' he said, blowing down into his cup, 'not that I'm complaining, it's always good to see my one and only godson.'

Robert wasn't quite sure how he should begin; he walked over to the couch and moved the newspapers out of the way so he could sit.

'What do you know about the Genesis Project?'

'The Genesis Project,' repeated William, he drank some of his coffee and clicked his lips together in appreciation of the taste and warmth. 'I haven't said that aloud for a long time, too long to remember.'

'You know about it then,' said Robert softly and carefully.

He knew fine well that William was a part of it but he would not make it known. It was obvious that the Genesis Project was shrouded in mystery, something that had been locked away so the ordinary eye could not wonder upon it. And William could honour this secrecy by keeping quiet if he felt pressured to divulge its origins.

'Yes of course,' said William brightly, 'before I took early retirement I was working on the Genesis Project, I oversaw construction of the facilities.'

Robert thought back to the night he visited the research and development centre, he had printed off a vast amount of pages and once he returned home he had the slow task of reading and sorting through. He had come across numerous designs of buildings and facilities that were going to be constructed on an island Frank had bought a few years before his death. That is what William must be referring to, overseeing the construction of these buildings. It meant nothing to Robert then, but he hoped in the next few minutes it would be like a jigsaw puzzle and that the pieces would start to fit together.

'What is it?' he asked.

He drank some of his coffee and as he swallowed it he almost retched; William had forgotten to add the sugar and it tasted awful. But he didn't want to offend the man who had worked on the Genesis Project and could tell him everything about it, so he drank some more to be polite.

'The truth was we were playing God,' said William. He drank the rest of his coffee and set the empty cup down on the hardwood floor. 'We took *His* deadliest creation, made it stronger, made it faster, and made it smarter. God created it and Frank nurtured it, aiming to create a Spectre.'

He began thinking of an easier way to put it when Robert's face displayed nothing but bewilderment.

'A – er – a Spectre was the term we used for a child from when it was first born it would be taught how to kill and how to survive.'

Robert drank some more of his coffee, this time the taste didn't even register to him. Had he heard right? A child from when it was first born would be taught how to kill and survive? Surely this was some sort of joke, William had a love for practical jokes, any minute now he would break into laughter and would tell Robert the truth.

But William's expression remained deadpan, no smile formed on his lips, no laughter came from his mouth. He leaned back in his chair, rested his elbows on the arms and began to drum his fingers together.

'Your father always made it sound dramatic,' he said irritably, 'he said the Spectres would ultimately become ghosts once they entered the battlefield, they would be able to move swiftly and kill their intended target without remorse, kill quickly, silently and efficiently, almost as if it were a reflex action. I found it difficult to share his enthusiasm, for me we were entering dangerous and unknowing territory.'

There was a brief silence in which William leaned forward and glanced down at his empty cup, he was about to make himself another coffee but reconsidered and leaned back in the armchair.

'We ran a selection programme,' he continued. '"Want to become involved in a scientific experiment and potentially earn £15,000." That was what we had advertised in areas with a high chance of successful applicants, obviously it was the local currency in the other parts of the world where we advertised. None of the people who applied knew that they were going to be apart of history, that was kept strictly confidential.' He chuckled. 'Besides a lot of them were most probably in it for the money, fifteen thousand pounds was a nice sum for anyone.

'Various tests were then carried out on the successful applicants to measure their intellectual and athletic capabilities, and then their family medical history was researched.'

'Why was that?' asked Robert, who had at last found his voice. It was a feeble question to ask to which he already knew the answer, but he had to speak, he had to say something to stop his body becoming numb with disbelief.

'The Spectre had to be of pure breed,' said William, leaning forward and raising his finger straight, 'a substantial amount of money was being invested in the Genesis Project, the last thing we wanted was for any of the Spectres to become ill with a genetic disease later on in their lives.'

Robert finished off the rest of his coffee, hoping somehow it would help clear his mind and make sense of what he was hearing.

'Fifteen men and fifteen women were selected as the final thirty,' he continued, as though he had not diverted in his explanation. 'Two years previous to this, your father had bought an island off the south coast of England and it was my job to hire architects and constructors and oversee the designing and building of the facilities. By the time the final thirty had been selected, the island had just been completed and they were taken there.' He leaned forward, picked up his teacup and stood. 'I'm sorry Robert,' he said, 'I must make myself another cup of coffee.' He smiled. 'All this reminiscing has made my throat go dry, would you like another?'

Robert picked up his cup and passed it to him.

'Don't forget the sugar,' Robert called, as William disappeared into the kitchen again.

Robert waited until he heard William filling up the kettle before he stood and walked over to the mantelpiece. He stared at the framed photograph of himself, Frank and William, all were dressed smartly in suits and were posing inside a marquee, it had been taken the day of Robert's welcome home party. It was hard to believe that his father was already heavily involved in the Genesis Project when this photograph was taken. Was the smile he portrayed fake, was he just trying to mask the unimaginable secret he harboured?

William walked back into the room, holding the two teacups in his hands and gripping a packet of unopened chocolate cookies with his teeth. Robert turned, took hold of the cup and sat back down on the couch. William dropped down into his armchair, rested his cup on the floor and opened the packet of biscuits. Grabbing two for himself, he offered the packet to Robert who held up his hand, before picking up his own cup of coffee and leaning back in the chair.

'Now where was I,' he said, dunking the cookie into his coffee, 'ah yes, the fifteen men and fifteen women, who never intermingled I might add, were kept on a strict diet and exercise programme for three months, making sure that their, shall we call it reproduction system was in the best shape it could be.' He paused a moment while he ate his soggy biscuit. 'The sperm and eggs were then taken, fertilisation took place in the lab, then the embryos were inserted into the surrogate mothers who were then kept under strict observation at the island. The men and women, once they had donated their sperm eggs did not stay.'

Robert drank some of his coffee, it tasted sweeter this time, but it did not clear his mind as he hoped it would, it still was swirling and laden with everything he had heard.

'The Spectres were born nine months later and all those who participated were made to sign confidentiality agreements preventing them from telling anyone what had happened, they then received their payment. Nine boys and six girls, all healthy, were born, it was strange staring down at them in their cots, knowing what they were going to become. I left before their second birthday and the next thing I knew was that Frank had killed himself.'

Robert shifted in the couch and William realised that the words he had spoken had come across quite harsh so he offered his apologises immediately.

'Why do you think dad wanted me to find out?' asked Robert, as he drank some more of his coffee.

William raised his eyebrows and Robert began to explain briefly, he told him about the leather bound journals left to him, how they led him to the research and development centre and how he was finally led here.

'It seems for redemption,' said William plainly, dipping his second cookie into his coffee, 'Frank was delving into things no man should, in the end I think he realised it and it proved all too much for him.'

'What are you saying,' said Robert, who felt slightly irritated by the words, 'it drove him to take his life?'

'Perhaps.' Again William paused to eat his biscuit. 'I cannot be certain of that, but one thing I do know is Frank changed because of it.'

'What do you mean, changed?' asked Robert, intrigued.

'The Genesis Project was like a drug to your father and once your mother sadly passed away, it took over his life, consuming him.'

Robert thought back to his father's long absences after the death of his mother. He just presumed his father was going through the grieving process, locking himself away to try and come to terms over what had happened to his wife.

'Before I left,' William resumed, bringing Robert back to his surroundings, 'your father was no longer the man I knew, I think.' He paused momentarily. 'No, I know a part of Frank died when your mother did, what remained was a bitter and twisted man who truly believed what he was doing was for the greater good.'

Robert slumped into the couch, he had heard so much this evening that his brain was still trying to process it all, trying to sort through it and put the revelations in some sort of neat pile.

'I must see this island,' he said, there could be no mistaking the determination in his voice.

He was determined to find the island, determined to travel to it, determined to see why it had driven his father to suicide. And no matter what William said to this, whether he thought it was a bad idea or not, it would not discourage Robert, he had made up his mind and that was that.

'You will not find answers there Robert,' said William softly, 'travelling to the island will only tarnish the good memories you have of your father.'

But as Robert looked at William he felt a deep frustration rising from within. Didn't William realise that he had to know? Had he no idea that he had to see the island for himself to see why the Genesis Project had drove his father to take his own life. Robert could not walk away now, not after everything he had been told. If indeed Frank did seek redemption before his death then Robert had to do all he could to honour it.

'I don't expect you to understand,' Robert said, 'but I have to go to the island, I think that is what dad wanted, why else would he leave me his journals?'

William leaned back in the armchair, rested his elbow on the arm and began to trace the outline of his lip with his finger.

'I see,' he said after a moment or two had passed. 'Well I wish you good luck; I hope you find what ever it is you're looking for.'

And that was the end of the conversation as far as he was concerned; he had told Robert everything he knew about the Genesis Project, what Robert did next was entirely up to him, he would not stop him. William set aside his cup on a small table nearby and leaned forward, about to stand.

'Before I go,' said Robert quickly, knowing he was overstaying his welcome, 'I need to know one more thing. Why did he do it? Why did my dad, the respected man he was, become involved in such a project? Why would anyone want to become involved?'

William chuckled, 'Come on Robert, surely you can't be that foolish, you're an intelligent man. After the fall of Nazi Germany in World War Two the US military ran a programme of acquiring German scientists and technicians for their scientific knowledge and expertise. I love my country but I know what she is capable of when she feels it's in her best interests. Think about what the Genesis Project would have represented, the prospect of having the Spectres, this new breed of soldier brought a great deal of interest, especially from President.'

William suddenly went quiet and for the briefest of moments he thought about the man who had never left his thoughts since his son had been laid to rest. *President Jack Carter,* the man who he held responsible for his son's death, the man who had sent Jack to fight in South Africa, showed a great deal of interest in the

Genesis Project. Although he was not directly involved in it he still knew it existed, still knew what Frank was planning, what he was creating.

'President Jack Carter,' William said as though he had not paused.

'The current President of the United States,' said Robert rather stupidly. He thought he must have heard wrong, somehow misinterpreted the words William had just spoken.

'He was not directly involved merely an observer, but he saw great promise in the Spectres. Obviously he wouldn't have seen them in all their glory while still in office, but he knew they could play an important role in the security of the United States once they had reached the age for operations.'

Robert drained the rest of his coffee, set the cup down on the table and stood, extending his hand.

'Find a woman called Dr Catherine Sutton,' said William as he shook Robert's hand, 'the last time I heard she was still living in England, she'll tell you everything else you need to know, she was working on the project right up until Frank died.'

'Thank you,' said Robert, 'I will.'

For a moment they looked at one another, then Robert said, 'Thanks for the coffee,' before walking past.

But before he walked out of the room, he turned by the doorway and stared at William. It felt odd at that moment, William seemed so old, so frail, he had played an important role in Robert's life, stepping into Frank's shoes when Frank wasn't around, offering Robert guidance, always there whenever he needed him, always strong and dependable.

But where was Robert when William needed him? When his son was killed? He was too wrapped up in his own life to even consider others, he'd never thought to write, to offer his condolences, to even ring him and say how sorry he was to hear about the death of Jack.

'Come with me,' he said, 'come to England, travel back to the island with me.'

The chances of William accepting the offer were slim, after all he made his views quite clear on the Genesis Project, it was as he said delving into things no man should, but Robert had to do something, he had to somehow ease the guilt which was pressing down on him.

'Just have a think about it,' he said when William remained silent.

He walked to the front door, grabbed his coat and folded it over his arm, then he opened the door and stepped out into the cool evening air. Michael was waiting for him by the car, and as soon as he saw Robert he climbed into the driver's side and brought the engine to life.

'I'll come with you to England,' William called from the front door.

Nothing was said after that, Robert smiled and waved in acknowledgement before getting into the car. As the car drove off William waved them goodbye and once he could no longer see them, he walked back inside the house and locked the door. Something warming was running through his body now as he wandered into the living room, there was still a glimmer of hope to bring justice for his son.

Chapter Sixteen

The Dreams of her Soul Mate

July 30th

She was walking along a deserted road in the warmth of the evening sun. Either side, riddled with the scars of war, high rising buildings shadowed over her. Could Mark be in one of these, she wondered, staring through the grime streaked windows. She called out his name, hoping that he would answer her back, but there was nothing ... only silence.

And then a terrible scream thundered across the empty street, a haunting sound that expressed pain and suffering in a way that she never thought possible, and without knowing it, she found herself suddenly running, running as fast and as hard as she had ever ran in her life.

'Stay with me,' she could hear someone shouting as she drew nearer.

And it was there, by the far ended building that eight shaven haired men were knelt around something. All were shouting and panic-stricken.

'Parker put pressure on it – no press harder –'

'Vasquez – Vasquez goddammit I need you over here –'

And it was then, as Lisa gazed down at what the eight men were knelt around, that she felt her mind go in a sudden freefall, unable to comprehend what she was witnessing, because this could not be Mark, his body broken and bloodied by the savagery of a battle that had once raged.

Feeling as though she was nothing more than a helpless onlooker, she could only watch – in horror – the many hands trying to staunch the blood that flowed from the wounds in his neck, arms and legs, as his adrenaline, which now surged through his veins, made his entire body jerk.

'I don't want to die,' he wept, his voice shaking uncontrollably.

'You are not going to die,' someone said, his voice was soft yet professional. 'Mark ... Mark ... listen to me, you are not going to die, understand? I am not going to let that happen, but I need you to fight this, okay?'

Lisa was suddenly nodding and was gripping her fists, urging Mark to fight through the pain and keep his life flowing through his veins.

And then quite suddenly, she heard a familiar voice say, 'Talk to him.'

And it was only when she felt a pair of eyes staring at her that she realised that Michael Parker was actually talking to *her*.

'Well what should I say? – I don't know what to say?'

But Michael, apparently, was no longer listening; he had turned his stare back upon Mark and continued to press down on his thigh.

Lisa walked around the mass of people, and knelt down by Mark's side, clasping his hand with hers.

'Hey you,' she said softly, the tears were now starting to form in her eyes, 'what have you been getting yourself into?'

Mark smiled and half coughed and laughed.

'Oh ... Lisa,' he said, his lips quivering from the effort in whispering the words, 'I thought ... I ... thought ... I ... I ... wasn't ... going to ... get ... the ... the ... chance to –'

'Shhh,' Lisa soothed, as she laid her index finger on Mark's dry, dusty lips, 'you need to rest.'

But he seemed determined to tell her something. He pulled at her hand, and she leaned in close.

'Lisa ... Lisa ... I ... I ... love ... you.'

'I know you do,' she whispered.

And as Mark smiled and looked past Lisa to stare at the darkening sky, he saw a woman standing not far from him. She looked to be in her fifties, dressed smartly in black trousers and a white blouse, with pearl earrings and a pearl necklace which suited perfectly. Her hair was dark brown with wisps of grey, it was tied back neatly in a ponytail and her make-up was immaculate.

'I ... I ... can ... see ... my ... my ... mom,' he said, smiling.

With tears now streaming, Lisa slowly nodded, fully understanding what was going to happen next.

'She's ... hol ... ding ... out ... her ... hand.'

'Go with her,' Lisa said, unable to stop the tears from streaming.

Mark stared into Lisa's watery brown eyes. They just looked at one another, both savouring their last moment together. And then, Mark looked past Lisa, and with great difficulty he raised his arm and grasped at, seemingly, thin air. For a moment, he just held it there, then, his eyes slowly closed and his hand thudded to the floor.

Whatever energy flowed through the man she loved, it had extinguished before her very eyes. Lisa kissed his still warm lips, tears rolling down her cheeks onto his dirt-covered face as she whispered her last words to him, 'I love you.'

She remained kneeling at his side, trying to take in the horrifying and none escaping truth presented in front of her eyes: that never again would she be able to hear Mark's laugh, to see his beautiful smile, to feel the beat of his heart. Never again would she be able to dance with him, to lay with him in an embrace. Everything that made him unique was gone ... forever.

It seemed that a long time had passed before she felt a pair of strong hands pulling her to her feet. She tried to fight it, wanting nothing more than to remain by Mark's side, but all her strength had been drained from her body. She stood, swaying, feeling as though her legs would give way at any moment.

'We need to move,' she heard a voice say, and Lisa neither knew nor cared who was talking to her.

'I'm not leaving him,' she said defiantly, gazing down at the empty shell of the man who had made her life whole, as tears continued to stream down her face making her eyes red and puffy.

'There's nothing you can do for him now,' the voice said rather coldly, 'he's gone, and we need to move – NOW!'

Somewhere in the distance, gunfire roared into the night, sending streaks of orange high into the inky sky.

'WE NEED TO GO NOW,' the voice roared with urgency.

But it was meaningless: the words ... the escalating gunfire ... nothing mattered to her now. Her 'everything' lay a foot away from her, perfectly still and peaceful looking, she could not bear to leave him, she would not, and she tore her arm away from whoever was gripping it and dropped down by Mark's side once again.

The man did not make an effort to hide his disgust. He cursed and turned away, bellowing to his comrades for them to get ready to move, but Lisa did not care if they were going to leave her, she would rather die here then live her life without the man who was without doubt her soul mate.

But then Michael Parker knelt down beside her and put an arm around her slender shoulders.

'Miss Anderson,' he said much calmer than the man before him did, 'we have to go, they're coming, it's not safe for you here.'

'I don't care,' she whispered, meaning every word of it.

'What would Mark want you to do?' he asked.

'What?' Lisa said, looking up now, surprised by the question.

'What would Mark want you to do?' he repeated in the same thoughtful tone.

Lisa's lips parted slightly, but no words came out.

'He would want you to come with me, wouldn't he?'

Lisa could no longer look at Michael now. He was right, and there was no escaping that fact.

'We have to go,' he said softly, 'it's not safe here.'

She did not fight against Michael when he lifted her to her feet and slowly led her away from Mark. She looked back, sobbing quietly as he grew further and further away from her.

And as the squad of soldiers began to quicken their pace, weaving in and out of the abandoned cars simply left on the road, Lisa had an unusual feeling that she, along with the rest of the men she was with, were being watched.

And then, without warning, a loud 'whoosing' sound tore through the silence.

'GET DOWN,' someone shouted nearby.

But before Lisa could do anything, before she could turn, or understand what was really happening, Michael pushed her to the floor, just as the car – about ten metres or so behind them – exploded.

The energy which rippled out from the car was unimaginably powerful and destructive. Lisa fell to the ground, hands covering the back of her head as dust and dirt from the street filled her nose and mouth. But barely a second had passed before she found herself scrambling to her feet, trying desperately hard to remember where Michael had fallen. He was right behind her, wasn't he? He would have fallen close by?

'Michael,' she called out, 'Michael.'

Her desperate cry echoed throughout the empty street, and she hoped, prayed even that it would be answered ... but there was nothing, only a cracking sound coming from the remnants of the exploded car.

Looking through the darkness, Lisa searched desperately for Michael, or any of the men that were with him, but they were gone, nowhere to be seen.

But then, out of the darkness a lone figure emerged. Lisa stopped, daring not to move, staring anxiously as the figure slowly approached her. She couldn't make out who it was, but whoever it was, it not very tall and it walked with a slight limp. The figure drew nearer, the space between them diminishing all the time, until it was no more than six feet from her.

It stopped, and Lisa could see the figure clearly. It was a man, a thin man with a bald head and a thick dark moustache. For a second, Lisa and the thin man simply stared at one another, her soft brown eyes meeting his cold dark ones.

And then, quite suddenly, the man threw back his head and shrieked into the night sky. A moment later, as though it was a response to it, hundreds of people emerged from the darkness all around. All were walking towards Lisa, holding their weapons high over their heads and shooting into the night sky as they shouted in their mother tongues.

Terror washed over her body. Lisa closed her eyes, and in that moment of fear and confusion, the shouts and escalating gunfire had faded away, for she was no longer there, she was...

Lisa opened her eyes, drenched in sweat she panted heavily in the darkness. She sat up, threw the duvet off her shivering body and scrambled out of the bed. Hurrying into the en suite bathroom, Lisa switched on the light and ran the cold water tap, staring into the mirror, staring at her horrified reflection as the water swirled down into the sink hole.

Cupping her hands, she splashed some of the water into her face, trying – in vain she knew – to rid herself from the nightmare, trying to wash it from her mind. The water felt cool and refreshing against her skin, but she could still see Mark, dying, gasping for breath, his eyes filled with fear. She gripped the sides of the wash basin and took long deep breaths as she closed her eyes. Her body stopped shivering as she did and she could feel herself becoming calm.

After ten or so seconds had passed, Lisa opened her eyes. And as she stared into the mirror once again, she could no longer see Mark, although the nightmare still lingered at the back of her mind.

She turned off the cold water tap and patted her face dry with a cream towel which was folded over the radiator. Then avoiding her gaze in the mirror she walked out of the bathroom, switching off the light as she went.

This wasn't the first nightmare she had had about Mark and she had already accepted the fact that it wasn't going to be the last. Normally she would climb back into bed, it now had almost become a routine for her but it suddenly occurred to her that Michael Parker had appeared in every single nightmare she had about Mark.

She had never thought to ask Michael about his time serving alongside Mark in the military. Undoubtedly it would be awkward, painful even to ask for his recollections; after all, it was common knowledge that Michael was there when Mark had passed away. Lisa had not bothered to ask what happened on that fateful night, denial had stopped her seeking out the truth. However, as the months passed by she wondered if the truth, which she was now willing to accept, would ease her heartache and end the nightmares which haunted her sleep.

She crossed over to the dressing table, dropped down onto the stool and stared into the mirror, her head pounding relentlessly, and although her heavy eyes itched and stung and longed for sleep, her thoughts were overwhelmed with *that* nightmare, the remnants of which showed no sign of leaving her brain.

Peering at the dark star-strewn sky through the sliver of gap in the curtains, guilt and grief weighing down on her heart, anger and frustration coursing through her veins, she clenched her fists as tears began to form in the inner corners of her eyes, she would not cry, she fought hard to stop the tears from running down her face, but in this silence, with her mind unoccupied, the tears were inevitable—

Wiping her eyes with the back of her hands, she opened the central drawer of her dressing table and pulled out the large red diary sitting at the very top. Then, switching on the small lamp, she turned the pages slowly and carefully, glancing at some of the things she had previously written:

...These past couple of months have been the most difficult of my life, the only thing keeping me going at the moment is Melissa. I don't think she really understands what is going on, Mark had spent the majority of her life away on tours...

...The American President has once again defended the South African war, the opposes of the war want American soldiers to be withdrawn. If that happens, what has Mark given his life for?...

...I visited Mark's grave for the first time since his burial. How did I feel when I gazed at the gravestone? No words I can write can really express how I feel, what I long for most is for the gaping hole deep inside of me to be filled...

Black watery blotches suddenly appeared on the page, and without realising it she was crying. Anger controlled her rationing from that point, the watery blob staining the page pushed her over the edge. She slammed the book shut and dropped it in the small plastic bin. The moment the diary thudded against the base, Lisa stood and threw herself down onto her bed. Not bothering to climb under the covers, she stared up at the darkened ceiling; the guilt already pressing against her heart seemed to become that much heavier with every passing second.

Although her diary was nothing more than paper bound together by card and glue, a trust had been formed between the pen and paper. She could become vulnerable in front of her diary, safe in the knowledge that it would not judge her, mock her, or divulge anything in the heat of an argument. She could tell it anything and everything and in a sort of strange way, it was the closest thing to a friend she had.

Exhaling deeply, she got off her bed, retrieved the diary from the bin then opened it once again, turning to a fresh page. Writing the date in the top right hand corner, she pressed the pen against her lips for a brief moment, thinking.

I had 'that' dream again (she wrote). *I've had it every night now for the past two weeks. But what does it mean? Perhaps I am ready to hear the truth surrounding Mark's death. It has been nearly two years, am I to spend the rest of my life in mourning?*

She paused and gazed up at the stars once again. Had two years nearly passed since Mark's death? It seemed odd, she was told that her pain would ease over time, and in her vulnerable state she wanted to believe them. But as the two year anniversary approached she now knew that it had all been lies, her pain would never ease, it would always be there, the passing months and years would just help her accept it.

The dreams have meaning, (she continued) *I know they do, but how do I seek answers to questions that have plagued my mind for months? Michael Parker, I think, holds the key. He has continuously reoccurred in the dreams, urging me to run with him. But how can I go about asking him? We have barely held a conversation since his arrival, can I really just go up to him and ask? I know he has something to tell me, but neither one of us will make the first move.*

Again she paused and again she looked up at the stars. How could she ask Michael what had happened when their only form of conversation had been wishing each other a good morning? But as she stared down at her diary and tapped her pen against the paper a thought occurred to her.

But on the other hand, do I really want to know the exact events surrounding Mark's death? Is it best for me to live in blissful ignorance? Would hearing the truth stop the nightmares or would it make things worse? It seems there is no easy answer and it appears whatever I do someone will get upset. I think I know what I must do.

She put the pen in the binding of the diary and closed the book. She opened the dresser drawer and as she replaced her diary she spotted something at the very bottom. Nestled in the far corner sat a small plain white envelope, which had slightly discoloured over time. Without thinking, she slowly reached for it and began to turn it over and over in her hands. It was addressed to her, in Mark's distinctive hand writing.

Reeling backwards towards her bed, she sat on the edge and closed her eyes, hoping and praying, trying desperately to convince herself that she had somehow misread or misunderstood what had been personally written to her. Sighing deeply, she reopened the envelope, pulled out the folded letter, and slowly and very carefully reread the words:

Dear Lisa,

South Africa is not what I expected it to be, as each day passes I realise that we don't belong here. The South African people don't want us here and I don't blame them, we are doing more harm than good. If I'm being honest I'm really scared, not of being injured or killed, (well I am a little) but that I'll never see you again, I'll never be able to see Melissa grow into a beautiful young woman. However, I know you are a great mother, and she's in the best of hands. Now, I know that if you get this letter it means that I am dead and I can only apologise for the burden I will be putting on you. I want you to know that I will always be with you in your heart. My life began the moment I set eyes on you and the years we had together have been the best in my life. You have given me a beautiful daughter and the day you accepted my marriage proposal was one of the happiest days of my life. I Love You Lisa and I will never stop loving you, and even though I will never be able to hold you again, my spirit will always be with you, looking over you. Whenever you feel lonely, just close your eyes and I'll be there, right by your side. You are the beat in my heart, the soul in my body, and I know that I have died fulfilled and complete. I only hope I have made you proud, that I did my job to the best of my ability and that I didn't fail my country. Take care of yourself my darling and never stop telling Melissa that her daddy loves her so very much.

Eternally yours
Mark
xxx

What was she really thinking? Did she really believe that Mark would have been alive after all this time? That it was all some sort of terrible mistake, that he wasn't dead but merely wounded and he would be home and walking through the door anytime soon.

And as she refolded the letter and placed it back inside the envelope, tears began to roll down her cheeks. The beautifully written words could not hide the fact that Mark was no longer with her, his body now buried under the earth, where it would lay undisturbed for an eternity, never knowing that his death was a simple statistic among the many others that had gave their lives in the South African war.

Lisa replaced the letter back inside the drawer and stood a moment, gripping the chest of drawers, trying to steady her swaying body. And in the silence and semi-darkness, with her eyes swollen from the tears she began to whisper.

'Whenever you feel lonely, just close your eyes and I'll be there, right by your side...'

She closed her eyes, wanting to believe that Mark would be by her side, holding both her hands, staring deep into her eyes, but in that moment of hopefulness, her world was suddenly ripped apart. The realisation hit her hard, and in that instance she knew that Mark wasn't with her, nor would he ever be.

And as soon as she opened her eyes, she wondered if she would ever be able to spend the rest of her life without him. Turning in the silence, she walked over to her bed, climbed under the covers and stared up at the ceiling once again. She always took a negative look on things when she was tired, everything would seem different once she had a few hours sleep. And with this comforting thought as an incentive, she pulled the duvet over her shoulders and closed her eyes.

But within an hour of her head hitting the pillow, she was suddenly awoken by Melissa, who ran into the room and jumped onto the bed.

'Good morning, mommy,' she said brightly.

Lisa rubbed her eyes, it took a moment for her to pull herself out of this sleepy state. She pulled back the duvet on the empty side of the bed and Melissa climbed under and cuddled into her.

The pair went downstairs, Melissa was first to reach the bottom and she ran into the kitchen expecting to see Robert. But only their bodyguard, David Tolland was sat at the table, newspaper spread before him as he drank his morning coffee. Lisa walked in a moment later, looked around for Robert and then immediately looked out of the window. The two specially built Range Rovers were gone and Marcus who usually cleaned and polished them at this time was nowhere to be seen.

'Good morning David,' Melissa said. She ran over and threw her arms around him, squeezing tight.

'Good morning Melissa,' David said plainly, as always remaining emotionally unattached as he hugged her back.

He offered his good morning to Lisa but before she could ask where Robert was, David's phone began to ring. He reached inside his trouser pocket and answered it.

'Hello sir.' He glanced at Lisa. 'Yes she is ... No not yet sir.' He checked his watch. 'In one hour ... yes that should be no problem, and should I tell – okay sir ... yes sir see you then.'

He ended the conversation and put the phone back inside his pocket.

'A helicopter is going to be arriving in one hour,' he said professionally, 'you need to pack enough clothing for you and Melissa that will last you both a couple of weeks.'

'Where are we going?' said Lisa, who immediately knew it was pointless to ask.

David checked his watch, 'You've got fifty-eight minutes.'

*

The helicopter, as promised, arrived within the hour, it flew overhead and landed fifty or so metres from the mansion. David along with Lisa who carried Melissa in her arms – who was carrying her favourite brown bear in hers – hurried out and climbed into the surprisingly spacious interior of the helicopter. They buckled themselves into the plush seats as the pilot welcomed them. He spoke for a minute or so, mainly to Lisa who he could see was apprehensive and then the helicopter was in the air, banking hard across Robert's vast estate.

As Lisa stared out of at the blur of greenery beneath her she could feel herself becoming increasingly uncomfortable and her heart began to beat that much faster. She hated flying at the best of times but her heart rate would have increased that much more had she known what would be waiting for her.

*

Lisa had no idea how much time had passed or where she was going. As soon as she settled herself into the seat and the helicopter was airborne, she closed her eyes and had kept them closed since.

'Mommy, Mommy,' Melissa said excitedly, 'look at that.'

'That's nice sweetie,' said Lisa, keeping her eyes firmly closed.

'No mommy,' Melissa said angrily, tugging at her mother's arm, 'you're not looking.'

Lisa slowly opened her eyes and immediately saw the enormous shape glistening in the distance, drawing nearer, and for a moment she wasn't quite sure what she should do. She stared out at the massive aircraft and her heart almost stopped.

As the helicopter settled down onto the runway besides Robert's plane and the blades began to slow, Lisa completely understood why the American press and indeed the entire world had nicknamed it after his attributes. Its official title was a specially constructed CyberTech Defence System 247-C Flightliner – built within the newly developed commercial side of the company – but it was referred to as the Titan.

'Miss Anderson?' a smartly dressed official with the CyberTech Defence Systems insignia stitched on the breast pocket of his navy blue blazer, appeared outside of the helicopter and opened the door for her. 'Mr Lane is waiting for you inside.'

Lisa stepped out of the helicopter with Melissa and the pair stared up at the stairs leading up to the cabin door. The plane was white with a blue underbelly; it was such a majestic sight, especially with the sun gleaming off it. Melissa held her bear close to her chest and grabbed hold of her mother's hand, squeezing it gently and Lisa returned the pressure, reassuring her daughter that everything was alright.

They began climbing the narrow stairway, while David and the smartly dressed official carried the luggage. Melissa was in front of her mother, pulling her upward, towards the darkened entrance.

The auburn-haired woman who greeted them inside had pale skin and a warming smile, she was dressed in a navy blue knee length skirt and blouse.

'Welcome Miss Anderson.' She knelt down so that her brown eyes were level with Melissa's. 'And this must be Melissa,' she said, and the little girl nodded with uncertainty. She stood once again. 'My name is Carmen,' she said softly, 'and if I can be of assistance to you in anyway, please do not hesitate to ask. Now if you would like to follow me please.'

She led them through a narrow corridor, they turned right and walked a short distance before arriving in a sumptuous and spacious cabin. Robert was already there, waiting for them, he thanked Carmen who wandered off to another part of the plane. Robert knelt down and opened his arms, but Melissa did not run into them, she stayed behind Lisa, holding the bear close to her.

'Where are we going?' she asked, half excited, half nervous.

'We're going on a magic journey Melissa,' said Robert, smiling, 'you have nothing to be worried about.'

Chapter Seventeen

Operation Restore Belief

Alone on his bed in his own private quarters, with a crossword resting upon his raised legs and a pen pressed against his lips, Michael Parker stared at the next clue of the crossword before him while the *Long Winding Journey* album of Naomi Andrews softly played in the background.

British Actress who has starred in such films as Diaries of a Sisterhood *and* I am what I am. *(5, 6)*

'Holly Hunter,' he said triumphantly as he began to write the name in block capital letters. He stared down at the next one.

Soccer star who has scored seventy-five goals for his country? (5, 7)

But before he could think of the answer there was a gentle rap at the door.
'It's open,' he said, dropping the crossword magazine onto the bed and getting to his feet. Lisa walked in, pale looking and tired.
'Miss Anderson,' he said, sounding slightly surprised, 'how are you finding the flight?'
'Well let's just say that Melissa's having a great time,' she said, forcing herself to smile.
Michael walked over to the small fridge and grabbed two chilled bottles of cola resting on the bottom shelf.
'Try drinking this,' he said, handing Lisa one of the bottles, 'it may ease the sickness.'
Lisa offered a word of thanks, twisted off the cap and took a gulp of the fizzy drink.

'I don't suppose you know a soccer star that's scored seventy-five goals for his country do you?' said Michael hopefully, as he was walking back towards his bed.

Lisa shook her head, 'I don't, sorry.'

'Well it was worth a shot,' Michael said, smiling. He twisted the cap off his bottle and took a sip. 'You don't have to stand, please take a seat.'

But Lisa couldn't. She had finally summoned the strength to ask him about Mark's death, but now she was here she couldn't ask. She just couldn't. But she had to know. Michael sat on the bed, looking up at her, slightly puzzled.

But before he could ask her what was wrong, Lisa suddenly found the courage.

'How did Mark die?' she asked, sounding a little less sensitive than she had hoped.

The feeling she felt was odd; moments before, an unimaginable weight pressed down inside of her, but as she said the words she felt a sense of relief, as though a valve had been turned, releasing all of the pressure that had formed.

Michael sat while Lisa stood, both just looking at one another. Neither knew how much time had passed before Michael said, 'I see.'

'I need to know,' Lisa said softly, sounding more sensitive now, 'I know you were with him when he died.'

'Yeah,' said Michael, who was now looking down at his bottle of cola as he turned it in his hands, 'I was.'

He took a long gulp of his drink, wiped his mouth with the back of his hand and sighed deeply.

'For the first couple of months,' he began, 'the war in South Africa was fought mainly from the air.'

Completely forgetting about her air sickness, Lisa slowly walked over to the small desk next to the bed and sat down on the chair.

'American planes flew night and day, targeting influential figures within the Liberators of South Africa.'

He took another drink of his cola; this sudden reminiscence had made his throat go dry.

'But the killing of these figures came at a heavy price; many hundreds of civilians lost their lives during the bombing runs. As a result, the Liberators of South Africa grew in numbers, thousands joined up to fight for their cause, and it became clear to everyone that the war would not be won in a couple of months as first predicted.'

Again he stopped to take another sip, Lisa still sat, watching intently.

'So having little other option, Operation Restore Belief was set into motion. It was a hearts and minds campaign, established to win the popular support from the South African people. We went on routine patrols, reassuring the locals that we were here to protect and help them. When I look back I realise that most of this was more for the benefit of the people back home.

'The South African war had been shrouded in controversy. The American people were becoming increasingly concerned with what was unfolding on their television and computer screens and in was only a matter of time before they begun to question the real motives of the war.'

Lisa sat there; a frustration was now beginning to form inside of her. This had been the very first time she had summoned the strength to ask Michael the details surrounding Mark's death. She wished he would just tell her what had happened on that fateful day, but as Michael finished off the rest of his cola and went to the small fridge to grab another bottle, he sensed her urgency to know.

'On the day Mark died,' he said, twisting off the cap of the second bottle, 'we were out on a routine patrol in Cape Town...'

And as Michael began to recount what had happened on that fateful day, Lisa felt herself drifting back with him...

The squad of eleven soldiers had been patrolling for the past twenty-five minutes. At the helm was the tall, burly figure of Michael Rodriquez. Rodriquez was African-American, he was tall and muscular and had handsome features. He was the embodiment of the American sergeant; strong, powerful, a fearless leader. The men under him all wondered why he had a Hispanic surname and Rodriquez added to the mystery by not revealing the origins.

Walking ten or so metres behind him was Private Andrew Wilkes. Wilkes was eighteen, but the desire to serve his country ran deep in his blood. He came from a long line of patriots; his father had served, and his father before him, and his father before him, they all belonged to the army, and Wilkes was going to be among them.

And walking behind him was nineteen year old Private Neil Lucas. Lucas was an aspiring writer, who thought it best to travel the world and gain a wealth of knowledge before writing his first novel. The unofficial rule in writing was to write about what you knew, and at his age Lucas knew very little.

'I miss my mom,' said Wilkes into his radio headset, 'I miss her home-made apple pie.'

'Yeah I miss your mom too,' said Lucas, looking at his comrade with glee, 'it's not because of the pies she makes.' He paused a moment, adding to the dramatic climax of the next few words he would say. 'It *is* because of her apples though.'

Only Rodriquez didn't find it amusing, the soldiers chuckles resounded in the ears of Wilkes.

'And what do you mean by that?' Wilkes fumed, unhappy that he was at the centre of his colleagues ridicule.

'Your mom's a very attractive woman,' said Lucas, smirking, 'if I play my cards right I could be your new daddy.'

The hilarity mounted. Wilkes was about to say something, but then reconsidered. He just walked, looking at the locals who were watching them with increasing anxiety.

'All right, knock if off,' Rodriquez said.

And the laughter stopped at once.

'So far the patrol had been uneventful,' said Michael, bringing Lisa back to her surroundings, 'some of the locals had shouted abuse at us but apart from that, it had been just an ordinary day.'

He took a gulp of his cola, and as he did he looked at Lisa. It was a look that suggested that he was unsure if he should continue. Mark had died from horrific injuries and his screams still haunted Michael to this very day. How could he explain to her knowing what he knew, knowing that Mark had given his life so that he could live. But Lisa sensed Michael's concerns, so she nodded and smiled in reassurance.

'The Liberators of South Africa,' Michael continued, 'were fearless men and women when it came to death; every one of them was ready to die for the cause. There was no leave no man behind, when they fought, they did so either until they won or until they were killed. Retreat would never be an option for them.'

He finished off the rest of his cola and just stared down at the empty bottle held in his hands.

'The Liberators were also good at adapting; they didn't have the sufficient weaponry to destroy our helicopters and planes, but they had ways of getting around that. Most of our intelligence had been gathered from the street. However, the Liberators had intimidated many of the locals we had been relying on for information. As a result, instead of bombs being dropped on apparent Liberators hideouts, they were being dropped on innocent people.

'As you can expect tensions grew, and more and more South Africans joined the Liberators cause. There was no other choice but to patrol on the streets to try and reassure everyone that we were here to help them, to give them a better future. The problem we faced was that more and more children were becoming involved in the war. They would persuade soldiers to pass them their footballs and would run away just as the ball, which had been carefully placed over a small home-made bomb, exploded; a simple trick which was claiming many American lives. We were told under no such circumstances should we listen to any children, because any one of them could have been brainwashed by the Liberators…'

And once again Lisa was drifting back to the South African street.

'Solider, soldier, please, please pass our ball,' said a group of children in broken English.

There were five in all; each one looked no more than ten years of age. They were standing on the other side of the road, pointing at a white tattered looking football which was on top of a pile of rubble. Rodriquez and the rest of his men stopped, but before he could take in the situation and fire a warning shot into the air to disperse the children, Wilkes ran passed him.

'WILKES,' Rodriquez roared, 'NOOOOOO!'

But the words came too late. The children had run off, their laughs were the last thing Michael heard before the ball exploded. Andrew Wilkes was consumed by flames as the energy from the blast rippled out across the street. The force was unimaginably powerful; Michael could do nothing but turn and shield his face with his hands. A fraction later he felt himself being forced into the air, he held onto his weapon as tight as he could as screams and yells from his fellow soldiers echoed inside his head as debris whistled all around him.

He landed hard on his back, he just lay a moment, waiting for that shot of pain to tell him his body was broken, wondering if this was death. He slowly opened his eyes and the street presented itself once again; the smoke and flames had cleared as quickly as they had been created. Half of him was buried under dust and bricks, bells resounded in his ears and something warm and wet was trickling from his neck.

And then a voice reached him through the silence, it was strong, steady and professional.

'Is everyone alright?' Rodriquez called out. 'Anyone hit? *Did anyone get hit?*'

Coughing murmurs came as the soldiers responses. But before Michael could shout out that he was okay, a sharp burning pain came from his neck. He touched his fingers against it and stared at the crimson blood on the tips.

'Parker, you alright?' Mark said, relieved that he was alive.

'I'm hit,' said Michael weakly. He pressed his hand hard against his neck, trying to stem the blood now dripping to the floor.

'PARKER'S HIT!' Mark shouted. 'WE NEED A MEDIC OVER HERE!'

Medic David Clark came rushing over and dropped to his knees.

'You're lucky,' he said, examining the wound, 'your jugular vein has been missed by about three millimetres.'

He began to rummage through this webbing.

'Hold still,' he said, as Michael winched when he began to clean and dress the wound.

And as Michael gritted his teeth and took the pain, he looked at the place where Wilkes had been standing. His body had been torn apart by the energy from the blast, leaving behind nothing more than streaks of blood, remnants of his uniform and small fragments of his skin and bone.

'This is why we never pass footballs to the children,' Rodriquez seethed.

Michael watched him walk to the place where the eighteen year old had died.

'I want every one of you to look at what's left of him, and remember it when any child asks you to pass them their ball.'

Losing a friend and fellow patriot was difficult for any soldier to take and once their adrenaline had stopped coursing through their bodies, a state of shock and loss gripped each of them.

Private Andrew Wilkes's death seemed so pointless and once again the purpose of this war went through everyone's mind. Wilkes was the one hundred and fifteenth American soldier to die in South Africa and he would be known not for the courage or bravery he had shown, but just for that statistic. This was a far cry from what was depicted in the war movies; Wilkes didn't have any last words, he didn't die heroically, he was blown up, there wasn't even a body to be flown back home under full military honours.

'Is he alright?' Rodriquez asked the medic.

'He'll live,' said David, 'he'll need a couple of stitches though.'

But Rodriquez was no longer listening; he was looking among the buildings, his eyes narrowing a fraction. An eerie silence had suddenly settled over the street, normally the locals would appear soon after an explosion to see what had happened. Many would come to the aid of the soldiers but there was no one, the street was quiet.

The medic stood, but before he could say a word a gunshot sounded through the silence. There was a horrific sound of cracking bones and blood sprayed onto the bodies of Michael and Rodriquez. For a moment that seemed to take an eternity the medic just looked at Michael, then his eyes lost all of their life, his body went limp and he fell to the floor with a thud.

'EVERYONE DOWN,' Rodriquez managed to shout into his headset, just as a hail of bullets began to rip past them.

He dropped to the floor and raised his weapon and looking through the sites he began firing. As quickly as it started, the rain of bullets stopped. The soldiers darted their eyes from place to place, wondering if they had won this brief firefight.

The street had fallen silent again but the soldiers didn't move, they didn't even speak, just in case they gave away their position.

And suddenly there was movement, the Liberators of South Africa emerged from the derelict buildings, there were fifty or so but the noise they made from their shouts and gunfire made them sound like hundreds. And as Michael watched them draw closer, fear raced down his spine. They were going to overwhelm them. He had heard of the horrific stories of what the Liberators did to their enemies. They would beat them within an inch of their lives, strip them and drag their naked bodies through the street.

'Fall back,' Rodriquez shouted to Michael.

He didn't have to be told twice, and in that instant, all logic, all that he had been taught and trained to do was irrelevant now, his survival was paramount to anything else. He gripped his weapon firmly, took a fraction of a second to compose himself and ran as hard and as fast as he had ever ran in his life. But then, quite suddenly his left leg buckled out from under him. It was a searing pain, as though someone had stabbed him with a white hot poker. He fell to the floor, his weapon falling from his hands as his palms became grazed from the stones on the dusty floor.

'PARKER!' he heard someone shout.

As he looked up he saw Mark running towards him.

'I've got you,' said Mark, there was no mistaking the panic in his voice, 'just hang in there buddy.'

Michael put his arm around Mark's neck and was lifted to his feet. Together they ran – or in Michael's case hopped – as fast as they could, with Mark constantly reassuring his friend that he would be alright. But then suddenly, despite the ear deafening noise going all around them, a horrific sound resounded in Michael's ears, the same sound he heard before the medic had died.

And in that moment time seemed to slow. It seemed dramatic how Mark's body jerked violently, he stumbled forward but before he could fall to the floor Michael caught him.

'I've got you,' he said.

They managed to get off the street and behind one of the derelict buildings, there Michael laid Mark sideways on the dry ground.

'Just hang in there – HELP – I NEED SOME HELP!' he bellowed towards the street, towards the soldiers fighting.

They were fighting for one another, they were fighting to survive this battle but he did not care; all he was concerned about was the dark stain of blood spreading across his back.

'I can't die,' Mark said slowly and with great difficulty, 'I promised my daughter.'

'This is nothing,' said Michael quickly, 'you're going to be fine, you're going to be alright, this is nothing but a scratch.'

He tore open his shirt and removed the body armour, the bullet had entered at an odd angle, it had torn through the back of his body unprotected by the armour, leaving behind a small hole from which it entered. Michael submersed his own pain by applying pressure on Mark's wound, trying all he could to stem the flow, nothing else was of concern now.

Mark tried to turn his head, but Michael did not miss this attempt and he leaned over. The dying soldier's eyes found his, and his lips trembled from the effort of trying to say the words, 'Tell … my…'

He did not finish saying the words instead he exhaled his final breath, and Mark closed his eyes becoming perfectly still.

Michael was back inside his room onboard the Titan.

'The last thing I remember before falling unconscious was Mark pulling me to safety. I woke up later that day in the camp hospital bed, I was told of the bravery he showed in trying to rescue me.' Michael could not tell Lisa the truth, to know that her fiancé had suffered great pain before he died. 'He was shot and was killed instantly during the attempt, he wouldn't have felt anything.'

Lisa wiped the tears from her eyes, smearing her mascara. Finally the truth after all this time, she now understood at last that Mark had died for his country, he had given his life so that Michael could live. He felt no pain, he had died quickly and that is all she hoped for, it was the best possible outcome.

She leaned forward and laid her soft hand on top of Michael's, squeezing it gently.

'I do not blame you for what happened,' she said, smiling.

She stood and headed for the door just as the pilots announced, 'Seat belts please, we'll be landing in five minutes.'

*

The CyberTech Defence Systems facility was a vast complex used to test its aircraft. Equipped with its own runway, hangers, control tower and numerous buildings, it was a world away from the derelict wasteland it had once been deemed as.

The facility already had advanced warning of Robert Lane's arrival and would follow a strict protocol, which he liked to be just so. The two custom-made S-Class Mercedes that were kept in his private hanger were to be fully fuelled with diesel, cleaned and polished, along with a customs official who would be waiting for the plane to carry out the mandatory documentation and luggage check.

The Titan descended into the gloomy morning rain of Great Britain. Robert had a special love for this country; it was a country of quietude and breathtaking views, a country with a rich history, with people who were passionate about their national teams in any sport they participated in. But what made his relationship all the more special with this country was that his mother had given birth to him here, his life had begun in England. And because of this the British people took great delight in reminding their cousins from across the water.

The Titan's tyres touched down on the runway with a puff of smoke and a spray of water and it began to decelerate. It taxied to Robert's grand, personal hanger situated in the vast complex of the testing area and began its routine one-eighty degree rotation within the hanger and rolled towards the front of it, making itself ready for its much later departure. The pilots brought the Titan to its final stop and powered down the engines.

Once the stairs had been positioned in front of the door, it opened and Robert began to descend, looking down at the two men waiting patiently for him. The man on the left Robert didn't recognise, he was in uniform and wore an identification badge. The man on the right was Simon Blackwood, director of this complex. He was a tall, thin man with a thick mane of black hair and wearing rectangular shaped glasses, the long black designer coat he wore had only the top button undone.

'Welcome Mr Lane,' he called out, 'so sorry about this miserable weather.'

Robert extended his hand and the pair shook.

'Mr Lane can I introduce –'

'My name is Lawrence Goddard,' the man interjected, his tone was stern, a man not to be messed with and Simon was taken aback, 'I'm from the HM revenue and customs.' He reached inside his pocket and showed his identity card. 'I understand that you've had a long flight Mr Lane, but I have a job to do, if you are fair with me then you will be on your way in no time at all.' He replaced his card back inside his pocket. 'Now, shall we begin?'

As promised, the documentation and luggage check was carried out without incident. Robert climbed into the back of the second Mercedes and settled into the plush leather seat. Michael dropped into the driver's seat and began adjusting the mirrors, seconds later he brought the powerful engine to life.

Robert stared out of the tinted window, watching Lisa as she settled Melissa onto her booster seat. They were only metres apart from one another but Robert felt an unusual loneliness here in the car. He pressed his hand flat against the window, wishing he could do more, wishing he could wrap his arms around her and kiss her deeply. If only she knew of the love he felt, if only she knew that he was looking at her now. He longed for her to turn round, to stare into her beautiful brown eyes, but she did not turn, she climbed into the car and sat down next to Melissa, holding on to her hand just as David walked over and closed the door.

Minutes later both cars were travelling out of the complex, Robert was still staring out of the window, watching the world slip him by. The Capri Rosa Hotel was a forty-five minute journey away, and he would savour and appreciate this time to recollect his thoughts away from Lisa. There were many things that would have to be done once he reached the hotel and now Robert began to think and try to understand what lay ahead of him.

Chapter Eighteen

The Keeper of Truth

August 2nd

'This just came for you Catherine,' Alan Sutton announced as he entered the kitchen and dropped a large brown envelope by his wife's empty breakfast bowl. 'It looks like it's from CyberTech Defence Systems.'

Catherine Sutton couldn't help but glance at the envelope. And in that brief moment, she felt the colour draining from her rosy cheeked face. Resting her elbows on the table, with her mug of tea clutched with both hands, she took a sip and stared up at her husband, who was busy looking into the small rectangular mirror as he fastened his silk blue tie.

'Really?' she said after taking another sip, trying her best to sound slightly intrigued.

'Yeah,' he said smartening his collar, 'I thought you had finished working for them?'

'I have – I did –' she could feel herself becoming flustered with the whole subject, she took another sip of her tea to calm herself. 'I suppose with Frank's son now taking over, he just wants to know what I did for his father. It'll be nothing important.'

'Well that's fine, but I hope they're not thinking of…'

But she was no longer listening, her eyes had averted from her husband's reflection back to the envelope by her breakfast bowl. And as she finished off her tea and picked it up, she could feel herself drifting back to the last time she spoke to Frank Lane…

Catherine Sutton was fuming. Storming down the corridor holding a printed sheet of paper in her hand, those she approached quickly stepped back against the wall, none wanted to be in the path of her wrath. She turned left, walked down the short corridor and ran her identification card through the security device on the thick glass door. It flashed green and she turned the chrome handle and stepped onto the blue carpet.

A lone door stood at the end of the hallway, she marched over to it, knocked twice and did not wait to be invited in. Frank was sat behind his desk and immediately looked up when Catherine stormed in.

'WHAT THE HELL IS THIS?' she raged, slamming the sheet of paper down on the desk.

She did not wait for a response.

'Eight years Frank,' she continued, her raging tone now subsiding slightly, 'I've given you eight years, and you tell me you're terminating the Genesis Project through an email!'

This wasn't the first confrontation the pair had had and it certainly wouldn't be the last. Both Catherine and Frank had a similar personality and traits, both were caring and warm, but without warning they could become stubborn and fiery and were always willing to fight for something they felt strongly about.

But Frank did not retaliate verbally, instead he raised his eyebrows, leaned back in his chair, and held out his hand, offering her one of the seats facing his desk. Surprised by this, Catherine pulled out the chair and sat. Frank smiled and opened the top drawer of his desk, withdrawing a half bottle of brandy and two glasses; this was something he had been planning in the days he had spent locked away here. He unscrewed the cap, filled both glasses and clinked them together. He drained his in one and as Catherine began to drink hers he told her the reasons of the termination, he told her everything.

Once she had heard Frank's explanation Catherine was no longer angry, the words had quelled the rage she felt only moments earlier. She finished off her brandy, put the empty glass on the desk and stared at Frank. He looked old now, an old man who hadn't slept or shaved in days, his eyes looked heavy and drawn and dark stubble shrouded his face.

'I've been a silly old fool,' said Frank desolately, 'William was right, he had been right all along.'

But Catherine did not believe a word of it, the Genesis Project would save countless lives and Frank was only casting doubt on it because of the depressive state he was in.

'Is there anything I can do?' she asked softly.

Frank screwed the cap back on the bottle of brandy and dropped it back into the top drawer. 'I've written a letter to Robert,' he said wearily, 'I don't know if he'll contact you, but if he does tell him everything about the Genesis Project.'

'Yes of course,' said Catherine, in a way that Frank hadn't needed to ask, 'I will tell him everything I know.'

'I want you to destroy all your work as well, everything that involved the Genesis Project.'

But at that moment Catherine was not so willing and she fell silent, destroying eight years worth of research, all that hard work was simply out of the question.

'Frank,' she said breathlessly, 'it's eight years worth, if I destroy it then what have I got? The idea of nearly becoming a part of history?'

'You have got your health,' said Frank, looking at her, 'I don't expect you to understand what I'm about to say but this is my last chance for redemption.' He leaned forward and rested his elbows on the desk, and then his voice took on a different tone, Catherine knew that it was only now, in this moment of final realities that forced Frank to say the next few words. 'Promise me you will destroy your work.'

'Okay,' she lied, 'I can't say I'm happy about it, but I will respect your wishes.'

Frank smiled. 'I've never been one for saying goodbye,' he admitted.

Catherine stood and extended her hand. 'Well, perhaps it's best if we don't.'

And that was the last words they had spoken to one another, not long after, Frank had died and Catherine could do nothing but wait for his son to get into contact with her. The weeks turned to months and then to years, but still she waited for him, never once had it occurred to her that he might never contact her even though Frank said that he might not, and yet she was surprised by the sudden arrival of the brown envelope with the CyberTech Defence Systems insignia marked in the top left hand corner, addressed so plainly in fine black italic handwriting there could be no mistaking it.

'…the table's booked for seven.'

Catherine heard her husband's voice once again; she looked up, her lips parted as she frowned slightly.

'Bob and Julie,' Alan repeated looking at her now, 'the table's booked for seven.'

He walked over to his wife and looked at her.

'You okay?' he asked. 'You look a little pale?'

'Yes, yes I'm fine,' she said forthwith, 'the table's booked for seven, got it. It should be a good night.'

She forced herself to smile reassuringly.

He kissed her on her cheek, said, 'I'll see you tonight,' pinched a slice of her toast layered thick with marmalade and left.

While waiting for her husband to leave, Catherine turned the envelope over in her hands and reached inside, pulling out two folded sheets of paper. Lying them flat on the table the uppermost one was a typed letter, she read it.

F.A.O Dr Catherine Sutton,

A few weeks ago I was asked how I would write to someone who I'd never met. At the time I couldn't answer as I hadn't ever had the task of doing it, but now I can relate. I have thought long and hard about how I should write this letter. My father had left me several journals in his will and over the past eight months I have read through them and have travelled and have met many people who my father spoke fondly of trying to find anything I could about the Genesis Project. Up until a few weeks ago I had all but given up hope, but a chance encounter with a man you might know, William Davies, has led me to the United Kingdom and to write this letter to you.

I was told that you were an important part of the Genesis Project and if this is to be the case, then perhaps the best person I should talk to about the project is you. By the time you receive this letter I will already be staying at the Capri Rosa Hotel, so could you ring me as soon as possible on the number below so that we can arrange a convenient time for us to meet. I look forward to hearing from you.

Robert Lane (it was signed in a handwritten scrawl)

The second sheet of paper which accompanied the letter was all of her personal information, her name, date of birth, her security clearance and her official job title. The photograph staring and smiling back at her in the top left hand corner was of a young Catherine, with vibrant auburn hair and brown eyes that had been taken eight years ago. It seemed such a lifetime away, now the signs of aging showed, masking her youthful looks with grey hair and wrinkles.

Holding the letter in her hand, Catherine stood and walked over to the cordless telephone base secured against the far wall. Looking at the number Robert had provided, she carefully dialled it, walked back over to the kitchen table and sat down just as it began to ring.

'Capri Rosa Hotel,' a professional female voice answered after two rings, 'how can I help?'

'Robert Lane's room please.'

'Whom may I ask is calling?'

'Catherine Sutton,' she said casually.

'One moment please.'

Classical music began to play when she was put on hold. Catherine placed her breakfast bowl on top of the small plate and took them over to the sink.

'I'm putting you through now,' the female voice said.

Catherine had no time to say thanks; it began to ring and was immediately answered.

'Good morning Dr Sutton, it's good to be finally talking with you.'

There could be no mistaking the voice, especially from all the media attention and coverage Robert Lane got.

'Yes it is,' Catherine could only think to say. 'I've received your letter,' she said, getting to the point, 'and I'm ringing to let you know I'm free tomorrow.'

There was a brief silence.

'Tomorrow,' said Robert, rustling pages could be heard, 'say at ten o'clock?'

'Ten o'clock tomorrow,' repeated Catherine, 'looking forward to it.'

She ended the call, walked back over to rechargeable phone base and dropped the telephone into it. Washing up what was in the bowl, she dried up and put everything away. Once she had finished, she unlocked the double doors which opened out into the back garden and walked towards the shed which stood against the far fence. Unlocking and removing the padlock, she pulled across the metal bolt and opened the door. Garden equipment, paint pots, tools and various other bits and pieces were strewn throughout, only the lawnmower wasn't layered with dust and dirt.

Slowly making her way through, watching her step as she went, Catherine knelt in front of the table laden down with bulbs, seeds, compost bags and plant pots. Despite her husband insisting he was a keen gardener, he spent very little in here and it suited Catherine perfectly. They had been married for over twenty years, but he knew nothing of the Genesis Project or any of the work she had done, not that he made much of an effort to find out, and even if he had he wouldn't have understood. She always referred to people like him as *those who were unable to think outside the box*. Through their ignorance they were unable to see the bigger picture, unable to see that the Genesis Project would have saved countless lives.

She pulled out the tattered boxes from under the table and began to sort through the very last one she got to. Removing the old dust sheet, countless folders and discs lined the bottom, everything about the Genesis Project was here in this box. Although she promised to destroy all of her research and work she could not honour the dead man's wish. The Genesis Project, regardless of the negative views it got, was the next evolutionary step in a rapidly evolving world. What lay in this box was eight years of hard work and research, which enabled the creation of the perfect weapon, a human, able to kill without remorse.

'Tell him everything,' she said aloud.

She hoped Robert Lane was the man his father made him out to be, because if he was blinded by ignorance, he would not understand what the Genesis Project represented, he would not understand why they created – in her eyes – the most advanced soldier the world had ever seen.

She began picking up the discs housed in their cases and put them on the table, there was much to be done.

Chapter Nineteen

The Capri Rosa Rendezvous

August 3rd

Later that evening Catherine cancelled the dinner arrangement with Alan's brother and his wife, and although her husband was unhappy about the decision he still went to the restaurant anyway, leaving his wife to have an early night. But sleep for her was practically impossible; she tossed and turned in her bed, getting up every hour or so to walk aimlessly around her home.

Now she was sat in the back of a taxi as it slowly made its way through the morning traffic, staring out of the window as her stomach rumbled in anticipation. Since reading the letter from Robert she wondered how she would start to explain the Genesis Project, it was not as though she could just talk about it, there was a complex history behind it.

The taxi rolled to a stop and the rear passenger's door opened a moment later, bringing Catherine back to her surroundings. Paying the driver, she stepped out into the wet morning air and was greeted by a tall, thin man dressed pristinely in a navy blue suit with matching tie and wearing white gloves.

'Welcome to the Capri Rosa Hotel,' he said in a professional manner.

'Thank you,' said Catherine, stepping onto the red carpet which led straight up the stairs to the main revolving door.

Noticing that there was no luggage in need of carrying, the man slammed the taxi door shut and returned to his position with haste.

Towering above the surrounding buildings, the six-star Capri Rosa Hotel was ideally placed just a few minutes walk from the capital. To stay there was to enjoy the ultimate in style, service and sophistication, this was a place purposely built for the rich and famous. Stepping through the revolving door, Catherine looked around in awe as she slowly walked across the highly polished marble floor.

The hotel lobby was regarded by many to be the most beautifully created in the world. The sumptuous and varied use of soft paints, vein white marble and walnut furniture and the breathtaking intricate chandeliers reflecting in the wall panelled mirrors, all combined to create one of the most magical interiors in the capital, endearing by day as by night.

The man who greeted her near the receptionist's desk was average in height and muscular, dressed smartly in a black suit. After his pleasant greeting, introducing himself as Michael Parker, he led her to the set of four lifts, he touched the pad to call it. The far end lift was the first to open, and out stepped a uniformed hotel porter who smiled pleasantly at the pair.

'Which floor sir,' he asked politely, once all had entered the lift.

'The Capri Rosa suite,' said Michael.

The porter pressed the top button on the numbered pad, the doors closed a moment later and the lift began to ascend. They waited, listening to the soft music playing in the background. In a hotel that enjoyed a worldwide reputation for style and luxury, the Capri Rosa suite surpassed all expectations. Without doubt the finest and most lavish suite in the hotel, the Capri Rosa took up the entire top floor and was split into two sections with dedicated staff for each. Both enjoyed marble floored hallways, a spacious and opulent sitting room and two bedrooms with en suite bathrooms. And that's where their similarities ended, the Capri suite had a study and gym whilst the Rosa suite had a Jacuzzi and kitchen.

'The Capri Rosa suite,' the porter announced as the lift came to a standstill.

The doors opened and Michael stepped out followed closely by Catherine.

'Have a nice day,' the porter said pleasantly. The doors to the lift closed and it descended.

A single walnut door stood either end of the long, grand hallway. Michael led Catherine left, towards the door which announced in beautiful italics on a golden plaque: *Capri Suite.*

Michael inserted the room card key into the lock of the door and turned the handle and walked inside once it beeped to do so. Welcoming warmth greeted them as they stepped into the hallway, which was majestic. White marble flooring, neutral coloured hand painted walls and soft ambient lighting hanging overhead. Michael requested Catherine's coat which he hung next to the others on the stand, and then led her to the first door on the left.

The sitting room was like no other Catherine had seen before, it was stylishly modern with a classic feel about it; soft rugs placed over the hardwood flooring, black leather couches and reclining chairs placed around a black glassed coffee table, a colossal flat screen television mounted to the wall, a mini refrigerator tucked underneath the tea and coffee making facilities and a whole range of walnut furniture placed throughout. The three sectioned window running along the entire far wall overlooked the city of London, the view it would produce if the blinds hadn't been closed would have been quite spectacular.

Catherine's eyes glanced over the four people who were already here, but only one was recognisable to her.

'Dr Sutton,' said Robert pleasantly, extending his hand, 'it's good to be finally meeting you in person.'

'Please, call me Catherine,' she said, shaking his hand.

'Catherine it is then … I believe you already know William.'

She looked over at the old, haggard looking man standing up from the couch facing away from her and it took a moment before she recognised who he was. Bill Davies was looking distinctly careworn from the last memory she had of him, she had seen that 'abuse of alcohol' look before in her ex-husband and it never boded well.

'You're looking well,' said William, forcing back the desire to smirk.

'Thanks,' said Catherine casually, 'shame I can't say the same about you … you always did love your alcohol Bill.'

William smiled uncomfortably. 'You haven't changed one bit,' he said bitterly.

'And neither have you.'

An uncomfortable silence followed the words, William's eyes flickered over Michael, standing next to the door, Marcus, standing by the window and then to Robert, who was staring back at him, and he spoke to those who would want to know where he would be.

'I'll be down in the bar if anyone needs me,' he said.

And without saying another word he buried his hands deep in his pockets and strode out of the room. Marcus and then Michael followed him out, closing the door as they went. Robert and Catherine were now alone and it was her that spoke first.

'I'm sorry about that,' she said, and she seemed to mean it, 'there's a lot of history between us, well, as soon as we began working on the Genesis Project together. A clash of personalities you see.'

'It's not a problem,' said Robert, smiling, 'would you like something to drink? I've got tea, coffee, bottled water.'

'Tea would be nice,' said Catherine, 'plenty of milk, no sugar.'

'Right, a cup of tea it is,' Robert said, walking over to the small kettle, 'please have a seat.'

Catherine dropped her bag next to the coffee table and sunk into the plush leather couch. Robert clicked the kettle to boil, tore open the two tiny cartons of milk and poured them into one of the teacups.

'William told me about the Genesis Project,' he said, dropping a teabag into the cup, 'he told me everything.'

'Bill's view is very narrow-minded,' Catherine scoffed, 'no doubt he said to you that he objected to the idea.'

'It was something to that effect,' Robert said.

Catherine shook her head disbelievingly. 'His opinion changed because of the death of his son, if Jack hadn't been killed then he wouldn't have retired, it was that reason and that reason alone, it was nothing to do with the Genesis Project.'

The kettle clicked off and Robert poured the boiling water into the teacup.

'My mom told me once that there are always two sides to a story,' he said, scooping out the teabag and stirring the liquid, 'so what's yours? Tell me your side to the Genesis Project.'

He grabbed a bottle of water from the fridge, handed the cup of tea to Catherine and sat opposite her.

'The Genesis Project was more than just creating 'mindless killers' as Bill would have no doubt put it,' Catherine said, 'what we were aiming to create was the most advanced soldier the world had ever seen. I accepted the fact that we were heading into the unknown, but if you took away the complexity of the Genesis Project and just left the ultimate aim, then there could be no denying that it was an exciting prospect.'

She paused a moment to take a sip of her tea.

'To achieve this we ran a selection programme, those who applied were then subjected to a number of varied tests, measuring their athletic and intellectual capabilities. Fifteen men and fifteen women were selected for the final thirty, they were taken to your father's island where they were kept on a strict diet and exercise programme for three months. The men's sperm and women's eggs were then taken and inserted into surrogate mothers.'

Again she paused to take another sip of her tea.

'All parties involved were made to sign confidentiality agreements' preventing them from talking about or discussing what was carried out on the island. And nine months later my babies were born.'

Robert had a look of bewilderment, it was hard not to. Why would she refer to the Spectres as her children? Why develop that emotional connection with them, knowing what they would ultimately become? His bemusement was not missed by Catherine who continued.

'I was placed in overall charge of the Spectres development,' she said, smiling broadly, 'when they were born, this phase was known as the Children of CS-13. The children were obviously the Spectres, CS represented my name, Catherine Sutton and the number thirteen was the amount of years it would be before phase two started.'

Robert twisted off the cap of his bottled water and took a gulp, hoping it would help clear his mind. William's version of the Genesis Project stood in stark contrast to Catherine's, her explanation to it all was of a well coordinated and well executed programme, but Robert knew that the words were all a façade, no matter what Catherine said, it could not disguise what the sole aim of the Genesis Project was. Those who were involved had no right to create life for such a purpose and Robert, all of a sudden, was disgusted with his father.

'If Frank hadn't ordered the closure of the project,' said Catherine, bringing Robert back to his surroundings, 'then the Spectres would have gone on to enhance their development—'

'So my dad ordered the closure,' interjected Robert, trying to get an understanding, 'why did he?'

Catherine let out a tiny sigh. 'The last time I spoke to Frank was the day he told me that the Genesis Project was to be stopped and I was placed with the responsibility. I was to do two things if you were to get in contact with me. First was to explain everything I knew about the Genesis Project and second was to take you to your father's island. He told me the reason for the closure but I cannot explain to you why, I also cannot tell you what happened to the Spectres.'

Robert took one final gulp of his water and screwed the cap back on. 'Perhaps I'm being naïve when I ask you this,' he said, trying to understand, 'but why did my dad do it? Why was he so desperate to create something like that?'

'A few weeks ago,' Catherine began, 'I watched this emotional documentary about a young soldier who had finished his first tour in South Africa. He was nineteen, in some respects naïve; he had this idea that being in the army would open doors for him. He believed the advertisements saying he would have a better life, he would lead a colourful life. But no matter how hard your training, nothing can prepare you for the horrific realisations of war.'

It was as though she was talking from experience, her tone grew sombre, and Robert looked at her, his eyebrows curving inwards slightly.

'He went to South Africa full of hopes and dreams,' Catherine continued quickly, 'truly believing he was going to make a real difference to the people there.' She seemed sad now, as though recalling the documentary was quite painful to her. 'He came back a broken man, his faith in the army shattered, his faith in everything shattered. He saw things that you and I can't even begin to imagine, it's nothing like what's depicted in the movies, it's very real and can break the mentality of any soldier, no matter how strong they are.'

She paused again to drink some more of her tea.

'The young soldier was unable to adjust to civilian life when he returned home, so traumatised he was over what had happened in South Africa that he drowned himself in the sea. At the end of the documentary the soldier's mother said it wasn't the water that killed her son, it was the army. If the Genesis Project had started twenty years ago then that young soldier would have been saved, his family wouldn't have had to go through the pain and suffering from losing him.'

She drank the rest of her lukewarm tea and set the empty cup down onto the glass topped coffee table.

'War has evolved now, it's not how it used to be; the media coverage alone is immense. And every time a soldier is killed, people begin to ask questions, they don't want to see dead soldiers being flown home, they want to see them winning, they want to see our soldiers playing football with the locals, they want to see them making a difference to the country. And the Genesis Project could have allowed that to happen, while the soldiers posed in front of world's cameras, reassuring everyone that they were making a real difference, the Spectres would be working in the background, and if any them of were killed then no one would be any the wiser, because as far as the world was concerned, the Spectres didn't exist ... That is why Frank did it, he saw great potential in the Genesis Project and knew it would ultimately save lives.'

Robert took a sip of his water and thought only for a moment. He would be lying if he said the Genesis Project didn't intrigue him, and yet the very thought of creating the wonderful miracle of life just for one sole purpose sickened him.

'There can be no denying that the Genesis Project if it worked properly could have saved countless lives,' he began and Catherine fought hard against the desire to grin broadly. 'However, in a lot of respects I have to agree with William.'

Catherine was no longer feeling complacent; this was most unexpected. Surely Robert was an intelligent man, surely he could see the bigger picture, he could not be so blinded by ignorance. Frank always spoke so highly of him, and yet here he was, unable to think outside of the box, to narrow-minded to understand what the Genesis Project represented.

'My father should have never allowed it to happen.' He rested his bottled water on the end table and leaned forward. 'You create this new breed of soldier but where does it end?' he asked rhetorically. 'You and my father had no right to do this.'

Catherine nodded. 'You're entitled to your opinion,' she mumbled, 'I think your wrong but that is of no importance now.'

'What you have to understand,' said Robert softly, 'is that my dad committed suicide, he deliberately crashed his plane because things got too tough for him. Now everything that I have either read or heard suggests the Genesis Project drove him to do so, he opened Pandora's Box and was unable to deal with the repercussions of doing so.'

Catherine fought hard against the urge to explain everything, *if you only you knew the truth,* she continually thought. Regardless of what Frank said the last time they spoke to one another she knew it was down to his depressive state, and it was because of this that had forced him to admit Bill had been right. For Frank to say that Bill was right was an insult to her and everyone else who worked on the Genesis Project, to admit Bill had been right meant her dedicated eight years was for nothing, and she would never be ready or willing to do that.

Robert leaned back into the couch and looked at Catherine for a long time. He was thinking, thinking about which path he should take, wondering if he really did want to see the island, to see the Genesis Project, to see the very thing that had drove his father to commit suicide.

'I will honour my father's wishes,' he said finally, 'but I want to make something perfectly clear.' He leaned forward and stared at Catherine determinately. 'I have no intention of restarting the Genesis Project.'

Catherine was unable to hide her dismay. 'I would be lying if I said I wasn't disappointment,' she said quietly, 'but I have to respect your decision.'

The last words she found difficult to say, how could she respect his decision knowing he had not been told the truth, knowing he had not been told all the facts. And as she stood, extended her hand and casually shook Robert's, she wondered whether there was still a glimmer of hope. She picked up her bag and rummaged through it, pulling out a single disk case.

'This is eight years of work simplified,' she said, handing it to Robert. 'I'll see myself out.'

And with that she swung her bag over her shoulder and left, leaving Robert to stare down at the case he held in his hands, the handwritten scrawl of which read: *The genesis project: the children of cs-13.*

Wandering into the lavish study, Robert powered up his laptop sat on the gleaming walnut desk and dropped into the black leather swivel chair. The exploration of the island would be the final piece to this complex puzzle, and yet, as his laptop finally finished loading and Robert opened the case and clicked the disk into the drive he couldn't help but think of his father.

'What did you do dad that scared you so much?' he whispered.

With every revelation the mysteries surrounding the Genesis Project only deepened, but soon he would know everything, he would be exploring the island, although still unaware of the dark secret it harboured.

Chapter Twenty

The Order of Cape Town

August 9th

Cape Town was in the shadow of a former glory, the land that had once been rich and vibrant and a popular holiday destination was now a distant memory. Most buildings bore a scar from the South African war, the roads and grassy plains were now covered with the blood of its people. Those who hadn't been killed, had either joined the fight or had fled to neighbouring countries, and the basic necessities such as clean running water and electricity, that many millions around the world took for granted, were nonexistent in most parts of the region.

Out on the deserted street that had once been home to the rich and famous, a large Boerboel dog slowly wandered down the litter-strewn pavement, sniffing at the empty cans hopefully as it passed them. The sun had been set for over an hour, but the moon shone brightly high above in the night sky, casting its light on the street below.

Then, all of a sudden, an American fighter plane thundered overhead. The deafening noise made the Boerboel crouch low to the ground, its eyes darting warily across the night sky, but the strange phenomenon had gone, its sound now fading away.

After a few moments the Boerboel resumed its search for food, but then it froze, its large brown eyes fixed upon the strange figure that had suddenly appeared from out of the darkness, breathing heavily. The figure stared out over the black scarf which covered its nose and mouth, seemingly taking in its surroundings. Then it set off running once again, the Boerboel, surprised by the sudden movement had disappeared into the house with the door hanging off its hinges.

The figure moved deeper into the deserted maze of once luxurious homes, its footsteps echoing on the paving stones as it passed numerous overgrown gardens and broken and boarded up windows and doors. The very last house the figure reached was far greater than the ones it passed; it was miraculously untouched from the South African war. Intricately formed in the wrought iron gates bore the sign: *Residence of Lenka Shone*.

The gate creaked loudly as it was pushed open. The once manicured and luscious gardens either side of the hand laid paving stone path were now overgrown with weeds. But instead of following it directly to the front door, the figure walked around the house to its back entrance, there it rapped on the door. Exhausted and breathing heavily, all it could do now was wait.

After ten or so seconds had passed, it heard someone moving from behind the door, and a moment later it opened a fraction. Illuminated by a candle he held in his small bony hands, a sliver of an elderly African man could be seen looking at the figure, an elderly man who had a weather-beaten face and short, thinning grey hair.

The figure pulled down the scarf. She was a young woman, who looked no more than twenty years of age. Her long dreadlocked hair hung down alongside a surprisingly beautiful face. The sweat that had gathered on her skin seemed to twinkle from the candle light.

'Naledi,' the man said in a dry whisper, looking and sounding a little surprised by the late hour, 'what do I owe the plea –'

But before Baruti Belling could finish saying the words, the visitor quickly stepped inside, blew out the candle, shut the door and slid across the two bolts. For a moment she stood, peering out of the single pane of glass. Then she walked quickly through the kitchen and hallway – with Baruti in tow – and into the large living room, which as you would expect, was majestic. The eight surrounding walls were painted a radiant ivory colour; a large mirror hung above a glowing open fire, the flames casting light upon a couch, two armchairs and a coffee table all of which were layered with a faint layer of dust. But despite the long thick curtains drawn across the windows and the open fire crackling, the room had a chilly feel about it.

'Naledi are you going to tell me what is going on?' Baruti demanded.

'The Order knows about our betrayal,' she said, hysteria evident in her voice. 'Themba, Kopano and Kefentse – they tortured them all before – before killing them – the Order of Cape Town knows everything.'

The words had drained the rich colour from Baruti's face.

'Then our worst fears have been confirmed,' he said calmly. He walked quickly across to the window and peered through the small gap in the curtains. 'We have little time before the Order arrives, we must act quickly.'

'We have no other choice,' Naledi said, whose voice was shaking from the effort of trying to keep it calm and steady, 'this is possibly the last chance we have to end this war, we must kill *him*, tonight.'

'It is too late for that,' Baruti said solemnly, 'killing him now will make no difference. The men and women in England have been contacted and are beginning their final preparations as we speak.'

'Well what should we do?' Naledi said, her voice still shaking.

Baruti turned but did not speak; he looked as though he was trying to work out something in his head. Finally he said, 'We have no other choice, we must inform the British of the impending attack in London.' He picked up his coat resting over the arm of the couch and threw it over his shoulders. 'Their base is not far from here,' he said, 'if I set off now I should be there by daybreak.'

'But the British,' Naledi gasped, 'they know who you are, they will treat you as a terrorist, you will be interrogated – tortured.'

'I will take my chances,' Baruti said, 'there are too many innocent lives at stake for me not to.'

'Well what should I do?' Naledi asked despairingly.

'South Africa is no longer a safe place for you or your husband and children,' said Baruti truthfully, 'as soon as you can, flee to one of the neighbouring countries. I will try and persuade the British to offer you and your family sanctuary in return for everything I know.'

'Thank you Baruti,' Naledi said, who knew the journey would be long and treacherous for him, 'you're a good friend.'

For a moment they just stared at one another, both knowing that this would probably be the last time they would be in each other's presence.

'You better go,' Baruti said, 'there is not much time.'

Naledi didn't need to be told twice, she nodded her head, said, 'Good luck,' and hurried from the room.

Four or five seconds later another American fighter plane thundered overhead, its deafening noise reverberating off the painted walls.

There was nothing left for it, Baruti reached inside his coat pocket and withdrew a stainless steel hipflask. He drank the remnants for Dutch courage, placed it upon the coffee table and buttoned up his coat. But as he hurried out of the room and arrived in the kitchen, he suddenly stopped, his eyes fixed upon Naledi. She was lying perfectly still on her front, the light from the moon shone through the wide open back door making the blood pooling out from under her glisten.

'Naledi,' Baruti whispered.

He dropped down by her side and rolled her over, cradling her lifeless head in his arms. Bullets had torn through her slender body; he could see the holes left in her clothing. She still had the look of fear etched upon her beautiful face, her eyes had lost all of their life and vibrancy and her lips were slightly parted. He ran his fingers over her eyes and mouth, closing them. She looked peaceful now. And as he gently rocked her back and forth, the shadow of a figure was cast upon them. Baruti wiped the tears from his eyes and looked up.

The figure's face was hidden behind the hood of its long coat, but as it threw it back, for a moment Baruti didn't recognise the young man ... then it suddenly dawned on him that this was his nephew.

Nobody knew who formed the Order of Cape Town. Legend had it that survivors had risen from the ashes and rubble the Americans had left in their wake and united through hatred and a desire to kill the South African Saviours. They forcibly recruited the children of Cape Town, putting them through unimaginable pain and torture, until every emotion within them was extinguished.

Thandiwe had totally changed from Baruti's last memory of him. They had said goodbye to one another at Thandiwe's fifteenth birthday party, and Thandiwe at the time was young and full of life, with short black hair and a pair of brown eyes that were caring and full of warmth. Now, two years on, Thandiwe looked old and gaunt. As he looked at Baruti the warmth had gone from his eyes, it was replaced with a look that only the Order of Cape Town could have given him, a deadened, abused look.

And in that moment of them becoming reunited, Baruti knew his fate, he was going to die, just as Naledi, Themba, Kopano and Kefentse had before him. He slowly stood, holding his hands up in defence.

Thandiwe raised his pistol, but before Baruti could reason with him, before he could do anything to stop his impending death, the gunshot tore through the silence and hit Baruti squarely in his knee. The burning pain was so immense, consuming the whole of his body that he could no longer stand. He fell to the floor, white-hot fire piecing through his left knee.

Whether it was the shock or fear that numbed his body he did not know, but the pain for whatever reason lessened. He reached out his hands to his nephew but he knew the end had come. There was no hope; there would be no memorable last words, no valiant attempt to disarm his nephew.

And as he watched Thandiwe draw closer to him, Baruti stared into the dull, lifeless eyes and hoped that everything would be over quickly. But as Thandiwe stopped about a foot away and raised his pistol something suddenly occurred to Baruti, this occurrence was well beyond fear or pain or reason, he could not die here and now without saying his final words.

'Thandiwe,' he said, his mouth had lost all of its moisture, 'don't let this hate consume you.'

But the words did nothing. A third American plane thundered overhead drowning out the gunshots.

Chapter Twenty-One

Exploration of the Island

August 10th

This was it, their plans and preparations were now complete. And as the morning sun began to rise, casting its light upon the runway, a silver helicopter with the CyberTech Defence Systems insignia marked upon it, gleamed in the morning light.

The vast complex which made up the UK facility had been built on land deemed to be derelict, which Frank knew at the time of buying would be the perfect secluded spot to test CyberTech Defence Systems aircraft. Built overlooking the giant runway which seemed to stretch out indefinitely in both directions, a black glassed 'viewing' tower stood. It had been created so that prospective buyers could watch the CyberTech Defence Systems aircraft in all their glory, but at this present moment in time it acted as a meeting room.

And it was inside this very room that Simon Blackwood, a tall, thin man with a thick mane of black hair and rectangular shaped glasses, stood at the head of the table. Sitting before him were the people who were about to embark on their journey to the island.

'Robert,' said Simon, there could be no mistaking the exasperation in his voice, 'I urge you to reconsider travelling to the island today, weather reports show a storm is approaching from the west, it will be hitting the island in a matter of hours.'

Every seat around the gleaming table was taken. Engineers, the pilot of the helicopter that would be taking them there, bodyguards and other influential figures were all sat, listening attentively to what the director of the facility had to say.

'I understand your concerns Simon,' said Robert casually, 'but we have covered every eventuality, which Michael will explain to you now.'

Michael, who was sat across from Robert, cleared his throat and spoke directly to Simon.

'I travelled along with Dr Sutton and the engineers when they went to restore power to the island,' he said.

He stood and walked over to the laptop which was set up next to the large projector screen against the far wall. Tapping a series of keys on the laptop, the large screen came to life.

'This is a detailed drawing I had made of the island.' He pressed the return key and red arrows suddenly appeared. 'These arrows show key areas I have identified which we could use to take shelter if needed. The helicopter will stay on the island and we will also take sufficient food and water in the event of us becoming stranded.'

The island was actually made up of three separate parts. One large, classed as the mainland, and two smaller, all were connected by road bridges.

Simon looked at the engineers hoping that they would raise a fault with Michael's idea, but each of them nodded their heads in agreement. He looked at Robert once again.

'Can I speak freely?' he asked him.

Robert leaned back in his chair and began to trace the outline of his lips with his finger. 'We're all friends here Simon,' he said.

'It's selfish of you to put me in this position.'

Gasps and murmurs quickly circulated the table, and it was only William who spoke.

'I think you're forgetting who you're talking to,' he said, a hint of anger in the tone of his voice, 'this isn't some snotty nosed kid fresh out of college, this is the president of the defence company who *you* work for.'

'I know who he is,' Simon said, looking William directly in his eyes, not amused, 'I do not need reminding of that.'

'Then you might do him the courtesy of showing some respect.'

'That's enough gentlemen,' said Robert, there was a steely tone he had never used in his voice before, 'I can understand your concerns Simon but we *will* be travelling to the island today, regardless.'

He stood and began to walk around the table.

'There has been increasing speculation from the British media as to why I am here, only a select few within this room know why that is. The longer I put off travelling to the island gives the media more time to speculate, which at this specific moment I cannot allow to happen. Perhaps you are right when you call me selfish,' he said, standing behind Simon now, 'and I don't expect you to understand as to why I have to travel to the island today.'

Robert walked back over to his seat and dropped down into it.

'If a problem should arrive, Simon,' he said, looking at him, 'then I have complete faith that you will handle it in a professional manner.'

Simon removed his glasses and dropped them onto the table, sighing deeply. The discussion was over, but he would have the last word.

'There is a problem with that island Robert,' he said, leaning back in the chair, 'it's an accident waiting to happen and it'll be the biggest mistake you make by going there.'

*

Robert always enjoyed the pleasures of morning in Britain, the rising sun, the cool air not yet touched by the early traffic, it was a new day that always brought with it a sense of hope and appreciation of being able to experience such a wonderful thing.

He was on the verge of travelling to the island, to see where the Spectres had begun their training. And as Robert climbed into the helicopter, and the shadow of its spinning blades were cast upon the runway, he took this moment to think about this journey of revelation he had undertaken. It was odd looking back, hard to believe it had taken nearly a year for him to reach this specific point in his life.

He stared out of the window, watching as the ground slipped by beneath him. Finding out the origins of the Genesis Project was more than just that, for Robert it was a journey that was emotional in every way. It also brought into focus the fact that Frank Lane was not the man he knew him to be.

Why would his father want to create such a thing? It was a question that he had asked himself a number of times during the course of his search since William had told him what the Genesis

Project was. And although that had been several weeks ago, Robert still found it difficult to try and make sense of it all. This whole idea of creating and developing this new type of 'soldier' – if you could call it that – seemed on the verge of surrealism, but it was very real, he was travelling to the island where it had all taken place.

Robert looked over at William, who was staring out of the window, looking deep in thought. *I love my country but I know what she is capable of when she feels it's in her best interests.* Those were the exact words he had said, and Robert remembered as though they were spoken just yesterday.

And as he turned his gaze back towards the window once again, he began to question if in fact he was naïve. Perhaps he wasn't the visionary his father had made him out to be, because no matter how open-minded he tried to be he could not see how the Genesis Project could be for the greater good.

'Magnificent, isn't she,' said Catherine, bringing Robert out of his pondering state.

She was smiling broadly and her finger was pressed against the glass window when Robert looked over at her. He stared out and saw what she was pointing at.

'Three miles long and almost that in width, it was the perfect spot for us. It was as though God specifically created the island so we could carry out the Genesis Project.'

William scoffed, although he did not avert his eyes from the window. 'That's what Adolf Hitler said when he began his eradication of the Jews, that God wanted him to do it. That is what you are implying isn't it, that God wanted you to do the Genesis Project?'

He looked at Catherine as he asked her the question.

'You are not so righteous Bill,' said Catherine, looking directly into his old eyes, 'and no matter what you say you still have no moral high ground, you were as much a part of the Genesis Project as any one of us.'

'My conscience is quite clear, Catherine,' said Bill silkily, 'is yours?'

It was a question Catherine did not answer; she averted her eyes from Bill and resumed staring out of the window.

'Such a beautiful island don't you think?' she asked Robert quietly.

'Yeah, it's something alright.'

'The island is self-sufficient,' continued Catherine, 'state of the art solar panels, wind and water turbines were installed for the island to generate its own power.'

They approached from the south, at the south end of the island the hills were the highest point, rising more than three hundred feet from the ocean, the helicopter began to climb and Robert stared in awe at the rugged cliffs and crashing sea below. The helicopter moved over the rocky cliffs to reveal the interior of the island: ridges and ravines heavily overrun with the dense forest. It was incredibly beautiful from the air, but as Michael gazed out he knew it was going to be difficult and daunting to navigate their way through the roads even with the high performance Land Rovers they had. He stared down and watched as the helicopter aligned itself with the large landing area which had been recently cleared of the grass and weeds and slowly began to descend.

*

Within moments of them stepping out of the helicopter, Robert, Michael, Catherine, Derek, William and Marcus had climbed into the two high performance Land Rovers which had been delivered earlier. They were laden with radio equipment, extra fuel, food, spare clothing and blankets, first aid kits and torches.

Sitting in the driver's seat of the leading Land Rover, Michael had a specially created map of the island spread out on top of the steering wheel, he preferred this old-fashioned method than relying on something much more technologically advanced. The road they were on twisted for about a mile before it reached a Y intersection where it split into two separate paths. Michael marked a cross next to the Y intersection with a pencil and then folded the map and put it onto the empty front passenger's seat, despite him travelling to the island only a few days ago with Catherine and the engineers, he nonetheless treated this journey as his first, it was safer to assume that he knew nothing.

He picked up the small radio and stared out of the front window as he spoke into it. 'Okay Marcus,' he said, 'ready to go?'

'That's affirmative, we are ready to go,' said Marcus a moment later.

Michael drove slowly and carefully, both Catherine and Robert seated behind him sat in silence, both staring out of their respected windows, and within seconds, they had left the landing area and were steadily moving through the dense forest, which was eerie yet wonderful at the same time.

There had not been enough time to renovate the entire island and although the road was overrun and in poor condition in some sections they made surprisingly good progress. After about five minutes, they came to the Y intersection, and Michael slowed and rolled the Land Rover to a stop, leaving it to hum idly. In the fork of the Y was a granite sign, the words engraved in it announced in bold letters:

$\Leftarrow$ *Accommodation*
$\Leftarrow$ *Complex B*
$\Leftarrow$ *Laboratory*
$\Leftarrow$ *Medical Centre*
Complex A $\Rightarrow$
Assault Course $\Rightarrow$
Outdoor Firing Range $\Rightarrow$
Lagoon $\Rightarrow$

Despite the sign showing them the way Michael nonetheless took nothing for granted, he unfolded the map and spread it out over the steering wheel and began to trace the route with his finger. According to the map, following the road to the right would lead them to the main complex just like the sign suggested, the road seemed a lot less twisty than what they had just travelled on. They would arrive at a security checkpoint after about half a mile or so and then the vast complex was about one hundred metres after that. And from what the map suggested, several buildings made up the main complex.

'We're going to take the right road,' said Michael, talking into the radio once again.

'That's understood,' replied Marcus professionally, 'taking the right road.'

Michael refolded the map carefully and followed the road to the right, which began to steadily descend through the ever increasing dense forest. And once again, as the map said that it would, they arrived at a concrete structure with a wooden road-barrier raised and secured with a thick chain and padlock. Everything about it indicated that this was the security checkpoint; it was in disarray and overrun by the forest.

Michael did not stop to recheck the map, he continued to drive, slowly and carefully down the road which was beginning to curve to the right. The surrounding forest grew sparse and through the gaps Robert could see something quite remarkable and he knew in that moment that they were about to enter an extraordinary and vast complex.

And then, suddenly, they emerged out of the forest and into the sunlight. Three substantial hexagonal buildings towered above the Land Rovers as they rolled to a stop in front of the stone steps, which led straight up to the portico main entrance. All three buildings were of identical build and design, with stone columns and panes of black glass – cracked and smashed in some places – that gleamed in the sun.

'What the hell is this place?' whispered Robert, which was overheard by Catherine.

'This Robert,' she said, looking at him now, 'is your father's greatest accomplishment.'

*

Two large thickly glassed doors at the entrance of the main building led into a darkened reception area beyond. The glass was scratched and streaked in dirt and the metal door panel was speckled with corrosion yet both doors gleamed in the light from the sun.

'Okay,' said Michael, looking down at the disturbed debris and dead leaves in front of the doorway, 'let's do what we've come here to do.'

He stepped through into the darkened reception area – which was surprisingly warm – with immense caution, he knew there was nothing to worry about but once again he took nothing for granted. He ran his hand up the wall, found the switch and turned on the overhead lights.

Their eyes encountered a scene of quietude and desertion. A large receptionist's desk with a flat screen computer monitor resting upon it stood in between two sets of double doors to the right of the entrance. Two black leather couches, separated by a square glass coffee table – which was piled with countless sports and women's magazines – were positioned against the left wall. A water machine, with a quarter full water bottle attached to the top, stood to the right hand corner of the room; thick dust layered over everything and on the wall behind the receptionist's desk were the letters: *Complex A*.

Michael moved deeper into the room, the dead leaves crunching underneath his boots as he walked along the blue carpeted floor.

'So this is Complex A?' Robert said, immediately looking at the wall sign as he stepped inside.

'That's right,' said Catherine, who was directly behind him, 'I wanted to call it Nexus but I was out voted on the idea.'

They made their way towards the left set of double doors with Michael once again first to step through. Robert walked through immediately after and found himself standing in a long corridor with a door standing at the far end, the cold air whistled through the broken windows along the right wall. The blue carpeted floor was stained, drenched and littered with leaves and rubbish from the large bin that had toppled over. A single door stood along the left black glassed wall, and although Catherine hurried past and headed towards the door at the end of the corridor, seemingly uninterested in the room she had passed, Robert, however, wanted to see it, he wanted to see everything on this island, regardless of the time it took.

'The stairs are this way,' Catherine called once she realised the rest were no longer following her.

'What's in here?' Robert asked her, pointing to the first door he came to.

'That's Conference Room A,' replied Catherine, somewhat impatiently, 'it's right there on the door. There's nothing of any use in there.'

And sure enough, there, stencilled in bold letters on the black glassed door were the words: *CONFERENCE ROOM A.*

Robert turned the chrome handle and walked inside, much to the displeasure of Catherine, who called out once again, 'There's nothing of any use in there.'

But Robert was no longer listening as he stepped into a grand room. Switching on the lights, he saw a long walnut table centred directly in the middle of the room with leather seats positioned around it and a laptop was set up next to a large projector screen against the far right wall.

'Every morning Frank would request a meeting in this room,' said Catherine nonchalantly, who was last to enter.

Robert ran his hand over the table, cutting through the thick dust.

'When your father ordered the closure,' continued Catherine, standing by the doorway, 'his last instruction was for everything in the entire complex to be left in its current state.'

'Why was that?' Robert asked her.

'That, I do not know the answer to,' replied Catherine, looking down the corridor. 'Like I told you in your hotel room, I am here to show you the island and tell you everything I know about the Genesis Project.'

Robert understood her irritation but it was necessary for him to see everything on this island, even though no one in this room would probably understand why. They walked out of the conference room a moment or so later and headed towards the door at the end of the corridor. They stepped through into the darkened corridor beyond and waited for the overhead lights to detect their presence.

They were standing in front of a set of lifts, a flight of stairs and a door either end of the long blue carpeted corridor. The large bronze sign secured to the plain painted walls in-between the lifts read:

Upper Fourth Floor
FITNESS SUITE, CHANGING ROOMS AND SAUNA

Upper Third Floor
LECTURE ROOM 1
LECTURE ROOM 2
LECTURE ROOM 3
LECTURE ROOM 4
RESTROOM

Upper Second Floor
RESEARCH AND DEVELOPMENT
LABORATORY
RESTROOM

Upper First Floor
CANTEEN

Ground Floor * *you are here* *
CONFERENCE ROOM A
CONFERENCE ROOM B
I.T. DEPARTMENT
RECEPTION
RESTROOM

Lower First Floor
LEVEL 12 CLEARANCE

Lower Second Floor
INDOOR FIRING RANGE
ARMOURY

Lower Third Floor
SWIMMING POOL AND CHANGING ROOMS

'Okay Robert,' said Catherine, staring at the wall sign, 'where would you like to go first?'

Chapter Twenty-Two

The Children of CS-13

When first told of the Genesis Project the whole idea seemed on the verge of impossibility to Robert, it was the plot to a movie or a storyline to a novel, it could not be real. And yet he was here, on the island that his father had bought and expanded, seeing the vast and lavish facilities that had been built. But with the revelations came this reality that his father had lived an entirely different life to the one Robert grew up knowing. Once again he was forced to admit that he knew very little about his father, for never once could Robert have believed that Frank would have led such a secretive double life.

However, exploration of the main complex had showed this entirely different world and although Robert still could not accept the Genesis Project's true purpose, he had to admit that what he had seen so far had been impressive. Despite the Spectres being only three years of age at the time of the island closing, they had already begun their training. They had begun learning how to read, write, count, communicate with one another, solve basic problems and every other aspect that would advance their learning. And they were learning at an alarming rate.

Now they were travelling in the Land Rovers and despite Simon's strong protest, the forecasted storm had yet to announce itself. Robert had seen so much already that he wondered if his brain would be able to take in anymore of this secretive new world. He was staring out of the window, his mind replaying what Catherine had explained during the two hours of exploring the main complex and the other buildings and facilities that surrounded it.

They were driving through another one of the island's forests, they had seen so many already but this one had an eerie sense about it, despite the sunlight streaming through the trees. It was the silence that made it so eerie, not a single birdsong could be heard and for the very first time since his arrival Robert could not help but feel he was about to see the darker side of the island. It was a feeling of uneasiness that would not go away until he heard the answer to something that had been troubling him since first learning of the Genesis Project from William.

'What happened to the children?' he asked Catherine, looking over at her now.

He could not refer to them as Spectres, because after all that's what they were, just children.

'They were taken to orphanages,' replied Catherine quietly, not meeting Robert's gaze.

Why didn't you tell me that in the hotel room? Robert thought.

They emerged from the forest and the view that greeted them was stunning. The waterfall towered thirty feet to the left of them, it was such a magnificent sight to see. And as the Land Rovers made their way over the secured bridge, Robert stared up at the surge of water spilling over and thundering into the pool beneath it.

'Beautiful, isn't she,' said Catherine admiringly, looking out through Robert's window.

'Yeah,' said Robert, 'she certainly is.'

'The medical centre is not far now,' Catherine said, resuming her staring out of her own window.

Soon Robert would know everything, this was the last piece to the Genesis Project puzzle, this final part of exploration would tell him one last thing and after nearly a year of searching he would finally know the truth. But then what? It was a question that had so much complexity around it, whichever path Robert chose next one thing was for certain, his father was a different person to him now. Frank Lane was not the man he grew up idolising, he was no longer the man Robert wanted to emulate and with this in his mind it seemed he had chosen his path.

'There it is,' said Catherine, bringing Robert out of his pondering state, 'there's the medical centre, that's where the Spectres were born.'

Robert leaned forward and stared out of the windscreen. The building was the same design as the main complex but was not as tall, the hexagonal black glassed structure stood perfectly alone on a cliff overlooking the sea; it was a lonely and secluded place.

Michael brought the Land Rover to a stop, and as he killed the engine faint spots of rain appeared on the windscreen. And then, quite suddenly, the storm began. Stepping out, Michael ran to the boot, opened it and grabbed his bag before closing it. Robert, Catherine and the others all stepped out and shielding their heads they ran towards the porch and out of the rain. Catherine pulled out the set of keys she had been entrusted with and unlocked the double doors.

The inner appearance of the building was just as majestic as the outer. They moved deeper inside and Robert looked around it, the floor of the circular entrance hall had been made from white marble and the curving surrounding walls were painted white, illumination came from the light streaming in through the high glass ceiling and the wall lights – which Michael switched on – dotted all around. Only an oak desk stood in the entrance area with a large plaque mounted above it that read: *WELCOME TO THE MEDICAL CENTRE.*

'This is where the surrogate mothers lived during the nine months of their pregnancy,' said Catherine, her voice resounding in the great entrance, 'everything here catered for their needs.'

A single door stood at the far end of the entrance area and Catherine led the others towards it while continuing to explain what her job was within the medical centre. As they stepped through, the sensors detected their presence and the overhead lights flickered on to reveal a short, plain narrow corridor with a single room on the left of it, everything stood in stark contrast to the grand entrance they had just left. The thickly glassed security door had been disabled prior to the visit and it stood ajar, the bold white stencilled letters read:

AUTHORISED PERSONNEL ONLY
MEDICAL MASKS AND OVERALLS TO BE WORN AT ALL TIMES
⇐ PLEASE COLLECT FROM SECURITY AND WASH HANDS THOROUGHLY BEFORE ENTERING

Catherine pushed open the door and walked through, stepping into a much larger corridor.

'This section was known as the clean zone,' she explained, once the others had arrived, 'it was paramount that this area remained free from infection. As explained on the security door, a number of measures were taken to stop this from happening.'

The corridor turned right at the far end, five white doors stood to the right and ten to the left, a single door stood at the opposite end to the entrance. The whole area was very plain with black vinyl flooring and the walls painted white, but it seemed that this was the area Catherine was most enthused to talk about, she began slowly walking down the corridor, pointing at the doors either side as she passed them. It seemed that she had finally come alive; she seemed quite irritable earlier when showing Robert and the others the main complex and the other surrounding facilities, but now she seemed calmer, more relaxed, as if she were at home and back in control of the situation.

'The surrogate mothers were kept under constant observation and had their own nutritionist, doctor and midwife,' she said. 'These are the rooms they used during the nine months, everything inside them catered for their needs, bedroom, en suite bathroom, their own little kitchenette and a living room.'

She continued to walk down the corridor.

'The dining room and recreational rooms were through there,' she said, pointing at the door directly ahead of them, 'which leads onto the walled garden.'

They turned right and stopped in front of a set of double glass doors which stood directly in the middle of two large rectangular windows, everything beyond was submersed in darkness. Once again, white bold lettering was stencilled on the glass door.

LEVEL 12 CLEARANCE ONLY (it read)
MEDICAL MASKS, OVERALLS AND GLOVES TO BE WORN AT ALL TIMES BEYOND THIS POINT

Level 12, as Catherine explained earlier was the highest clearance on the island, only those directly involved in the Spectres development had this clearance, those personnel remaining were told very little about the Genesis Project only that they were working on something of great importance.

'Eleven boys and four girls were successfully delivered through there,' said Catherine.

'I don't want to appear sexist,' said Robert carefully, 'but why would you want the girls to become Spectres, would it have been better if it was male dominated?'

Catherine smiled. 'I had the same discussion with your father,' she said, 'but I will tell you exactly what I said to him. What women lack in physical strength they more than make up in speed and agility.'

There was no malice in the words, just a general explanation.

'So how were you going to deal with the problems of monthly periods?' said Robert, feeling it was an important question to ask.

'Several options had been discussed,' said Catherine, 'but the most logical solution would have been for them to have their ovaries removed, this would have eliminated the problem of their menstrual cycle. However, removing them would have led the female Spectres to immediately go through the menopause, hormone replacement therapy would have restored the lost hormone levels and help the body function normally again.'

Catherine unlocked the double doors and pushed them open, she fumbled for the light switch and the overhead lights flickered on to reveal a large room with tall lockers lined against the left wall, a window which partially ran along the far wall next to a singular door and two sinks which were against the right. They walked across the black vinyl flooring, dotted throughout were signs reminding those entering to wash their hands thoroughly. Robert looked through the window, the room beyond was in darkness.

The large light switch next to the singular door operated the sectioned lights in the room beyond, Catherine walked directly over to it and pressed down the top row of buttons. The lights at the entrance of the room beyond came on, Robert opened the door and walked inside. The second set of lights came on, and Robert could see the room beginning to reveal itself.

It was clear that this was the delivery room, on the right side were individual rooms, birthing beds and medical cots could be seen through the window. The room continued to light up further down, revealing the sheer scale of it all.

'Were you present at any of the births?' Robert asked, looking over at William who was walking behind.

'Yes,' said William simply, who had spoken very little throughout the exploration. 'We watched from up there.'

He pointed up to the window which was suddenly brought out of the darkness by the overhead lights. Robert stared up at it, a set of metal stairs led up to the door next to the window which overlooked the room.

'Up there was your father's office,' continued William, 'from there we watched all fifteen being born.'

The room was fully alight now and as Robert drew his gaze away from his father's office and looked directly ahead of him, he suddenly slowed. Against the far wall stood fifteen circular glass containers, each was about two metres in height and a metre or so in diameter. Something was submerged in the emerald green liquid.

'It cannot be,' Robert whispered as he drew close. 'Please let this be some kind of nightmare.'

But this desperate plea did nothing to stop the horrific image now searing itself in his brain. And quite suddenly his legs buckled out from under him, time seemed to slow from that moment, he fell to the floor, his eyes unable to tear themselves away from the naked body. No one came rushing to his aid, all were paralysed from what they were seeing.

The young boy looked to be about three years of age, he looked peaceful, as though he was sleeping. However, seeing the young boy naked had taken away what little dignity he had. Robert looked at the other containers, the remaining girls and boys were all the same, all at peace, all naked, all submerged in the emerald green liquid.

Catherine stood quietly behind Robert, William, Michael, Derek and Marcus, she was smiling broadly, after all these were her children. She had no emotional connection with the Spectres, and yet as she gazed upon them her smile faded slightly, her sadness came from the fact that she had never had the chance to see what they would have ultimately become.

'What the hell did you do Catherine?' William asked, although Robert barely heard him do so.

'I have regretted it everyday,' said Catherine quietly. 'I never wanted it to end this way.'

The words felt like a white hot poker searing the inside of Robert's stomach. What he felt was well beyond anger, but whatever was surging through his body gave him the strength to stand up and face the woman who had taken away the children's lives.

'You regret it,' he said, his voice was shaking from the effort of trying to keep it steady, 'is that all you can say, that you regret it.'

The rage flared up inside him like wildfire.

'YOU SAID THEY WENT TO ORPHANAGES.'

'You honestly believe that if I had told you the truth you would have wanted to see this place,' said Catherine calmly and steadily. 'The last thing I wanted was to do this, you think I wanted to administer the lethal injection. No, I didn't, but I had no other choice, Frank was a very persuasive man, he was not one you said no to.'

'DON'T TALK ABOUT MY FATHER LIKE THAT,' Robert raged.

She had no right to talk about Frank like that, and for a moment Robert forgot all about his father's involvement in the Genesis Project, defending his honour was the only thing of importance now.

'You can never justify what you've done,' he said, his rage subsiding slightly, 'and nothing you can say will ever hide the fact that you are a murderer.'

'I'M A SCIENTIST,' Catherine bawled.

Robert's words were perhaps the greatest insult he could have said to her, and for once there was a show of emotion, she was no longer calm. She wanted to run at Robert, beat him for being so ignorant; couldn't his feeble little mind grasp the fact that the Genesis Project represented hope? That it would benefit the lives of millions of people throughout the world.

'Aren't they one of the same,' said Robert coldly.

They just stood and stared at one another.

'Do you know how it feels to see someone you love come back from serving his country a shadow of their former self?'

Catherine asked, whose voice was almost as cold and calm as Robert's now.

'What are you talking ab –?'

'Do you know how it feels?' repeated Catherine, more forcefully this time.

'No,' said Robert simply, having no idea where this conversation was leading.

'Then you have no idea what it was like for me to watch my first husband slip away into depression, and to see that he would rather drink himself to death than to talk over his experiences with me. I could have saved him – I COULD HAVE SAVED HIM!' she screamed.

The sudden silence in the delivery room was absolute, and as Robert stared at Catherine – whose mascara had become smeared from the tears now rolling down her cheeks – he was beginning to understand why the Genesis Project meant so much to her. But the question was, did she honestly believe in it, or had the guilt of losing her husband driven her towards it? Only Catherine knew the answer, but whichever it was neither could justify what she was responsible for.

Without saying a word Robert walked past Catherine and headed towards the door they had entered through. He switched off the lights above the glass containers, it wasn't much but he hoped that this little act could help restore some sort of dignity to the fifteen children who had had their lives cruelly taken away from them.

'These children are to travel back with us,' he said, walking towards the flight of stairs, 'and then I want everything on this island to be destroyed.'

He did not wait for a response from anyone; he climbed the metal steps and did not bother to wait for the others as he entered his father's office. His eyes encountered a depressive scene, it appeared that Frank had spent the last few months of his life here. An old looking mattress lay on the blue carpeted floor, empty beer and cola cans, crisp packets and chocolate bar wrappers were strewn across the mahogany desk and floor and unwashed shirts were hanging over the back of the leather chair.

Robert moved deeper into the office and picked up the framed group photograph of Frank, Mark and him which was on the desk.

It had been taken on the day of Robert's welcome home party, that in itself seemed to be a lifetime away.

'What happened to you dad,' he said quietly.

'Frank watched me administer the lethal injection to the Spectres from up here,' said Catherine, 'that was the last time I saw him alive.'

Robert did not reply, he replaced the photograph, walked around the desk and dropped down into the leather desk chair. So this was it, the final piece to the Genesis Project, and yet he could not help but think there was something missing. He wasn't quite sure why but he opened the top drawer of the desk, and as he looked inside there was a disk case, scrawled on the front of it were the words: *To my son.*

Robert reached for the case, opened it and withdrew the disk. Something was resting on the desk, and as Robert looked up he saw that Michael had taken the laptop out of his bag and powered it up. Once the laptop had finished loading up, Robert inserted the disk into the drive.

The screen came to life, and there was Frank, slightly blurred standing a foot away from the camera, the automatic lens took a moment to focus itself then Frank became that much clearer. He took a single step backwards and spread out his arms.

'You're not the only one who looks good on a television screen, Robert,' he said, smiling broadly.

'Oh my god,' Catherine gasped, moving her hand involuntary to her mouth.

Chapter Twenty-Three

The Recorded Message

After his 'modest' introduction, Frank's expression hardened slightly. He turned away from the camera and walked towards his desk, the automatic zoom adjusting as he did. The video message had been recorded in his office in the main complex.

Frank walked around his desk, pulled out the leather chair and sunk into it. He was looking distinctly haggard, he was gaunter, greyer and unshaved compared to the last memory Robert had of him, he had never seen him like this, he looked very ill.

'This is such a beautiful place, don't you think?' he asked, he swivelled in the chair and stared out at the window, the last remnants of light streamed through the glass.

Robert gave acknowledgement even though his father would never hear him do so.

'I bought it not long after your mother died,' Frank continued, still staring out of the window, *'and for the first couple of years I set to work getting the island expanded and constructing all of the roads and buildings you see. The actual Genesis Project didn't become a realisation until fours year later.'*

He turned around, rested his elbows on his desk and stared deep into the camera lens.

'Before I tell you everything I want to take a moment and thank you for giving me the opportunity to explain myself. You probably hate me, and that is perfectly understandable; you have lost your mother, brother and now me, but I promise you that once I explain you will understand why I had to take my life, you will understand everything.

Frank sighed heavily and leaned back in his chair.

'Difficult to know where to begin,' he said wearily, *'no doubt you will have heard so many different views on the Genesis Project, some will be true, others greatly exaggerated and some negative.'*

Catherine shot a sideways glance at William, who caught the look and couldn't help but smirk.

'But now it is time for me to tell you everything about the Genesis Project.'

He paused a moment, as though he was wondering how best to begin his explanation.

'I was nine years old when I first thought of the Genesis Project, well when I say thought, it was actually a dream I had, which is still as clear to me now as it was all those years ago. It begins with me standing in a country that has been ravaged by war, and although it is nightfall, the moon is high in the sky, casting its ambient light on the toppled buildings and the burnt out cars.'

Robert turned up the volume of the laptop and leaned forward on his elbows.

'I am nine years old in body and in mind but I do not fear this place, it's as though I have been here before. I begin to walk slowly and then pick up my pace, I walk past all the destruction that surrounds me, walking until I see figures emerging from the shadows. I stop, neither knowing if they are my friend or my enemy. I just stand there as they approach me. There are fifteen in all, all identically dressed in a black, what could only be described as, combat suit. Their faces are concealed by a strange, odd looking helmet, they appear to be more machine than human, and I neither know if they are men or women or a combination of both. They stand around me and one of them asks about their orders, but before I can reply, a large explosion illuminates the night sky and screams follow shortly after.

'And it is in that moment that I realise what I have to do, these 'soldiers' that I command must help liberate the people of this country, and as I tell the fifteen this, they hurry off and I awoke immediately after.'

He paused again, running a hand over the dark shroud covering his strong jaw and dimpled chin.

'I only had the dream the once but when I woke the following day I knew I was destined to make it become a reality one day. As the years past I became obsessed with the idea of these futuristic soldiers, drawing countless pictures of how they would look, expanding the whole idea of them.

'I wanted them to be able to kill quickly, quietly and efficiently and to disappear into the shadows immediately after. From birth they would be taught and trained how to do this as well as many other things in a controlled, highly disciplined environment.

'As each year passed my idea evolved, becoming more and more complex. I drew all of the buildings you see here, I thought of a variety of lessons that would be taught, and devised an intense fitness regime that would be followed. But more importantly, the children would be known as Spectres.

'I didn't know it at the time but when I reached my twenties the whole idea of creating the most advanced soldier the world had ever seen had taken hold of me, but still I hadn't even attempted to turn it into a possibility. I founded CyberTech Defence Systems, Mark was born, I married your mom and then you came along and the desire to create the Spectre had in some respects loosened its hold on me, I had a family and other responsibilities now but it was still there, waiting patiently, knowing that sooner rather than later it would consume my entire body. It sounds dramatic but that was the reality of it all.'

He opened the top drawer of his desk and withdrew a thick leather-bound bible.

'The day your mother died, a priest came to the hospital to offer me some words of comfort.' He presented the bible to the camera. 'He gave me this and said I would find the answers I was looking for. This book saved my life, it gave me a purpose, it helped me travel back to the road I had lost my way on.'

He rested the bible in front of him, staring down at it for a brief moment before looking back into the camera.

'I took the death of your mother hard and I'm ashamed to admit that I found solace in alcohol.'

Robert winced; he too had followed the same path his father had, seeking comfort in alcohol to numb his pain. But unlike his father he had conquered his desire, it was a part of his life that he was ashamed of and would never want to repeat.

'And it was during one of my drunken states that I began to read the bible the priest had given me. To this day I still don't know why I did it, perhaps I thought it appropriate to mock the Almighty, perhaps I was just destined to, either way I came across *a particular section which seemed to make perfect sense to me, and in that moment of revelation I knew what I had to do.'*

He opened the bible and began to read aloud the short passage which had proved of great interest to him. And as Robert listened to the words, he understood how his father could have misinterpreted them. The grief that had consumed Frank's body had plunged him into a dark solitary place; these words unlike the alcohol, offered him hope and light.

'Reading these words gave birth to the Genesis Project,' he said, closing the bible shut and looking back into the lens, *'and I knew then what I had to do. So I began my long journey of creation, buying this island, employing Bill to oversee the design and construction of all the buildings you see and working closely with Catherine on the selection program. At times it proved tiresome but once the fifteen healthy babies were born and as soon as they took their first breath I knew that they were destined for great things. The Genesis Project was more than just developing 'mindless killers' as some would put it, it was about creating the most advanced soldiers the world had ever seen.'*

William scoffed and could no longer listen to what he thought was complete and utter nonsense, he turned away and walked towards the door.

'It was a vision that brought a great deal of interest from Jack Carter.' William stopped at once with his hand upon the door handle and looked over at the laptop when told of this. *'Although he thought it too much of a risk to joint fund it, he nonetheless wanted to be kept informed of all developments, this was something he knew would benefit the United States.'*

And then his voice took on a sombre tone, he sighed deeply, unable to look into the lens of the camera.

'Except that it didn't, and like all fairytales an end was inevitable.'

It seemed that Frank had reached the subject he was most eager to talk about, the real reason why he wanted Robert to see this island, something that was far greater than him understanding the Genesis Project.

'I have cancer,' he said quietly, as though this was still something he still found hard to accept.

The moment was odd and the words seemed to linger for a long time. Robert sank deep into the black leather chair. The idea of his father becoming ravaged by the disease of cancer made him feel quite ill.

'It's advanced rapidly,' Frank continued, and Robert raised a hand to his mouth, *'it's spread too far to be operated on.'*

Frank could no longer look at the camera now and he dropped his gaze down to his lap.

'When you are told something like that, when you are told that you are going to die, you look back on your life and try your best to correct the mistakes you have made during it. I admit that I haven't been a perfect man but I've tried to live a life, and it has been a colourful one at that.' He smiled faintly. *'I know now that Bill was right, the Genesis Project was something that no man should ever delve into. I created fifteen lives from my own foolishness and fifteen died because of it.'* He sighed deeply once more. *'I had no other choice but to put the children to rest, they did not belong in this world, it was the kindest thing I could do.'*

He seemed determined to explain something to Robert and he stared deep into the camera once again.

'I saw what cancer did to your mom,' he said, and his eyes began to moisten from the painful recollection, *'she was no longer recognisable in the end, the brutality of chemotherapy and the savages of cancer had left her a ravaged skeleton. I couldn't bear that to happen to me, being nothing more than a spectator, watching as the cancer diseased and decayed my body. I'm a proud man Robert, I would rather have no life than only being able to live half a one as I wait for my death to come. I would rather be remembered for taking my own life than being another statistic of dying from cancer.*

'And so by the time you see this I will be dead, the cancer will be consumed in the plane crash, leaving behind no trace of it even existing. I have ordered the complete closure of the island and I have explained to your grandmother what she needs to know as she will have taken control of things, making sure that you will be somewhat shielded from the immense media interest my death would have generated at the time. Don't blame her for keeping it from you, she was just honouring my final wish ... I needed you to see this island ... I need you to carry out something that I can

only trust you to do. This may not make sense to you Robert, but I have my reasons for doing this.'

Frank stood, walked around his desk and leaned against it.

'I have never had much faith,' he admitted, avoiding his gaze in the camera, *'but if there is a higher judgement in another life, I don't want to be held accountable for what I have done, I want to be reunited with my wife and son and I want to be happy.'* He stared deep into the camera lens. *'And now, once again I must ask for your help. I have asked so much of you already but I need you to give the children a dignified burial and then destroy everything on the island, this is my last chance for redemption.'*

He walked towards the camera, the automatic zoom trying its best to stop the picture from becoming blurred. He stood in front of it and reached his arm to the side, about to stop the recording but then reconsidering.

'You may perhaps have wondered why I never told you about the cancer.' There could be no mistaking the sadness in his eyes. *'I must confess that I thought you had enough to deal with, what with Mark's untimely death.'*

A single tear rolled down the left side of his cheek and the screen went black.

Chapter Twenty-Four

The Betrayer of Friends

After almost a year of searching, Robert had finally learnt the truth, sitting in front of the laptop screen he now understood why he had to explore this island. His job was to destroy the entire complex so that his father could have redemption. He ejected the disk, replaced it back inside the case it had come from and closed the laptop.

He sat in the silence, a mixture of emotions now flowing through his body. Questions began to explode inside his head, questions that only his father could answer, and that could never be. It was some time before Robert stood, and although he still found it difficult to forgive Frank for what he had done to the children – regardless what he had said and thought – he would nonetheless follow his wishes.

'Catherine,' he said, 'what I want you to do is to collect as many blankets as you can, I want to restore some dignity to the children.'

Catherine nodded and headed for the door.

'I cannot allow that to happen,' said a cold, clear voice.

Robert looked over at the man standing by the door, but before he could say a word William Davies grabbed Catherine by her hair and stood behind her.

'What are you –' Catherine cried.

He pulled hard on her hand exposing her neck, then he reached inside his trouser pocket and withdrew a penknife which he pressed against her skin.

'Let's just all remain calm,' said Michael calmly, raising his hands, 'there's no need for anyone to get hurt.'

'I am perfectly calm,' said Bill, whose voice was still calm and clear, 'it was perhaps the biggest mistake you made Mr Parker, giving me this penknife.'

Robert could only stand there, his mind racing, unable to process what he was seeing.

'I'm afraid I haven't been honest with you Robert,' said Bill regretfully, 'you see, ever since my son died I have been living a half life. It is only natural, I helped bring him into the world and I watched him grow. He died for his country and although I was heartbroken I felt proud that he had given his life for a cause worth fighting for.' He sighed deeply. 'But the South African war is not worth fighting for is it, and so you can understand my anger and contempt when the realisation that Jack died for nothing dawned on me.'

He lowered the knife pressing against Catherine's neck a fraction, she could no longer feel the blade pressing against her skin.

'And since then,' continued Bill, 'I have done everything I could to hold those responsible for Jack's death, to expose those who sent him to fight for nothing. But bringing about the downfall of Jack Carter's Presidency was a difficult task, in which I nearly lost hope. However, it was you Robert that carried an unknowing ray of light for me.'

The realisation settled over Robert, everything started to become clear now.

'You've been planning this from the moment I asked you to travel to the island with me,' he said, finally finding his voice.

'Yes,' said William regretfully, 'and that is why I offer my apologies.'

He could see the expression of shock and betrayal on Robert's face, but once he had explained everything Robert would understand, he would understand why he had to do this.

'There is so much to tell you,' he said quietly, staring directly into Robert's eyes, 'so much that you do not yet understand.'

'And I'm ready and willing to listen to you,' said Robert softly, 'just let Catherine go.'

There was a moment's silence, then William let go of Catherine's hair and lowered the knife from her throat. Overwhelmed with terror and fear Catherine's eyes rolled upwards, she crumpled to the floor and Michael rushed over to her. William walked over to the window but did not peer through.

'Death has such a complexity surrounding it, don't you think?' he asked in a tone Robert had never heard before. 'One moment your loved one is there, but in a blink of an eye they are taken away without a second thought.'

He glanced out of the window at the darkened area where the Spectres were.

'You never knew my son Jack, did you Robert?' he asked, turning and looking at him now.

'No Bill, I never had that pleasure.'

'But you can relate over how I am feeling,' continued William, 'you lost your brother and I lost my son. They both fought bravely and gave the ultimate sacrifice … but they died for nothing.'

'Yes I can relate,' said Robert calmly, 'I loved my brother very much and I too was angry when I was told the news that he had been killed. I went through exactly what you're going through now Bill, but I realised that Mark wouldn't have wanted that, he would want me to live my life, remember the amazing memories I have of him. And I'm sure Jack would want you to do the same, because no matter what you do Bill nothing will ever bring him back.'

'You are right Robert,' said William after a momentary pause, 'Jack is dead and he will always be, but there is one thing I can do, and that is bring him justice. You see, I knew of the interest Jack Carter showed in the Genesis Project, but it had not dawned on me until the night you came to see me. Telling you what I knew about the project brought back many memories, which I am sure had been repressed due to my son's death. But I knew the President was a smart man and I knew that he would have made sure that nothing implicated him in the Genesis Project. However, Frank has unknowingly given me what I needed in his recorded message. Jack Carter took away my son, so I find it fitting that I take away the most important thing in his life, once I expose his interest it will ultimately bring about the end of his Presidency.'

'But they are just my father's words,' said Robert quickly, 'Jack Carter can just deny them.'

William chuckled. 'Well of course he will,' he said, smiling, 'he's not going to admit it is he? Jack Carter will have no other option but to lie, but in doing so a political storm will gather. Once the newspapers back home get a hold of the story they will do their utmost to discover the truth, and once they see this place, he will have no other choice but to step down as President. His reputation will be destroyed, and I would have finally brought justice to my son and to all those who fought in the pointless war in South Africa.'

'Jack gave his life so that the world could be a better pla –'

'He gave his life for nothing,' raged William, 'he died because of Jack Carter's lies and betrayal, he is the man responsible for every single American soldier's death in South Africa. He sent them to fight for nothing, my son died for NOTHING!'

And in that moment Robert knew, he knew that the man standing before him was not the William Davies he respected and admired. The death of his son had turned him into a madman, who seemed he would not stop until he achieved justice, and that in itself could prove deadly.

Robert was thinking hard, endless options of what he should do next ran through his brain. He looked at the disk case on the desk, smashing it could put an end to Bill's plan, but at what cost? Robert quickly tried to think of all the repercussions it would cause, but it did not matter, because at that moment Marcus picked up the disk case, walked directly over to William and handed it to him.

'The man makes a lot of sense,' he said, 'Derek and I fought alongside Jack in South Africa, we were with him when he died. He got no recognition for his ultimate sacrifice, none of us did. We came home and we were branded murderers by our own people,' he said in disbelief, 'by the American people, do you have any idea how that feels?'

'You've been planning this all along,' breathed Robert, his body now shaking.

'Yes,' said William, 'both Derek and Marcus visited me shortly after Jack's death, we had a little discussion and it was clear that we all felt the same.'

Robert could no longer stand, he dropped into the leather chair and looked over at Michael who was still comforting Catherine. Was he among this betrayal? He dismissed the thought at once, out of all the bodyguards Robert had struck up an unlikely friendship with Michael Parker. Catherine was opening her eyes now, Michael looked up at Robert, and from his expression he knew what their fates would be. But then something unexpected occurred and Robert could only watch in horror as Michael stood.

'Everything is clear to me now,' he said, avoiding Robert's eyes as he turned to face William and Marcus, 'ever since I returned from South Africa I have been carrying this weight on my shoulders. Mark Lane died trying to save me, and I thought I owed it to him by protecting his brother once I had finished my time in the army. I thought it was the honourable thing to do, but I now realise that I must let the whole world know what Jack Carter is responsible for. I can save many lives by doing so.'

'Are you beginning to understand?' William asked him softly, delighted that Michael was now with them.

Robert could not find the words to reply.

'You see, I'm not the only one who feels betrayed by the President Robert, this is what we have to do.'

Robert felt a blade pressing against the skin of his neck, and he could only watch as Marcus pulled out a penknife from his combat pocket and walked over to Catherine.

'I regret it,' said William coldly.

He felt no remorse, no guilt as he headed towards the door. It was time for him to leave this island and expose all of its dark secrets, but before he could turn the handle Michael stopped him.

'Not here,' he said, 'it will be the biggest mistake you make killing them in this room.'

William stopped and turned round to face him, he raised his eyebrows urging Michael to continue.

'This is Robert Lane,' he explained, pointing at him, 'perhaps the most famous man in the world, do you think you can simply murder him and get away with it?'

It seemed with all of William's careful planning he had not considered this.

'Kill them outside,' continued Michael, 'and then drop their bodies in the river. The current will take them out to sea and by the time they are found there will be nothing to suggest that either one was murdered. We can tell the world it was an unfortunate accident, everyone will go into mourning, it will be such a tragic loss.'

'You heard the man,' said William, looking at Derek and then Marcus, 'take them outside.'

Robert felt himself being pulled to his feet, he did not fight back, the whole of his strength had been torn from his body. It had been the ultimate betrayal, and this island of death was about to claim two more lives.

*

They were led outside and were forced to their knees on the patch of grass. It had started to rain, Robert could feel the drops on his face, his body was no longer numb now, the disbelief had come and gone, his feeling was one of acceptance, he had accepted the fact that he was going to die.

He thought back to what William had said earlier, the complexity of death as he had put it, death was not complex, it was cruel. And how cruel it was for his life to be ended like this and that very thought pained him.

And yet, on the verge of death, something entered his mind that held a shred of hope for Catherine's and his survival, and he found his voice to ask William that very thing.

'What have I done to you that was so bad it justifies killing me?'

There was a long silence, all eyes were on William now as he stared at Robert. Surely there was still compassion left in him, it was just the anger he felt that had masked it. William would soon see, soon understand that this was madness, that killing Catherine and him and then revealing the President's interest in the Genesis Project would never fill the gaping hole inside of him.

But it seemed that William had nothing but evil inside of him because he smiled and said coldly, 'You deserve to know why I'm going to kill you Robert. I have always been fond of you, after all I am your godfather, but the truth is you are too much of a liability. You have the same traits as your father and I know that you would not be able to walk away from the island in silence, I have betrayed you and I know you would do your utmost to stop me. You would inform Jack Carter about my plans and that Robert I cannot allow to happen.'

Catherine began sobbing and Robert knew that this was the end, there could be no reasoning with Bill or anyone else for that matter.

'Michael,' said William, 'as it was you that suggested we should kill them outside perhaps you can do me the honour of doing just that, call it a show of alliance.'

Michael did not hesitate, he withdrew his penknife from its pouch secured to his belt and unfolded it. He walked over to Robert who in turn felt a deep anger and hatred burning inside of him, at the man who was supposed to protect him, at the man who Mark had died saving.

'I TRUSTED YOU,' he raged, and he spat at Michael, who immediately wiped it from his face.

'Sometimes honour is more important than trust, Robert,' said William through a long sigh, 'I'm sorry that it had to end like this.'

He nodded at Michael, who in turn walked around Robert and gripped his hair, pulling back his head. He could feel the sharp blade pressing against his neck, tears rolled down his temples, he closed his eyes, he would not think about his death. He pictured Lisa, beautiful, elegant, the woman he had never told how he felt about her. What he would give to have that chance now, that chance to explain everything to her.

Time seemed to lose all meaning, Robert could only wait for his death, it was such a horrific feeling to experience. He continued to think about Lisa, smiling, laughing, the woman he had loved for a lifetime. But then, quite suddenly, the blade was no longer pressing against his skin. Was this death? He could feel his heart beating, he could feel the cool air being sucked into his lungs. He opened his eyes, slowly and fearfully, but Michael's eyes did not meet his, he was looking directly ahead.

Robert pulled his hair from Michael's grip and moved his head forward to immediately see what everyone was looking at. The helicopter above looked to be spinning out of control and was heading directly towards them.

Chapter Twenty-Five

Death and Persistence

The pilot fought hard against the controls of the helicopter as it spun widely out of control.

And quite suddenly everything slowed, became blurred. The spinning helicopter increased in speed, Michael was the first to act, he pulled both Robert and Catherine up from the ground and all three ran. However, fear had rooted Marcus, Derek and William firmly to their spots.

And as William watched the helicopter draw closer with unprecedented speed, his thoughts flashed upon his son Jack, and he hoped, prayed, that he never had to endure fear like this before his death.

The helicopter crashed on its side in front of the two Land Rovers and as its momentum carried it along the ground it collided with them. The fuel from all three ignited from a spark and a large orange fireball emerged from the wreckage, the explosion was ear deafening. The flames and energy rippled out, consuming anything and everything that stood in its way.

William could only watch, his life didn't flash before his eyes as death approached him like he thought it would, his last thoughts were, *I'm going to die.* He fell to the floor and shielded his face as the flames tore through his body. Marcus and Derek shared the same fate, impossible it was for them to survive such a destructive force; both were burnt to death as they tried in vain to run away.

In the shear panic Robert suddenly became separated from Michael and Catherine, running on pure adrenaline, his eyes were wide and filled with terror from the prospect of death.

He could hear the flames behind him, they were closing in on him fast, there could be no way of him outrunning it, and he knew in that moment that he was going to die, it was such a horrible feeling to experience.

But then, quite suddenly, the ground before him declined dramatically and Robert lost his footing and could not stop himself from falling. In a shower of leaves, flailing arms and legs, he crashed through the thick foliage with a sickening impact and he was in a sudden freefall, rapidly approaching the river below.

Semi-conscious, Robert tried to keep himself as straight as possible and yet as he hit the water feet first, the very air within him was knocked suddenly from his lungs. The icy water that engulfed him made every part of his body scream in agony, the skin on his face and hands felt like it was being burnt by the flames he had narrowly avoided.

He could hardly breathe; his lips and fingers trembled violently as he broke the surface and gasped desperately for air, the force of the current was unimaginably strong, pulling him along effortlessly. He tried to see where Michael and Catherine were but was suddenly pulled under. He kicked against it widely, trying to push himself back to the surface, trying to keep himself afloat, but his drenched clothing and boots just pulled him deeper under the water.

He looked up, the light streaming through the murky water was getting further and further from him. With stars now dancing in front of his eyes he pulled at his boots in a last ditched effort, but his numb fingers were unable to loosen the laces. His heart thudded slower with every passing beat, and his eyes grew heavy, death would soon be upon him, but still he fought, he sunk deeper … deeper … deeper …

He could feel life pouring back into his lungs and heart, coughing and vomiting up the river's water, soaking and shivering uncontrollably he came round, lying on his back on what seemed to be mud. Somewhere around him, someone was panting heavily, it was hard to tell where they were or who they were with his senses dazed and disorientated.

Robert had no strength to open his eyes let alone lift his head to see who had prevented death from wrapping itself around him. All he could do was take long, deep breaths and just savour and appreciate being alive. Then he heard a voice, panting yet steady, speaking to him from above.

'Mr – Lane – are – you – okay?'

Nothing but the disbelief of hearing *that* voice could have given Robert the strength to open his eyes. And there, stooping before him was Michael, drenched through to his skin, remnants of the river still dripping off his shivering body.

Robert wanted to scream 'traitor', at him but no sound came out, he curled his left hand into a fist and hit Michael hard on his cheek.

'What are you doing?' cried a voice hysterically, it was Catherine although Robert didn't see her.

But Robert did not answer her, Michael Parker had betrayed both Catherine and him. Michael fell backward, clutching his left cheek. With his body still shaking violently, Robert staggered to his feet and – cursing profusely – pummelled Michael's face and stomach with heavy punches.

'Stop it!' Catherine shrieked, 'stop it!'

Michael pleaded in a vain attempt also, he shielded his face with his hands but not even they could stop the force of Robert's punches.

'Mr Lane,' he said, 'I'm not going to hurt you.'

'Liar,' Robert roared, punching Michael harder, 'you were with him, you were going to kill us.'

'I had to say those things,' said Michael desperately, 'I had no other choice, I needed to make them believe I was with them, it was the only way we had of surviving William's murderous attempt.'

'I believe him,' said Catherine.

Robert stopped his incessant punching and looked up and saw her standing not far from them, drenched to the skin, her shoulder length hair plastered to her pale-looking face.

'If he wanted to kill you he would have let you drown,' continued Catherine. 'I saw him jump into the river and rescue you.'

It seemed that Robert had never considered this, he looked down at Michael, his face was bleeding and beginning to swell. Robert then looked at his own hands; his knuckles were stained with Michael's blood. What Catherine had told him seemed to encase Michael in an invisible barrier, protecting him from any further pain. This man had rescued him; he had just brought Robert back from the brink of death.

'I'm sorry,' said Robert, unsure what else he could say.

'You have nothing to apologise for,' said Michael weakly, 'I would have done the same in your position.'

Robert stood and helped Michael to his feet and as they stared at one another's bloody faces, Michael caught hold of something being washed up on the muddy shore.

'That's a spot of luck,' he said, smiling.

And from that moment Robert and Michael had become friends again, the broken bond had repaired itself and would forever remain strong. Michael walked over to the edge of the water and picked up his bag.

'I thought I had lost it,' he said to both Robert and Catherine, walking towards them. 'I had to take it off when I hit the water, damn thing nearly drowned me. I did the rookies' mistake and kept all of my stuff in here.'

He knelt down, unzipped his bag and withdrew a small tobacco tin which he opened on his raised knee. Windproof matches, a condom, a roll of fishing wire, a safety pin, cotton wool, a needle and thread and a fire lighter lined the inside of the tin.

'Gives a whole new meaning to the phrase be prepared,' said Catherine, looking at the blue foil wrapping of the condom.

Michael looked up. 'It's surprising how much water a condom can hold,' he said.

He began to look among the forest floor. Michael was unsure if there was going to be a rescue helicopter sent, and none of them had the luxury of just waiting in the hope that it would. Their first priority was to dry their clothes and then find adequate shelter, the rain had eased slightly now but none knew if this was the end of the predicted storm, all they could do then was just wait.

'We need to make a fire and dry out our clothes as best as possible.'

He began to clear away dead leaves and weeds from the forest bed with his hands, saying to Robert and Catherine, 'Could you look for some stones.'

They wandered among the forest, and by the time they arrived back five or so minutes later with a handful of stones each, Michael had found some dry twigs from under the forest bed and had stripped the bark from a nearby fallen tree with the second penknife he kept in his bag.

'Form a circle with the stones,' Michael said to them, 'don't make it too big, we don't want to make the fire unmanageable if it gets out of hand.'

Once the surround for the fire had been constructed, Michael broke the firelighter in half, struck one of the windproof matches and lit the corner, then slowly and very carefully he placed it directly in the middle of the stones. He began adding the tinder, one piece at a time to try and get the fire established, and once it had, he began to add the twigs and other firewood.

The flames were welcoming and gave the three of them a sense of hope. Michael rummaged through his bag once again and pulled out a rope and a couple blankets – rolled up in separate plastic bags – which he passed to Robert and then to Catherine. He tied the rope to two of the trees nearest to the fire and then removed his drenched jumper, T-shirt, trousers and socks and hung them over the rope.

'We have to dry out our clothes,' he explained, standing before them in his vest and boxer shorts, 'to stop the advances of hypothermia when the temperature begins to fall tonight. You can always get undressed behind one of the trees if you feel embarrassed.'

'And risk getting stung by nettles,' said Catherine at once, 'you can both turn away if you don't like what you see.'

She undressed to her underwear and threw the blanket around her shoulders, Robert did exactly the same and Michael hung their clothes on the makeshift washing line. And then an explosion shattered the silence, they looked across the river and saw a plume of black smoke rising into the air.

And it was clear, as the three of them sat around the fire, that in the minutes after they had narrowly escaped with their lives the explosion from the helicopter had caused devastation on an unimaginable scale. It was hard to tell from where they were sitting but the flames from the explosion must have torn through the medical centre and ignited the flammable bottles.

How long they stared at the black smoke rising, none of the trio knew, but whether each one would admit it or not they all thought about the four who had perished.

'Let's hope none of them suffered,' said Catherine quietly, as she watched more and more black smoke fill the air.

'Yeah,' said Michael, 'let's hope.'

Robert didn't say a word, he sat with his knees tucked under his chin and breathed silently. Although the last thing he wanted was for William to suffer before he died, he still found it difficult to make that known to Catherine and Michael. William was going to kill both Catherine and him and expose the Genesis Project to the whole world, how could Robert forgive him for such a thing?

'Is another helicopter going to be sent?' Catherine asked, there could be no mistaking the desperation in her voice.

Michael let out a tiny sigh. 'I don't know,' he admitted, 'but we can't stay here in the hope that it will.'

He stood a moment later, walked over to the hanging clothes and ran his hands over them, frowning as he did. He picked up some more firewood, fed it to the fire and then rubbed his hands together. But then a rumble of thunder could be heard overhead, which made every one of them look up through the forest at the dark clouds beginning to drift toward them.

'A storm is coming,' said Michael, 'we don't have much time. Quickly get dressed.'

He pulled on his clothes and then began to look among the trees and forest bed, he walked deeper into the thicket, picking up sticks as he passed them, frowning, then throwing them back down onto the floor. Robert and Catherine gave each other quizzical looks as they started getting dressed in their now smoky damp clothes.

After a few minutes of searching, Michael had finally found what he was looking for. The branch was thick and strong and when he stood it up it was taller than him. He rested it against the tree it had broken from and making sure there was a bit of an angle on it, he raised his foot and stamped down hard on it. It broke cleanly in the middle.

He picked up his pocket knife by the fire and began to strip the bark about six inches or so from one end. He did the same to the other and then walked over to Robert and Catherine who were now fully dressed.

'It's not much,' he said, passing the makeshift walking sticks to each of them, 'but it's better than nothing.'

And as they said their thanks, Michael clipped the pocket knife back in the holder on his belt and then reached inside his bag, more in hope than anything else. He withdrew a folded white sheet of paper which had been laminated. Kneeling on the ground, he unfolded it as Robert and Catherine stood around him. It was another detailed drawing of the island Michael had asked to be made, and as it had been laminated it had been protected when it plunged into the water.

'We're somewhere about here.' He tapped the map with his finger. 'This water runs straight through the island, if we follow it downstream it will lead us to a lagoon.' He looked up at Catherine. 'What would that have been used for?' he asked her.

'Scuba diving and snorkelling training.'

'Would there have been a storage facility near it?' he asked, refolding the drawing and sliding it inside his trouser combat pocket.

'One was being built,' said Catherine, 'but I don't know how much of it was completed before the island was closed.'

'We'll have to risk it, we don't want to get caught up in this storm.' Michael began to look around. 'We don't have the time or the resources to build a raft,' he said, 'we'll have to walk.'

*

The rain showed little signs of easing by the time Simon arrived at the Capri Rosa hotel. His decision to allow the exploration of the island had proved a costly mistake to make and he was unable to shake the pilot's last words from his mind, but he had to at this present moment, because he was about to fulfil a duty Robert had asked him to do in the event of something happening to him.

'Keep Lisa informed,' he had said to him, *'tell her everything if she asks.'*

Inside her hotel suite, unaware of what was about to befall on her, Lisa was sat in the living room with Melissa. David was sat on the couch, reading the morning's newspaper.

'More tea, Mommy?' Melissa smiled brightly, as she picked up her yellow plastic teapot and held it above Lisa's small pink cup.

'Oh yes please Melissa,' said Lisa in a high pitch squeak.
And she pretended to pour.

They were sat on a large blue blanket on the floor. Melissa had sat her favourite bear next to her with a pink cup resting on its legs. And as she watched Lisa about to take a pretend sip of her tea, she said in a warning tone, 'Be very careful mommy, it's very very hot.'

'Okay,' said Lisa, 'I will.' She began taking several sips. 'Oh this is a lovely cup of tea Melissa.'

Melissa giggled with her shrieks of delight, but they were suddenly cut short by the telephone ringing. David folded the newspaper and dropped it onto the coffee table as he stood and walked over to pick it up.

'Hello?' he said, and Lisa looked at him. 'Yes ... one moment.'

He put his hand over the mouthpiece and looked at Lisa.

'Do you know anyone called Simon Blackwood?' he asked her.

'Simon Blackwood,' Lisa repeated, 'yes, Robert spoke of him.'

David removed his hand from the mouthpiece. 'Yes send him up, I'll meet him outside of the elevator ... thank you.'

He replaced the telephone, checked to make sure he had his room card key on him and walked out of the room, leaving Lisa and Melissa alone.

'Would you like some cake, Mommy,' said Melissa, breaking the silence.

Lisa looked at her daughter, she was holding out a small pink plate with a piece of plastic cake balanced upon it, she was smiling brightly.

'Thank you,' said Lisa weakly.

She took the cake off the plate and pretended to eat it.

'This is a lovely piece of cake,' she said, trying her best not to think of what Simon wanted, 'did you make it?'

Melissa giggled. 'Of course not, Mommy,' she said, rolling her eyes at her mother's foolishness, 'it's not real you know.'

'Oh silly me,' said Lisa, and she kissed Melissa on her forehead.

David arrived back not long after he left, accompanied by a tall, thin man with a thick mane of black hair and rectangular shaped glasses.

'Lisa Anderson,' the man said quite coldly, 'my name is Simon Blackwood.' He did not extend his hand. 'I believe we met briefly when you landed.'

'Yes we did,' said Lisa, standing.

'Would you like some cake Simon?' asked Melissa cutely, balancing the cake she had given her mum on a pink plate.

Simon did not give a reply and began looking around the room, unimpressed of the little girl sitting on the floor. 'Is there somewhere we can talk in private?' he asked Lisa, avoiding her eyes.

'Melissa sweetie,' said Lisa softly, looking at her daughter, 'why don't you put Antony bear to bed, he must be really full up and tired after eating all that cake.'

Melissa picked up her favourite bear and cradled it as though it was the most important thing in the world to her.

'Okay, Mommy,' she said.

She stood, but before she left the room she waited for Simon to look at her. He did after a moment or two of waiting and she stuck her tongue out at him before running out of the door, giggling. Lisa raised a hand toward her mouth to mask her growing smile.

'Charming kid,' said Simon sarcastically.

'With all due respect Mr Blackwood,' Lisa said calmly, 'you don't know my daughter and I would appreciate if you didn't talk about her like that.' Simon raised his hands in defence. 'Now, is there a reason why you are here?'

'There's no easy way to say this,' said Simon, he walked over to the couch and dropped down into it, 'so it's probably best if I come straight out with it.'

His pause was long and unneeded and this silence was unbearable for Lisa. And she knew from the tone in which Simon had spoken that something terrible had happened, she walked over and sat down opposite him.

'How much did Robert tell you, about what he was doing today?' Simon asked finally.

'He – er – he said that he was travelling to an island Frank owned,' Lisa said.

Simon nodded. 'He travelled there by helicopter, which I objected t –'

'What's happened to Robert?' There was no politeness in the words, Lisa wanted to get straight to the point.

'If I'm being truthful I don't know, I have no idea if he is alive or dead, and there can be no way of telling.'

'What do you mean no way of telling,' Lisa fumed, fuelled by Simon's words, 'send another helicopter, search for him.'

'That is simply out of the question,' Simon said callously, 'I cannot afford for another helicopter to crash. The first crashed because of a technical failure, the others could have the same problem, and a series of tests have to be run on each of them before I allow anymore to be sent.'

Lisa was shell-shocked, she was unable to process what Simon was saying, how could he just sit there and be so casual towards Robert being missing? Surely he should do all he could to save him, and yet he wasn't, he wasn't prepared to do this.

Simon stood. 'I was just keeping you up to date on proceedings; I will contact you if any news should arise.'

The words were like a series of fireworks going off inside of Lisa's stomach, a fury rose from deep within her, overpowering the timid and often conservative Lisa Anderson, making her strong and able to speak. She stood and slapped Simon hard across his cheek.

'Now you listen to me you son of a bitch,' she said as Simon reeled back in horror, clutching his cheek with his hand, 'I'm going to say this once and once only, you're going to send another helicopter and you're going to find Robert.'

Simon made a sudden movement, as though he was on the verge of physically pushing Lisa, but David quickly stood in front of her, protecting her from any such action.

'You are in no position to give me such orders,' Simon said, a smug smile curling upon his lips.

'That's where you're wrong,' said Lisa defiantly, 'because if you don't make every conceivable effort in finding Robert I'll make sure you're held responsible for his death, and that's not a threat, that's a promise.' She looked at David. 'Escort him out will you, I have nothing left to say to him.'

And as David led Simon out of the room, the fear of losing Robert overwhelmed Lisa, she sank into the leather couch and could not stop the tears from falling.

Chapter Twenty-Six

A Cruel Turn of Events

August 11th

The wind and rain was harsh and unforgiving and Michael Parker had been a soldier long enough to know that it could break the strongest of hearts and minds.

The storage building they hoped to seek shelter in was nonexistent and the relentless wind and rain made it impossible for them to head back to the main complex. The only hope they had of surviving this was to use the wooden shed – which housed canoes and oars – not far from the lagoon as shelter.

Michael, Robert and Catherine quickly got to work, using the rope from Michael's backpack they secured the discoloured canoes over the gaps in the shed. The makeshift walls were not the best but at least they stopped most of the rain from coming through.

It was damp and confined inside when the door was shut, but this did not stop the elation from surging through each of their bodies; they were finally out of the rain, they had a chance of surviving this.

Michael dug a shallow hole with his hands and made a small fire from cotton wool, fire lighters and the wooden handles from the oars, the warmth and light produced was minimal but it was welcomed and emitted a sense of hope. They ate some of the food rations not long after making the fire and although it looked disgusting it tasted delicious and it eased their hunger pains.

But the rain drumming overhead was cruel and as the time passed the hope that each of them carried began to dwindle like the fire. The fear of dying from hypothermia overwhelmed Catherine and she was the first to break down, sobbing quietly in her hands. Robert put an arm around her and offered words of comfort and reassurance, the heated words exchanged earlier in the day were forgotten now, surviving this had fused together their broken bond of friendship.

Now it was ten o'clock, Michael held his hands above the glowing ash and rubbed them together, trying to send some warmth back into them, trying to ease the numbness. He looked through the darkness at Dr Sutton, she was asleep and had been for about an hour or so, and although he couldn't see her properly he could hear her breathing. He listened a moment before resuming the warming of his hands. It was only a matter of time before hypothermia began shutting down her body, both Robert and he would share the same fate, but with strength still left in his body he would do all he could to keep her alive.

Robert sat opposite, cupping his hands together and blowing hot air into them, the momentary warmth he felt was nice. Then he began to rub his arms and legs, trying all he could to stop his body from shivering.

'We're not going to make it, are we?' he asked.

'No,' said Michael, whose lips trembled from the cold.

Robert exhaled sharply through his nose.

'I'm scared,' he said quietly, trying to converse what energy he had left.

'Try and think of it as just going to sleep Mr Lane.'

And with that nice warming thought, Michael used his last remaining strength to lie down on the floor, tuck his legs under him and cross his arms.

'I'm sorry I couldn't save you Mr Lane,' he said, squinting at Robert through the darkness.

'You don't need to apologise,' said Robert still quietly, 'I'm the one who should be sorry for ever doubting you.'

Michael closed his eyes and sighed wearily. His mind had finally been broken, he had finally accepted the fact that he was going to die, whether it be in the next few minutes or hours his soul would finally accept defeat and he would drift off to an eternal sleep.

The last of the glowing ash died out a few minutes later, the light and warmth had finally extinguished. Robert lay down and rested his head on his outstretched arm, he could feel his eyelids beginning to close, but he fought to keep them open. From this odd sideways view, he took in the last moments of his life, it seemed almost cruel that the island he had finally uncovered after months of searching was going to take his life.

And yet he could feel his heart pounding fiercely in his chest. How strange it was that on this brink of death it pumped that much harder, in a valiant attempt to keep his blood flowing, to keep him alive.

Terror, unlike he had ever experienced before washed over him as he lay on the mud, would his death hurt? Of all the times he had thought about taking his own life, he had never thought of death itself, his desire to end the tormenting demons had always overshadowed the idea of it. And yet as he waited, waited for his end to come it never occurred to him that he was no longer in control of his death, he could not choose when, where or how, it was going to happen now, and it was that that scared him.

At last his shivering slowed, it had failed to warm his body and finally admitted defeat, and Robert welcomed it. He could feel his muscles beginning to stiffen and his shivering eventually stopped.

'Lisa,' he whispered, the name he spoke was slow and slurred. 'I ... love ... you.'

He wanted his last thoughts to be of her, he tried to picture her, tried to see her beautiful smile, to see her face, to see her brown eyes, to see everything that made her so special, so unique. But he could not, he could not picture her, he could not see her, he could not see anything, it was as though his brain was concentrating on keeping him alive, too preoccupied doing this then using its last remnants of energy to unlock all of the amazing and beautiful memories he had stored away of Lisa.

His breathing began to slow and oddly, with his ear resting upon his wet jumper, he could hear his heart, it seemed to be growing slower with every passing beat.

Confused and apathetic, his mind, body and soul on the brink of death, a noise came to him from overhead. It was a bizarre sound, a distant rumbling, like another storm beginning to gather, Robert opened his eyes a fraction, the effort alone doing this was immense.

A bright light was streaming in through the gaps in the oars and shed, casting itself onto his body. This was death, he knew it was, he was going to be collected, going to be reunited with his mother, his father, his brother, all the loved ones who had passed away. And then something quite unexpected happened, something was spreading throughout his body, he could feel it despite the numbness, it was well beyond warmth, peace perhaps? At last he was at peace? Was it preparing itself for the crossing over into the next world? Robert did not know, but the idea of dying no longer scared him.

With one final effort he closed his eyes and drew the faintest of smiles on his lips.

Chapter Twenty-Seven

A Second Chance

Finally, eternal peace, and yet as Robert opened his eyes slowly, this was nothing like he thought it would be. He was lying on his front, with the left side of his face pressed into the mud, which was neither soft nor hard. He was still inside the shed, but Michael and Catherine had gone.

And as he stood slowly and looked around, they were nowhere to be seen. He was not concerned over this, on the contrary, he felt a sense of joy, of elation, he felt at peace with himself. He was fully clothed and not a single part of him ached, he looked at his hands, turning them over as he moved his fingers. He was neither hot nor cold, he was perfectly in the middle, if there was such a thing.

He walked, slowly and carefully, to the door, pushed down the handle and stepped through. Bizarrely, however, he suddenly found himself standing in a long corridor, with gold coloured writing on the walls that he did not understand. He turned to go back through the shed door, but as he did, the door had vanished; the carpeted corridor was all he could see now.

He looked in both directions, the overhead lights showed that it seemed to stretch out indefinitely both ways. He stood there, wondering which direction he should take, wondering if it made a difference at all. But then, quite suddenly and unexpectedly, he caught hold of something out of the corner of his eye, he turned to see a figure walking towards him.

He just stood, feeling not one bit intimidated or afraid as the figure drew closer to him. But then something extraordinary happened, he looked at the woman in utter disbelief, she was dressed smartly in black trousers and a white blouse and was wearing pearl earrings and a necklace which always suited her perfectly.

'Mom?' he said slowly and quietly, 'is – is that you?'

Margaret Lane smiled. 'Oh Robert,' she said softly, 'my beautiful boy, look how handsome you've become.'

'Momma,' Robert cried, and he ran towards her and threw his arms around her. 'I've missed you so much,' he said, his voice muffled by her clothing, 'I love you, Momma.'

'I love you too, baby,' she soothed.

They pulled away from one another and Margaret wiped away the tears from her son's cheeks.

'I'm so proud of you,' she said quietly, 'you have conquered your demons and have forgiven your father … you have become a great man Robert.'

She looked sad now, as though what she was about to say next pained her to do so.

'Am I dead?' Robert asked her.

'You are in the cross over,' she replied softly, 'between the worlds of life and death.'

'And … are you here to collect me?' said Robert, urging his mother onwards.

'Yes,' she said quietly and regretfully.

Robert nodded and sighed deeply. 'Okay,' he whispered. What else could he say? He had found out he was about to die, there was nothing else he could say to that.

He looked around at his surroundings, if this was indeed the eternal resting place they stood in, it was not what he imagined it to be, there were no clouds, no Pearly Gates, just this corridor that seemed to go on forever in both directions. And for a long time they stood silent, Robert looked at his mother, looked at the tears rolling down her cheeks, twinkling in the overhead lights. The realisation of what would happen next began to settle gradually over mother and son.

'Will it hurt?' Robert asked her finally.

'Of course not,' she reassured softly, 'it's like drifting off to sleep. You have nothing to worry about, I will be by your side throughout.'

'I love you, Momma,' said Robert.

Margaret smiled and held out her hand. 'Take hold,' she said quietly.

Robert reached out, his fingertips were millimetres from his mother's, but then she reconsidered and pulled away sharply.

'You have so much yet to give to the world, my beautiful beautiful boy, I cannot allow this to be your time ... I couldn't give Mark a second chance,' she said regretfully, 'but I can for you ... However, in order for this to happen I must leave you now.'

'No, you can't,' said Robert, who felt an overwhelming sadness. 'Don't leave me, Momma, I need you.'

But the words that were said with so much emotion did nothing to keep his mother from leaving him. And as she took a step back, her body seemed to glow and looked to be getting smaller and smaller, as though she was being pulled away from him. But she was not, she was still in front of him, just growing lighter and smaller.

'MOMMA,' Robert called, now just nothing more than a helpless onlooker, 'MOMMA, DON'T LEAVE ME.'

And in no time at all, her body form had gone, she was nothing more than an orb, perfectly spherical in shape, brilliant white in colour with a tint of blue. And for a moment it just stayed there, gently bobbin up and down, Robert stared at it, mesmerised by its alluring colour. And then, without warning, it zoomed off.

'Momma,' he called after her, 'Momma come back.'

But before he could chase after it, his entire body, without warning, began to shiver uncontrollably. He fell to the floor in excruciating pain; his quivering body unable to support his weight. He just lay there, unable to do nothing more than to watch his mother rapidly fade from his sight.

'MOMMA,' he screamed, 'HEEEELLLLP MEEEEEEEEE.'

And quite suddenly, the lights behind him began to extinguish. He was no longer calm, fear unlike anything he had felt before gripped his shivering body, the darkness was advancing rapidly, it was closing in on him. Gritting his teeth, he began to crawl across the carpet, trying all he could to somehow out crawl it, but he could not. The darkness enveloped his pulsating and suffering body and in that instant the fear that had surged through his veins telling him to try and crawl away now paralysed him.

His breathing came in short, shallow gasps in the darkness; he looked up and watched as the overhead lights continued to extinguish further down. He lay there, shivering uncontrollably, more frightened than he had ever been in his life, having no idea what was happening or what was going to happen to him next.

But then something odd but at the same time wonderful happened. The orb returned, emerging from the darkness, it was such a beautiful thing to see. The ambient light it emitted was cast upon him, ebbing away all of the fear he felt. He stared at it, watching it move gently up and down, and then someone emerged from the darkness and into the orb's light.

And as it circled the figure, Robert looked up and saw that it was a woman who was standing over him. From what he could see, she was tall, thin and graceful, with gently curled golden hair, which came down to her slender shoulders. The circling orb gave her an eerie effect.

'Robert Lane?' she said, ever so softly.

'Yes,' replied Robert with great difficulty.

The woman surveyed him for a long time, then she inclined her head and said, 'It is not your time.'

The orb continued to circle her for a moment longer, then she held out her hand and the orb moved towards Robert.

'Take hold of it,' she said softly, as she disappeared into the darkness.

With great difficulty, yet through sheer determination, Robert reached out his hand and grasped the orb, which absorbed into his skin as soon as he did. It travelled up his arm, eradicating the shivering as it went, his mother was giving him life again. The lights flickered on overhead a moment later, and as soon as the illumination was cast upon him, his pain and fear ended at once.

He could feel his heart beginning to pulsate, feel the blood coursing through his veins, he began to breathe, long deep breaths he took, how wonderful it was to experience such a thing. He stood, not a single part of him ached, he felt alive, felt hope, joy, elation, felt so many wonderful things.

He looked around, he was completely alone, but he did not care, he was happy, so very happy that nothing else even entered his mind. The overhead lights grew brighter, pure white, and it engulfed him, he was no longer in the corridor now, he was far away from there now, he was...

Robert slowly opened his eyes and gazed around at his surroundings. He was lying on a bed, his head propped up with pillows, in a small, quiet room. A moment later, the head of a middle-aged woman came into his view.

'How are you feeling, Mr Lane?' she asked him professionally, her accent was Scottish.

'Where am I?' Robert asked wearily.

'You are at the medical centre,' the woman said, 'my name is Lillian Tyler, I'm one of the nurses here. I don't think we have ever had the pleasure of meeting one another.'

Robert winced as he tried to sit up, every joint in his body screaming in protest as he did. And then everything came suddenly rushing back to him and he remembered.

'The others! What about the others!'

'Mr Parker and Mrs Sutton are both fine,' the nurse reassured him, 'you have nothing to worry about.'

Robert slumped into the pillows and winced once again from the pain in his joints.

'What happened?' he asked her. 'How did we get off the island?'

'A rescue helicopter was sent as soon as the rain had eased,' she said, straightening the sheets of the bed as she walked around, 'all three of you are extremely lucky to be alive, if you were found any later then you would have died from hypothermia.'

Robert lay there, lost for words. Lillian plumped up his pillows and checked her watch.

'I'll tell Dr Timmons you're awake,' she said pleasantly.

And she left, leaving Robert to look around. It was a handsome room he was in, no doubt his father would have had some sort of influence in its make-up, it seemed to emanate his sense of style and sophistication.

And as Robert interlocked his fingers and closed his eyes, he thought about his mother. She had appeared when he had drifted off to sleep, beautiful and alive and there to greet him. Had he came so close to death? Had his mother given him a second chance to live again? It was hard to remember what she had said to him, it seemed to be trickling from his brain, and the harder he fought to stop it, the quicker it flowed, until only sketchy details remained.

But as he opened his eyes a more pressing matter came to his attention. Although he, Michael and Catherine survived, four people still died on the island, and the media attention over this would be immense. He would have to do all he could to stop the story from being leaked, at least until he planned what he would announce in front of the news cameras.

The bodies of the Spectres had been destroyed, eradicated by the exploding helicopter, the buildings that remained represented nothing out of the ordinary, the classrooms, swimming pools and private sleeping quarters could have been used for the 'rebuilding program' Frank was working on, a place where wounded soldiers would go for rest and recuperation.

Robert began to think deeply, trying all he could to devise a history to this fabricated idea. If thought through properly then this could be the perfect smoke screen.

But within five minutes of him expanding the 'Forgotten Warriors' program, Simon Blackwood arrived, grim faced.

'We have a problem Robert,' he said, 'somebody has leaked the story to the press, they've begun to arrive outside the facility gates.'

Robert cursed under his breath. 'We don't have much time,' he said quickly, 'if I don't deliver a statement within the hour, they'll start thinking I have something to hide, the last thing I need is for them to start digging around.'

He swung his legs out of the bed and hobbled over to the chair in the corner, but before he could pick up his clothes folded neatly over the arm nurse Tyler walked in.

'What are you doing out of bed,' she said, stern faced, the pleasantries of earlier were nonexistent now, 'you need your rest.'

'Nurse Tyler,' Simon began indignantly, 'I don't think you understand the situation we are in, four people are dead and somebody has leaked that to the press. It is paramount that Robert delivers his speech now before pandemonium breaks out there.'

The nurse looked less than impressed.

'Maybe so,' she said quite calmly, 'but that will have to wait, Mr Lane needs his rest. If the press are as eager to know the truth as you claim they are, then they will wait.'

Simon did not make an effort to hide his disgust. 'I think you're forgetting who you are talking to,' he said, his lips curling into a snarl, 'I don't take kindly to being talked down to like that.'

'I know perfectly well who I am talking to, you're Simon Blackwood and you're an ignorant pig!' Simon looked taken aback by the remark, nurse Tyler continued. 'You might think you're something special within the facility, but in this room your say means nothing. Now you,' she looked at Robert, 'get back to bed, and you,' she looked Simon directly in his eyes, 'get out now before I call security.'

Simon looked at Robert, standing by the leather chair, and then to nurse Tyler, who in turn said, 'Well!'

He nodded curtly and left at once.

'Dr Timmons is busy seeing to Mrs Sutton at the moment but he will be along shortly,' nurse Tyler said, 'in the meantime you have a visitor, I have a right to turn her away, but she has been so worried about you, and it wouldn't be fair on her.'

She left the room and a moment later Lisa walked in, clutching a bag of grapes.

'Good morning,' she said, her voice was the most beautiful voice Robert had ever heard, 'how are you feeling?'

'I've felt better,' Robert admitted, raising a smile.

'I believe these are supposed to brighten up your day.'

She put the bag of grapes on the bedside table, sat on the edge of the bed and sighed deeply.

'I feel like I should give you a hug or something,' she said quietly, avoiding Robert's eyes, 'I think I'm still in shock over what had happened ... I came so close to losing you.'

'I'm sorry I put you through that,' replied Robert at once, who had no intention of hurting Lisa.

Lisa chuckled. 'You have no need to apologise,' she said, wiping away the tears from her eyes, 'it's been an emotional twenty-four hours, ignore me, it's just me being silly.'

Robert hobbled over to the bed and sat down next to her, and as he did, Lisa took hold of his hand.

'I don't know what I would have done if I had lost you,' she breathed, 'you mean so much to me, you've been the constant rock in my life.'

Both stared in each other's eyes, and in that moment of becoming reunited, Robert wanted nothing more than to lean forward and kiss Lisa, to wrap his arms around her and press his lips against hers. What he would give to share such a moment.

He would do it now, he would kiss her, tell her everything, regardless of the consequences, if surviving the island had taught him anything it was to appreciate and embrace life, to seize every opportunity that presented itself. But once again fate dealt its cruel hand, and this perfect opportune moment was shattered by Melissa running into the room.

'I thought I told you to stay with David,' Lisa said to her, stern faced.

'But Mommy Uncle Wobert *needs* the card I made,' said Melissa in an almost pleading tone. 'You forgot it.'

She ran over to the bed and jumped onto it, thrusting the folded piece of paper into Robert's hand.

'I drawed this for you Uncle Wobert,' she said, bouncing up and down on the bed, 'do you like it?'

'I love it,' said Robert at once, staring down at the colourful drawing on the front of the handmade card. He opened it and read what Melissa had written.

to my uncle robit,

i hope you get beter soon i have missed you lots and lots and will be hapy wen you come home

love you lots from melissa
xxxxxxx
and mommy xxxxx

'Thank you,' he said, smiling broadly, 'I will treasure it always.'

'Okay Melissa,' said Lisa softly, 'Uncle Robert needs his rest now so we have to go.'

Melissa leaned forward and kissed Robert on the cheek, she then dropped down off the bed and took hold of her mother's hand when she held it out for her.

'I'll come and see you tonight,' Lisa said.

Robert raised a roguish grin. 'I can't wait,' he said.

'Bye Uncle Wobert,' Melissa said, waving to him, 'get better soon.'

'I will,' Robert called out as they left the room.

Now alone, Robert's thoughts were once again on Lisa Anderson, she was the woman he had loved since the moment he laid eyes on her, but she was the woman he could never have, and that fact pained him.

Chapter Twenty-Eight

The Truth behind an Answer

August 14th

'Mommy,' Melissa said, her nose was pressed against the window, 'why are there lots of people standing outside?'

But before Lisa could reply, Melissa, who had turned her head to hear her mother's response, caught something on the television. She jumped off the chair she was standing on and ran over to it.

'Mommy, Mommy,' she said rather excitedly, 'Uncle Wobert's on the television.'

Lisa, who was on the couch with a magazine resting upon her raised knees, swung her legs out and leaned forward. Melissa knelt on the floor.

In the top right hand corner of the screen were the words: *Earlier today*. Robert was standing at a podium somewhere within the CyberTech Defence Systems compound. The podium bore the CyberTech Defence Systems insignia on the front of it. He was talking into six microphones, all of which were positioned so that his voice would be heard clearly.

The screen suddenly switched to a brown eyed brunette, she was sitting behind a news desk.

'I believe we can now go live to our reporter Chris Chapman who is outside the CyberTech Defence Systems facility for us now.' She spun in her chair to look at the screen materialising behind her. *'Chris how do you think the statement went for Robert Lane today?'*

The screen switched again to show a middle-aged man standing in front of the entrance to the facility. He was tall and clean shaven with short dark brown hair. The long black coat he was wearing had only the top button undone.

'Well Andrea,' he began in a professional manner, *'this was obviously an emotional statement delivered by Robert Lane. Let's*

not forget that four people died on the island he had travelled to, among the deceased was pilot Jim Watson who braved the bad weather conditions in an attempt to rescue Mr Lane and his colleagues.'

'Did Mr Lane explain why he travelled to the island in the first place?' the newsreader asked, although the screen did not switch to show her doing so.

'He touched upon it briefly, he explained that his father had bought and expanded the island to use it as a base to develop and test warships. He also went on to say that he wanted to see if he could use it as the centre point for the Nethuns project, the multibillion pound deal to build four revolutionary aircraft carriers for the Royal Navy.'

'He has come under serious scrutiny as of late,' the newsreader said, *'so do you think this statement could be the start of the rebuilding process for him?'*

'Well it has been a turbulent couple of years for him, there can be no denying that, as we all know he lost his broth –'

The screen went dead. Melissa turned her head, her mouth slightly open from the disbelief as she looked at her mother who was holding the television remote control.

'Time for bed,' said Lisa, smiling brightly.

Melissa now knew it was pointless in trying to argue or change her mother's mind. She got to her feet and slowly made her way to the bathroom, trying her best to extend the time before going to bed.

And as Lisa heard the tap running in the bathroom, her bright smile faded. Once again Mark's death had hit her like a brick wall, she sat back into the couch and tried her utmost to subdue the tears welling in her eyes. During Mark's funeral, mourners had offered their condolences, and each one had said that the pain she was feeling would ease over time. The two year anniversary of Mark's death was next month, and the pain she felt on hearing of his death was still as raw as that fateful day.

'I've brushed them, Mommy,' Melissa said, showing her pearly white teeth.

'Well done,' said Lisa. And as she wiped away the small beads of tears her mascara smeared slightly. 'Would you like to have a story read to you tonight?' she asked.

Melissa looked at her mother, wondering what could have possibly upset her. She did not ask though and she simply nodded her head.

'What story?' asked Lisa, who was now on her feet.

'*Rupert Rabbit and Friends* please Mommy,' Melissa said, who was excited from the prospect of having her favourite book read to her.

She ran off into the bedroom, jumped on and climbed into the middle of the king size bed and pulled the covers over her. Lisa walked in a moment later, swinging the small brightly coloured book with a grey rabbit, white owl and green tortoise illustrated on the front in her hand.

She sat next to Melissa and wrapped her arm around her, but before she had even opened the book Melissa looked up.

'Why did daddy die?' she asked.

And as the words resounded around the room, an icy cold shiver ran down Lisa's spine. Why did Mark die? She had asked that exact question herself to her mother, the priest who talked at Mark's funeral and even God. Was it all part of *his* plan? Did her fiancé die so that many others could live? Did she actually believe that anymore? With all the American soldiers dying in South Africa everyday she found it difficult to believe in anything.

But as she sat on the bed, looking down at her daughter, she knew she had to put aside what she felt for the sake of Melissa. What right did she have not telling her what happened on that fateful day, of the bravery her dad showed? She thought for a moment about what she would say.

'Did daddy tell you why he was going away?' she began softly.

Melissa nodded but did not say anything, instead she sucked her thumb.

'Okay, well daddy went to a country called South Africa to stop the terrible war over there, do you know what a war is?'

Melissa nodded and continued to suck her thumb.

'Well, daddy was out one day looking for the bad people when he was killed.'

Melissa pulled her thumb out of her mouth. 'How did daddy die?'

Lisa fought hard to stop the tears welling in her eyes; every one of these questions was like a knife stabbing at her heart. 'Daddy was fighting when he got killed,' she said, her voice breaking slightly from the emotion.

'But why didn't Uncle Wobert stop him from dying?' Melissa asked, a hint of anger could now be heard in her soft, innocent voice.

'Oh Melissa,' Lisa said, through a long sigh, 'uncle Robert *couldn't* stop him from dying.'

'Daddy told me he was going with some friends,' began Melissa, still the anger could be heard in her voice, 'and that's why the bad people weren't going to hurt him. I thought Uncle Wobert was daddy's friend, why didn't he save him?'

And as Melissa told her mother this fact, Lisa, for the very first time since his death was angry at Mark. He had no right to fill Melissa's head with this fairy tale. Had he no idea of the repercussions it would cause? That telling her such things would form a rift between uncle and niece if he died. But as Lisa sighed deeply and pulled Melissa close to her, her heart instantly forgave the man who she loved deeply, he had done what he thought was best.

'What you have to remember Melissa,' Lisa said, kissing her forehead, 'is that Uncle Robert loved your daddy very much. Yes he was his friend, perhaps his best friend, but Uncle Robert isn't a soldier sweetie.'

It seemed that Melissa had never considered this, her expression softened slightly as she looked up at her mother.

'We have a lot to be thankful for Melissa,' Lisa continued, 'Uncle Robert pays a lot of money for you to go to your school, think of all the friends you've made, Abbie, Jessica, Alice, you wouldn't have met them if is wasn't for him. We live in a lovely home and we've been on some wonderful holidays, all because of Uncle Robert.'

Melissa looked down at the book and began to run her finger around the outline of the rabbit.

'What you must never forget,' said Lisa softly, 'is that your daddy was a very brave man and you shouldn't be angry with Uncle Robert.'

She opened the book to the first page and began to read. 'This story begins with a grey rabbit called Rupert...'

A few minutes later Lisa quietly walked out of the bedroom and slowly and carefully closed the door behind her. She had only read five pages of the book before Melissa could no longer keep her eyes open and fell asleep, now in the small hallway, alone, Lisa stood against the wall and slid to the floor.

She had remained strong while answering the questions Melissa wanted to know about Mark's death, but this explanation had brought back so many painful memories that she was no longer strong enough to fight back the tears. She began to sob quietly, but immediately became frustrated in allowing herself to become this emotional wreck.

She wiped away her tears and took long, deep breaths; she could not stay here, in this awful silence, with the painful memories of Mark as her only company. She took a few more moments to try and compose herself, then she stood and walked into the living room to find David closing each of the windows and drawing the curtains.

'David,' she said, 'I need to ask you for a favour.'

*

When Robert looked back he realised that he had very few recollections of the past few days, it was as though they had passed by in a continuous blur. The memories he did have were very painful to him and there was one particular one that was still raw and fresh: the emotional meeting with the widow of pilot Jim Wilson that took place the day after Robert left the CyberTech Defence Systems medical centre.

'I'm so sorry,' Robert had said to Barbara Wilson, who had set out an afternoon tea for his arrival.

'Jim died doing what he loved,' she replied, dabbing away her tears with a tissue, 'he was a man who was born to fly.'

Robert tried to write out a cheque for her, to offer her some sort of compensation for the loss of her husband, but Barbara leaned forward and laid a hand on Robert's, stopping him from writing.

'Your money will never bring my husband back Mr Lane,' she said softly, not meaning any malice in the words. 'I do not blame you for what happened to Jim, you should not feel guilty.'

But it was difficult for him not to; he had defaced the memory of the brave pilot by the lies he had told to the news cameras. Now Robert was sat alone on the couch in his living room, holding the cup of coffee which was gradually growing cooler in his hands. He thought about the island, four days ago he was there, he came close to death and yet he had survived, he was alive. His brother, however, had not shared the same fate as he, he had been shot and killed, he was dead, buried under the earth, his life journey was ended by the Liberators of South Africa, but Robert's was still going.

Of all the times he had thought about suicide, nothing had scared him as much as staring death in the face that day on the island did. The simply truth was that he could control the aspects of his death. He could choose where, when and how, but four days ago that choice was taken from him. His experience on the island had brought into focus how fine a line there was between living and dying, in a blink of an eye everything could have ended.

And in this vulnerable state the painful memories came flooding back. The children on the island, encased in liquid in the glass containers lurked in the back of his mind, they did not appear in front of his eyes, they were just there, tormenting him. William Davies was also there, lurking, the man who had been his godfather, his father's best friend, the man who had tried to kill him so that he could expose the island's dark secrets. Marcus and Derek also tried to kill him, the two bodyguards had been swayed by William's words, all three were killed by the exploding helicopter.

Robert put his now cold coffee on the table, closed his eyes and buried his face in his hands. He tried to push the memories from his mind, tried to lock them away until he was ready to deal with them, but there were so many that were overwhelming his body. He took his face out of his hands and looked over at the complimentary welcome basket resting not far from him on the coffee table.

A small packet of chocolate biscuits, crackers and nuts along with an array of different types of tea, coffee and jam and a small bottle of brandy had all been nestled in the basket. The handwritten tag attached to the handle read: *With compliments, Mr. Lane.*

Only the brandy was left now and Robert was being drawn to it, he wanted to drink it, to numb the overwhelming memories swirling in his mind. He reached over and picked it up, turning it in his hands, staring at the label, at the liquid gurgling inside. He tried to convince himself that drinking this brandy wouldn't hurt; he just needed it to help him relax, to help him numb his thoughts, it would never go back to the way it was before, where the desire for alcohol was all consuming.

He twisted off the metal cap, but before it had reached his lips there was a timid knock at the front door. No doubt it would be Michael, although he had a card for this room and his knock was always strong and powerful. Robert set the brandy down next to the basket, walked over to the door and was surprised to see Lisa standing there when he opened it.

'Hi,' she said, smiling, 'I was just wondering if you wanted to get some dinner?'

'That would be nice,' he said, without even thinking about it.

Robert was hungry but the thought of him and Lisa going out to dinner together made his stomach flutter with sickness. They would be alone, in a romantic setting, this would be their first date and he was already nervous.

'Great,' said Lisa brightly, 'pick me up in an hour?'

'An hour,' replied Robert, who was trying his best not to make an issue of this dinner date, 'are you sure that's enough time for you?'

'Hey, I'm not that bad.' And she tapped him playfully on the arm. 'So pick me up in an hour?'

'I look forward to it,' said Robert calmly, despite Lisa touching his arm like that.

And as she walked back to her room opposite and Robert watched her go, he seemed to fall in love with her all over again, finally the painful memories were no longer tormenting him.

Chapter Twenty-Nine

Their First Date

Michael had been given the night off and could order anything he so wished, compliments of Robert. So tonight he was happy enough just to stay in his room, order the deliciously appealing grilled rump steak with chips and Caesar salad and see what was on the television. David had not been so lucky however, his job for tonight was to look after Melissa, who after being woken when Lisa was getting ready was excited over the prospect of being able to stay up late and couldn't stop jumping on the bed.

Spending an evening with Lisa Anderson, just the two of them was something Robert had wanted ever since falling in love with her. Now, with butterflies in his stomach he stepped out into the sumptuously decorated hallway, closed the door of his room behind him and headed towards her room opposite.

He took his time, checking his breath, rubbing down the arms of his suit jacket and making sure his tie was adjusted and centred, everything would have to be perfect for tonight. And seemingly in no time at all he was standing before her door, knocking three times and waiting patiently.

It seemed to take forever for it to be answered, but when it did, and Robert stared at the woman framed by the doorway, he knew it was worth the wait. Dressed beautifully in a long, dark red dress with matching heels, Lisa's shiny brunette hair was tied up in a French knot which was held into place by two wooden sticks that criss-crossed, her make-up was as always immaculate and her slender fingernails were French tipped.

'See I told you I would only be an hour,' she said, smiling brightly.

'You're beautiful,' said Robert louder than he meant to, and his cheeks began to redden because of it.

'Robert Lane,' said Lisa softly, 'are you blushing?'

'Me, blushing,' said Robert casually, despite his heart racing, 'do you know how hot you get wearing a suit like this.' He grabbed the lapel of his jacket. 'Which, I might add, I look good in.'

'Yes you do,' said Lisa, looking Robert up and down now, 'see, you can look handsome when you make an effort.'

Unable to think of a quick witted response to this, Robert walked backward to the lifts and pressed the button to call it. Lisa closed the door behind her as she followed him.

'Although the insults have been fun,' he said suavely, 'we have a dinner that awaits us. Why else have I gone to so much 'effort'?'

The doors to the elevator opened with a ping and he stepped back to allow Lisa to enter first. They arrived in the lobby a minute or so later, they walked out onto the gleaming floor, said their good evenings to the female receptionist on duty as they passed her and made their way down the short flight of steps and through the double doors.

The Maitre 'D who greeted them at the entrance to the restaurant was tall and dapper, dressed in a tuxedo. He had thick silvery hair which was neatly brushed to one side and warm, welcoming blue eyes.

'Good evening Monsieur Lane,' he said, extending his hand, 'zo glad you are joining us.' He spoke impeccable English but there could be no mistaking the French in his accent.

'Good evening Jean-Claude,' said Robert pleasantly.

And as he extended his hand, Lisa caught a glimpse of the money folded discreetly inside his first two fingers and felt a pang of sadness. Mark would do exactly the same whenever they went to a restaurant, this 'money handshake' as he liked to call it ensured they would get the best treatment, although Robert's celebratory status alone could achieve that without the need for money.

'And who iz zeez lovely vision you 'ave brought wiv you this evening,' Jean-Claude asked, looking at Lisa now.

'Jean-Claude, may I introduce to you Lisa Anderson.'

Jean-Claude bowed his head, took hold of Lisa's hand and kissed the back of it.

'Zee pleasure iz all mine,' he said, still holding Lisa's hand.

He stood straight, smiled at the pair then picked up two burgundy leather-bound binders that were laid flat on the wooden stand by the entrance.

'Zis way please.'

And as he stepped into the restaurant and lead them through, faint whispers drifted to them as they passed countless occupied tables.

'That's not – is that Robert Lane?'
'Vivien – Viv, look who it is.'
'Is that Robert Lane?'
'That's Robert Lane, luv look.'
'Who's that woman he's with?'

Jean-Claude led them to the Capri Rosa room, it was a small, secluded dining room which was separated from the main restaurant by draped velvet curtains. The table – which was set out with cutlery and carefully folded napkins and a tall white candle centre piece – could seat up to ten, however, tonight it would just be the two of them. Jean-Claude offered a seat to Lisa, then to Robert, and once they were both seated he handed them their menus, lit the candle and said, 'Would you like to order your drinks now while you look through your menus?'

'Just a still water for me Jean-Claude,' said Robert, as he opened the menu and began to look through the starter meals.

'Very well zir, and for madam.'

'Still water will be fine,' said Lisa, smiling.

Jean-Claude smiled and said, 'I zhall not be a moment with your drinks,' before hurrying off.

'So this is how the other half lives,' said Lisa admiringly once they were alone.

Robert glanced up from the menu. 'It has its downsides,' he said, raising a slight smile.

Lisa believed it too, Robert was hailed as America's 'golden boy' when he first came to the nation's attention, but as he started to slide into the pit of depression, and began to make rash decisions – most notably his infamous appearance on *Questions & Answers Time* – he suddenly became hated, portrayed as a greedy businessman who had an addiction to sleeping tablets and alcohol. One newspaper printed that he had 'bedded a string of beauties' in a matter of days. None of it was true, even his fondness of alcohol had been greatly exaggerated as Lisa was quick to defend if she heard anything to the contrary.

Jean-Claude arrived with haste, bearing a silvery tray with two large glasses of water placed upon it. He laid the drinks in front of Lisa and Robert, tucked the tray under his arm and said, 'I will be back in one moment to take your orders,' before hurrying off again.

'I don't think I've ever thanked you, have I,' said Lisa as Robert closed his menu having decided what he wanted to order, 'thanked you for everything you have done for Melissa and me.'

Robert drank some of his water; it hydrated his dry throat, he could speak once more. 'It's nothing, really, I'm sure you would have done the same if the roles were reversed.'

Lisa leaned forward and placed her soft hands on top of his; as soon as she did his heart began beating that much faster.

'I just didn't want you thinking that I didn't appreciate what you've done for us.'

'I would never have thought that,' said Robert softly.

If only she knew the truth, if only she knew of the love he felt. He would tell her now, tell her everything, tell her he loved her the moment he had seen her. And so as they sat there, holding each other's hands, staring into each other's eyes, Robert on the verge of telling Lisa everything, Jean-Claude's voice broke this idyllic moment.

'Are we ready to order?'

*

They spoke about everything and anything through the starter and main meal, which were both superb, and as their desserts – chocolate cake with cream drizzled over the top and strawberries cut in half placed around the shape of the plate – were placed in front of Lisa and then Robert, it was he that continued.

'Truth was,' he said, sliding his folk through the cake, 'I always wanted to be an actor. Well I wanted to be an actor ever since I saw the film *The Outback.*'

'Is that the one with Tom Douglas?' said Lisa before dipping one of the half-cut strawberries into the cream and eating it.

'Yeah,' said Robert, delighted, 'Tom Douglas starred as the fiery, weather-beaten bushman who helps an up-and-coming author write her book set in the outback. It's one of those films that I never tire of seeing and it always takes me back to when I was eleven and saw it for the first time.'

He paused to eat another piece of cake.

'Everything seemed so simple back then, you had nothing to worry about, well, apart from the constant worry if a girl liked you or not.'

He chuckled and so did Lisa.

'So why didn't you become an actor then?' she asked, intrigued.

'I had this natural gift for business,' he said, his smile fading, 'when Mark and I were kids we got money for helping around the house, and while Mark spent his money on comic books and video games I saved my money up and started my own little business.'

'Really,' said Lisa smiling, 'I never knew that.'

'Yeah,' said Robert, who couldn't help but grin, 'I made my own lemonade and would sell it to the kids at school at a profit. Anyway my dad showed a great deal of interest in my first business venture, so I think I was destined to follow in his footsteps. Well even if I wasn't I had no other choice.'

He smiled and Lisa knew he was forcing himself to do so, trying to mask the tint of sadness he felt.

'I always envied Mark because of it,' he said, his expression hardening slightly, 'he did what he wanted to do, regardless ... and he always got the girl.'

The final words were spoken aloud unintentionally and Robert immediately regretted saying them, it made him sound resentful about his dead brother. Lisa looked at him, her fine eyebrows raising, puzzled as to why he would say such a thing.

'He was always so popular with everyone,' he said quickly, 'I was always second best in that respect.'

'And which high school did you go to,' said Lisa rhetorically. 'Do you know how many girls at our school had a crush on you? Sophie Green was heartbroken, actually heartbroken when you didn't go to the prom, she wanted you to be her first.'

'Oh,' said Robert quietly, avoiding Lisa's gaze, 'I didn't know that.'

'There are a lot of things you don't know Robert, you were the one all the girls wanted to be with ... except me,' she said, grinning broadly, 'I saw beneath all that suave and sophistication, I knew what you were really like.'

Robert felt like he had hit a brick wall, the girl he loved through high school felt nothing for him, he knew this already but it did not stop his heart from sinking.

'Mark told me everything you used to get up to when you were kids,' she said, eyeing Robert with amusement.

'Don't believe a word of it,' said Robert and Lisa couldn't help but laugh, 'Mark tricked me into thinking it was for the good of the country.'

'So stealing apples from the neighbour's tree when you used to visit your grandma that was for the good of the country?'

'Well of course,' said Robert silkily, 'there was no way that family could've eaten all that fruit, we were helping them out. Think of all the wasps that would have been attracted by it all, and you know what wasps are like, they can be aggressive little buggers, especially when you stand in the way of the apples.'

Lisa couldn't help but chuckle. 'Okay,' she said, 'what about throwing eggs at the windows of old lady Wilson's house?'

'Now that was in retaliation to what she did to my ball,' said Robert in his defence, 'the cantankerous old bag took if off me and burst it when I did nothing wrong, it wasn't my fault her flowers got squashed.'

'Of course it was,' said Lisa, disbelieving, 'you were the one who kicked the ball onto them ... You've got a roguish side to you Robert Lane.'

For a long time, neither one spoke, it wasn't an awkward silence, more a silence from which they could eat the rest of their desserts and finish their drinks.

'Why didn't you go to the prom?' asked Lisa.

Robert dropped his fork onto the plate and wiped his mouth with his napkin. 'The girl I wanted to go with was already going with someone else,' he said quietly, unable to meet Lisa's beautiful brown eyes. 'I just wouldn't have been able to watch her dancing with him.'

Lisa's eyebrows arched with intrigue. 'Who was it?' she enquired. 'It wasn't Chloe Simons, was it? Mark said you had a thing for her.'

It was you, I have loved you ever since the moment I saw you, Robert longed to say, the love he felt had burdened his heart for over twenty years, if only he could tell her, tell her everything.

'Have you enjoyed this evening?' asked Robert softly.

'It's been interesting,' said Lisa, thinking it best not to press the matter further, 'I've seen this whole other side to you.'

'I'm not as extravagant as what people make me out to be.'

Lisa stared at the limited edition Jean-Paul Henry diamond encrusted watch on his right wrist, something that would have cost hundreds of thousands of pounds, and raised her fine eyebrows a fraction. Robert caught hold of the look and immediately spoke in his defence.

'I never bought this,' he said at once, 'it was a gift.'

He unclipped his watch and as he handed it to Lisa their fingers brushed against one another, causing Robert's heart to miss a beat this time.

The watch was surprisingly light in her hands, Lisa turned it over and stared at the writing engraved on the back.

Jean-Paul Henry (the writing curved at the top)
Black Ice Limited Edition 1/25 (it curved at the bottom)

But something was engraved in between the curved words, the letters were small but Lisa managed to make them out.

I'm proud to call you my son. Dad x

Lisa knew Frank had every right to be, she handed the watch back to Robert and said smiling, 'You're a good man Robert Lane, and you're going to make someone very happy one day, I know you will.' She wiped her mouth with her napkin and stood. 'Excuse me I need to go to the rest room.'

Robert stood and watched her go, and as he sat a moment later he couldn't stop the disappointment from crashing over him. Lisa and him would never be, and yet he still couldn't accept that fact. Her heart belonged to Mark, he was her first and only love, they had brought Melissa into the world, they had planned to get married as soon as Mark finished his tour in South Africa and had left the army for good. They were on the verge of starting a whole new life together and a cruel turn of events stopped them from doing so.

Mark Lane was a man Robert idolised, he was everything a brother could be: strong, dependable, a man of great character, and Robert loved him deeply. And yet here he was, having dinner with the woman he would have married had he not given his life for the country he loved deeply. What gave him the right to do so? Mark was dead and buried and here was Robert, just continuing on with his life, as though nothing had happened, a total disregard for what his brother had sacrificed.

And yet – and it seemed cruel to even think it – life moved on whether you wanted it to or not, it had no regard for death. Life did not stop and mourn because you lost a loved one, it carried on as normal.

Jean-Claude arrived with the final bill and Robert paid it in cash, something which he always preferred to do, as well as giving the Maitre 'D a generous tip. He stood, stretched his arms above his head and grabbed his jacket off the back of the chair, which he had taken off earlier in the evening.

And as he carefully folded it over his arm and turned, he saw a young woman standing by the entrance to the secluded area. She looked to be in her late teens but she was strikingly beautiful. Her long, graceful black dress flowed down to her feet, her nails were impeccably filed and painted black and her make-up suited her pale complexion perfectly, but what made her stand out from the rest of the people in the restaurant was her hairstyle.

It was copied off French supermodel Evony Dubois who had wowed catwalk audiences earlier in the year. This woman's hair was jet black and came down to her shoulders, but the tips had been dyed a crimson colour and were flicked outward.

Robert smiled pleasantly at her but before he could open his mouth, she spoke.

'I'm sorry to disturb you Mr Lane,' she said, 'but, well my mum is such a great fan of yours, but she's too scared to ask for your autograph.' She rolled her eyes discreetly at her mother's foolishness. 'So I've been sent to ask you for it.'

Robert couldn't help but smile. 'What's your name?' he asked her.

'It's Kerri, Kerri Summers.'

'Well Kerri Summers, I would like to meet your mother,' he said, much to the young woman's surprise.

'Well – er – yes, right this way then.'

And with that she led him into the main part of the restaurant which was nearly empty now due to the late hour. They headed towards a table where an unsuspecting woman sat, there could be no mistaking that they were mother and daughter.

'Mr Lane,' Kerri said, 'this is my mum, Marie.'

The woman looked up, and there was Robert smiling broadly at her. And in that moment Marie Summers felt an elation she never even knew existed, trembling with excitement she could not stop a nervous laugh from escaping.

'I'm so sorry,' she said at once, her cheeks blushing from the embarrassment, 'I'm just so excited to be meeting you.'

'No need to apologise,' said Robert pleasantly, easing her worries. 'I'm just an ordinary guy ... So are you celebrating anything special?'

'Something like that,' Marie said, a lot calmer now, 'Kerri got accepted into university –'

'We don't know that yet, Mum,' the daughter interjected.

But Marie was having none of it, she shook her head and said at once, 'Of course you're going to get accepted, you're a straight A student.'

'What are you going to study?' Robert asked Kerri.

'Aeronautical engineering,' she said proudly.

Robert nodded his head in agreement. It seemed such an odd choice from a woman with such beauty, and Robert would never have guessed that that was her chosen career path. 'That's an exciting field to get into,' he told her, 'so who would you like to ultimately work for then?'

'Well,' she began slowly and unsurely, 'you probably here this all the time, but I would like to work for you.'

'That's a good choice to make,' said Robert, delighted.

He fumbled inside his jacket pocket and withdrew a pen, then grabbing one of the napkins left on the table he wrote down his CyberTech Defence Systems e-mail address.

'I tell you what,' he said, handing over the napkin, 'when you're accepted at university get in contact, perhaps we can arrange for you to do some work experience.'

Kerri took the napkin and thanked him several times, the shock of it all made her unable to say anymore. Then he took another napkin and wrote: *To Marie, many thanks for the support, Robert Lane.*

Unable to hide her excitement she accepted it with trembling hands and stared down in wonder at what he had written. And as he replaced the pen inside his inner jacket pocket, there was Lisa, smiling brightly and waiting patiently for him by the entrance to the restaurant. Although he always felt humbled meeting fans he could not pass on this opportunity, and so he wished the pair a goodnight and walked towards Lisa.

What he felt for her now was well beyond love, love would never be able to do justice in explaining what he felt for her. And yet having such feelings were futile, their hearts would never become one, this path he was unwittingly on would never lead to happiness, what he felt was absurd and yet he had no control over it, he could not quell his feelings which, he longed to do.

*

'I've really enjoyed tonight,' said Lisa as the doors opened on the elevator and she stepped out.

'I'm glad you have,' Robert said, following her out.

The elevator doors closed with a ping and they both stood, staring at one another.

'Goodnight Robert,' said Lisa.

She leaned towards him and kissed him gently on the cheek. And as she smiled and walked away, Robert brushed his fingers against his face.

'Would you like a cup of coffee?' he asked her.

Lisa turned. 'Coffee would be nice,' she said, 'just give me a minute will you, I just want to check on Melissa, make sure she's okay. I'll meet you in your room.'

Running his room key through the electronic lock, Robert turned the handle and walked in. He dropped his wallet on the small table and laid his jacket over the leather couch next to it as he passed them and walked over to the kettle and filled it with water. And as he clicked it onto boil, there was a timid knock at the door.

'Milk, two sugars, correct?' he asked Lisa after opening the front door.

'Yeah, that's right.'

She sank into the leather couch, removed her shoes and began to massage her aching feet, but as she did she caught hold of Robert's wallet resting on the small table with what looked to be a photograph folded inside of it. She was not one for going through people's private belongings, but her intrigue got the better of her. Glancing over at Robert, who was busy pouring milk into the two teacups, she picked up the wallet and turned it over in her hands. Then, sliding out the photograph slowly and carefully, she unfolded it and instantly felt shocked, unable to comprehend what she was looking at.

The photograph was the last one to be taken of her, Mark and Robert all together. However, Mark had been cut from the middle and the two end pieces had been taped together, showing just her and Robert, cheek to cheek, both smiling, as though they were in love.

Although she felt unsteady on her feet, Lisa nonetheless stood, her mind repeatedly asking why he would do this as she looked over at Robert.

'What's this,' she said surprisingly calm, holding up the photograph.

Robert turned, the smile he had curled upon his lips immediately vanished, replaced by a look of utter horror.

'Why would you do this?' Lisa demanded to know.

'It's – it's not what it looks like,' he stuttered, still reeling.

And he instantly regretted saying the words, it was possibly the worst thing he could have said. *Of course it's what it looks like!*

The kettle suddenly clicked, but Robert did not know or care that it had, so determined he was to explain himself that nothing mattered now. He sighed deeply and stared down at the two teacups, the grounded coffee was beginning to mix with the milk.

'I love you,' he said quietly.

And as soon as he did, the invisible weight that had pressed down on his body for over twenty years lifted.

'You ... love me?' Lisa said, her legs felt terribly wobbly, she had to sit down.

'I've loved you since the moment I set eyes on you,' he said, still staring down at the two cups, 'although I was only a kid and didn't know what it was.'

Questions exploded inside of Lisa's head, but then anger controlled her from that moment.

'That's why you asked Melissa and me to move in with you,' she said, understanding everything now, 'so you could sleep with me the first opportunity you got, that's all you've ever wanted, isn't it.' She looked furious and disgusted. 'ISN'T IT?'

'I would never have dreamed of doing any such thing,' said Robert, hurt that Lisa would even accuse him of such a thing, 'I respect you to much to take advantage. The truth is Mark came and saw me before he went to South Africa, he asked me to look after Melissa and you if anything were to happen to him. I would have done that anyway, not to sleep with you, why would I want my first time to be with a woman who didn't feel the same love I felt for her.'

'Your first time,' Lisa repeated quietly, 'you're ... you're a virgin?'

'Yes,' said Robert, avoiding her eyes.

'You can't be,' said Lisa, stunned, 'what about that Italian woman?'

'She wasn't you,' said Robert quietly, looking up at her now, 'and if I couldn't have you I wouldn't want anyone else. Why would I, you are perfect in every sense of the word, you made me want to give up the alcohol, you made me want to become a better person. I have loved you for as long as I can remember and I will carry on loving you for the rest of my life. My heart will always belong to you.'

Lisa could not speak, she now knew that the love Robert felt for her was far greater than she ever thought possible.

'I don't understand,' she said, finally finding her voice, 'why didn't you say anything – when we were teenagers – why didn't you tell me then?'

'Because I knew you would reject me,' said Robert truthfully, 'your heart belonged to Mark, and even though I loved you – and still love you – very much I loved my brother more.'

There was a long pause, an awkward silence as Robert and Lisa just stared at one another.

'I'm sorry you had to find out like this,' said Robert regretfully, 'I never wanted you to.'

Lisa looked down at the photograph, feeling a pang of sadness. Robert had loved her for what seemed like an eternity, but she did not feel the same, her heart belonged to Mark, and would be until she was reunited with him. And yet what she would give to have one more night with him, to feel his beating heart, to feel his lips against hers, to have him hold her in an embrace. She looked up at Robert, at the one man who could perhaps attain Mark in a spiritual connection. And without saying a word, she walked over to him, her lips millimetres from his.

'Am I supposed to be a grieving war widow for the rest of my life?' she whispered.

She interlocked her fingers with his and slowly pulled his body closer to hers, Robert felt like his heart was going to burst through his chest at any moment. Lisa gently brushed her nose against the dimple in his chin and whispered, 'Make love to me Robert.'

And as Robert closed his eyes and inhaled her soft fragrance, wanting nothing more than to do just that, Mark suddenly appeared in front of him. His older brother, the man who he looked up to, who he idolised, who gave his life so that Robert could ultimately live in a world of peace. And in that moment he couldn't, he couldn't betray him, he couldn't do it to the man he loved.

'I'm sorry,' he said quietly, 'I can't do it to him.'

Lisa let go of his hand and the embarrassment of the rejection came crashing over her. She walked over and picked up her shoes, and was unable to look at Robert as she hurried towards the door.

'You don't know how hard it is for me,' said Robert desperately, 'to see you walk away like this.'

Lisa's hand was on the door handle, but she did not turn it.

'For twenty years I have wanted nothing more than for us to be together. I love you Lisa, my heart will always belong to you no matter what, but I can't betray Mark. I can't betray my brother.'

Lisa turned. And as both she and Robert looked at one another, it was he that felt burning conflictions, should he follow the path in his head or in his heart?

Simply calling Lisa beautiful could never do her justice, she was more than that. And before he knew it, he was walking towards her, driven by passion, lust and love.

Lisa dropped her shoes as Robert wrapped his arms around her waist and pulled her closer. He kissed her deeply, her body rising as they both became lost in the embrace. And as they pulled away and stared deeply at one another once again, Robert felt a sense of hope surging through his body. And without saying a word, Lisa took hold of his hand and led him towards the bedroom.

Closing the door behind them, she slowly pushed him towards the bed. He sat on the edge and watched as Lisa unzipped the back of her red dress, allowing it to fall to the floor.

Robert stared in admiration, in wonder at Lisa, who was wearing nothing more than black laced underwear. He watched as she slowly moved closer, walking in a seductive manner, until she was directly in front of him. She straddled his lap and began to run her fingers through his thick, dark hair.

And as Lisa threw back her hair and closed her eyes, she pictured Mark, just as Robert began to gently then more hungrily cover her in kisses.

Chapter Thirty

Idealism of a Would-Be Terrorist

When meeting Elliott Grant, he appeared to be a pleasant nineteen year old, with high ambitions. But over the past twelve months, his persona had gradually altered. Throughout school, college and university – although he spent only one year there – he was hailed a star student. He was popular with both pupils and teachers, was captain of the local football team and was the first in his family to be accepted into one of the most prestigious universities in the world. Life was going well for him, but one week after his eighteenth birthday, his picturesque life was ripped apart.

Elliott had arrived home after football training to find his mother in the kitchen, head in her hands, crying profusely.

'What's wrong?' he asked, dropping his sports bag by the kitchen door.

'Your father,' she sobbed, 'he's … he's dead.'

Elliott fell to the floor, his legs now unable to support his weight. His father was a soldier, he was strong, he was a leader but with this noble profession came the possibility of him being injured or even killed that simply came with the job. But like many people with loved ones in the military, Elliott always assumed it would happen to someone else, never him.

'It's a mistake,' he said loudly.

His mother shook her head to this, but Elliott didn't believe it. He ran out of the kitchen, and headed up the stairs to his bedroom. He dropped down at his desk, switched on his laptop and waited agonisingly for it to load up. It seemed to take forever for the display background of glamour model Lucy Marsh to appear on the screen. He double clicked on the Internet icon and as soon as the screen appeared, he didn't waste any time in loading up one of the news websites.

As soon as the page loaded up, its main headline announced:

British soldiers killed by American friendly fire.

With his body now numb with the haunting reality that his father had been killed in South Africa, Elliott wasn't aware that he clicked on the headline. The screen changed and the new page loaded up instantly.

The headline was at the top of the page, but it was a picture of the machine, terrorising the South African sky that dominated the entire screen. The caption directly underneath it read:

An American RS-15 Black Raven helicopter flying over Johannesburg, South Africa. It is believed that one is at the centre of the incident.

Without realising it, he was scrolling down, reading the article typed underneath the caption.

An investigation is under way after a British patrol came under attack from an American helicopter. Three soldiers died in the incident which occurred at 9 a.m. local time. The soldiers have yet to be named but their next of kin have been informed. More to follow...

Elliott fell out of the chair and onto the floor. Now on his hands and knees, he couldn't stop his body from shaking.

The media coverage was immense, his father was among the first to be killed from a friendly fire incident in South Africa. The Americans had regularly boasted how they had learnt from their mistakes and friendly fire incidents would now be a thing of the past. How wrong they were.

After the funeral Elliott fell from grace; he left university and returned home, becoming a recluse, spending most of his days in his bedroom, just sitting in front of his computer, curtains drawn and listening to dark, depressing music.

Having a mother who came from a wealthy family certainly had its advantages. Never needing to work, Elliott created the website: *Stop The War In South Africa.* Thousands became members and every one of them printed off the petition and sent it directly to the Prime Minister. But after four months British troops were still there, fighting, dying for a cause people found hard to believe in.

But then something quite unexpected happened one day. Elliott had received a private message from someone who gave no name.

It seems you and I share a common interest (the person had written), *however, that is where our similarities end. I already know that sending petitions off to the Prime Minister will not end the war, you still hold on to that hope.*

If you want people to listen you first have to get their attention. We live in a society in which to gain their attention, you must bring their own little world to a standstill. If you believe the South African war should be ended as much as you say you do, then help us bring the world to a standstill, make it listen.

Everyday for about a week, Elliott read the message over and over but he did not reply. And each time he did, he felt an odd sensation in the pit of his stomach every time he read the words, *help us bring the world to a standstill.*

It was clear that in order to make the world stand still and take notice you would have to do something unimaginable, something so horrific that people had no choice but to listen to what you had to say. But Elliott would never kill innocent men and women in order for his voice to be heard.

But as the weeks and months passed, more and more horrific stories came out of South Africa. Finally Elliott admitted defeat and although this was the last thing he wanted to do, he replied to whomever it was who had sent him the message and they arranged to meet at a café not far from where he lived.

Elliott arrived with great trepidation but felt instantly eased when greeted by the bald headed, dapper dressed man who introduced himself as Charles Piennar. They talked over coffee and breakfast, and although Elliott didn't know it, it was the day that the seed of radicalism was planted in his head. Now, six months on Elliott had become radicalised and was ready to give his life and take others to stop the war in South Africa.

And as darkness began to creep over the quiet house of his mother's, Elliott was alone in his bedroom, sitting in front of his laptop, copying what he had written on a sheet of lined paper.

By tomorrow the world will have changed in ways that not even I could have comprehended (he began to type), *and as this declaration is given to the world's media and read out across the globe, I, Elliott Ethan Grant, have no doubt in my mind that many will question my motives.*

Many will say that the death of my father made me join the militants cause. THIS IS NOT TRUE. I am fighting with the militants because there is a strong injustice in South Africa which needs to be brought to everyone's attention.

The South African war is such a controversial issue and so many people are divided on the matter. Is it right to be in the country? Well if you believe what the Prime Minister has to say, then what we are doing in South Africa is beneficial to the whole world. Written below is an extract from the Prime Minister's last speech.

The campaign in South Africa has been hard and we have sustained heavy losses, but we are winning the war. Most of the South African people support the war and we are working closely with them, building new projects such as homes, roads and schools, we are providing them hope and giving them a brighter future.

I particular like the words: building new projects such as homes, roads and schools. Aren't these the exact things that British planes have destroyed time and time again when searching for the Liberators of South Africa?

And when the Prime Minister states that many of the South African people support the war. The only problem is what other choice do they have? If they fight alongside the militants then they are branded terrorists, if they support the war then their homes, their loved ones, everything that they hold dear to them is destroyed.

The South African war concerns the whole world and it is time for everyone to come together and find a solution to this devastating problem that endangers the lives of men, women and children of South Africa every day. The people that will be demonstrating at Trafalgar Square tomorrow should not be embracing this war, how can they vindicate the senseless butchery towards the people who have done nothing towards them?

As for those who will condemn this well-coordinated attack, you will scrutinise the Trafalgar Square bombings in every possible way. You will not look at the causes which have led the four of us to give our lives for what we believe in: putting an end to this mindless violence. I urge you all not to be so ignorant and arrogant, research the history of this conflict and you will begin to understand.

So what we will be carrying out tomorrow is in response to what has happened in South Africa, I just hope that my family don't think any less of me, but this is something that I have to do. Do not shed any tears for me, I do not fear death; death is something that should be celebrated not feared, and my story will be told and retold for many, many years to come until it becomes legendary.

Elliott finished typing and for a brief moment he stared at the cursor blinking on the screen, then he reread what he had written, set his laptop to standby mode and swivelled round in his chair. He looked around at his room slowly and deliberately, because this would be the last time he would be able to do so.

His bedroom was grand and emanated style and sophistication; handcrafted wardrobe, chest of drawers, bedside cabinet and computer desk made from oak and a chocolate leather king size bed frame with an ultra soft mattress. The framed posters on the beige papered walls were of scenic sunsets and yet there was one that demonstrated his teenage defiance.

And as Elliott stared into the hazel eyes of glamour model Lucy Marsh he couldn't help but chuckle. His mother did not hide her disgust when she walked into his room one day to find the picture of the brunette posing on a bed, topless, secured proudly to the wall. But despite this rebel act he nonetheless had to compromise the nudity and make the poster more 'tasteful' as his mother had said.

And as he stared at the words, *Nudity is nothing more than liberation from your clothes* printed on paper and placed on the glass to hide the bare chest, quite suddenly his room became illuminated from the outside security light streaming in through the gap in the curtains. Elliott stood and walked over to the window, staring down at the silver M6 Coupé BMW rolling to a stop. He narrowed his eyes a fraction when he saw the tall, well-dressed man stepping out of the driver's side of the vehicle and walk around the front to open the passenger's door.

'Oh Edward,' his mother's voice sifted through the window, 'you're such a gentleman.'

Elliott looked at her with deep disgust and as he watched the pair link arms and head towards the front door he could no longer look at them. He closed the gap in the curtains, crossed to the wardrobe and pulled open the doors, he reached for his backpack and unzipped it. And just as he was about to put his clothes in it, he spotted the clear plastic container sitting at the bottom.

Elliott didn't know why he was doing it, why he was lifting the container out of the bag, but he dropped the bag to the floor and he held the container in his hands, becoming transfixed with the ball bearings it housed. There were two hundred or so, all highly polished, all perfectly spherical in shape.

They had an unusual innocence about them, it seemed impossible that something so simple, so pure, so – in some respects – beautiful was going to be a part of something world changing, responsible for many deaths. But before he could begin to question himself on whether this was the right thing to do, Charles's voice began to reverberate inside of his head and he could feel himself drifting back to the conversation he had with him a week after they learnt about the demonstration being held at Trafalgar Square.

'What you must never forget,' Charles had told Elliott when he had raised concerns, *'is that the people who are demonstrating at Trafalgar Square support the war in South Africa, they believe it is a war worth fighting for. But I ask you this Elliott, did any of them offer their condolences to you or your mother when your father died?'*

Elliott shook his head to this.

'Of course not,' Charles continued softly, *'because your father's death meant nothing to them, they do not care about him or you or your mother. It pains me to tell you this Elliott but your father will never be remembered for the courage he showed or the sacrifice he made, he is just a statistic; one of the first to be killed*

by the Americans. And the demonstrators feel it is acceptable for more and more soldiers to die for their country, for them to die in this needless war, don't you see that we must kill them in order to save many...'

Now back in his bedroom Elliott's mind seemed to go into freefall after that moment of reminiscence. His father was a hero, a man with courage, who was brave, who had given his life so that his son and indeed everyone else for that matter could live in a world free from terror and tyranny. But none of this could hide the fact that his father's decaying remains lay under the soil, British soil, the ultimate sacrifice, never knowing that his son was going to be apart of history, never knowing that his son's actions would ultimately free South Africa from the perils of war.

And without realising it tears began to run down his cheeks, he wiped them away as quickly as they had formed and forced himself to fight back this breakdown of emotion. He placed the container carefully back in the bag and began to grab his clothes and folded them neatly over it.

By the time Elliott arrived in the living room he was so angry with his mother that no matter what she said to him he would take it as an insult to him and to his late father. He walked in and found her and Edward drinking wine and laughing on the leather sofa.

'Elliott,' she said pleasantly, wiping away the tears formed by her laughter, 'would you like some wine?'

Elliott stared at Edward, stared at his hand caressing his mother's thigh, and anger began to swell deep within him.

'You bitch,' he said suddenly and sharply, 'dad hasn't been buried for five minutes and here you are already shacking up with him.'

'How dare you talk to your mother like that,' Edward raged, ready to jump to his feet.

'It's okay darling,' Elliott's mother said, gently patting Edward on his leg as he leaned back. She finished off her wine and looked at her son. 'What do you expect me to do Elliott, become a grieving war widow for the rest of my life? The world does not stop because your dad died, it keeps on going, and I know that this sounds harsh but we all have to move on with our lives.'

Elliott stood there and a smile began to form on his lips. 'Goodbye, Mother,' he said plainly.

And that was it, the last conversation he had with her, there would be no last kiss, no last embrace, no kind words offered, and it seemed almost fitting. He would die tomorrow and his mother would remember this moment for the rest of her life, an eternity of torture. And with this pleasing thought he turned and walked out of the room. He picked up his bag which he had dropped by the front door and stepped out into the cool evening air, which began to show the first signs of rain.

And as the droplets became heavier as they fell upon his body as he walked towards his car, Elliott began to laugh in fits of hysteria.

Chapter Thirty-One

Meetings and Plans

Twenty-five minutes had past, Elliott had now calmed down but the rain had not. He indicated and turned left onto a quiet, privately owned road, which was bordered on both sides by high, manicured hedges. In the distance, the extravagant cast-iron gate that had barred his way the last time he visited was now open.

Illuminated by outside spotlights, the home of Charles Piennar stood perfectly alone. All of the downstairs lights were on, twinkling in the long sash windows as wisps of grey smoke spiralled out of the chimneys into the night sky. The others had already arrived.

The gravel crackled underneath the car as Elliott rolled it to a stop next to the stone fountain. Killing the engine, he stepped out into the pouring rain and quickly gathered his things from the boot. Then, with a mixture of excitement and anxiety now beginning to develop in his stomach, he shielded his head against the pounding rain and ran to the front door. He was about to raise his fist and knock, but the door immediately swung open from within.

Charles stood before him, dressed in a pristine three piece charcoal suit. His black loafers were highly polished and his blue tie was centred and tied perfectly. He stepped aside at once to allow Elliott to enter.

'I have lived here for two years,' he said, removing Elliott's soaking coat from his back, 'but I shall never get used to this dreadful weather of yours.'

He stared out at the rain pounding off the gravel and smiled to himself, not even this miserable weather could dampen his spirits this evening. He closed the door and turned around.

'The others are already enjoying the food I have laid out for them, please go along and help yourself, I will be with you shortly.'

Charles hung Elliott's coat on the stand and headed for the kitchen. Elliott ran a hand through his long wet hair, took a long deep breath and walked towards the double set of doors which led into the dining room. Dingane, Limpho, Thaba, Mosa, Mamello, Mandisa, Kajiso, Uuka, and Rupa were, as Charles said, enjoying the food and drink that had been laid out on two long side tables.

And as Elliott greeted those he passed, he stopped by the table and looked at Rupa, who was busy chatting to Mamello and Mandisa. She glanced over at him, smiled, then quickly went back to the conversation. The relationship they now had had quickly blossomed after Elliott had taken Rupa home on that rainy evening, hard to believe it was over six weeks ago. A few days later they met at a small coffee shop and just talked about anything and everything and both were surprised over how much they had in common; they had the same taste in music, films and books.

And after that, they became inseparable, spending every day together, both knew that what they felt towards one another was more than just friendship. They knew that their relationship wouldn't last long but neither cared, they would live for now.

And as Elliott began to walk alongside the table, staring down at the various food laid out, he wondered if he actually had fallen in love with her. He had never been in love before so wasn't really sure what it was all about. All he knew was that he couldn't stop thinking about her when he wasn't with her, he would get butterflies every time he saw her and when they kissed, it was like a thousand fireworks exploding in the sky, spectacular and unforgettable.

The more he thought about it as he filled his plate with sausage rolls, canapés, vol-au-vents, chicken pieces and sandwiches, the more he began to smile. He *was* in love with her and this realisation felt wonderful.

'You made it then,' a soft voice said excitedly.

Elliott had just put three chicken and stuffing sandwiches on his plate, he looked around and saw Rupa standing there, dressed in a black sequined top and plain black trousers, looking beautiful as always. She stared at his wet hair, frowning slightly.

'Is it raining outside?' she asked, trying her best to remain straight faced.

'This hairstyle is going to be all the craze,' he said casually, 'I'm going to call it the typical English weather look.'

'I don't think it'll catch on somehow,' said Rupa as she tucked the long strands of blond hair behind his ear.

'Something this radical takes time to be accepted, but you'll see, this time next year.'

Rupa chuckled softly and took a step closer, her lips were millimetres from Elliott's as she stared deep into his blue eyes.

'Your hair looks ridiculous,' she whispered.

And before Elliott could say a word, she kissed him on the lips, much to the delight of onlookers who whistled and clapped. The pair broke apart, and embarrassed by the sudden attention, Rupa took hold of Elliott's hand and led him out of the room.

'I was just wondering,' she said, her voice seemed dry as she spoke the words, 'well what I mean to say is that seeing this is our last night together, I was wondering – well hoping that you want to sleep with me tonight.'

Elliott nearly dropped his plate; this was totally unexpected. He looked at Rupa totally speechless; she seemed to be getting redder by the second.

'It doesn't matter,' she stuttered and turned away, heading for the door, 'it was a stupid idea anyway.'

'I would love to,' said Elliott suddenly.

Rupa turned and looked at him again, her beaming smile lit up the entire hallway.

'Although,' Elliott admitted, 'I've never *been* with a woman, if you know what I mean.'

Saying this made him feel uncomfortable, as though it was something to be ashamed of, but Rupa stepped closer to him and wrapped her slender arms around his waist.

'It's okay,' she softly said, 'it's nothing to be embarrassed about, I think it's sweet.' She gave him a peck on the cheek and whispered in his ear, 'I haven't either.'

Elliott began to chuckle and as Rupa realised what she had just said, she tapped him playfully on the arm.

'You know what I mean,' she said, and she began to laugh too.

Elliott smiled, 'Yeah I know what you mean,' he said.

The pair were no longer laughing now. Both looked at one another, both knowing that this would be the last night they would be alive, and both happy that they would be spending it with one another.

A moment later Charles appeared, glasses clinking as he carried a crate filled with cans of beer and lager, bottles of champagne and various wines and spirits.

'Shall we get this party started?' he asked the pair, his eyes twinkling.

*

It was nearing eleven o'clock when the last of the food had been cleared from the table. Now gathered on the leather sofas, Charles Piennar stood in front of the dwindling open fire with a glass of water in his hand.

'I just want to say a few words before we retreat up to bed,' he said, his voice, despite the late hour, was still deep and powerful. 'Many years ago racial segregation divided our country, for those of you who were lucky enough not to live through it, the aim of apartheid was to maintain white domination while extending racial separation. Those who fought against the regime were branded terrorists; many were jailed, many were tortured to death.' His voice broke slightly from his reminiscing. 'But as soon as the apartheid rule was abolished those who fought were no longer regarded as terrorists, they were hailed as the heroes and patriots who had given South Africa a new hope.'

He slid his hand in his trouser pocket and began to pace up and down in front of the fire, staring down at the water in his glass as the people sat before him began nodding their heads in agreement.

'By tomorrow evening the world will have branded *us* as terrorists,' he continued, a tone of disappointment could be heard in his voice, 'there will be no escaping that. But once we have won the war in South Africa, in time *we* will be regarded as liberators, and those who give their lives for the cause tomorrow will be hailed as patriots of South Africa.'

Elliott, Rupa, Kajiso and Limpho all smiled with delight, their deaths would not be in vain; they were going to change the course of the South African war.

'What you will carry out tomorrow will be told and retold for the years that follow our liberation. Tomorrow will be the day that ended the war in South Africa.'

He stopped and raised his glass towards the four.

'For tomorrow's victory,' he said passionately.

'For tomorrow's victory,' the rest repeated.

And in unison they all drank the contents of their glasses in one. The water would flush the alcohol from their bodies, hydrating them for tomorrow's day of importance.

'Now everybody get some rest,' Charles said, his black eyes seemed to glisten in the lights, 'tomorrow we are going to change the world.'

Chapter Thirty-Two

The Trafalgar Square Message

August 15th

Robert awoke slowly, and for a fraction of a moment he wondered whether last night – the best of his life without doubt – had really happened. He was lying on his side near the edge of the bed, he could see his clothes which had been thrown to the floor in the heat of passion, but Lisa's ... Lisa's were nowhere to be seen.

He could not bring himself to roll over, to have the disappointment crash over him, he would just rather lay there in blissful ignorance. But as the minutes passed, more of him needed to know, had Lisa slept next to him throughout the night, or had this first experience been so awful for her that she had to leave as soon as he had fallen asleep? And so he rolled over, half expecting, half not expecting to see the beautiful brown eyes of Lisa Anderson gazing back at him, but no eyes met him, that side of the bed was empty and looked to have not been slept in.

The golden dials on his Jean-Paul Henry watch read: *6:55 a.m.,* before Robert sat up and swung his legs out. The deep-piled carpet felt soft underfoot as he walked across the room to the dressing gown hanging over the chair which stood in the corner. Throwing it over his shoulders, he glanced at the empty bed and felt his heart sink, had he been that bad that Lisa couldn't have brought herself to sleep next to him? But then, something sudden and quite unexpected happened. The toilet flushed in the en suite bathroom, and a moment later water could be heard coming from the taps.

Robert turned sharply and watched as Lisa walked out of the bathroom, switching off the light as she went.

'Good morning,' she said, smiling.

Lisa was wearing different clothes to those she had on last night, her hair was shiny and immaculately brushed and her make-up was flawless, she looked even more beautiful if that was at all possible. Robert just stood there, lips slightly parted but no words came out.

'I'm sorry that I had to leave you,' said Lisa, and she seemed to mean it, 'I didn't want Melissa waking up without me being there.'

Robert was nodding his head, but still he couldn't find the words, so elated he was to see Lisa standing there.

'When I came back you were still asleep,' she said, slowly moving towards him, 'you looked so peaceful, I just didn't want to wake you.'

Robert had met and greeted some of the most powerful and richest people in the world, but he was so taken aback with what Lisa had just told him, he said quickly 'you should of,' before thinking it over first.

Lisa smiled and Robert did too as he walked towards her. His eyes gazed deeply into hers as he put his arms around her slender waist.

'Last night,' he whispered, his lips only millimetres from hers, 'was the best in my life, thank you so much.'

He kissed her passionately, and Lisa fought hard against the desire to pull away.

'I'm going to have a quick shower,' he said, 'and then we'll get some breakfast, sound a good idea?'

Lisa nodded.

Kissing her lips once again Robert began to hum his favourite song as he walked into the bathroom and closed the door behind him.

Now alone, Lisa stared at the unmade bed, and as she did the night's events came rushing back. It was unbearable for her and she wanted nothing more than to leave this room, she turned quickly and hurried towards the door. She stepped into the hallway, trying all she could not to think about what she had done with the brother of the man she loved. But in this silence it was all she could think about.

'It was a mistake,' she kept whispering to herself as she clenched her fists.

As soon as Robert had fallen asleep after they had sex – for Lisa it was not love, she did not love Robert, she had foolishly thought that she would somehow achieve a spiritual connection with Mark if she had slept with Robert – she left him and returned to her suite. With Melissa fast asleep and oblivious to all that went on, Lisa hurried into the bathroom, quickly undressed and slid the glass doors around her in the walk in shower.

But the powerful jets of water did not cleanse her body, and no matter how many times she washed her skin, she could not get rid of the dirty feeling she felt. And a moment later she slid to the floor, tucked her knees underneath her chin and could not stop herself from crying.

Now in the hallway, Lisa could not stay there a moment longer, to have this unimaginable guilt and heartache pressing down on her entire body. But before she could leave, the front door opened and Michael walked in with a newspaper tucked under his arm.

'Good morning Miss Anderson,' he said, smiling, although somewhat surprised.

Lisa froze, staring at the man by the door, at the man who had fought alongside Mark in the South African war, at the man who Mark had died trying to pull to safety.

'Last night was a mistake,' she said quickly and frantically.

And as soon as she said the words Michael Parker understood everything.

'You don't have to explain yourself to me,' he said mechanically, 'I'm just a bodyguard.'

He walked into the sitting room and dropped the newspaper onto the coffee table. And yet despite this, Lisa felt a need to and she hurried after him.

'You don't understand,' she said with haste, 'he told me he loved me, I was caught up in the moment – it was a mistake what we did, I don't love him, he means nothing to me.'

'If what you say is true,' began Michael, adjusting the blinds to allow the morning sun to stream through, 'shouldn't you be telling Mr Lane that?'

'I can't' said Lisa at once, shaking her head, 'it'll break his heart, I just can't do that to him.'

'And lying to him won't when he finds out,' said Michael, looking at her now, 'because he will find out sooner or later.'

Lisa didn't answer this; instead she sat on the leather couch and buried her head in her hands.

'Listen,' Michael said kneeling, his voice was a lot softer now , 'regardless of your reasons not to tell him, you know what the right thing to do is, you owe him that.'

Lisa took her head out of her hands and looked at him through her red and puffy eyes.

'I just wanted to be with Mark,' she said quietly, 'I miss him so much, I just want this pain to stop.'

And then something quite strange happened. Michael put his arms around Lisa and hugged her.

'The pain will ease over time,' he whispered.

And they just stayed like that, Michael kneeling, Lisa sitting, both happy in this embrace, both knowing that they had spoken only on odd occasions, but both knowing that it didn't matter now.

*

A sumptuous breakfast was created by the chef and was wheeled into the dining room by the butler and placed in front of Robert, Lisa and then Melissa. Sitting at the opposite side of the table to him, Robert looked up at Lisa every so often and smiled. Lisa smiled back although this was the last thing she wanted to do, she wanted to tell him everything, she wanted to tell him that last night meant nothing to her, she wanted to tell him that what they had done was a mistake. She wanted to tell him all these things and yet she could not bring herself to do so, she could not break his heart like that.

'How's your French toast?' Robert asked her.

'Fine, thank you,' she said wearily.

'My French toast is weally yummy Uncle Wobert,' said Melissa, her mouth full of food.

'Ah brilliant Melissa,' said Robert, smiling broadly.

Lisa leaned inwards towards Melissa.

'What have I said to you about talking with your mouth full,' she said sharply.

'That I'm not to do it,' said Melissa quietly. 'Sorry Mommy.'

They ate the rest of their breakfast in silence, which was unbearable for Lisa. The guilt bearing down on her was so intense that she wanted to scream.

'Melissa,' she said, once the table had been cleared by the butler, 'I want you to pick out the clothes you want to wear today.'

'I'm going to wear my Rupert Rabbit clothes today, Mommy,' said Melissa, smiling brightly.

'You can't,' said Lisa at once, 'they're too dirty for you to wear today.'

'Ah please, Mommy.'

'MELISSA,' Lisa retorted, startling Robert, 'just do what you're told.'

'Don't shout at me please, Mommy,' Melissa said quietly and tearfully.

'I won't ask you again.'

Unable to stop the tears from rolling down her cheeks, Melissa dropped off her chair and cried as she disappeared out of the room. The moment she'd gone, Lisa buried her face in her hands. As well as feeling terrible over last night's events she now felt guilty that she'd snapped at her daughter.

'What's the matter?' Robert asked her softly.

Lisa took her face out of her hands and looked at Robert. She would somehow summon the courage and tell him everything.

'Last night,' she breathed, 'it…'

Meant nothing…

Was a mistake…

Shouldn't have happened…

'…really meant a lot to me.'

Robert beamed brightly. 'It meant a lot to me too,' he said, 'I'm just so happy that my first time was with you.'

Lisa smiled, although deep within her heart sank. This whole moment was unbearable for her, she could not continue this lie, she would tell Robert everything here and now. Something deep within gave her the courage to do so, and she looked at him now, knowing what she was about to say would break his heart but knowing it was best for her to do so.

But before she could say a word there was a loud double knock at the door and Michael walked in a moment later, his hand covering the mouthpiece of the cordless telephone.

'Sorry to disturb you Mr Lane,' he said, 'but there is a Samuel Potter waiting downstairs wanting to meet with you.'

'Samuel Potter,' repeated Robert, looking puzzled.

The only Samuel Potter he knew was the activist who had publicly opposed the idea of CyberTech Defence Systems facility in Britain. Surely it could not be him. Robert drank the rest of his coffee, wiped his mouth with his napkin and took the phone off Michael.

'Hello ... yes speaking...' he said, walking out of the room.

Michael stood for a moment longer, looking at Lisa who could only shake her head. He didn't say a word after that, he nodded and left the dining room.

Now alone, Lisa stared down at her lap and sighed deeply.

'I'm sorry Mark,' she whispered.

But the apology did nothing, it did not ease her heartache or anguish and in that instant she knew. She knew that no matter how many times she said sorry it would never alter the fact that she had slept with Robert. She had betrayed Mark and would have to live with that for the rest of her life.

*

Samuel Potter was a man who fought for what he believed in, regardless of the consequences it would pose. He had been at the heart of protests and demonstrations for the past forty years and he was also the man who Frank Lane had so elegantly put it once, *'the constant pain in my ass'*.

When CyberTech Defence Systems began to grow and flourish, Samuel was quick to announce to the world that Frank Lane and the rest of his 'cronies' were nothing more than greedy businessmen who prospered on death and destruction. And when the company reached the shores of the United Kingdom, Samuel organised a mass protest and held a sixty hour sit-in outside the proposed building site. The protest was to no avail and Samuel was subsequently arrested with countless others.

And yet despite his mammoth reputation and the fact that Robert had never met the man in person, he was nothing like what he imagined him to be. The man walking into the sitting room was short and frail-looking with long white hair tied in a ponytail and slimline glasses perched in front of a set of green eyes, nothing like the man pictured in newspapers, magazines and on the television.

'Mr Lane,' he greeted Robert cheerily as he shook his hand. He took a step back and looked directly into his hazel eyes. 'Oh yes,' he beamed, 'you've definitely got the look of Margaret alright ... a remarkable woman your mother was, I'm afraid to say that I only had the pleasure of meeting her the once, however, she left a lasting impression on me.'

Robert smiled, although he was unsure about this larger than life character standing before him.

'Would you like something to drink Mr Potter,' he said, offering him one of the couches.

'My dear boy no need for formalities,' said Samuel at once, 'please, call me Samuel ... and yes, a nice cup of tea would do wonders for me.'

The butler on duty clicked on the kettle and put a teapot, two teacups, a jug of milk and a bowl of sugar cubes onto a silver tray. Once the water had boiled, he filled up the ceramic teapot and carried the tray over to the coffee table and set it down. Nodding courteously at the pair, the butler left the room to allow Robert and Samuel to talk in private.

'So what can I do for you Samuel?' asked Robert, adding milk and pouring tea into his cup.

'Well first of all,' Samuel began, adding sugar cubes to his tea, 'I would like to take this opportunity to say how sorry I am to hear about what had happened on the island, ghastly business that was.'

Robert accepted the offer of condolence, although he was transfixed by the amount of sugar Samuel was putting into his tea.

'And I suppose with all that going on in your life,' continued Samuel, still adding the sugar cubes, 'you are unaware of the protest being held at Trafalgar Square today in regards to the South African conflict.'

Robert was about to take a sip of his tea but reconsidered, instead he looked Samuel straight in the eyes. 'With all due respect Mr Potter,' he said in a scornful tone, 'if you are protesting over the South Af –'

'No, no, my dear boy,' interjected Samuel merrily, 'it seems that we have come to a misunderstanding, I very much believe in the South African war. I will admit that your father and I had our differences, however, I would never feel it inappropriate to disrespect the ultimate sacrifice his brave son made. The reason for the protest is to make known the disgust we hold towards our government, they have sent our brave men and women to fight in South Africa without the resources they need to do the job properly. How can a builder build a house if he has not got the right tools to do it?'

He paused a moment to stir his tea, then rested the spoon by the sugar bowl.

'My mother, God rest her soul, taught me three things,' said Samuel, he took a sip of his unimaginably sweet tea and smacked his lips together in appreciation of its taste, Robert grimaced, 'never speak ill of the dead, always fight for what you believe in and always admit when you are wrong.'

He leaned forward and rested his teacup on the glass table.

'Your father and I had little respect for one another,' he said, 'and I'm not going to sit here and tell you a fairytale that we were the best of friends. What I am going to do however, is swallow my pride and ask you for your help.'

Robert eyed the man sitting opposite him with great intrigue.

'I've been organising protests and demonstrations for forty years now, but I'm not as young as I used to be. It's a young man's game really and my wife has been pestering me for some time now to give it all up. Today's protest at Trafalgar Square will be my last and as you can understand I want it to be memorable, and what better way to achieve this than to have the most famous man in the world there ... I know all about the unfair publicity you have received over the years, perhaps this could be the start of a new chapter for you.'

Robert had never thought he would finally have the chance to re-launch himself into the public eye. Finally this was the opportunity he had been longing for.

'Will it be televised?' he asked.

'Of course,' said Samuel smiling, 'I wouldn't have it any other way. Accept the proposed offer Mr Lane and you my friend will become a part of history.'

Robert smiled and extended his hand. 'Well Samuel,' he said, 'how can I refuse such an offer?'

Samuel began to laugh as he shook his hand. 'Mr Lane, this is going to be one hell of a day.'

At that exact moment many miles away, the mother of Elliott Grant was reeling in horror, screaming for Edward, who was running up the stairs taking two at a time. She had just come across what her son had written on his laptop.

Chapter Thirty-Three

The Flaw in the Scheme

Despite Michael continually raising concerns over Robert's safety and security, they nonetheless arrived at the giant stage which had been constructed within Trafalgar Square.

'Mr Lane,' Samuel called, 'so glad you made it.'

'I wouldn't have missed this for the world,' Robert smiled. 'May I introduce to you my dear friend Lisa Anderson and her daughter Melissa.'

Melissa smiled and waved when Samuel greeted her and Lisa.

'Now if you will excuse me Mr Lane,' said Samuel pleasantly, 'I shall be just one moment.'

And he walked off into the bustling crowd of technicians, security staff, PR officials and all others involved in the mass demonstration. The noise from the waiting protesters was electrifying, unimaginable, on the same par as fans waiting at a concert for their favourite artist to appear on stage.

'Are you nervous?' Lisa asked who was holding Melissa in her arms.

'It's eight thousand people,' said Robert, sounding braver than he actually was, 'I've never talked in front of this many before.' He smiled faintly. 'I suppose there's a first time for everything.'

'You'll be great,' Lisa said.

But the reassuring smile which accompanied many of Lisa's, *'You'll be fine'*, *'You'll be great'*, *'Don't worry'*, never came. The smile that she gave him seemed to be forced; as though this was the one thing she was unable to do naturally.

'Is everything okay?' he asked. 'You don't seem yourself.'

Lisa quickly looked at Michael, who was looking at her now. The look he gave her was one that suggested that this was neither the time nor the place to explain everything to Robert. But he was wrong. Lisa could not keep on pretending that last night meant something to her, she had slept with Robert in the hope that she would have had some sort of spiritual connection with Mark. She did not however, and although telling this to Robert would hurt him deeply it was best for him to know.

'Last night,' she began quietly.

But before she could admit her guilt, a casually dressed man wearing a headset strolled over to them. He was tall, with spiked blond tipped hair, a designer goatee and slim designer sunglasses, which did look odd on him, because the sun was hidden behind a mass of clouds.

'Mr Lane,' he interrupted, 'a quick word with you please.'

The timing couldn't have come at a worse time. With deep frustration, he nevertheless smiled at Lisa and said, 'Hold onto that thought.'

He followed the man as he headed towards Samuel Potter and the three grouped together.

'Okay this is what's going to happen,' the man began quickly, 'Sam, you're going to go on stage first, get the crowd warmed up, after you've ran through your speech, come off and Mr Lane it'll be your time to shine.' He glanced at his watch. 'We're a little behind schedule, so you'll have to keep it brief.' He touched his fingers to the earphones of his headset. 'Okay Sam you're up now, get yourself over to Kimberly and she'll get you sorted with a microphone, good luck gentlemen.' He walked off quickly.

Samuel extended his hand to Robert, 'Good luck, Mr Lane,' he said pleasantly.

He slowly walked up the short flight of steps, and once he was handed a microphone he hobbled onto the stage, much to the delight of the eight thousand strong protestors. The noise was unimaginably deafening, Melissa, who was startled by the sudden uproar, covered her ears with the palms of her hands, even Robert who was standing by the steps Samuel had just walked up was surprised by the reception.

Over a minute had passed before the crowd fell silent. Samuel Potter stood directly in the middle of the stage, feeling immensely proud, as he looked down at the men and women who were hanging on his every word.

'Ladies and gentlemen,' he said, holding the microphone close, 'welcome to Trafalgar Square.'

Once again the noise was deafening; cheers, screams and swearing thundered across Trafalgar Square. Every man, woman and child knew that they were going to be a part of history and each gave it their all.

'We all know why we are here today,' Samuel continued, he held up his hand and the entire crowd fell silent once again, 'we are here because our Prime Minister, a one Mr Thomas Gordon and his Cabinet have sent eleven thousand of our men and women over to South Africa in an attempt to put an end to the violence occurring in the country.'

He slowly began to pace back and forth on the stage.

'We are not here to protest against the war, on the contrary, we all agree with the decision, we all believe in the South African cause, don't we?'

His response came; the entire crowd erupted once again in cheers and claps, with every man and woman agreeing with him.

'Yes, yes we all believe in the South African cause, our forces are doing an excellent job over there, providing the people with much needed hope. But there is something that is troubling me, when the news of Zuberi Jacobs's death reached us, Thomas Gordon was quick to announce that the war was effectively over and British forces would be returning home within a year.'

He stopped and stared out at the crowd.

'The one year anniversary of that statement is fast approaching, and yet our brave men and women are still in South Africa, they are still fighting, they are still dying, so much for the South Africa war being over, and so much for our troops coming home within a year...'

And as Samuel continued his speech, Robert was still standing by the steps, he looked over to where Lisa was standing. She was talking to Melissa, who she still held in her arms, but she looked over and their eyes met. She smiled in hope of reassurance, but it was a smile that had a hint of sadness, she looked away a moment later but Robert still stared at her, a horrible thought now beginning to creep into his mind, infecting the wonderful thoughts he had of last night. Perhaps last night meant more to him than it did to her. To him they had made love, but maybe it was just sex to Lisa, meaningless, perhaps she did it out of pity, knowing how he felt about her.

He looked away and bowed his head, closing his eyes; he would have to know how she felt. He would ask her now; how could he go on stage with this uncertainty hanging over him? He opened his eyes, but before he could turn, Samuel Potter's voice resounded throughout the back of the stage; his speech was coming to an end.

'Now ladies and gentlemen, I have a very special guest with me today. A lot of you will wonder why I invited him to talk on this stage; well I believe he hasn't been given a chance to tell his side of things. So people do not prejudge him, just listen to what he has to say.'

Samuel hobbled off the stage and down the flight of steps, to an eruption of claps, whistles and shouts.

'You'll be fine, Mr Lane,' he said to Robert with a wink as he passed him the microphone.

Although this was the last thing he wanted, he would have to wait before he could ask Lisa how she felt. He took a long, deep breath and began his walk up the narrow, makeshift staircase. He arrived on the stage, his heartbeat increasing with every step he took, he gripped the microphone tight with both hands it gave him a sense of reassurance doing so. The crowd had fallen eerily quiet, Robert stared out, looking out at the different faces all of which were displaying nothing but shock at the sight of this 'special' guest.

'I received a phone call this morning,' he began, his throat had become completely dry, 'and it was Samuel Potter. He wanted to know if I was willing to come here today and speak to you all, to have my say.'

He started to walk the entire length on the stage, back and forth, staring down at his shoes as he went.

'I didn't have to think about accepting the offer, it was a chance to become a part of history, to become a part of this mass demonstration. But what do you do before you arrive? Do you write your speech down, or do you talk directly from your heart? There is a risk from doing either, if reading something you have written, then you can be accused of being robotic, if you talk from your heart then the immense pressure you are under to talk in front of such a large a crowd can make you forget important things.'

He stopped directly in the middle of the stage and stared out at the crowd once again.

'Ladies and gentlemen I choose to talk directly from the heart, fully aware that there is a risk of doing so.'

He resumed his pacing up and down the stage, and as he approached the side he appeared on he saw a woman standing at the top of the stairs. She was holding up two of her fingers, he had two minutes to talk to the crowd.

So as Robert continued to talk, three figures carrying rucksacks on their backs walked swiftly around the outside of the crowd.

'We must give Elliott more time,' said Rupa quietly, 'I know he will be here soon.'

Before Elliott, Rupa, Kajiso and Limpho had departed Charles's home they were told not to travel together, they had to travel to Trafalgar Square alone, it looked less suspicious that way. But because of this the three were unaware that Elliott had been arrested by the police twenty minutes ago.

Limpho checked his watch, the digital numbers read: *13:24:58*

'We do not have time,' he said quickly, 'we have to get into our positions.'

Rupa's brown eyes glistened from the tears forming. She had spent the most wonderful night with Elliott; they had made love and fell asleep in each other's arms. It seemed the perfect way to spend their last night together.

'Come on,' Limpho pressed, 'we have less than one minute.'

Rupa looked hopefully among the crowd, Elliott was among them, she knew he was, he would be walking towards her any moment now.

'Rupa,' Limpho said, grabbing her violently by the arm, 'get in your position, NOW!'

She quickly wiped away her tears and hurried into the crowd, pushing past people as she went.

'Ladies and gentlemen,' said Robert, still pacing up and down on the stage, 'my brother, Mark Richard Lane, gave his life for the South African war, he fought bravely and he died a hero. From that moment the war in South Africa became a personal matter to me, I had immense wealth and power but none of this could save him.' His voice shook slightly from the emotional reminiscence. 'All I could do was make sure that all of the South African Saviours had the best equipment available to them, it was no longer about profits, it was making sure that the war in South Africa could be won, it was making sure that no more lives were going to be lost. Impossible I know, death is always an inevitability in war but I had to do all I could –'

A terrible, bloodcurdling shriek stopped him finishing the sentence. He looked out among the crowd, wondering who had made such a sound. Many of the demonstrators were turning their heads, realising that something unexpected had just transpired. And then a circular gap began to form, the demonstrators stepping back from the middle-aged African man carrying a backpack.

With a terrible smile forming on his lips, he threw his head back and looked to the sky.

'FOR THOSE OF YOU WHO SUPPORT THE MURDER AND DESTRUCTION IN SOUTH AFRICA,' he screamed as loud as his throat would allow, 'THE BROTHERHOOD OF SAKARABRU SEND YOU THIS MESSAGE.'

He began to laugh, a laugh filled with insanity before he exploded into a ball of flames and smoke. The noise was ear deafening and those stood around the man were killed instantly, their bodies torn and mutilated by the energy from the bomb.

Everything around Robert seemed to slow and go hazy and like many others he instinctively dropped to the floor. And then fear and panic and confusion suddenly rippled out from where the man had took his life. And the survivors of the bombing began to run and clamber over any security fence which barred their way.

'Lisa,' whispered Robert.

He scrambled up from the wooden floor but before he could get off the stage he was forced to the floor by the fleeing crowd.

'LISA!' he cried out, 'LISA!'

And as his body was stood on repeatedly as people clambered over him, he had no way of knowing if Lisa was safe, he tried to get to his feet but more and more people obstructed him, not caring or perhaps not knowing he was under them. And then quite suddenly a powerful hand gripped his and he was pulled to his feet.

'I've got you Mr Lane,' said Michael, sounding calmer than he actually was.

'I have to get to Lisa,' Robert said dazed and disorientated, his face and hands bloodied and beginning to bruise.

'They'll be safe,' said Michael still trying to remain calm, 'David won't let anything happen to them. I must get you out of here.'

But before Michael could seize his arm, Robert jumped off the stage and over the metal barrier and ran into the petrified demonstrators. Men and women, young and old, raced in all directions, and as he pushed past them and having no idea where he was going or what he was doing, a short portly man with a thick mane of hair crashed into him and the pair fell to the floor.

Dazed and disorientated, Robert sat up and everything around him slowed once again. He looked through the mass of people and with a sudden surge of horror rising from the pit of his stomach his eyes focused on the top of the stairs which led to the National Gallery. An African man stood there and despite the noise going on all around, his hysterical scream reached the ears of Robert. He threw his head back and as Robert searched desperately, he saw Lisa and David, who was carrying Melissa close to his chest, and they were heading towards the stairs.

'LISA!' Robert screamed, 'LISA, LISA! NOOOOOOOOOOOOO.'

But the words could not be heard from the panic and fear and the African man was suddenly consumed in a ball of smoke, fire and noise, enveloping and killing all those around him.

But Robert knew Lisa was alright, David was with her, she had not been caught by the explosion, they had sought cover, she was fine and would be running out of the smoke any second now...

But as each slow second passed, they did not reappear.

And in that instant, a terrifying realisation entered his mind. 'NO!' he screamed, 'LISA! GOD NO! NO! LISA!'

But his cry was unanswered.

Scrambling to his feet, adrenaline and fear pulling at his heartstrings, he managed to run three steps before Michael's powerful hands seized him around his arms, holding him back.

'What are you doing?' said Michael.

'I've got to get her, she's alive, she's alive, I have to save her, let me go ... LET ME GO!'

'There's nothing you can do.'

'GET OFF ME,' he yelled, and he fought hard against Michael who refused to let go, 'I MUST GET TO H—'

Then he heard a terrible shriek that stopped him from forming the words, a shriek filled with insanity and hatred, and both Michael and he stared at the young Indian girl who stood not far from them, whose eyes burned with a desire to kill.

'FOR THE BROTHERHOOD OF SAKARABRU,' she screamed.

Robert felt himself being pulled backwards, but he was unable to tear his eyes away from the woman who was ready and willing to die for whatever cause she stood for. And then his world became a complete blur, he found himself suddenly falling into the Trafalgar Square fountain.

His entire body shuddered and screamed in agony as the cold water splashed over his skin. Gasping and shaking he scrambled to the central column and cowered behind it, having no idea what had happened to Lisa or what would happen to himself, he began to tremble violently as tears started to well in his eyes. Scared and alone, he wrapped his arms around himself and buried his head.

A second or so later an ear deafening explosion extinguished all the panic and fear. Daring not to raise his head, Robert closed his eyes tight as smoke began to engulf his shivering body.

Chapter Thirty-Four

The Stranger of Hope

The sudden silence was eerie. The explosions and the petrified screams that had terrified Robert had now stopped. Surely this was death, impossible it was for him to have survived the third attack, despite Michael's heroic attempt to shield his body.

He opened his eyes slowly, not knowing what to expect. Faint wisps of smoke were drifting overhead and as Robert looked around, he found himself still lying in the Trafalgar Square fountain. But it was odd, the water had drained away, it was empty. He looked at his hands, and then ran his fingers over his face and neck; his cuts and bruises had vanished. He began to pat down his body and legs, not a single part of him ached as he did. Even his clothes were untouched by the explosions.

And then he began to look around for Michael, wondering where he might have got to, but as he looked all around him he was nowhere to be seen. The whole thing was odd, but before Robert could even try and understand what was happening, Lisa suddenly occurred to him, he had to get to her. He would have to look for Michael later so he got to his feet and climbed out of the fountain.

A gentle breeze now ran through Trafalgar Square, and as Robert revolved on the spot, wondering which way he should head, a woman suddenly appeared from the clearing smoke. She was tall, thin and graceful, with vibrant ocean blue eyes and rich soft, gently curled golden hair, which came down to her slender shoulders. And despite the smoke swirling around her, her olive skin and long flowing white dress with silver coloured straps still radiated exuberance.

She walked barefoot across the stone flooring, her white dress gently flapped around her ankles as she went. Robert felt drawn to the natural beauty she had about her that he walked towards her. But then he saw both Lisa and Melissa, they were walking up the steps, hand in hand as they headed towards the National Gallery.

Robert suddenly ran past the woman, who in turn turned and called out, 'It's not your time.' But he didn't take any of it in, he didn't care what she had to say; he had found Lisa, that was the only thing of importance to him.

He ran as fast and as hard as he could, calling out Lisa's name as he went, but still she didn't turn, perhaps she couldn't hear him. They went through the doors of the National Gallery, they would wait for Robert in there, he was sure of that. He sprinted up the steps, taking three at a time and pushed through the doors.

But then he suddenly found himself standing in a long burgundy carpeted corridor, its surrounding walls had an ivory coloured wallpaper plastered on them with some sort of gold coloured writing which Robert couldn't translate. He had seen this place before, he was sure of that, but where? The overhead lights showed it seemed to stretch out indefinitely. Perhaps Lisa and Melissa had gone through a different door he wondered, and as he turned to go back outside, the doors had vanished, replaced by the corridor. He looked in both directions, wondering which way he should go, wondering if they had actually walked down here.

He called out their names once again but once again to no avail. On and on the corridor went as he walked down it, and it really seemed that it would not end.

And then quite suddenly sharp pains began to spread over his entire body, he looked at his hands and arms and watched in horror as the bruises and cuts that had vanished now began to appear on his skin, causing the blood to drip from his body. His clothes became torn and burnt and he tried to stem the flow with his hands but it all seemed irrelevant, because at that moment the lights behind him began to extinguish.

Fear gripped hold of his body and without even thinking about it he ran, ignoring all of the pain now circulating through his body. The darkness was advancing rapidly, it was closing in on him, he could not outrun it but still he pushed hard. His legs suddenly buckled out from under him, and it seemed to take an eternity for him to fall to the floor, his palms burning from the deep-piled carpet. The darkness enveloped his bloodied and bruised body and in that instant the fear that had surged through his veins telling him to run now paralysed him.

His breathing was shallow and erratic in the darkness; he looked up and watched as the overhead lights continued to extinguish further down. He lay there, shivering uncontrollably, more frightened than he had ever been in his life, yet still with an overwhelming feeling of déjà vu, but having no idea what was happening or what was going to happen to him.

But then something odd but at the same time wonderful happened. An orb materialised from the darkness, it was white with a tint of blue and was perfectly spherical in shape. The ambient light it emitted was cast upon Robert, ebbing away the fear he felt. He stared at it, watching it move gently up and down. And then without warning it zoomed off.

'Wait,' he said weakly, 'come back.'

Whatever this thing was perhaps it could show him the way out, or at best show him where Lisa and Melissa were. And with great difficulty he reached out his right hand, holding it out for a couple of seconds before he could no longer and dropped it to the floor. It stopped about ten metres or so down the corridor and for a moment Robert thought it would travel back to him, but then someone emerged from the darkness and into the orb's light. And as it circled the figure, Robert recognised it as the woman who he saw in Trafalgar Square, the effect the orb gave her while circling her was eerie.

'Help me,' said Robert desperately.

'It is not your time Robert Lane,' the woman said softly, the orb continued to circle her for a moment longer, she held out her hand and the orb moved towards him, plunging her back into the darkness. 'Take hold of it,' she said softly.

The orb stopped in front of Robert, casting its welcoming light onto him.

'Who are you?' he asked weakly into the darkness.

'My identity is not of importance,' said the woman softly, 'you must take hold of it, you do not belong here.'

'I can't,' said Robert breathlessly, 'I have to find them. I cannot leave them here.'

'Take hold of it Robert,' the woman said, she was no longer speaking softly, there was a demand to her voice now, 'it is not your time, you do not belong here.'

'You do not understand,' said Robert, who now had the same tone to his voice as the woman's, 'I cannot leave them here, I must find them.'

'Everything will be alright,' the woman reassured, 'take hold of it, you must trust me. You do not belong here.'

Robert reached out and grasped the orb, which absorbed into his skin as soon as he did. He felt it travelling up his arm, healing the cuts and bruises as it went, it was like life itself was flowing through him, giving him warmth. The lights flickered on overhead, and as soon as the illumination was cast upon him, his pain and fear ceased. He got to his feet and looked down at his entire body, every part of it was now miraculously unscathed, even his clothes were in pristine condition.

Whatever was flowing through his veins was giving him a sense of hope, a sense of reassurance, and he now knew that everything was going to be alright. The lights grew brighter and brighter, he looked up just as the pure white light engulfed him.

Chapter Thirty-Five

His Darkest of Fears

He was lying on his back once again and cold water was washing gently over his bruised and bloodied body. An overwhelming smell of smoke filled his nostrils with every shallow breath he took. And as he slowly opened his heavy eyes and allowed his vision to clear, he found himself submerged in one of the Trafalgar Square fountains, faint wisps of smoke drifted overhead. He had been caught by the explosion, he could feel his body throbbing and bleeding, but it was the shock and fear of what he had just witnessed that kept him from moving.

And then murmurs from those that had survived the attack travelled across the square to his ears, it was a pitiful plea for anyone who could come to their aid.

Having little thought for his own well-being and more for Lisa and Melissa's, Robert's strength came from that very concern, and he forced himself to sit up. And as he looked around, he saw that he and Michael were apparently alone in the fountain. Michael was near the central column, lying quite still on his back, his face looking the other way.

'Michael?' Robert whispered, his voice was dry and hoarse. 'Are you okay?'

But Michael did not answer, he did not even stir.

And then a terrible thought came crashing over him, but he shook the very idea from his head. This was Michael Parker, the man who survived the South African war, he was a fearless warrior. He was just winded, taking a few moments to compose himself before he got up.

Robert struggled to raise himself out of the water that was still lapping over his body. He stood, swaying slightly, and wiped away the blood trickling down his face from a deep cut over his right eye before staggering towards Michael. Splashing water as he went, he dropped down by Michael's side and stared at him.

The surrounding water was beginning to mix with the blood seeping out from under him and he knew he was dead.

Michael looked peaceful, as though he was simply asleep; his eyes were closed and the faintest of smiles had formed on his bruised lips. But it was still difficult seeing him like this: on his back, his body broken and bloodied, his earpiece hanging over his face.

How long he knelt by Michael's body, Robert did not know, but something within him knew that staying here was never going to bring him back. He removed his drenched jacket and laid it carefully and gently over the lifeless shell of his bodyguard, his friend. He was sure Michael would have preferred this, than having complete strangers staring down at him.

He did not look back when he clambered out of the fountain. And as he stood there, with his clothes soaking and dripping wet and all of his senses still confused and disorientated, the devastating after-effects of the explosions presented itself in front of his eyes. Countless bodies, some intact, others mangled and disfigured littered the entire square, their blood had transformed the stone flooring into a sea of red. The whole scene was horrific and in that instant Robert could not stop himself from dropping to the floor.

It had become all too much for him and he was unable to stop the incessant shivering running through his body. But as soon as this emotional breakdown started it suddenly stopped. His sole purpose now was to find Lisa and Melissa, and it was this very thought that had numbed this emotional state.

He got to his feet and very slowly and carefully he began to walk amongst the dead. There seemed to be no one who had survived the terrorist attack, every body lay perfectly still as he passed them. But as he walked swiftly towards the steps near the National Gallery, he all of a sudden slowed; his eyes were fixed upon the little girl lying face down at the bottom of the stairs. The little girl who was wearing the same coloured dress, the same coloured coat and clutching an identical teddy bear as Melissa had. And then without warning his legs buckled out from under him. He hit the ground hard, the grazes on his palms deepening.

He scrambled to his feet, this could not be her, this could not be Melissa. He ran, faster and harder than he had ever done in his life, his heartbeat intensified with every step he took, and as he drew closer to the little girl he saw David lying spread eagled not far from her. And in that instant Robert knew, although still he couldn't accept it and still he kept thinking, *it cannot be her.*

He knelt by the girl's side, a part of him unable to roll her over, the other part needing to. He put a hand on her shoulder and with so many things gripping at his heart and lungs he turned her onto her back.

Melissa's face, arms and legs were awfully bruised and swollen, the look of shock and fear was still etched upon her face.

'Melissa,' he whispered, staring into the empty brown eyes.

But the little girl did not stir.

'No, no, no, Melissa, no.'

The whole idea of his niece dying like this was too awful for him to process. He pulled the teddy bear from out of her small and badly grazed hand and held it tight when he scooped her up.

He walked up the stone stairs, taking one step at a time, slowly and carefully, it was indescribable how he felt now, his body was overwhelmed by so many emotions that it seemed to have shut itself down from everything occurring around him. Unknowingly tears formed and rolled down his cheeks, dripping onto Melissa's coat, absorbing immediately and forming little round wet patches.

But as soon as he reached the topmost step horror rose from the pit of his stomach; for there was Lisa, lying on her back and staring up at the world as she gasped for breath.

Robert tried to cry out her name as he ran towards her, still holding Melissa close to his chest, but he could not form the words. He dropped down by her side and suddenly became no more than a helpless onlooker. Her lemon coloured shirt was torn and stained with her blood.

Lisa looked at Robert, her eyes were filled with fear.

'Where's Melissa?' she asked him with great difficulty, never seeing or knowing of the little girl he held in his arms.

'She's fine,' lied Robert without hesitation, 'I have her here, she's just sleeping.'

He gently laid Melissa's body in Lisa's arms. With her own body on the brink of death Lisa did not know her daughter had perished and she smiled from the comfort of holding her. She tried to raise her left arm so she could rest it on Melissa's head, but the strength had left her body, this attempt wasn't missed by Robert, however, who very carefully and gently moved Lisa's hand to where she wanted it.

'Mommy's here,' she said softly, stroking Melissa's hair, 'mommy's here for you sweetie.'

Tears began to roll down the side of her head, streaking the patches of blood, as she looked at Robert.

'I'm ... sorry,' she sobbed.

'It's all going to be alright,' Robert reassured, his voice shook from trying to keep it calm.

He could not just watch the woman he loved die, he would do all he could to save her, nothing was more important now. He tore open the bottom half of her shirt, her stomach had suffered several deep cuts from the explosion. Robert ripped off the arm of his drenched shirt and began to wipe away the blood, but only more replaced it. He pressed down hard on the wounds with his bloodied hands, trying all he could to stop the blood from issuing from them.

Lisa found a glimmer of strength from somewhere and with great difficulty and through great pain she moved her hand from Melissa's head towards Robert's hand and held it. He looked at her, his eyes were red and filled with tears.

'Please don't die,' he said desperately, 'I don't want you to die. I don't want you to leave me.'

He could no longer look at her now, still he wiped away and tried to stop the flowing blood.

'You're going to live,' he sobbed, 'you're not going to die. I WON'T LET YOU DIE.'

Anger masked his last spoken words now, she wasn't going to die, she was going to live, live through this, she was strong, she was a survivor. Lisa applied the smallest amount of pressure on his hand and Robert looked at her once more.

They just stared at one another, both crying, both knowing that nothing could be done. Then, somewhere in the distance, the sound of sirens could be heard through the silence, bringing hope.

'Look Lisa,' said Robert relieved, he looked over to where the noise was coming from, 'help's coming, see?'

But Lisa did not. The fear in her eyes had vanished, replaced by emptiness, and in that instance, Robert knew she had gone. The pain was tearing at his heart, he cradled the bodies of both Lisa and Melissa and gently rocked back and forth. His scream of anguish reverberated around Trafalgar Square.

Chapter Thirty-Six

A Time for Mourning

The Trafalgar Square bombings had brought the entire country into total disarray, rolling news coverage of the attacks were broadcasted by the various news channels, uninterrupted right up until a few minutes ago. Mobile phone networks were inundated with calls, forcing them to initiate emergency procedures to prioritise emergency calls. And security across the United Kingdom was raised to its highest alert level, forcing bomb disposal experts to destroy any suspicious packages found in controlled explosions.

It was seven o'clock now, the downpour of rain that was falling over the south of the country had been falling for the past hour, washing away the remnants of blood that had not been cleaned from Trafalgar Square. The façade of 10 Downing Street was now quiet, the reporters that had gathered earlier to listen to Prime Minister Thomas Gordon's statement were now gone, writing up their articles for tomorrow's newspapers.

Sitting alone in the room he regarded as his study, the Prime Minister was reading through countless official documents. The words slipped through his mind, leaving behind no trace of meaning. He was waiting for the commissioner of police to whom he requested to see, and between wondering when he was going to arrive and trying to quell the terrible day's events, it was no wonder the words meant nothing to him.

He had done all he could for tonight, he had addressed the nation in an attempt to send out a calm and clear message, approved contingency plans so the country could be protected against further attacks, and had held discussions with all the foreign nationals who had rung to offer their condolences. He knew that there was nothing more that could have been done, but it did little to ease the uncomfortable feeling now tightening in his throat and chest. He dropped the documents onto his desk and undid the top button of his shirt and loosened his tie.

'How could I have allowed this to happen?' he said quietly and regretfully.

And in this silence, with this uncomfortable feeling now spreading throughout and pressing against his entire body, he began to think over and question the decision he had taken to become involved in the South African war.

It was always going to be a controversial decision whatever he made, but his stance against terrorism was clear: anyone who threatened the lives of the people he was sworn to protect would be dealt with with extreme force. It was a position that was black and white, it was a position that was clear and precise and to the point. And yet the South African war was not so, it was a subject that had many grey areas in it, and it was because of this that doubt was created and began to creep into his mind.

Going to war was the last resort he had; there were no other options or alternatives left. There would be repercussions, but in some respects it could be justified when he explained that going to war would ultimately bring peace, lives would have to be sacrificed so that many could survive, it was easier for him to think of it like that.

And yet the brave soldiers who had fought and gave their lives for the war in South Africa did not prevent the terror unfolding in Trafalgar Square, they paid the ultimate sacrifice but still over five hundred protestors had perished today.

The Prime Minister removed his glasses from his face and dropped them onto the table.

'What am I responsible for?' he said as he massaged the temples of his throbbing head.

His decisive actions were ultimately responsible for the attack on Trafalgar Square, he had chosen wrongly, there could be no denying that, but whether he would publicly acknowledge it was an entirely different matter. Now he had arrived at this crossroads and would be judged on which path he took next. Apprehend those behind the atrocious act then more lives would be lost, withdraw from South Africa then those who had died for their country had done so for nothing.

And yet how many more lives would have to be sacrificed in order for there to be peace in South Africa? How many more families would be torn apart by the deaths of their loved ones?

Was it really worth the sacrifice? Was the war justifiable now because of the Trafalgar Square bombing?

The questions ran in an endless loop in his brain, he didn't know what he believed in anymore. The legacy he wanted to leave after he had served his time as Prime Minister was of the man who led the country in a new direction bringing with it hope and prosperity, now that was all tarnished, he would always be remembered as the politician who led the country into a controversial war.

He sighed wearily, picked up his glasses and continued to read through the documents. What other choice did he have other than to continue the fight in South Africa? Retreat was an option that could never be considered, he and the country would always stand strong against their adversaries. But how many more lives would be claimed because of this?

But before he could consider and comprehend the repercussions of the continual involvement in the South African war, there was a gentle rap at his door.

'Yes,' he said drained, removing his reading glasses and looking up.

The door opened and his secretary's head peered around.

'David's here to see you Prime Minister,' she said respectfully.

'Thank you Victoria,' he said, standing, 'send him in, and will you ask Mary to bring us some tea.'

'Very well, sir,' she said nodding, and then disappeared at once.

The Prime Minister re-buttoned his collar and adjusted his tie, then he walked around his desk to greet the bland featured police commissioner who arrived moments later dressed pristinely in his uniform, clutching an executive looking black folder close to his chest. After their pleasantries, shaking one another's hands the Prime Minister offered the commissioner one of the chairs facing his desk before he resumed his seat.

'So what do you know about the young man who was arrested earlier?' he asked nervously.

The commissioner crossed his legs, rested the folder against his raised thigh and opened it, then removing the pen from its holder he opened the notepad attached to the right hand side.

'His name is Elliott Ethan Grant,' he said through a long sigh, pressing the pen against his lips as he glanced down at the hand written notes he had made, 'in some respects he doesn't fit the typical profile, highly intelligent, an overachiever at school, college and university before he became a dropout.'

'So what does that say about the state of our country?' the Prime Minister interrupted. 'Have you got any insight as to why, a bright young man like that would want to try and take the lives of so many people?'

'His father was sergeant Harry Grant,' David said and the Prime Minister recognised the name at once and immediately slumped in his chair because of it, 'after his father's death, he became alienated from his mother and her current partner as well as his friends, seemed the ideal choice –'

There was a couple of knocks at the door and one of the household staff walked in when called to do so, carrying a silver tray with two cups of tea, a small jug of milk, a bowl of sugar and a small plate of chocolate biscuits placed upon it. She carefully laid it down on the Prime Minister's desk who in turn said, 'Thank you Mary.' The tone in his voice suggested that she should leave the room at once, she nodded politely at the pair and did exactly that, closing the door quietly behind her.

The Prime Minister picked up his cup, adding a drop of milk and stirring a spoon full of sugar into his tea.

'As you were saying David,' he said before taking a sip, savouring and appreciating its warmth and taste.

And as the commissioner continued to read through the hand written notes he had made, the Prime Minister leaned back in his chair and simply allowed the words to wash over him, they were meaningless now, not after what he had just been told. The death of sergeant Harry Grant had made his son become vulnerable, and in his vulnerable state he had been manipulated, manipulated to give his life for a cause that he was *made* to believe in.

Harry Grant was among the first to be killed in a friendly fire incident involving an American helicopter, something that brought a great deal of sadness to the Prime Minster when he was told. It was always distressing to hear that any soldier had to sacrifice their life for the country, but to be told that those who you were fighting alongside were responsible was difficult to accept. The media interest was immense, bringing with it the reality that the casualties of war were not only the soldiers, it was also the loved ones they left behind, they had to try and pick up the pieces and rebuild their shattered lives. Elliott Grant was such a casualty, so confused and angry he must have been to try and take the lives of the Trafalgar Square demonstrators.

'We had no reason to become involved,' he said glumly, although he was unaware of doing so aloud.

'With all due respect Prime Minister,' David said, looking up from his notepad, 'we could not have predicted this.'

The words ignited something deep within the Prime Minister; his calmness had been consumed by something that was far greater than anger.

'Really David,' he enraged and he slammed his cup down on his desk, spilling most of the tea, 'you're telling me that we were so arrogant not to even think that the conflict in South Africa was never going to reach us here?'

'There was no evidence to suggest it would,' said David calmly, 'as far as we were concerned the Brotherhood of Sakarabru were working with us, we had no idea they were planning something like this.'

And yet being told of this did little to ease this uncomfortable feeling, a feeling that was well beyond guilt or anger or fear. In spite of everything he had read over the last few hours, the involvement of the Brotherhood of Sakarabru in the Trafalgar Square bombing had never been regarded, not until now. The resolve of the Liberators of South Africa had been broken; Zuberi Jacobs and other high-ranking members had been killed almost a year ago, their bodies obliterated by the bombs dropped onto the building they were in by the Americans. The end of the war was quick to be announced by both Jack Carter and himself, their arrogance blinding them from seeing that the Brotherhood of Sakarabru were fooling the world with their integrity all the while relentlessly planning an unspeakable act of terror. Their believable lies had brought the entire world to a standstill.

'You did the right thing Prime Minister,' said David, trying to reassure the gloomy-looking man sitting opposite him, 'the Liberators of South Africa were a genuine threat to our security –'

'This was never about our security,' the Prime Minister said, 'this was about maintaining the strong relationship with America, they asked for our help and we obliged.'

He stood and walked over to his window, staring out at the night sky.

'And as a result we have stirred up a hornet's nest.' He sighed deeply. 'I have failed our brave men and women fighting over there and I have failed the people here.'

He turned away and began to walk around his office.

'Lives have been lost because of my foolish judgement.'

And there could be no escaping that haunting fact, the repercussions of becoming involved in the South African conflict had proved costly, and the 15th of August would always be the day that reminded him of that.

Chapter Thirty-Seven

A Time for Celebrating

The rain that had pressed against the windows of 10 Downing Street had now eased over the magnificent residence of Charles Piennar. Congregated in the dining room, the nine stood around the long mahogany table, holding each of their glasses filled with champagne aloft.

'To victory,' Charles said proudly.

'To victory,' the eight repeated.

There was a brief silence as they all took a sip of their champagne.

'Today's attack on Trafalgar Square was met with unparallel success,' Charles continued, 'ladies and gentlemen we are about to embark on a new chapter, one that will see us ending the war.' He took another sip of his champagne. 'Now I know a lot of you will be frustrated by Elliott's sentimental actions, but the killing of the Trafalgar Square protestors was not our ultimate aim. Today's attack was to send out a message to the entire world, and ladies and gentlemen, there will be no doubting who is responsible for the bombings of Trafalgar Square; we have achieved what we set out to do.'

And as each of the guests acknowledged Charles's words with cheers and whistles, there was one man who did neither.

What have I become apart of, Mamello Galpin thought as he stared down at the champagne in his glass.

*

The celebrations grew late into the evening.

Standing alone in Charles's garden, Mamello Galpin was walking aimlessly across the fine wet grass. With his hands buried in his pockets, he thought about the day's events. It had started off as a justified cause, a cleverly thought-out plan that would ultimately put an end to the South African war. But how could he celebrate, knowing what he did, knowing what he was responsible for?

The grief and anguish he felt after the death of his daughter had gradually turned to hate under the influence of Charles Piennar. He had been told that killing the Trafalgar Square protestors would bring justice to six month old Kefilwe.

'Your pain will ease once we send out our message', Charles had said to him, *'I can promise you that my friend'.*

But Mamello now knew that was a complete fabrication, it was like a game of chess, and he was the pawn in it, someone to be used and sacrificed if needed. And the more he thought about it, the more he knew that he was no better than the men who killed his daughter. How could he judge them now, when he himself had killed over one hundred innocent men and women?

He continued to walk around the garden, his trainers were now soaked through from the wet grass. Despite what had happened today, it was such a beautiful night: the sky was now clear and cloud free and the stars twinkled in the distance, Mamello stopped walking and looked up at them, trying, if he could to make out the various constellations. And as he did, faint strips of pop music could be heard coming from the house.

An invisible barrier – created from his guilt and grief – now separated him from the people inside the house. It seemed impossible to him that they could be celebrating like this. Everything had changed so much in the past twelve hours; did they honestly believe that the end would soon be near in South Africa? Because Mamello couldn't see it.

'There you are,' Mandisa Galpin said, startling her husband.

And Mamello turned to see his wife standing by the garden archway.

'What are you doing out here?' she asked quizzically, walking towards him. 'You're missing the karaoke,' she said, looking as though she was trying to contain her laughter, 'Charles is doing his rendition of One Thousand Days, I don't think he would mind me telling you that he's awful.'

She stood behind her husband, wrapping her arms around his waist and resting her chin on his back.

'Would you like to do a duet with me?' she asked softly. 'Maybe that Vanessa Burns one you like.'

'How can I,' he said, pulling away, 'knowing what I've done.'

'What you've done,' she repeated, bemused, 'I don't understand. What do you mean?' She moved closer to him and put a hand on his shoulder, but once again Mamello pulled away.

'What we did today weighs heavily on my heart Mandisa,' he said quietly. 'We're responsible for the murder of so many innocent people.'

'Innocent people?' Mandisa repeated. It was a strange moment that followed, it was almost as if the two words were spoken from a different language, for how could her husband – the love of her life, the man she regarded so highly – even suggest that the supporters of the war were innocent, it made no sense. 'How can you call them innocent?' she asked. 'They supported the men and women responsible for killing our people that is what they were protesting at Trafalgar Square for, for better equipment to be supplied to the soldiers fighting in South Africa.'

Mamello turned around at the sound of these words.

'Do you really believe that?' he asked his voice no higher than a whisper.

Mandisa tilted her head a fraction and parted her lips slightly, but no words seemed to come out.

'Do you really believe that?' he asked again, however, there seemed to be an urgency in his voice this time, a need to know how his wife felt.

'Well, yes,' Mandisa said, and it was clear from Mamello's expression that he expected this answer, 'of course I do, why else would I fight?'

But before Mamello could answer there was a clearing of a throat. And both he and Mandisa turned to see Charles standing not far from them, leaning on his shoulder against the garden wall.

'I hope I'm not interrupting anything,' he said, his voice was as cold as the air that surrounded them.

'Of course not,' said Mandisa, quickly avoiding Charles's dark eyes, 'I was just asking Mamello if he wanted to sing with me.'

She laughed nervously as Charles continued to stare at them both, his face expressionless.

'I see,' he said, his eyes narrowing slightly, 'well before he does I would like a quiet word with him.' He parted his hands. 'If that is okay with you Mandisa.'

'Yes of course,' she said anxiously.

She quickly glanced at her husband, raising a smile to him before she hurried out of the garden, avoiding Charles's eyes as he passed him.

Now that they were alone, Charles reached inside his jacket's inner pocket and withdrew a cigar which he prepared to smoke.

'It has been an emotional day for us all,' he said, placing the cigar in his mouth, 'so I will pretend that I did not hear your conversation.'

Mamello said nothing; he simply had his hands in his pockets and felt himself brave enough to stare back at Charles, who in turn smiled.

'I admire your courage,' he said silkily.

There was a brief silence as Charles fumbled for his lighter in his trouser pocket. He lit his cigar and immediately became surrounded in its smoke as he took several long draws on it.

'I am returning to South Africa tomorrow,' he said before taking another long draw of his cigar. 'I suggest that you at some point do the same, then you might think twice about calling our enemies innocent.'

And as far as Charles was concerned that was the end of the conversation, he turned away and left a trail of smoke behind him as he started to walk back towards the house.

'I no longer want to fight, Charles,' Mamello called out with surprising confidence, 'I don't believe in the cause anymore.'

Charles spun round, hurried over and grabbed Mamello violently by the arm, pulling him closer.

'I would be very careful in what you say next,' he said in a restrained manner, 'because I will not be held responsible for my actions.'

'This is not what I joined up for,' Mamello said indignantly, tearing his arm away.

'You joined because your six month old daughter was killed by British soldiers,' said Charles coldly, 'but not only were they satisfied with killing her, but they thought it appropriate to mock her while recording a video of her mutilated body.'

The cruelly spoken words had caused tears to well in Mamello's eyes but he would not give Charles the satisfaction in seeing him in this weakened state. He turned quickly and closed his eyes, but the words had achieved the desired effect and he could feel himself breaking down from within himself. The more he fought against it the more this feeling spread throughout his body, within seconds it arrived to his brain revealing every horrific thought and image he had kept locked away.

And with all these particular memories flooding back to him, there was one that he could feel himself drifting back to…

The sun had not yet rose when the British planes – laden with bombs – flew overhead, leaving death and destruction in their wake. The first of the explosions brought Mamello out of his deep slumber. Uncertain what was happening, he along with Mandisa – who woke immediately after him – both climbed out of the bed and crawled along the floor, panic-stricken.

'What's going on?' Mandisa cried.

'I don't know,' said Mamello, whose voice shook from the fear, 'stay here and keep low to the ground, I'm going to get Kefilwe.'

He scrambled to his feet and headed for the bedroom door, as soon as he pulled it open the petrified screams from his daughter reached him just as another plane thundered overhead.

'It's okay Kefilwe,' he called out reassuring, 'daddy's com –'

The air suddenly exploded. Mamello had his hand on the handle of his daughter's bedroom door, when an unimaginable force tore apart his world. He could do nothing to prevent himself being thrown into the air, his daughter's terrified screams reverberated inside of his head and he had no way of knowing what had happened to her –

Mamello didn't know how much time had passed before he found himself opening his eyes and seeing the world presenting itself before him in pain and semi-darkness. He was half-buried under bricks and remnants of furniture that had once made up his home. His face was bleeding; he could feel the morning air brushing against it and as his vision cleared he could see that his daughter's bedroom had been completely destroyed.

A torrent of emotion overwhelmed his battered and bruised body, tears formed in his swollen eyes and rolled down his bloody cheeks, dripping onto the debris that covered him.

'Kefilwe,' he whispered with great difficulty.

And then voices reached him through the silence. Loud and clear, they spoke in English accents and were cursing in enjoyment over the death and destruction that the planes had achieved.

'Look at this poor bastard,' he heard a man say, there was an immaturity to his voice, 'didn't stand a chance did he?'

For a moment no one gave a response to the heartless words but then someone with the same cruel sense of humour said, 'Hell no.' There was a long pause. 'There's not much left of him is there?' he said rhetorically.

And again there was a pause. Mamello could hear their footsteps approaching closer. He was sure that these men were British soldiers, but in any case he would not call out to them for help. He deeply mistrusted all of the South African Saviours ever since they arrived to the country he loved so dearly.

'What's that?' the immature spoken man said.

'It's a girl, I think,' the second man said uncertainly.

'That's the sickest thing I've ever seen.' The immature spoken man paused briefly. 'Tell me you're not recording it?'

'I've gotta take this back home and show it to my brother,' the second man said casually.

The words crushed Mamello's heart; the anguish he felt was so indescribable and so overwhelming that his eyes grew heavy and he drifted out of consciousness. He woke several hours later to find himself lying on his back on a soft mattress. Dim lights from oil lamps were all around him and he could smell cool, earthy air. And then the face of a figure appeared over him a moment or two later, bald headed with designer facial hair, he spoke in fluent English, 'My name is Charles Piennar,' he said, his voice was deep yet welcoming, 'you are safe here.' He held out a full bottle of what looked to be like water. 'Here,' he said, handing the bottle to Mamello, 'drink this.'

'My wife,' Mamello said suddenly, his voice was dry and hoarse, 'where is my wife?'

'She is right here,' said Charles pleasantly.

Mandisa came into his view as soon as Charles said the words. She had been crying, her eyes were red and puffy, and the tears had left lines down her face which was covered in dust. She gripped Mamello's hand, squeezing it gently in reassurance.

Wincing in agony, Mamello sat upright. The cuts he had sustained during the attack had been cleaned and dressed, he looked around the earthy room before turning to Charles who looked a little out of place with his navy blue shirt and charcoal trousers.

'Where are we?' he asked him.

'Safe from the South African Saviours bombs my friend,' said Charles softly, 'we are in one of the abandoned rooms once used by the Liberators of South Africa.'

Mamello took the bottle off Charles, unscrewed the cap and took several sips. The water hydrated his aching body and cleared his groggy mind, and with it came the horrific thought and truth that his daughter was dead, no longer would he be able to see or hear everything that made her so unique. And in this silence he could hear her terrified screams echoing inside of his head, it grew louder and louder until he could no longer take it.

'How did you find us?' he asked, and the screaming stopped at once.

'I came to look for survivors as soon as I heard the explosions,' said Charles, 'you and your wife are the only ones who I found alive.'

The pair bowed their heads, Mandisa squeezed Mamello's hand, who returned the pressure. He had many more questions he wanted to ask Charles, but before he could say another word Charles spoke, 'I have no children,' he admitted, 'so I would not be so arrogant to say that I know how you are feeling.'

Both Mamello and Mandisa looked up at him.

'I know what happened to your daughter,' he said sympathetically, 'I saw what the British soldiers did, I saw how they made a mockery out of her.'

Mandisa buried her head in Mamello's shoulder and began to sob quietly.

'Your pain will lessen in time my friend,' said Charles.

But Mamello found that impossible to believe, he would never, could never accept the death of his daughter.

'Your pain will lessen once we send out our message,' Charles said, and a smile began to form on his lips, 'I can promise you that my friend.'

Mamello stared deep into Charles's dark eyes and as he did they seemed to go cold. And in that moment Mamello could feel something grow inside of him, bigger and bigger it grew, consuming his grief and pain, and giving him a desire to avenge.

'What is this message?' he asked.

Now back inside the walled garden Mamello's thoughts returned to what he and the others were responsible for. Now he understood that Charles had manipulated his grief, turning it into a black poison that flowed through his body, infecting everything that it touched. It had turned him into the man he vowed he would never be: a man consumed by hate and revenge.

But now Charles was no longer injecting the poison into him from the words he spoke, his words meant nothing. At last Mamello was free and at last he had found his voice.

'I still bear the mental and physical scars the day my daughter died,' he said quietly. He turned and faced Charles, staring at him determinately. 'We had the moral high ground then,' he said clearly, 'every one of us had a justified reason of why we fought against the South African Saviours. But how can we judge now, when we ourselves have murdered innocent people.'

Charles raised his hand and struck Mamello violently across his face with the back of it. The gold ring he wore on his little finger cut into the skin causing it to bleed slightly.

'You called our enemies innocent once and I forgave that,' he said calmly, 'but to do so again is an insult to the cause.'

The very thing that had brought them together and formed their friendship had now severed it. Both Charles and Mamello looked at one another with deep disgust.

'You are now a traitor to the cause,' said Charles coldly, 'and you will be held accountable for this.'

'Every one of us will be held accountable on the day of our judgement,' Mamello said confidently. 'Your threats mean nothing to me.'

'I'm glad your daughter isn't alive to see you now,' said Charles cruelly, 'because she would be ashamed.' He took a final draw on his cigar and he discarded it into the rose bush.

Mamello said nothing to this, he turned and walked across the damp grass. But as he wiped the blood from his cheek, he saw Mandisa standing by the garden archway. And as he was met with an impassive stare and before he could say anything, something hard wrapped around his neck and he was pulled backwards. He fell on top of Charles, who pulled on the leather belt harder and harder. Mamello gasped for air, doing all he could to loosen the belt with his fingers.

'Help ... me,' he gurgled.

He reached out towards Mandisa, a plea for her to come to his rescue, but she simply turned, the tears running down her cheeks seemed to glisten in the moonlight as she did.

Mamello's dying heartbeat resounded in his head. His eyelids felt heavy, he tried to fight it, and once again he tried valiantly to loosen the belt, but his eyes began to close. A moment later his grip on the belt slackened, he was dead.

Charles removed the belt and rolled the limp body off him. He stood, breathing heavily as he wiped the sweat from his face with his hands. Then, without so much as a backwards glance, he replaced his belt and walked out of the garden, closing the gate as he went.

'Mamello was a traitor to the cause,' he said to Mandisa, who was stood with her arms crossed, shivering uncontrollably. 'I couldn't allow him to live, knowing what he did.'

There was a brief pause. Surely explaining his actions could never justify killing her husband, but Mandisa understood completely.

'I know,' she said, looking at him now, 'we have come too far.' She looked at the walled garden, her eyes narrowing slightly. 'The man in there is not my husband,' she said without hesitation.

Neither of them spoke but, together they walked, arms linked, back towards the house to continue the celebrations.

Chapter Thirty-Eight

The Offer of Sympathy

August 16th

The sun was beginning to rise: the pure, beautiful colouring looked so innocent to him, for it would have never had to experience the events of yesterday. Robert sat on a bench inside one of the many walled gardens, welcoming the warmth pressing against his face. Simply being alive to experience this awesome sight should have brought comfort to him, but the whole of his body was still numbed from all he had witnessed yesterday ... Michael's lifeless shell in the bloodied water of the Trafalgar Square fountain ... Melissa's little body lying face down by the steps leading to the National Gallery ... Lisa slowly dying in his arms, her face etched with fear...

The silence and stillness in this garden was suddenly broken by a faint dripping, he averted his eyes from the colourful plants and stared down at his left arm. Without knowingly so, he had dug his fingers deep into the cuts, tearing at the stitching. His blood was now slowly dripping down his arm, onto the wooden bench. But he did nothing to stop it, he just resumed staring at the plants.

I had all this power, this wealth, and I couldn't save them. And that was the simple truth of it, for all the influence and authority he possessed in the world and the vast fortune he owned, none of it could ever bring them back. He had somehow found the strength to deal with the untimely deaths of both his parents and his brother, but never, up until this very point, had he felt so alone and powerless.

Overwhelmed with Lisa dying in his arms, Robert fell unconscious soon after and had been brought to this private hospital as soon as the emergency services recognised him. It was the best place for him they thought, offering anonymity and security the surrounding hospitals couldn't guarantee.

And since then his body had seemed to just shut itself down, he was going through the motions, he was neither happy nor sad, if there was such a thing of being in the middle then he was in it, completely emotionless. Still he sat on the bench, still he looked out at the colourful flowers, still feeling nothing.

But then, this early morning silence and stillness, which was only broken by the dripping of his blood and the occasional bird song, became suddenly overpowering. He stood and began to walk around the quiet, beautiful garden, his breathing coming in short, shallow gasps, trying all he could not to think about the events of yesterday, but in this garden, in this quietude, it was all he could think about ... there could be no escaping the haunting truth.

It was his fault that Lisa, Melissa, David and Michael had perished, it was his entire fault, if he had not been so selfish, so self-centred to thrust himself into the public eye then they would all be alive still.

It was unbearable, he curled his hands into fists and rapped them against his head, trying all he could not to think about it, he could not stand it, there was an unimaginable hollow deep within him, the place where Lisa had been, where Lisa had been taken from him. He did not want to live his life without her, the woman he had loved from the moment he saw her, he did not want to live with this dark hole that would never be filled.

Robert could not stand this, he could not stand this overwhelming feeling, he had never felt so trapped inside of himself, never had he wished as he did at this moment, that he was with Lisa in that eternal resting place.

The door which led into the walled garden opened and Robert turned to see a tall, sombrely dressed man with prominent cheekbones and thinning brown hair entering, he was wearing a white strip around the front of his collar and was clutching a red book of some sort close to his chest.

'Good morning Mr Lane,' he said softly, 'my name is Father Harold Dalton, I work in the chapel here at the hospital. I hope I didn't startle you.'

Robert shook his head.

'Would you mind if I sat?' the priest asked him, pointing to the bench.

Again Robert shook his head.

The priest walked over to the bench and as he sat down and rested the book upon his knees, his eyes caught hold of Robert's bloody arm.

'I shall call one of the nurses to see to that,' he said, concerned.

'No,' said Robert, his voice was loud and strong and determined.

'Very well,' the priest said, calmly. 'I want you to know that you are quite safe here, there is nothing that can hurt you.'

Robert didn't say a word to this. It seemed that the priest was reminding him as to why he had been brought here, reminding him of the actions that had taken away the life of the woman he loved. And although the priest was looking at him with great concern and not of judgement, Robert could not bear to meet his eyes.

'Do you have faith my son?' the priest asked, as he continued to look at him. 'Do you believe in the Almighty?'

'A long time ago,' Robert said simply, still avoiding the priest's eyes, 'not anymore.'

The priest nodded in a sort of understanding way. 'I took it upon myself to see you today,' he said, 'perhaps in the hope of offering you some words of comfort.'

Robert was happy enough just to stare at the orange lilies in the large brown ceramic pot.

'I have counselled many families,' the priest resumed softly, 'so I can understand how you are feeling.'

'How can you possibly understand,' said Robert quietly, talking to the lilies.

'I do understand how you're feeling,' said the priest, still softly, 'you're feeling an unimaginable amount of pain and suffering, and it stands to reason. And no doubt with me being here, you're probably thinking, how can I preach about God to you, when He allowed the atrocities of yesterday to happen.'

Robert turned away and stared determinately at the flowers climbing the stone wall, the colours of which became blurred from the tears forming.

'Alas,' continued the priest, although Robert barely heard him, 'that is a question that is as old as religion itself and it is a question I feel that any answer I give, will not be sufficient. Why does God allow bad things happen to good people?' he asked rhetorically. 'Like most people I have struggled myself to understand the complexity of the Lord's actions. Why does God allow men and women to be raped? Why does He allow children to be abducted and murdered? Why did He allow the Trafalgar Square bombings to happen yesterday?

'If God is as powerful as what we are made to believe, if He created the world, man and the various species, then why not protect them all?'

Robert did not answer, he was letting the words simply pass over him. They were insignificant; for nothing could ease his heartache, nothing mattered to him now, the explanation would never bring Lisa back, it would never erase the events of yesterday. He closed his eyes and thought about Lisa, the woman whose life had been cruelly taken away from his, their one and only special night together was to be their last. He should have told her sooner, explained the love he felt for her when they were at high school together.

Had he told her everything, then things would have been different he knew that for certain, he would have led a different life, Lisa would have given him the belief and encouragement to pursue his dreams, she would have made his life complete, the woman who he had loved for a lifetime.

'I suppose in some respects,' he heard the priest say, 'yes, God does allow bad things to happen, however, He does not cause them. God gives freedom to his people, we are free people Mr Lane, not simple puppets on a string. But with this liberation comes great responsible, for bad things take place in the freedom that comes with the gift of life –'

'Instead of Him resting on the seventh day,' said Robert suddenly, his voice shaking from the effort of keeping it calm, 'maybe He should have spent that day learning about love and compassion.'

'Yes He should have,' replied the priest softly, 'but like every one of us He is not perfect, and He has made mistakes in some of His greatest creations. However, I believe God has a plan for you Mr Lane, and I know you are to do great things.'

It was all too much, the words made Robert turn and he stared directly into the priest's eyes.

'THEN I DON'T WANT TO LIVE,' he screamed hysterically.

He tore open his shirt, exposing his bandaged chest and looked skyward.

'TAKE ME,' he cried, 'I BEG OF YOU TAKE ME, TAKE ME INSTEAD OF HER.'

'There is no shame in what you are feeling Mr Lane,' said the priest calmly, who was unaffected by this outburst of rage, 'it is good to show emotion, it is a good quality to have, it separates you from those who committed the horrific attack on Trafalgar Square yesterday.'

The priest's calmness had ignited a deep hatred in the eternal emptiness of his stomach, he wanted to hurt the man sitting on the bench, he wanted to beat the calmness out of him, to make *him* feel the same pain and regret he was feeling.

'SHUT UP,' he bellowed, 'I DON'T WANT TO HEAR ANYTHING ELSE YOU'VE GOT TO SAY!'

And he picked up the ceramic plant pot and threw it hard across the garden; it shattered into several pieces against the stone wall.

'LEAVE,' Robert yelled, 'I WANT YOU TO LEAVE, NOW!'

There seemed to be little air left in his lungs, he stood, panting heavily, shaking uncontrollably, as he stared at the priest.

'Very well,' said the priest quietly.

He clutched the book, stood slowly and hung his head, sighing deeply. Robert carefully watched him do so, but this show of sadness, or weariness, or whatever it was from the priest portrayed did not calm him. On the contrary, his anger – which had subsided for only a fraction of a moment – now flared inside of him once again. How dare the priest show this sign of emotional weakness, he had no right to do so, he did not share the same fate as Robert yesterday, he had not seen what he had, he had not had the woman he loved die in his arms, he had no idea how much he had suffered.

The priest presented the book he held in his hand and looked at Robert. 'You have a lot of anger inside of you Mr Lane,' he said clearly, 'I hope you can find solace in this.'

He gently laid the book on the bench and left without saying another word. The sun was beginning to rise properly now, bathing the garden in its light. The silence was absolute; the birds had flown away from the screams of hysteria.

For a long time, Robert just stood in the garden, gazing out at the colourful plants once again, trying not to think about Lisa or to remember the one and only night he spent with her, the ultimate connection of love.

The gardener arrived not long after and Robert wiped away the tears with the back of his hands and hurried over to the book left on the bench, the gold bold lettering of which read: *THE HOLY BIBLE.*

Chapter Thirty-Nine

The Trafalgar Square Vigil

August 20th

For the days that followed the Trafalgar Square massacre a vigil had been held. Uniting against the terror which had unfolded, thousands of people had visited the square to pay their respects to the five hundred and seventeen people who had lost their lives. Flowers, poems and messages had been laid and written, whilst candles had been lit and placed around Nelson's Column.

Under a dark blue sky in which the night's first appearance of stars were beginning to glimmer, Robert Lane stood at the top of the National Gallery stairs, staring down at the square, clutching four beautifully made white candles close to his chest. Despite the late hour, mourners still walked aimlessly across the stone flooring, their cries of sorrow echoing into the night sky.

However, Robert could not bear to walk among them, to have their gazes set upon him, to have their sympathy offered to him, the man who the newspapers were calling, "the miracle man of Trafalgar Square".

And so he waited, waited until he was ready to walk down these steps and head for Nelson's Column. In the distance Big Ben chimed for nine o'clock and with it came the realisation that he'd had been standing there now for fifteen minutes.

Taking several long deep breaths, Robert finally summoned the strength from within to take the first step. He walked slowly down the stone steps, trying not to relive the tragic last moments he had with Lisa, trying not to look at the place where she had died in his arms. And in no time at all he was walking among the mourners, none looked up as he passed them, each man and woman was overwhelmed by their own grief to even acknowledge him.

And as Robert drew closer to Nelson's Column, his chest grew tighter with every step taken, every emotion he felt was weighing down on his heart and lungs making it difficult for him to breathe. And before he knew it he was standing before the iconic structure, staring up at the statue of Admiral Horatio Nelson.

Letters, flowers, balloons, poems, candles and teddy bears covered the entire base. And as Robert slowly walked around to find a spot to put the four candles, he caught a glimpse of handwritten notes and poems as he passed.

To my darling Sophie, (it read in beautiful handwriting)

I miss you more than words can say. You were my first and only love, and I know my life will never be the same without you. Even though I know you would want me to move on with my life, I will never be able to. I love you so much and the pain I feel will never ease over time.

Always yours
Danny
xxx

Another was written on a small piece of card attached to a beautiful bunch of brightly coloured flowers.

To my Eric,

A loving husband, a devoted father, taken from us at the age 37, you will be forever in my heart and thoughts.

Your loving wife and sons,
Mary, Craig and Joshua
xxxxx

The next was written above a beautifully painted picture of a large man with a moustache. He looked to be walking with a small black dog whilst a little blonde-haired girl sat on his shoulders.

To my daddy, (it read in a child's handwriting)

I miss you lots and lots and I cried when mommy told me you had gone to heaven. You were the best daddy ever and I will miss you forever.

love you lots daddy
from Jessica
xxxxx

    It felt odd reading the words and in that split second Melissa suddenly appeared in front of his eyes. She was sitting at the kitchen table, happy enough just to draw wonderful and colourful pictures.

    And tears began to run down his cheeks because now his niece was gone, in the blink of an eye her life was extinguished and he hoped that she knew nothing about her death, that she died quickly and painlessly, the little girl who had turned his life upside down, the little girl who was the much needed ray of sunshine in his dark and depressive world, the little girl who was no longer here.

    Still he walked, more slowly this time, still trying to find a suitable place to stand and light the candles, still looking at what people had written for those that they had lost.

> *I miss you more than words can say,*
> *I think of you always,*
> *You will be forever in my heart.*

    What he read next was handwritten on a small white card which was stapled to a bouquet of red roses.

Sam,

You fought for what you believed in and that is what we both admired in you. Rest in peace son.

Mam and Dad
x

The very last thing he read was typed on an ivory coloured card which was leaning against a framed photograph of a handsome man, smiling merrily as he posed with what looked to be his wife and three children.

Graham,

We have lost a son, father, husband, brother and uncle. Heaven has gained an angel.

Still he walked until he found a place near one of the giant bronze lions. He set the candles out in a line and lit each one, with care and deliberation, trying his best to remain strong. For a moment he just stared at the flickering flames, then he knelt at the base and closed his eyes. As soon as he did Lisa flittered in and out of his mind ... her last words echoed inside of his head ... the look of fear etched on her face appeared in front of him...

He shook his head and opened his eyes, staring at the flames through watery eyes. He should have done more than light four candles, he should have written something or brought some flowers at least. As soon as he stood he wanted to leave, arrangements had been made for him to stay at a holiday retreat. There he would think about what he would do next. Another ten minutes had passed before the August chill forced him to leave. He turned and walked away, wiping away the tears with his hands as he went.

Chapter Forty

The Deception

August 24th

THE DAY GREAT BRITAIN STOOD STILL

SUICIDE BOMBERS TARGET TRAFALGAR SQUARE IN DAY OF TERROR

It was a horrific and nightmarish moment for those that had been involved in the Trafalgar Square demonstration. What started off as a peaceful protest for better equipment to be supplied to the British soldiers fighting in South Africa ended in well-calculated outbreaks of terrifying disbelief, signified first by the haunting words of the first suicide bomber, the detonation of his rucksack and the panic-stricken demonstrators scrambling for their lives.

Those that were trying to escape the flying debris and flames came under further attack from two more suicide bombers that detonated their rucksacks near the steps leading towards the National Gallery and in between the two Trafalgar Square fountains. It suddenly became clear to those running for their lives that nowhere was safe.

Continued on Page 4

MORE ON THE TRAFALGAR SQUARE ATTACKS

A MOTHER'S GRIEF: *Final declaration by the fourth suicide bomber found by his mother before he could carry out his task*   Page 11

OFFICIAL SUSPECT ARAPMOI SEBOTHOME?: *Witnesses say they heard the first bomber announce he was a member of the Brotherhood of Sakarabru*   Page 17

***TERRORISTS EXPLOIT WEAKNESSES:** Investigators have criticised the lack of police present at the march* *Page 26*

Lenka Shone finished reading the front page of the eight-day old English newspaper, he took a long draw of his cigar and studied carefully the photograph centred directly in the middle of the paper. Trafalgar Square looked like a scene from a nightmare; countless bodies littered the entire area, spilling their blood onto the stone flooring and into the water of the two fountains.

The writing directly under the photograph read:

The Massacre Of Trafalgar Square: *Three huge explosions engulf parts of Trafalgar Square as suicide bombers detonate their rucksack bombs. Hundreds are feared dead in day of terror.*

Lenka took one final draw of his cigar, then, crushing it in the ashtray he stood and poured a whiskey for himself. He sat back down once he had filled his glass and licking his index finger and thumb, he began turning the pages until he found page seventeen. The black and white picture which topped the article was of Arapmoi Sebothoma. He was standing outside, dressed in his uniform as he overlooked South Africa. It was a beautifully set scene which had been taken and included in an article written about him. The caption underneath read:

Is He Responsible?

Lenka picked up his glass of whiskey and took several sips as he began to read the article.

Yesterday's devastating and astonishingly well-coordinated attack on the mass demonstration held at Trafalgar Square plunged Great Britain into a state of disbelief.

The whole country – possibly the whole world – shook, as three suicide bombers successfully detonated their backpacks equipped with explosives. The sense of security and self-confidence that all the people of Great Britain feel took a serious blow from which recovery will undoubtedly be slow. The after-effects will be nearly as bad, as hundreds, if not thousands of people discover that friends and family died awful, unimaginable deaths. There had been no official count, but Prime Minister Thomas Gordon said that over five hundred people had perished, and in the immediate aftermath, the disaster was already being ranked as one of the worst and most devastating terror attacks in Great Britain's recent history.

PRIME MINISTER'S RESPONSE

In an emotional statement delivered last night, Prime Minister Thomas Gordon vowed to respond, with force if necessary, against those responsible for the attack on Trafalgar Square, declaring that he would "bring justice to all those who perished on the fifteenth of August".

The speech came hours after a day of terror that seems destined to define his time as Prime Minister. Seeking to calm the nation and make known his determination to exact retribution, he told a country numbed by the horrendous loss of life:"It is through terrorism that the people who committed this atrocious act of murder express their principles, and it is now, at this very moment, that we must demonstrate ours."

BOMBER'S ANNOUNCEMENT

Now his attention will turn to who carried out this devastating attack, the nightmare scenario for him and the security services is that this was the South African group the Brotherhood of Sakarabru and their leader Arapmoi Sebothoma who were responsible for the Trafalgar Square bombings. Survivors of the attack all say that the first suicide bomber announced he was a member of the Brotherhood before detonating the explosives.

If what was declared was true then not only would this group find it easy to evade detection and suspicion, but their capture by any of the 'South African Saviours' could spark a furious response by the South African people, in effect dramatically heightening unrest in the country.

Until recently there was no firm evidence to suggest that the Brotherhood of Sakarabru were planning such an attack against

Great Britain, although many have become increasingly angered by the 'South African Saviours' and have spoken publicly.

Initial information suggests that the operation was planned by dedicated extremists. The bomb makers used sophisticated techniques and high explosives, suggesting that they had a vast knowledge in bomb making.

LIBERATORS OF SOUTH AFRICA INVOLVEMENT

There has been speculation that surviving militants of the Liberators of South Africa could have planned and executed the Trafalgar Square bombings. A security service insider said it is possible but highly unlikely.

Lenka had finished reading the first page of the article but he had read enough, he closed the newspaper, leaned back in his chair and started to swirl the whiskey around the glass as he held it in his hand. He knew Arapmoi would never plan such a horrific attack, regardless of the final words he had spoken in their last conversation.

'Never again disrespect this monument.'

And even though he had said it with severity, Lenka knew that Arapmoi would never kill the Trafalgar Square protestors, but the darker side he showed that night would work in Lenka's favour if need be.

He drained the rest of his whiskey, stood, and walked around his office, tying to think of who would plan and execute such an attack. Not that he would do all he could to apprehend them, on the contrary, he would want to thank them. Whoever they were had cast aspersions on Arapmoi, a continuous thorn in Lenka's side and a genuine threat to his Presidential ambitions.

But there would be repercussions which Lenka didn't need, especially at this critical point in South Africa. Questions would need to be answered, investigations and inquiries would be carried out, and Lenka would have to show willing, willing to help with everything. But the South African people loved and embraced Arapmoi, and they would not believe his involvement in the Trafalgar Square bombings until the man himself admitted it—

There was a loud double-knock at his door and Lenka slowed. Luthuli Dros had been away, trying to persuade an ex-politician to join the Council. No doubt this would be him, having achieved what he had been asked to do and ready to bask in all his glory.

But Lenka would not allow him this personal satisfaction, where Luthuli had been was in the middle of nowhere and the chances of him knowing about the Trafalgar Square bombings were slim, and he would use this to his advantage. He would appear distressed and distraught in front of him and if anyone cast doubt on Lenka then Luthuli, like the faithful assistant he was, would be quick to defend. Lenka stopped and looked over at the door.

'Yes?' he said sharply, a faint smile curling upon his lips.

The door opened inwards and Luthuli strolled in, seemingly pleased with himself as he looked at Lenka's deadpan expression.

'WHERE THE HELL HAVE YOU BEEN?' Lenka raged.

Luthuli stopped and raised his eyebrows. He was taken aback, for never once had Lenka spoke to him in such a manner before.

'Sir you know where I have been,' he said quickly, 'I've been trying to persuade—'

'Yes, yes,' said Lenka irritably, 'never mind that now, have you heard the news?'

'News, sir?' Luthuli said, looking perplexed.

Lenka stormed over to his desk, grasped the newspaper, and read aloud the headline. 'The day Great Britain stood still,' he said, trying to keep his voice calm and steady, 'suicide bombers target Trafalgar Square in day of terror.'

The words echoed throughout the now silent room, and it took a while for Luthuli to find his voice.

'Impossible,' he could only manage to say.

Lenka opened the newspaper and continued to read. 'Now his attention will turn to who carried out this devastating attack,' he said, his voice now beginning to break, 'the nightmare scenario for him and the security services is, that this was the South African group the Brotherhood of Sakarabru and their leader Arapmoi Sebothoma who were responsible for the Trafalgar Square bombings. Survivors of the attack all say that the first suicide bomber announced he was a member of the Brotherhood before detonating his explosives.'

He stopped and looked up, and Luthuli could not believe what Lenka was implying from his expression.

'Surely there must be some kind of mistake,' he said. Feeling as though his legs were going to buckle out from under him, he sat in the chair facing Lenka's desk.

'Read it yourself then,' Lenka said indignantly.

And he threw the paper onto his desk as he passed it, unwavering he was, as he picked up his empty glass and headed to the whiskey to refill it.

Feeling slightly numbed by Lenka's unusually sharp, confrontational personality, Luthuli was unsure what he should do. He did not want to appear to be questioning the competence of the man he regarded highly, but on the other hand this was a serious accusation that Lenka was accusing the Brotherhood of Sakarabru of. Deciding it was probably best if he should read the articles for himself, he forced a slight smile as he leaned forward and grabbed the newspaper.

Lenka remained standing, taking sips of his whiskey as he shook his head incessantly.

'How could he do this?' he said, massaging his temples with fingers.

The question was more for himself than for Luthuli to answer, who was still reading the newspaper, slowly and carefully.

'And with the election due to be held soon.'

He finished off the rest of his whiskey, walked wearily back to his desk and sat down in his chair. He did not know how long it took for Luthuli to read the newspaper, nor did he care. But finally he folded the paper and dropped it onto the desk. What he had just read had obviously shaken him, his eyes were a little wider from the shock and the colour in his face had drained away.

'It's a mistake,' he said quietly, 'it's a misprint, a misunderstanding by the survivors, the Liberators of South Africa are a part of th –'

'Or perhaps you are clinging onto a false hope,' said Lenka quite calmly.

'Sir?' Luthuli said, his lips quivering, 'I hope you are not suggesting that Arapmoi was somehow involved.'

'That is exactly what I am suggesting,' said Lenka, much to Luthuli's surprise, 'I know what Arapmoi is capable of, I have seen first hand that he is willing to kill. The day he saved my life I saw a madness in his eyes that has never left my thoughts.'

He leaned back in his chair and buried his face in his hands.

'And yet the people will not believe a word of it, Arapmoi will never admit to the attack and any accusations that are made towards him could send the country into a crisis.'

He slid his hands from his face and looked at Luthuli.

'And for the first time I do not know which path I should take.' He sighed deeply. 'What should I do?' he asked despairingly.

'I'm afraid you cannot put that responsibility onto my shoulders,' Luthuli said regretfully.

Lenka smiled wearily. 'I know you are right Luthuli,' he said, 'and it is unfair of me to put you in that position.'

'Whatever you decide,' said Luthuli softly, 'I am certain that the Council will respect your decision and fully support you.'

After a moment or two had passed, Lenka stood and began to smarten his tie and suit.

'I must first calm the nation,' he said, 'I will not place blame on Arapmoi I will just explain the facts.'

'That is all you can do sir,' said Luthuli.

Lenka acknowledged Luthuli's words with a pat on his shoulder as he passed him. Walking over to the door he turned the handle and stepped out into the hallway. And as he walked across the carpeted floor he began to smile, Luthuli Dros had fallen for his deception, and it was time for him to do the same to the country, it was in the best interests of everyone after all.

Chapter Forty-One

Hidden Truths

That evening, Lenka Shone, the man predicted to be the next South African President spoke in front of news reporters and cameras. As promised he did not blame Arapmoi for what had happened, instead he explained the facts, and yet because of this he still deceived the nation. He knew that Arapmoi wasn't responsible for the attack on Trafalgar Square, but he did not tell the world this, as far as Lenka was concerned his relationship had ended when Arapmoi had turned down the generous job offer on the Council.

And so, as the South African people tried to understand what Lenka had said, Arapmoi and Tebogo, who after many weeks of travelling, had finally arrived at the cottage Clarence Sauer had spent his last years in. They stood in front of the thickly rusted gate under a sky which had lost most of its light. The cottage stood perfectly alone, the garden either side of the narrow path which led straight up to the front door, had been allowed to grow wildly in the years the cottage had been unoccupied. But miraculously the cottage and the small amount of land that surrounded it appeared to be totally unscathed by the war that once raged in South Africa.

'I wonder why no one ever took care of his garden,' Tebogo said, squinting through the darkness at the various weeds advancing through the plants and grass.

'Perhaps someone did,' Arapmoi said, 'but a risky business it would be pulling out weeds with bombs exploding all around you.'

He turned the handle of the rusty gate and it squeaked in protest as he pushed it open. They walked down the narrow path and stood in front of the door, a large bronze plaque was secured to it, the words engraved upon the metal read:

At the turn of the millennium Clarence Sauer, after many years of fighting, finally lost his battle against lung cancer. On the day of his funeral, as a final mark of respect, his cottage was locked and this plaque was placed upon this door, to act as a lasting memorial to Clarence Sauer and to remind all South Africans of the hope and joy he once brought.

Those who had come to see where Clarence Sauer had lived the last part of his life had left their mark around the plaque, as a way of paying their own tribute. Some had simply written their initials in permanent ink, others their names, but a select few had taken the time to carve their beautiful messages into the dark wood of the door.

South Africa will miss you Clarence Sauer no one can ever replace you.

You are a King amongst Kings Mr Sauer.
God bless your soul.

Rest in peace Clarence Sauer, you brought so much hope and happiness to the children who had none.

Thank you for giving me a second chance in life.

'Should we replace this door?' Tebogo asked as he looked at the engraved words.

'No,' Arapmoi said at once, running his fingers over the grain of the wood, 'they took their time to honour his memory. Clarence Sauer would have been glad they did.'

The decision to use this cottage as a central point was one that had not been an easy one to make and Arapmoi had thought long and hard about it for many months. He had been a close friend of Clarence Sauer, he admired and respected him deeply. He had spent his remaining years here and ultimately passed away in his sleep, as a result of this and as a final mark of respect, the cottage was locked, never again to be opened. But a lot had changed since then; South Africa had plunged into war, and Arapmoi knew that if his friend was still alive today he would want this cottage to be used to help rebuild the country. And it was this nice warming thought that had been the deciding factor.

But still it felt strange and almost kind of eerie for Arapmoi to be back here after all this time, and yet it was one of those odd moments when it felt like it was only yesterday.

The key to the cottage was housed among many other things at the monument in a glass cabinet. Arapmoi didn't take it, he didn't want Lenka to know what he was doing or where he would be staying. But this idea of invisibility presented a problem: how would they get in?

The pair began to walk around the cottage, wondering which window was big enough for them both to climb through but could also be easily boarded up until it was replaced. They walked around twice and finally decided on the single side window on the right hand side of the cottage. Removing the rucksack from his back, Tebogo knelt as he unzipped it and pulled out a tattered blanket. Then, picking up a rock from the garden, he held it in his hand and wrapped the blanket around it. He looked away and shielded his face as he broke the window, and once all the shattered glass had been cleared from the window cill and frame he climbed through.

The room he dropped down into was narrow and dark. Arapmoi handed him a torch and as Tebogo shone it around, it became clear that Clarence Sauer used this room for storage. The shelves on the walls to the left and right were filled with all sorts: paint cans, tools, a variety of cleaning equipment, screws, nails, nuts and bolts.

Resting the torch on the shelf, Tebogo grabbed hold of the two bags with sleeping bags secured to them and the handcrafted walking stick. He put them down and as he reached out his arm, Arapmoi gripped his hand and he was pulled up. Now cramped in the room, Arapmoi took hold of the torch and pointed it towards the door as he turned the handle and stepped through.

The living room was simple, two threadbare couches and an old round coffee table were grouped together in front of an open fire which would be the only source of light once lit. Dust layered over everything and the air that greeted them was stale. Clarence had designed this cottage for simplicity; no electricity, no running water, only a well at the bottom of the garden, and it was because of this and the late hour that Arapmoi decided that they should call it a night.

'We will begin tomorrow,' he said.

They set up their sleeping bags in the living room. The pair made makeshift mattresses from the seats of the two, two seated couches, their feet stuck out from the bottom, but it beat sleeping on the hard floor. Tebogo rolled up some of his spare clothes and rested his head against them.

'Night sir,' he said, closing his eyes.

'Sleep well Tebogo,' Arapmoi said a moment later.

But Tebogo barely heard it, he was already asleep. Sleep for Arapmoi on the other hand was the last thing he desired. He lay on his side, staring into the darkness, his mind now wondering if he had chosen wisely. But then he quashed the thought at once, there was nothing left for him back home, he was needed here; to watch Lenka carefully and make sure that the power he had did not corrupt him, to make sure that he kept all of the promises he had made, to make sure that the man did not become a tyrant. Ten or so minutes had passed before Arapmoi finally drifted off to sleep.

Soon he was walking in the calmness of night. Surrounded by trees and bushes, Arapmoi had his eyes fixed firmly upon the grey stoned cottage, which gradually grew closer to him. Its one and only window glowed softly in the darkness and its entire façade was covered in exotic wall climbing plants. And in no time at all he was upon the wooden door, knocking on it twice and waiting, looking up at the full moon high in the sky, casting its light onto him.

The door opened inwards a moment later. A small elderly man stood before him, frail-looking with white bushy hair and large circular glasses, he seemed unfazed by the late hour.

'Arapmoi,' he greeted with a smile, 'my dear old friend. It has been a long time.'

'My apologies,' said Arapmoi, 'I have been meaning to visit for some time.'

The man stepped back, opening the door a little wider. Arapmoi extended his hand as he walked inside, but the man's eyes twinkled as he smiled.

'You know me better than that Arapmoi,' he said heartily.

The two friends embraced, the man patted Arapmoi on his back several times as they did. Then he closed the door and hobbled as he led Arapmoi into the small living room. The warmth from the open fire, gently cracking away against the far wall, stung Arapmoi's face as he entered. The room was simple, two threadbare couches and an old round coffee table were grouped together in the illumination of the fire, which was the only source of light. A black, old-fashioned kettle hung above the glowing ash.

'So what do I owe the pleasure?' the man asked.

'Zuberi's dead,' Arapmoi said at once.

'I know,' said the man, offering Arapmoi one of the seats, 'I might live in the middle of nowhere but I still saw the fireworks, why else would the people be celebrating if it wasn't for Zuberi's death?'

'Yes of course,' Arapmoi said sitting. 'I should have come to see you sooner.'

'You have no need to apologise Arapmoi,' the man said softly, 'I know you have been busy.' He picked up one of the logs resting in the wicker basket and threw it on the dwindling flames. 'So how do you feel about the death of Zuberi?'

'The war is finally over,' Arapmoi said, staring into the fire.

The man smiled. 'That is not what I asked,' he said, 'I know of the relationship you had with Zuberi.'

The warmth seemed to fade from Arapmoi's face. The softly spoken words had unsettled him.

'You had more of a relationship with him than I did,' Arapmoi said quietly.

'I see,' the man said, looking attentively at Arapmoi through his large circular spectacles. Then he glanced over at the black kettle and said brightly, 'Will you be staying for a cup of tea? No doubt you will be accustomed to it having spent all those years in England.'

'That would be nice,' Arapmoi said after he had finished chuckling.

The man stood and hobbled out of the room. Arapmoi heard the opening of cupboards and the clinking of cups, and the man came back a minute or so later bearing an old tray with a small milk jug, a bowl of sugar with a spoon resting in it, and two ceramic cups with a single tea bag in each of them, placed upon it. He put it down on the table and asked Arapmoi, 'Milk? Sugar?'

'No sugar, just a drop of milk.'

'So where will you go from here Arapmoi,' the man said as he began to make the tea, 'will you be returning to England?'

'No,' he said, shaking his head, 'I am needed here. It is going to take a long time to rebuild South Africa to what it once was; the country needs all the help it can get.'

'And is that the only reason you are staying?' He handed Arapmoi his tea and once he had made his own sat down opposite. 'Do not get me wrong it is very honourable but there are many people ready and willing to rebuild South Africa.'

Arapmoi took a sip of his tea and let out a tiny sigh.

'I think Lenka will become corrupt with his power.'

The man raised his eyebrows and surveyed Arapmoi through his large, round glasses.

'He is becoming a tyrant,' he said taking another sip of his tea. 'If this is correct then the celebrations have been short lived. Lenka Shone's power and influence will only grow, but that will not be enough for him. Men who are consumed by power and greed only want more, and they will not let anyone stand in their way of achieving their goal.'

Arapmoi already knew this but still his eyes widened slightly. And then his mind drifted back to when Lenka offered him a job on the Council now knowing the truth behind it. Lenka obviously saw him as a threat to the Presidential election, it was a common fact that the South African people loved and respected Arapmoi. If Arapmoi had accepted the proposal then Lenka would be in control; he would be able to watch him closely and make sure he did nothing untoward.

But Arapmoi had not accepted the offer, and he didn't know it at the time, but in doing so he had suddenly become a problem for Lenka –

'Sir,' Tebogo's voice echoed around the room, *'sir, wake up.'*

'I must go,' Arapmoi said urgently. He put his half-drunk cup of tea on the table and stood.

'Sir, someone is coming.'

'Be careful Arapmoi,' the man said, who also stood.

Arapmoi had just put on his long, hooded coat, but before he could say a word, he was awoken suddenly by a pair of powerful hands seizing him.

Arapmoi opened his eyes just as a black trainer came crashing down on the left side of his face. The pain was so intense that he almost blacked out because of it. He screamed out in agony as he felt himself being dragged away. Through his watery eyes he tried to see if Tebogo was being subjected to the same sort of beating, but the sleeping bag he had been in was now empty.

Arapmoi was dragged out of the cottage, the front door stood wide open, it had been unlocked; the air was cool against his bloody face. A car was parked not far from him, its bright headlights made his eyes sting; he winced and turned his head.

And as he did, he saw Tebogo lying perfectly still on the floor. His face and hands were bloody and swollen, and as Arapmoi was forced to his feet and pushed against the bonnet of the car, there was no way of telling if he was dead or alive.

And then suddenly and quite violently he was punched hard in his kidneys. His legs buckled out from beneath him as he slid partly down the car bonnet, he lay on his front, the blood from his face now pooling onto the white rusty paintwork.

He raised his head, wondering if he could somehow force his wounded body to climb into the car and drive off, but someone was sitting in the driver's side. And as Arapmoi narrowed his eyes a fraction, he recognised the person as Mosegi Joubert, the young man who had been guarding the door of the Clarence Sauer monument the day Zuberi had been killed.

Mosegi sat, drumming his fingers on the steering wheel, his expression one that suggested that he wasn't quite sure what he should do.

'Help me,' said Arapmoi weakly.

But Mosegi didn't, he looked away just as Arapmoi was grabbed by his ankles and pulled off the car. His face thudded off the dusty ground, the pain was indescribable, he just lay there, hoping, praying even that they would kill him soon.

Powerful hands rolled him onto his back, the man standing over him had a look of pure hatred and insanity about him. He was short and gaunt looking and the pistol he held in his hand was pointed directly at Arapmoi, who wanted nothing more than to close his eyes but couldn't because of the fear that had numbed his body.

'WHAT ARE YOU DOING?' someone shouted close by.

Arapmoi watched as a figure suddenly emerged, pushing the man away just as the gun roared. The bullet hit the ground, spraying dirt into the air.

The man cursed. 'He is responsible for the Trafalgar Square bombings,' he said, there was hysteria in his voice.

Trafalgar Square bombing, Arapmoi thought, unable to make sense of it.

'Lenka wants him alive,' the second man said.

'We can end this now,' the man said in shrieks of madness, 'he is too dangerous to be kept alive. Killing him now will end all of this – we must – we must.'

'He will be held accountable for what he has done,' the second man said, trying his utmost to remain calm.

But the reasoning did little to convince the man. And Arapmoi, through his swollen, watery eyes could see him, standing not far away, the gun in his hand still raised directly at him.

Fear unlike he had ever known gripped his entire body. Death was upon him, but he could not have his last thoughts to be of this. He closed his eyes and thought of nice warming thoughts. The gun roared for a second time. He knew this was death, this time the bullet had tore through his skull, killing him. But the moment was odd, his pain had not lessened, a tunnel with light shining at the end of it did not appear in front of his eyes announcing his death. He was still very much alive, breathing, bleeding, still lying on his back.

'What are you do –'

'On the floor now,' he heard someone say. The voice sounded familiar to him. 'Put your hands behind your head.'

Arapmoi opened his eyes slowly, unsure what to expect. The man that had been standing not far from him was now crumbled on the floor, he was dead. Mosegi was standing over the second man pointing the pistol directly at his back. Once the man had done what he had been told to do, Mosegi walked quickly over to Arapmoi.

'You once told me that if you try and fool others you are only fooling yourself,' he said calmly, pointing the pistol directly at Arapmoi's head.

'That's correct Mosegi,' Arapmoi said weakly, 'I did.'

'So I'm going to ask you this once and once only.' His pause was only momentarily. 'Are you responsible for the bombings at Trafalgar Square?' he asked, his weapon still raised.

Yet again this bombing of Trafalgar Square was mentioned, but still Arapmoi had no idea what it was all about.

'I know nothing about the Trafalgar Square bombings,' Arapmoi said at once, staring into Mosegi's dark eyes.

Mosegi looked a little unsure with what Arapmoi had just said.

'Three suicide bombers killed over five hundred people when they held a demonstration at Trafalgar Square. People are holding you responsible for the attack, is what they are saying true?'

'No,' said Arapmoi, 'I had no involvement.'

'Then who is responsible?'

The only sound to break this silence was Tebogo's low groaning and coughing. Arapmoi looked over at him, to the young man whom he regarded as a son, who he loved, who he trusted with his life, who was still young and naïve enough to be tricked and manipulated...

'I don't know,' he said, pushing the thought from his head at once.

Silence followed the words. Mosegi looked at him for a long time before slowly lowering the pistol.

'I believe you. South Africa is not a safe place for you now, sir.' He helped Arapmoi to his feet and sat him on the bonnet of the car. He then glanced over at the man still lying on his front with the hands over the back of his head before walking over to Tebogo and kneeling by his side.

'How did you know we were here?' Arapmoi asked, once the pain in his face lessened.

Mosegi explained briefly, how the three had been ordered by Lenka to watch and follow Arapmoi and Tebogo, and they waited for the pair to enter the cottage and fall asleep before unlocking the front door and grabbing them.

Arapmoi wiped away the blood from his lip with the back of his hand, and as he did, Mosegi stood and walked over. Pulling a tatty-looking handkerchief from his pocket, he offered it to Arapmoi who said a word of thanks.

'Lenka is holding you responsible for the Trafalgar Square bombings,' Mosegi said, 'but I think he may have had something to do with it.'

Arapmoi's body seemed to slump a little. His worst fears had become real, Lenka was a tyrant, a man who was corrupted by the power he now held and he would not let anyone stand in his way.

And as Mosegi knelt down by Tebogo's side once again and Arapmoi held the handkerchief against his bleeding lip, it was becoming clear to him why Lenka had planned and executed the attack on Trafalgar Square. He recalled what the old man had said to him in his dream: *'Men who are consumed by power and greed only want more, and they will not let anyone stand in their way of them achieving that.'*

Lenka had offered Arapmoi a place on the Council, an offer which he turned down. And because of this he was considered a threat to Lenka and his Presidential aspirations. Killing the Trafalgar Square protestors and then accusing Arapmoi eradicated his problem. Arapmoi would be captured and then put on trial and there was nothing he could do to prevent it from happening.

A few more minutes passed before Tebogo awoke from his unconsciousness. Groggy and in pain, he put his arm around Mosegi's neck and was helped to his feet.

'You need to get as far away from here as you can,' Mosegi said as he and Arapmoi put Tebogo into the car and fastened him into his seat.

Mosegi ran into the cottage and emerged a minute or so later with the two backpacks, sleeping bags and Arapmoi's walking stick in his hands. He threw them into the back of the car and as he shut the door he looked at Arapmoi.

'Come with us,' said Arapmoi.

'My journey ends here sir. I have already failed in my duty, I cannot possibly go on.'

And as Arapmoi extended his hand and Mosegi shook it, he said, 'No matter what anyone says, you will always remain a hero to me.'

He climbed into the car, and as he shut the door and brought the vehicle to life, he looked across at Tebogo, whose face was bloodied and bruised.

'Did anyone mention killing the protestors at Trafalgar Square to you?' he asked calmly.

Tebogo's mouth was badly swollen; he could only shake his head.

'Are you sure? You weren't mislead into thinking it was a good idea.'

Tebogo shook his head again.

Arapmoi heard all that he needed, he put the car into gear and drove off.

But Mosegi did not watch them go; instead he stood behind the last man whom accompanied him on this journey of apprehension.

'What have you done?' the man vented his anger.

Mosegi did not give an answer, raising his pistol he killed the man where he lay and then pressed the nozzle firmly against his temple.

'It has been an honour to fight with you sir,' he whispered, closing his eyes.

The gunshot echoed across the land and a fraction of a moment later Mosegi's body thudded to the floor.

Chapter Forty-Two

A New Council

September 1st

The deaths of the three who had been sent to apprehend Arapmoi and Tebogo had brought the whole of South Africa to a standstill. Everyone could not understand it. Arapmoi Sebothoma responsible for such an atrocious act; it could not be possible. Arapmoi was an inspirer, a leader, a man who had given the country hope, and yet ... he and Tebogo were gone, nowhere to be found. And people now began to wonder if he was not only responsible for the deaths of the three but also for the Trafalgar Square bombings.

And since then South Africa seemed to have lost all of its direction; those that were expected to lead it through this dark time had hidden themselves away in the Clarence Sauer monument. Even Lenka Shone, a man who never shied from the television cameras took a week to deliver his address. But even this was forgettable, it was nothing like the inspiring and trademark speeches he usually delivered.

'I can confirm that both Arapmoi Sebothoma and Tebogo Jeppe are now wanted in connection with the Trafalgar Square bombings,' he had said plainly in his official address. *'I had issued an order for their arrest which unfortunately resulted in the deaths of three security officers.'*

As soon as he had finished he was immediately bombarded with question upon question but Lenka answered none of them, he turned and walked away, without so much as a backwards glance.

Now Lenka Shone was in the 'green zone', the part of South Africa which had been declared safe from the Liberators of South Africa. Since the death of Zuberi Jacobs many of the Liberators had disbanded and the select few that still believed in the cause had either been captured or killed. South Africa now faced a new enemy, an enemy which had been created by Arapmoi Sebothoma to protect the country.

And as Mosegi's coffin was gently lowered into the earth and the final few words were said, the dozen people who had gathered to pay their last respects now watched as Mosegi's mother dropped a colourful flower into the hole. She stood for a moment sobbing quietly then she turned and buried her puffy face into the shoulder of her husband.

Lenka felt no remorse, no guilt, no sadness, only a pure loathing as he stared down at the dirt being thrown onto the wooden box.

This man was loyal to Arapmoi Sebothoma, he thought, *he killed the other two, he is a traitor to South Africa.*

Removing the designer sunglasses from over his heavy, drawn eyes, Lenka folded the arms and slid them inside the top pocket of his black suit jacket. With Luthuli Dros close behind him, the pair walked over to the grieving mother and father.

'I appreciate you being here today, Mr Shone,' the father said quietly, extending his hand.

Lenka shook it. 'It is an honour,' he lied, 'Mosegi was an outstanding individual, he will be sadly missed.'

'Thank you Mr Shone,' the mother said between her sobbing, 'Mosegi often told me how privileged he felt to be working for you.'

'Yes,' Lenka said softly, 'he played a very important part within the Council, and I will do everything in my power to find Arapmoi Sebothoma and Tebogo Jeppe.'

Mosegi's mother gave a watery smile and both her and her husband nodded. Then they linked up their arms and cuddled into one another as they watched their son's coffin becoming buried underneath the earth.

Lenka did not stand there a moment longer than he had too, he turned away, reached inside his inner jacket pocket and withdrew a cigar. Once Prepared he lit it and left a trail of smoke behind him as he and Luthuli walked in silence towards the sleek car waiting for them. The driver stepped out and opened the passenger's door but before Lenka could climb in, an American army four by four vehicle, heavily armoured, pulled up alongside.

The passenger's door opened at once and out stepped a tall, clean shaven, burley figure of a man.

General James Perez was a new face to South Africa; he had been drafted in to help lead and restructure the country, in the hope of giving it a new direction. He stood with his wide shoulders thrown back and his strong dimpled chin held above his chest. He had the unmistakable authority of an army general: Strong, powerful, a natural leader who was proud to wear the American insignia on his pristine, immaculate uniform.

'General Perez,' Lenka said pleasantly, smiling, 'what do I owe the pleasure?'

'I want a word with you Lenka,' the general spoke in a way that indicated that this was not a request, this was an order. His voice fitted his commanding stature: deep and fearless.

'Of course,' Lenka said silkily almost sarcastically. 'Anything for the South African Saviours.'

He told Luthuli – who was already waiting inside the sleek car – that he would be only a minute, then he climbed into the surprisingly spacious army vehicle and as he closed the door he was soon surrounded in a haze of cigar smoke. The smoke clung to the lungs of General Perez, but he fought the desire to cough, he would not appear weak in front of the politician.

'I'm sorry,' said Lenka, who eyed the general's discomfort with great enjoyment, 'where are my manners.'

He reached inside his inner jacket pocket and withdrew a cigar. He offered it to the general who in turn held up his hand and shook his head.

'That is right,' Lenka said, smirking, 'you Americans now lead uneventful lives; you grow old and die of boredom.'

He replaced the cigar inside his jacket pocket just as general Perez clicked down his window a fraction.

'You've been a difficult man to find Lenka,' he said, looking at the world through the dust-streaked glass.

'I have a country to rebuild general Perez,' said Lenka, who took another long draw of his cigar, 'surely you of all people understand that.'

He exhaled the smoke in the direction of the general, who could no longer prevent himself from the inevitable coughing.

'One day last week I had the best night's sleep,' general Perez said quickly, 'which surprised me because we still are at war.' He smiled and began to drum his fingers underneath the window. 'I woke up refreshed and revitalised, I showered and shaved and had a hearty breakfast. I thought the day would be a good day, I was full of optimism. So you can understand my disappointment when, while I was drinking my cup of coffee I was told that you had given the go ahead for Arapmoi Sebothoma and Tebogo Jeppe to be arrested. When told something like that, questions begin to circulate around in your head, you try to make sense of it all, try to give reasoning, but it's difficult.'

He turned his head and stared at Lenka, narrowing his green eyes a fraction.

'They say you have a unique sense of humour, but I strongly advise you not to play games with me Lenka, I'm not as laid back as my predecessor. So I'm going to ask you this once and once only.' He paused briefly. 'Why did you order three of your men to arrest Arapmoi Sebothoma and Tebogo Jeppe?'

The general's eyes seemed to darken and grow cold from that point. They had seen an unimaginable amount of pain, suffering and death, Lenka knew this because he had also seen the same. But the general's stare did little to intimidate Lenka who had experienced his fair share of intimidation over the years, he continued to savour and appreciate his cigar and deliberately took his time in answering the general's question.

'I was afraid that you would follow an ancient American tradition and shoot Arapmoi and Tebogo first and asked them questions later,' he said smugly.

General Perez was a poker playing man who had perfected the ability to remain expressionless. He glanced down at the gun resting in the side holster and brushed his fingers against the metal.

'What you fail to understand general,' Lenka said quickly, knowing he was walking a fine line, 'is that South Africa is at a pivotal moment.' He glanced at the cigar held in his fingers but suddenly lost the desire to take a draw from it. 'The people are becoming increasingly frustrated with your presence here, if I allowed you to go ahead with the capture of Arapmoi and he was killed during the attempt, then South Africa would have fallen into complete chaos.'

'We would have never allowed that to happen,' Perez said confidently.

'You promised the entire world that you would capture Zuberi Jacobs and make him stand trial,' Lenka scoffed. 'What did you do?' He did not wait for an answer. 'You dropped a bomb on him. Arapmoi is hailed as a hero by the locals and many believe that he is not responsible for the Trafalgar Square bombings, if he was killed then you wouldn't be dealing with a few militants, it would be hundreds of thousands.'

'Innocent men do not run Lenka,' Perez said, looking back out of the window.

'Yes they do general; they do if the people chasing them are wielding guns.'

And having the last word, Lenka opened the door and stepped outside. But it seemed that general Perez had finished with him anyway.

'I will be seeing you Lenka,' he called out.

'Not if I see you first general Perez,' said Lenka silkily as he dropped his cigar to the floor and crushed it under his highly polished shoe.

Then he slammed the door shut, and did not watch the car as it drove away. He climbed back into the sleek waiting car, chuckling to himself, much to the disapproval of Luthuli.

'Regardless of what you think of the Americans,' he said sternly, 'we still need them. The last thing we need at this critical moment is for them to withdraw.'

'They won't withdraw,' Lenka replied, smiling confidently.

'You cannot be sure of that sir.'

'Of course I can,' Lenka said, looking at Luthuli now, 'I know they won't withdraw now because Jack Carter isn't shaking my hand in front of the world's media, congratulating me on winning the Presidential election. Then, and only then will the American soldiers leave the country. They have lost too many of their own, if they withdraw and South Africa falls into disarray what have they died for?'

'Do not be too sure of that,' said Luthuli, shaking his head, 'President Carter is campaigning for a second stint in the White House. The Presidential elections will be held later this year and

South Africa has become an unpopular war with the Americans, he may have to withdraw troops to save his Presidential career.'

Lenka's confident smile slowly began to fade when told this.

'I will apologise to Perez tomorrow,' he said.

'I do not think that will be enough,' said Luthuli quietly, 'you must break all ties with the Brotherhood of Sakarabru.'

Lenka's face displayed nothing but shock, Luthuli might as well have said that he was going to run for President.

Luthuli let out a tiny sigh. 'What happened last week was a tragic loss, but it was made apparent that Arapmoi has more influence than what we gave him credit for. How many more has he influenced? How many in the monument?'

It was clear that Lenka had never considered this, he glanced over at the driver, wondering if he was as loyal as he claimed to be. Then he thought about everyone inside of the monument, some of Zuberi's people, those that he had trusted, had plotted to kill him, what was preventing the Council members from doing the same to him?

Luthuli leaned inwards, his voice was no higher than a whisper. 'Address the nation tomorrow,' he said, 'condemn Arapmoi's attack on Trafalgar Square.' He could see Lenka was about to speak, but Luthuli felt it paramount for him to continue. 'Support the South African Saviours, people are losing their loved ones everyday, honour their sacrifice by creating a new Council, by doing all you can to find Arapmoi and Tebogo and bring them to trial. Convince the doubters and objectors of the war that our country is worth fighting for...'

Luthuli's voice trailed away: Lenka was thinking, the idea of creating a new Council intrigued him. The original Council had been formed by the surviving politicians, Lenka had become leader only because no one else wanted to do so. But now he could think of at least a dozen who could, and most probably would, run against him when the Presidential elections got underway.

What gave them the right to do so? Lenka had risked his life daily, he had made himself seen and heard, he had done all of these things while the other Council members burrowed themselves away inside the monument. In creating a new Council he could pick people that he could manipulate and use to do his bidding. He looked over at Luthuli, he like many others was a simple pawn in this game of chess, and that is what Lenka wanted for the new Council: men and women he could use and sacrifice if needed.

And as he looked out of the window a grin began to form on his lips; *Arapmoi's sudden disappearance could work in my favour,* he thought.

Those that he felt could threaten his Presidential ambitions could be accused of working with Arapmoi, no proof would be needed, South Africa was in complete disarray. *And I am the man to lead us through this.*

Regrettably people would die during the reform, sacrificed in order for the country to become great again. *For a tree to grow and flourish, the parts that threaten its health must be cut from it.*

'Have you got a pen and some paper?' he asked Luthuli, looking at him.

Luthuli rummaged through his jacket and trouser pockets and pulled out a pencil and a small notepad, which he opened to a fresh page.

'Good,' said Lenka softly, smiling.

He turned his head and looked out of the window again, watching the world slip by him.

'Write this down.'

Chapter Forty-Three

The Bringer of Hope

September 3rd

He was walking along the stone flooring of Trafalgar Square, up ahead Lisa and Melissa both stood on the National Gallery steps, both smiling at him, both waving.

Robert waved back.

'LISA,' he called out, smiling brightly, 'MELISSA, YOU'RE BOTH OKAY.'

Neither Lisa nor Melissa replied, they just stood there, still smiling, still waving. And as Robert began to run towards them, a bloodcurdling scream thundered through his ears and a fraction of a moment later both Lisa and Melissa erupted in flames.

'NOOOOOOOOO!' Robert screamed.

He opened his eyes at once, they were wide in terror from the nightmare. He was sat underneath a large oak tree overlooking a gleaming lake, the whole of his body was soaked in sweat and he was shivering uncontrollably.

Since his arrival at the holiday resort he had spent most of his time in the secluded lodge. But the silence and stillness this morning was so unbearable to him that he could no longer stay inside, and so he ventured outside. He had been walking around the vast complex for about thirty minutes before he came across this tranquil spot. He had sat under the oak tree and stared out over the lake, before his physical and mental exhaustion had eventually pulled him to sleep.

He had not been asleep for long before the nightmare had awoken him. It was the same setting every time he closed his eyes, Lisa and Melissa were both standing in Trafalgar Square and moments later they were consumed by flames. Robert was nothing more than a helpless bystander, and no matter how hard he tried, he could not save them, he could only watch their burning bodies and hear their screams of agony.

The last remnants of the nightmare had left his mind now, and Robert wiped the tiny beads of sweat from his forehead. And as he sat there, he could see a young couple making their way down the long, winding path. They walked hand in hand, the man was carrying a wicker basket, and the woman was laughing, possibly over something her partner might have said.

It seemed practically impossible to Robert that these two had a desire to eat and laugh. How could the pair be acting as though nothing had happened? Didn't they realise that people had died at Trafalgar Square? Didn't they realise that Lisa, Melissa, Michael and David had all perished? Or perhaps they did, but didn't care. Too wrapped up in their own little world to even think about others.

Robert just sat there and waited for them to pass before he got up and walked to the edge of the water. He picked up a handful of pebbles and began to skim them off the gleaming surface.

His decision not to fly back with the bodies of Lisa, Melissa, Michael and David had not been an easy choice to make. Lisa's parents had rung him several times, but Robert had ignored each of their calls, sending them straight through to voicemail. Although they were heartfelt messages, not blaming him for what had happened, he could not bring himself to ring them back.

How could he? Knowing what he was responsible for. Knowing that Michael had raised concerns. Knowing that he hadn't listened to them. Knowing that his ignorance and arrogance are what had killed all four of them.

Throwing the last of the pebbles, Robert now looked out across the water. Where would he go from here? His grandmother was arriving tomorrow, Robert knew better than to argue with her; if he refused then she would have come anyway. But regardless of this, how could he return home? The home where Melissa's shrieks of delight could be heard every morning, the home which Lisa graced. Now his mansion would be silent and empty.

How could he spend the rest of his life living like that? No matter what he did, the guilt and loss tearing at his heart would be with him always. No amount of time could ever heal him, he couldn't live like that. He would walk, walk until he reached the bottom of the lake. Then he would be at peace, he would be reunited with all the people he loved dearly.

He stood at the edge of the lake, the water gently lapping over his trainers. But before he could take his first step, a black dog, big and powerful swam effortlessly through the water. Carrying a long, thin stick in its mouth, it emerged from the lake, water dripping off its soaked body as it dropped the stick by Robert's feet. It shook itself widely then sat, wagging its tail and panting loudly as it stared up at Robert.

'Boomer,' a woman called out.

The dog turned its head quickly and suddenly, then it picked up the stick and ran over to the woman who was walking over. Robert looked over at her, she was young, perhaps early twenties and was wearing a body warmer, jeans and colourful wellingtons.

'He won't do you any harm,' she said pleasantly, stroking the dog's head, 'he's just full of energy.' She knelt down and the dog excitedly began to lick her face and neck. 'Aren't ya, yes you are.' She patted his neck softly. 'Good boy.'

She stood, and as she looked at Robert, her fine brown eyebrows curved inward a fraction, as though she recognised him. And then it dawned on her that this was Robert Lane, *the* Robert Lane, the man who was the president of one of the most powerful defence companies in the world, the man who had appeared in countless magazines, the man who had survived that horrific bombing at Trafalgar Square.

And yet he looked nothing like his photographs, dark stubble shrouded his upper lip, cheeks, chin and neck, his eyes looked heavy and drawn and his hair was thick and uncombed. The man who was once regarded as the sexiest man on the planet had fallen dramatically from grace, and it was no wonder, he had lived through one of the most horrendous terrorist attacks ever to reach the shores of Great Britain.

'It's such a beautiful sight, don't you think?' the woman asked, looking over at the lake.

'Yeah it's something alright,' said Robert quietly.

She was about to offer her condolences to him, she had heard what had happened to his family, but it seemed odd that she should, she didn't know him and the last thing she wanted to do was upset him. And yet some part of her felt that she should mention it.

'I'm sorry about your family,' she said. 'And I'm sorry about what happened to you.'

Robert's eyes, all of a sudden, began to glisten that much more in the sun which would soon be setting. He stared out over the lake, unable to look at the woman who was kind enough to offer her sympathies.

'You probably won't want to hear this right now,' she said softly, 'but time is a great healer, in time your pain will ease.'

Robert tried to say 'thank you', tried to say anything for that matter, but the words became lodged in his dry throat. But the woman caught hold of this attempt and smiled pleasantly, reassuring him that it was alright as she walked passed him and called out to her dog, which ran straight to her.

The thought of walking into the lake raced through Robert's mind. He looked over and watched as the woman walked away, throwing the stick to her dog and every time he brought it back to her. He could not walk into the water now, not after talking to her, she had been nothing but kind to him, he just couldn't bring himself to do it.

He picked some more pebbles and began to skim them off the surface once again. The sun had set before he realised the cold air had began to numb his hands. He wiped the dirt from them and returned to the lodge he was staying at, unable to stop the tears from rolling down his cheeks.

*

It was nearing ten o' clock now, Robert was fast asleep, snoring loudly, on the four seater couch, and the film he had been watching had just now finished, the last of the end credits were disappearing off the top of the television screen.

'Up next is the news,' the off-screen man announced professionally.

The exclusive four bedroom lodge Robert was staying in was among a select few dotted around the country retreat, this one overlooked one of the large, gleaming boating lakes. The executive lodges were designed for those who wanted complete relaxation with a private outside hot tub inside an enclosed garden. It ideally suited Robert who wanted nothing more than to escape the outside world.

Before he arrived here the entire staff at the retreat were made to sign a confidentiality agreement preventing them from mentioning Robert's whereabouts to anyone. He was also to be given menus from the four restaurants within the retreat, and three times a day someone would place his order and then deliver it directly to him. Tonight's meal was roast duck with baby potatoes and a variety of vegetables, although not overly hungry Robert ate about half before drinking his way through the entire contents of the mini bar refrigerator, which were now strewn throughout the open planned living room.

'The time is ten o'clock,' the off-screen man announced, *'now the late night news with Kirsty McNeil.'*

A bald-headed African man with designer facial hair suddenly appeared on screen, he was standing behind a podium with microphones in front of a large grey stoned building.

'I will do everything in my power to aid in the capture of Arapmoi Sebothoma and Tebogo Jeppe.'

The screen switched to show a smartly dressed middle-aged female news presenter seated behind her desk.

'Defiance,' she said, *'that was Lenka Shone's strong message today as he assists British and American forces in the capture of the Brotherhood of Sakarabru leader Arapmoi Sebothoma and his lieutenant Tebogo Jeppe. Also on the programme –'*

'LISA!'

Robert's blood curdling scream resounded throughout the lodge. He lay flat on his back, breathing hard and sweating profusely, his arms were outstretched trying to grab hold of Lisa but he was grasping thin air. He scrambled off the couch, hurried over to the mini bar refrigerator and pulled open the door. It was empty and he looked around the room desperately, his eyes looking at each of the bottles hoping that there was some alcohol left in them.

And then his eyes fell upon the full bottle of whiskey, next to the glass tumbler on the square oak coffee table. He rushed over to it, twisted off the cap and half drunk, half poured it down his throat. The whiskey was drained in a matter of seconds and with the alcohol now flowing through him he dropped down onto the couch, bowed his head, buried his face in his hands and waited for it to calm his still shivering body. The nightmare he had just awoken from was now a faded memory but still he sat, his face still buried in his hands.

Once again the decision not to travel back with the bodies of Lisa, Melissa, Michael and David and ultimately attend their funerals played heavily on his mind. It was the right thing to do, wasn't it? He did not fear funerals; he was not stranger to them. Over the years he had attended his grandfather's, mother's, brother's, father's and many of his friends, he had stood in front of the mourners and delivered speeches. From an early age he had been looked upon to be strong, his mother had told him once that he was the glue that kept all of the family together.

He shook himself mentally. A moment later he stood, turned off the television, crossed over to the window and drew back the curtains. His view was majestic, overlooking a large gleaming lake, but not even this could quell the horrific nightmares that he had when he slept and the vast emptiness inside of him that he had when he was awake.

He turned the handle of the window, unhooked the security latch and opened it as far as it would go. And as the cool night breeze started to drift in he began to walk aimlessly around the room. Despite the fact that he witnessed the Trafalgar Square bombings first hand, despite the fact that it played on everyone's lips, that it was sprawled across all the newspapers and was still mentioned on all the news channels, in some respects he still denied that it had ever happened.

The last moments he spent with Lisa had been locked away deep within his mind, never to be opened, never to be explored. Perhaps that's why he couldn't attend the funerals; going there would be admitting that Lisa was dead, admitting that she would be buried under the earth forever.

He walked over to his bags left next to the stairs, picked up the smallest one and sat back down on the couch. He unzipped it and began to rummage through, not looking for anything in particular just trying to keep his mind occupied. He threw the bible the priest had given him and some of his clothes onto the couch opposite him but then he stopped.

He stared down at the soft brown bear he held in his hands. It was Melissa's, it was her favourite bear, the same bear she had with her when she died. He hugged it close to his chest, unable to stop the tears welling in his eyes.

'I'm so sorry,' he cried.

He just sat there on the couch, rocking back and forth, his tears dripping onto the bear he still clutched close to his chest. And then the silence was suddenly broken, which made Robert jump slightly, by a loud flapping sound. Through his red puffy eyes, he looked up and watched in wonder as the white bodied owl with golden coloured wings soared through the open window. For a moment he admired its elegance and gracefulness in the air, before it landed on the window ledge and stared at him through its huge black round eyes.

How long they stared at one another, neither knew nor cared. The owl did not move, nor did it attempt to fly away, when Robert wiped away the tears from his eyes and cheeks. He stood, still holding the bear in his hand and slowly walked towards it. The owl stayed on the ledge for a few more moments longer before launching itself back into the air, disappearing into the darkness. Robert shut the window and closed the curtains but as he turned and walked wearily back towards the couch, his eyes caught hold of the bible resting open.

Robert suddenly stopped, although he was unaware of doing so. He was staring at the words, staring at them for a long time, trying to make sense of them, wondering if this was what his life was leading up to, wondering if this was the plan God had for him, the one the priest had told him about.

And then Robert walked over to the bible and picked it up, staring at the bold lettered words at the top of the page which read, *THE FIRST BOOK OF MOSES CALLED GENESIS.*

And in that moment of revelation he knew. He knew what he had to do. At last he understood why he had survived, he had a purpose, that purpose was so crystal clear to him now that he couldn't understand why he had not seen it before.

This is a sign from God, he thought, *I know what he wants me to do.*

And with that realisation came a sense of peace that now flowed through his entire body.

Right, where to begin.